Book 1
of
The Dimension Guardian Series

Dimension Guardian
The Realm of Beasts
The Guardian Tournament

K.J. Amidon

www.the-amiverse.com

2nd Edition Copyright © 2010
3rd Edition Copyright © 2013
4th Edition Copyright © 2021

Website: www.kjamidon.com

Published by K.J. Amidon

ISBN: 978-0-9832280-5-9

Cover art by K.J. Amidon

4th Edition © K.J. Amidon 2021

Printed in the United States of America

Dedication

I dedicate this book to itself. This story has sparked a love for storytelling and truly pulled me through some of the darkest times in my life. This book deserves recognition for everything we've been through together.

My 12-year-old self, who thought the original write of this series was good enough to publish, my 23-year-old self became brave enough to rework it so it was fit for reading, my 28-year-old self remained unsatisfied with this particular book in the series, my 30-year-old self finally fell madly in love with this book.

It has been a journey, so I must thank this book for enduring the roller coaster with me.

Table of Contents

Chapter One

Guardian Peter Hendricks slumped against the outer wall of the Dimension Protection Council compound, cringing at the pained groan from the man slung across his back. The dark stone nearly concealed the blood pouring from the two men, the moonlight causing it to glisten with deceptive beauty.

"Stay with me, Scott," he groaned, tightening his grip on the other man's wrist and pulling him higher on his back.

Continuing without jarring the horrifically-injured Scott was an impossible task while dragging a struggling, chained woman behind him. She struggled against her restraints and the restriction spell Peter had cast on her, but she had no success, even as Peter's exhaustion slowed his gait.

He faltered as he climbed the deserted stairs of the Guardian Branch building within the Dimension Protection Council compound. Stumbling, he managed to get his feet under him, the sound of Scott hissing in pain keeping him upright.

"Almost there..." he whispered to his colleague. "Don't you die on me, Scott..."

After dragging the struggling woman and hauling Scott for nearly forty minutes from the nearest portal, Peter's legs were ready to give out in fatigue, but he pressed on, pushing open the great doors with his shoulder, his breath heaving in exhausted pants, sweat dripping over his skin, making it difficult to keep hold on Scott's wrist.

It was eerily silent within the Guardian Branch. The moonlight shone through the large windows, casting cold shadows over the statues of honored Guardians adorning the vast halls. It would be three hours before the sun would rise and Guardians would flood the building to perform the menial, paperwork-related aspects of their job protecting the five worlds. But in the early morning hours, Peter knew only a few Guardians would be present.

"Help!!" he bellowed. His voice echoed among the columns, but rather than carry his cry further, the massive structure swallowed the noise. Struggling to take a full breath, Peter trudged along the hallway, dragging the woman over the marble floor, trying not to slip on the blood that fell from Scott's gaping wounds.

"*Help*!!" he cried once more, reaching a juncture of hallways in the heart of the building.

Three Guardians peered out from a meeting room and immediately ran to Peter when they saw the streak of blood in his wake.

"What happened?" one man demanded. Peter nearly fell to his knees as the others approached, breathing hard, his body trembling.

"We were attacked," he choked. "My entire group. Everyone else is dead."

"Who attacked you?"

Peter retreated from the second man, his eyes narrowed with hatred.

"Stay the hell away from me, you filthy demon."

The second man blinked, taken aback. He opened and closed his mouth, too stunned to respond. When he finally turned his eyes away from Peter, unable to protest the term, his eyes fell on the woman bound and gagged behind the wounded Guardians.

"Amaria!" he gasped, starting forward.

"Not another step!" Peter barked, stepping between them. "Don't come near her! You demons can't be trusted!"

"Peter," the female Guardian said, raising her hands peacefully. Peter's eyes briefly flicked to her, but returned to the demon Guardian. Peter did not recognize the woman, though he knew she was a human Guardian from his home realm merely by her appearance. "Yes, Brikin is a demon, but that doesn't mean you can talk to him that way. You know he can be trusted. He has been vouched for by the Dimension Protection Council."

"I wish that meant something," Peter scoffed. He kicked the bound demon Amaria, though his eyes remained focused on Brikin. "This one is also vouched for, but she turned around and attacked us. Seven human Guardians and one demon, and only Scott and I survived. Scott is barely breathing..." His pleading eyes finally turned to the human Guardians. "The demons are turning against us, even demon *Guardians*. You have to help me. Get Scott to the healers and take Amaria into interrogation. She sabotaged the mission and tried to kill us to cover it up. We need to find out *why*."

"Peter, you're delirious," Brikin said. "We're not—"

Peter dropped his grip on Amaria and reached for his gun, pointing it at the male demon Guardian.

"Don't move," he ordered. The other Guardians raised their hands, stilling immediately.

"Peter, put the gun down."

"I used to rally for you, you know?" Peter said with a broken laugh, his hand shaking as he glared at Brikin. "I tried not to be afraid of your strength, or speed, or your skills in magic. I heard all the horror stories of your kind, how you *murder* for sport, but I never believed it…until *this* bitch," he kicked Amaria once more, "murdered five human Guardians *right in front of me.*"

Peter steadied the gun at Brikin.

"But it's all true, isn't it?" he choked. "You're planning to take over the Dimension Protection Council, and then take over the other four realms. Amaria killing those Guardians proved to me that demons, even demon Guardians, cannot be trusted."

Brikin was still for several long moments before taking a deep breath.

"You're right."

In the blink of an eye, Brikin had lunged forward and grabbed Peter's wrist, yanking the gun out of his grasp and flinging Peter and Scott to the ground. Peter had been so wrapped up in the confrontation with the other demon Guardian that he had not noticed Scott's breathing slow as his injuries began to overwhelm him.

As Peter tried to orient himself to sit up, Brikin's foot on his chest pinned him to the marble floor.

"You're a fool, Peter," the demon said. "If you know demon Guardians can't be trusted, why did you come back *here*? To the Guardian Branch where there will certainly be demon Guardians?"

Scott coughed, drawing Peter's attention just in time to see a bullet rip through the younger Guardian's head, putting him out of his misery.

The two human Guardians with Brikin immediately set to untying Amaria, one of them muttering the counter-spell to the magical binding Peter had used.

"You…but they're…." He looked between the humans and demons, his eyes wide with fear. "They're *human.* They're—"

"You're a hundred years too late," Brikin cackled, turning the gun on him. "It's bigger than you and me, now. It's unfortunate that you have to die knowing that you will never be able to tell those precious humans you protect that they're in danger."

"Wait, wait!" Peter cried. He was surprised when Brikin did loosen his finger on the trigger. "I-I-I can help. Tell me what you want me to do. Spare my life and I will help your cause."

"You really think I'm that stupid?" Brikin said. "You mean you want to infiltrate us. You're a Guardian, Peter. It's what you've been trained to do, and letting you live past tonight would only allow you to tell others what you know, and while there's no way to stop what's about to happen, it would be annoying to have even more altruistic Guardians like yourself trying to get in the way."

Amaria hurried forward, standing at Brikin's side and baring her teeth in a half-growl, half-grin.

"Let him stay," she sneered. "We could always use more able-bodied Guardians for muscle."

"Don't be an idiot."

"I can be useful!" Peter gasped. "I swear!"

"You're more useful to me as a corpse."

Brikin pulled the trigger, but Peter used his own magic manipulation, skills every Guardian was taught as a child, to redirect the bullet to the ground by his head. He tried to scramble to his feet, though his exhausted legs only carried him a few steps before a bullet bit into his thigh and he crumpled to the ground once more.

Amaria squealed excitedly, skipping to Peter and kneeling in front of him.

"Feeling a little tired?" she asked mockingly.

Brikin kicked the fallen Guardian onto his side, aiming the gun at his head.

"The dragons will not allow you demons to destroy everything," Peter warned, staring down the dark barrel of his own gun. "You'll all be killed for this."

"In case you haven't noticed, the dragons don't give two shits about what happens around here," Brikin said. "I doubt a few dead Guardians will be enough to get their attention. It hasn't been enough so far."

Peter looked at the four sets of dark, contemptuous eyes.

"Y-You'll be tried by the council for murdering another Guardian," he stuttered.

"Allow me to fill you in on just how powerless you are," Brikin said with a haunting smirk. "If you really are more valuable alive than dead," he cocked the gun, "then my master will simply bring you back to life."

Another gunshot rang through the halls of the Guardian Branch building and Peter's limp body fell flat on the bloodied floor.

"What the hell were you thinking?" the human woman snapped, glaring at Amaria. "You were supposed to kill *all* of them and make it look like an accident."

"I tried!" Amaria retorted. "This bastard was a lot tougher than he looked."

"Master Yokouro will not be pleased you killed him here in the Guardian Branch," the man said to Brikin.

"Then we better clean up and make it look like he was killed somewhere else," Brikin said shortly. "Or, we put a gun in his hand

and make it look like he had snapped and was coming to kill other Guardians."

"Are you crazy? We can't let the bodies be discovered in here!" the woman said.

"Master Yokouro wants war," Brikin reminded her. "We're giving him a reason to wage it. If the Guardians are too disjointed to fight against him, and they begin fighting each other, he can dominate the realms with ease." Brikin turned to Amaria. "You better start crying," he said. "After all, Peter attacked the other Guardians. And as a last resort," he handed the gun to her, "you had to defend yourself."

"No one is going to buy that," the female human said, rolling her eyes.

"Don't doubt my ability to sell it," Amaria said confidently, preparing herself for the charade.

Chapter Two

"Dimension Protection Council is now in session! Silence is ordered!" a guard announced. The talking slowly ceased in the circular hall as the council members found their seats and faced forward, waiting for the meeting to commence. When the room was quiet, Elder Jonathan Teban, a man about eighty years of age from the Human Realm and the most powerful man in the council, stood.

"I am sure you have all heard the reason for my calling an emergency session today," he started. "A group of Guardians, all of whom were highly-ranked, were killed earlier this week. Another Guardian's testimony, which you have before you, states that Guardian Peter Hendricks murdered those in his party, and then, in a fit of psychotic rage, yelling about demons being the dominant species, tried to kill any he found in the Guardian Branch building before being shot and killed."

Those in the Dimension Protection Council murmured among themselves, unnerved and anxious about the direction of the emergency meeting.

"It is clear that the situation in our unsettled realms is getting worse by the day," Elder Teban continued. "Neighbors and families are turning against each other in the Human Realm, mostly out of fear of the demons. Our Guardians are trying to settle each of these cases peacefully, but the people are not willing to listen to them, insisting that the Guardians seem unable to complete their jobs and are no longer a viable means of protection for the realms."

He cast an eye around the room, the cold gaze unsettling to all those who were close enough to be under its full intensity.

"There is no need for me to explain the riots that would occur if we were to let news of what happened with Guardian Peter Hendricks reach the people. Guardians turning against one another, claiming complete demon domination...the panic would be catastrophic."

Elder Syrus Ari of the Beast Dimension was the next to speak. A lion who had taken a human form for the purpose of representing his realm in Council, he was the youngest of the five Elders, but held just as much, if not more respect as the older Elders.

"This problem is not exclusive to the human-inhabited realms. In the Beast Realm there have been reports of hunting parties that slaughter anyone suspected to be a demon. These lynching parties have even led to the killings of three Guardians. If we do not find a way to curtail this violence, more Guardians will die and, without the Guardians, we cannot maintain order over the people, nor protect them from any real and present danger that may arise."

The next to speak was Elder Constance Lunar, the representative of the Dimension of Darkness—a realm that had been named after a loose translation of the original dragon appellation.

"Unfortunately, I have also heard horrible news about the Guardians from my realm. What happened yesterday is not a unique occurrence. My Guardians are beginning to fear the people they protect, causing them to be hasty in their decision to end the lives of anyone who moves too suddenly around them. Several of my Guardians have even gone into hiding to avoid punishment for such crimes, believing the Dimension Protection Council is not to be trusted, either. I sent Guardian Eclipse Retani to retrieve some of them, but he discovered that three had committed suicide. Two others have been dishonorably discharged from the Guardian Branch and committed due to mental instability."

The Representatives of each realm, who were seated on the ground level of the meeting chambers, did not seem as surprised by the news as the Protectors, who sat in balconies above. The Elders looked over the five sections of the room with a critical eye, gauging reactions of those from each of the five connected worlds.

The Elders knew it was very important that the members of the Dimension Protection Council did not panic. If they were to let fear and anxiety dictate their decisions, it would be easy for inequality among the realms to be noticed and called out, strengthening the argument that Council could not protect their people. It would also cause a quick spiral into anarchy and rebellion, decimating the peace Council had managed to maintain for millennia.

Elder Abigail Celeste of the Realm of Light spoke once the murmuring had quieted.

"The peace agreement between our five worlds has faced many difficulties in the four thousand years it has been in effect, but this kind of fear in the people has not been documented since the original formation of our alliance and the solidification of the portals." She was silent for a few moments, casting her eyes about the room, choosing her words cautiously. "I understand that no one wants to actually say it, but we know that the cause of tension has to do with the Dimension of Demons. Demons are very powerful creatures, and the Guardians were originally created to protect the realms against them."

"With all due respect," one Representative from the Dimension of Demons started, standing, "the demon Guardians have been an immense asset to the DPC. Without their strength and knowledge, there are countless magically-gifted *humans* that could have overrun the realms. Demons are not the only dangerous creatures in existence. I would venture to say that the realms have been more often endangered by *humans* than rogue demons."

"That may be the case," Elder Celeste agreed. "But we cannot ignore the panic demons create by their mere existence. Even human *Guardians* are afraid of demons."

"What is it you suggest we do?" a demon Protector sneered. "You want to strip demon Guardians of their position? You want to deny our realm what little representation we have fought to achieve in Council? That would anger the demons in the realm to war."

"We have reason to be concerned. After all, there have been numerous Guardians through the years who have heard of demons planning to overthrow the Dimension Protection Council and destroy the peace alliance of the five worlds," the female Elder reminded him.

Ignoring the gossiping of the Representatives and Protectors from the other realms, the demon Representative continued to speak, his voice controlled.

"Perhaps you have forgotten that our world would lose just as much from the destruction of our alliance as the human realms. And, for that matter, you seem to think that our rulers do not have any control over their subjects. The Old Blood Lords would not allow demons to plot against the Dimension Protection Council."

"Yet they seem *not* to have control, nor do they seem interested in the number of demon criminals caught in the last year alone," Elder Teban said. "We have not heard the Old Blood Lords express that they wish to correct the situation with their subjects, or even acknowledge the damage their subject have inflicted on our realms."

The demon Representative was about to retort, several other demons standing as well to defend their Old Blood Lords and their realm, but the fifth Elder stood, motioning them silent with his hand.

A shiver of anticipation filled the room as the Elder from the Demon Realm, Elder Demetrius Renard, commanded everyone's attention. He was the oldest among the Elders—as demons lived impossibly long lives—but his strength was never doubted. He often frightened others in Council merely by the strength of his aura.

"There is no need to attack the Dimension of Demons, the Old Blood Lords, or the Dimension Protection Council," he said. "Bickering about these things will not solve the problems plaguing our people. All demons can agree that we strike fear in the hearts of humans. The Elders do not wish to remove the representation of the

Demon Realm from Council, but we do seek a way to curb the violence against our Guardians that is perpetrated out of fear of demons."

Those who had stood to defend the Dimension of Demons slowly returned to their seats.

"This is a very serious problem we must address," he continued. "What occurred with Guardian Hendricks did not involve civilians—the crime was committed by one Guardian against other Guardians. This is a very disturbing situation. If our Guardians are turning against one another, then they will certainly turn on the general public under the right circumstances. Chaos will take over the realms, the likes of which has never been seen before, even when the alliance was first formed."

The demon Elder turned to the other four Elders, getting the approving nod from Elder Teban before continuing.

"More frightening still," he added, "is a discovery we made regarding the Dimensional Holding Seal that keeps the five realms secured. This seal has, in fact, fractured in two places. It is clear that these breaks are not accidental, but are the result of a deliberate attack. Someone is trying to destroy the seal."

The council room came alive, the terrified chatter downing out the last words of Elder Renard's announcement. He lifted his hand, waiting for the room to silence.

"This confirms our suspicions. Without the seal in correct placement and at full strength, the realms will collide. Holes will rip in the dimensional fabric. This could swallow entire cities and drop them into other realms...which means that the Dimension of Demons could be linked to any of the human-inhabited realms and we would be unable to stop it."

At the realization of the imminent destruction, the room erupted in a cacophony of panic.

"However, we must consider the seal that we are discussing," Elder Renard continued, raising his hands to silence everyone again, though he was nearly shouting to be heard. "The Dimensional Holding Seal was placed by Lord Vestera Hizoku himself, the leader of the dragons and most powerful creature in the known universe. To break this seal, the perpetrator would need extensive knowledge of magic and energy manipulation. While it might be easy to point at the demons, we realize that a group of humans could also break the seal, if armed with the correct information."

Elder Renard's shoulders slumped, his eyes dropping to his feet.

"Considering the account of those who survived Guardian Hendricks' attack, and the apparently-growing number of

Guardians turning against the council, it is entirely possible that a group of Guardians is responsible for breaking the seal."

Unlike before, the room was filled with a dull murmur rather than a boisterous roar. The severity of having the Guardian Branch turn against the rest of the Dimension Protection Council settled heavily over the room, causing tensions to rise to an uncomfortable level.

"As you are all aware, the Guardians are the strongest magical protection force we have in the realms. However, that also makes them an enormous threat if that power is used *against* the realms. Therefore, in order to prove themselves to the Elders, the Council, and the rest of the Guardian Branch, we have decided to host a Guardian Tournament."

One Protector from the Realm of the Beasts stood abruptly, his voice ringing loudly over the shocked shouts of other council members.

"My Elders, I respect your judgment, but holding a Guardian Tournament is dangerous and reckless! I must ask you to rethink this course of action. We have no proof that the Guardians were involved!"

"We know the dangers of a tournament. That is why we are *not* going to notify the dimensions' people when the tournament starts. Only Guardians and the Dimension Protection Council members shall be allowed to attend. Remember, we are using the Guardian Tournament as a *test*, not a spectacle," Elder Ari answered.

A Protector from the Demon Realm stood.

"Elders, I agree that you should reconsider. It is too dangerous, and if we are facing the ones disrupting the peace between the realms, we should be extremely cautious because, as you said, their power must be exponential. What if this is the same perpetrator from the last Guardian Tournament? We would be playing right into their hands. The massacre from the last tournament should be reason enough to never use the practice again, even in these extreme circumstances."

"As we just stated, we understand the risks. But the Guardians are too dangerous *not* to be investigated thoroughly," Elder Renard defended. "If we bring them under intense scrutiny and interrogation, we might insight a rebellion within the branch. If we can determine the culprits, and identify those who wish to undermine the work of Council under the pretext of a Guardian Tournament, we can keep the framework of Council intact, while being sure not to anger other Guardians into turning against us. But, in light of your concern, and the very real danger of repeating the carnage of the Guardian Tournament Slaughter, we shall bring the decision to Council."

"All in favor of reinstating the Guardian Tournament," Elder Teban said, "stand."

The sounds of chairs scraping on the floor filled the room as most council members rose to their feet. Younger members were fearful of what might happen in the tournament, but they were more interested in keeping the Guardians contained, regardless of the dangerous tactic. The older members who remembered the last tournament remained in their seats, but they were outnumbered.

"Very well, majority decides. The tournament shall begin in two months' time," Elder Teban announced.

"For those of you who do not already know the rules, booklets will be given for you to distribute to your Guardians," Elder Celeste explained. "They must form teams of five. It is not realm-specific. There must be a designated team leader, whose first name the team will compete under. For the purposes of this tournament, in the next two months the old stadiums will be opened, cleaned, and brought up to code for competition."

The noise flooding the council hall was a mixture of anxiety and excitement as everyone sat again. The younger members knew of the slaughter that had disbanded the Guardian Tournament forty years previous, but they were sure that there would be enough changes to ensure that nothing of the same magnitude occurred again. Older members were either trying to warn the younger ones of the danger of the tournament, or were sharing worried, knowing looks.

"Though the teams can be comprised of Guardians from any realm, the Elders have decided that it would be wise to place the top-ranked Guardian from each realm in a single team to be Council's eyes inside the tournament," Elder Teban added. "Not only will this give us insight to dangerous Guardians competing, it will protect our Guardians, as our top-ranked Guardians will not be scouted into teams of those seeking to destroy Council, nor will there be favoritism to the teams that have one of these Guardians."

Everyone sat rigid in their seats, waiting for the names to be announced, though most already knew the top-ranked Guardians.

"From the Human Realm we have chosen my grandson, Dalton Teban, to lead the team, as he is the top-ranked Guardian, both in the Human Realm and in the entire Guardian Branch. From the Realm of Darkness we have chosen Eclipse Retani, and Mitoki Ecaep has been chosen from the Realm of Light." Elder Teban hesitated before mentioning the next name. "As for the Beast Realm, we have chosen Hanyi Treneke. His paperwork has already been processed and he has been unretired for the duration of the Guardian Tournament."

A concerned humming reverberated through the meeting hall. A Protector from the Beast Realm scrambled to his feet.

"Sir, was Hanyi made aware of the fact that he was to be unretired?"

"We will send a convoy to inform him tonight," Elder Ari answered indirectly. Many were unsettled that the Elders would unretire a Guardian without his consent—particularly considering the circumstances under which Hanyi Treneke had resigned.

"Sir," the Protector protested, "Hanyi Treneke *will not* join this tournament, even if you decide to put him back in the Guardian Branch. He is one of the survivors of the Tournament Slaughter. You cannot expect him to walk back into a stadium after that. We have not been in contact with him in over thirty-five years. We have no way of being sure he is still alive."

"He is alive," Elder Ari assured. "We have been keeping a very careful watch over him."

"I still must protest," he said, exasperated. "Hanyi followed his partner's lead and left the Guardian Branch only days after the slaughter. He could not even conduct the investigation on the massacre because he was traumatized. He is not the same Guardian he once was."

"Well, if he followed his partner's lead out of the branch, perhaps he will follow his partner back in." Elder Teban smiled thinly, as if amused, however annoyed, by the protestations. "We are going to reunite them. From the Demon Realm we have chosen Keito DeVero. He has also been unretired for the duration of the tournament."

The announcement of the well-known name created a louder wave of uncertain mumbling. A Protector from the Demon Realm stood, his eyes downcast.

"Elders, much like Hanyi, Keito refuses to have anything to do with the Guardian Branch. He is the only other survivor of the Tournament Slaughter. He watched his team be murdered. The last Protectors we sent to him for information came back with broken limbs. He wants nothing to do with any of this. You have *no* idea what—"

"They *must* join this tournament," Elder Teban interrupted sternly. "They are the survivors of the slaughter forty years ago, and we understand how difficult it will be to get them back, but their inside knowledge is crucial. These are the same Guardians that were champions of the tournament for eight consecutive years. We need the best of the best to find these culprits and guide our human Guardians. This tournament is too dangerous for us not to utilize *all* of our resources, and that includes two of the best Guardians in recent history." He paused and fixed the standing Protectors with a sharp glare. "They will not decline our request if they are not given a choice."

Silence gripped the room. The meaning of the words hung menacingly in the air. The demon Protector bowed his head. The Beast Realm Protector sat slowly, clearly uncomfortable with the order.

"Announce the tournament to your Guardians. As for the five that we have selected, we want them brought to the Elders' Chambers tomorrow at midday," Elder Celeste added when she knew there were no further objections. Everyone in the Dimension Protection Council talked amongst themselves, discussing the tournament with varying degrees of enthusiasm and fear.

Chapter Three

Keito DeVero stared into the dying embers in the fire pit, sipping the last of his broth from a crude ceramic bowl. The older woman by his side ladled herself another serving from the pot above the fire pit, settling back against the cave wall. She pretended not to look over Keito's tense shoulders and drawn expression. A pang of worry radiated through her chest when he set the bowl aside after a half portion of supper.

"Not hungry?" she asked, trying to sound casual.

"Not really."

"You should eat more, Keito," Lady Todac said. "You're looking thin."

Keito did not respond, falling back into his pensive silence.

Despite all her years of knowing him, she still had to deliberate if it was wise to ask Keito what was bothering him. Unlike many demons in the realm, she did not fear him, but she feared upsetting the demon she considered a son—she could not stand seeing him in pain.

"Something is troubling you," she finally said. "What is it?"

He heaved a sigh, hesitating.

"While I was hunting, I heard some demons in the woods discussing the DPC and the Guardians."

"Do you regret leaving the Guardians?" she asked, trying to read the younger demon's expression, though Keito was far too skilled at hiding the emotions behind his sharp golden eyes. His response was simple and short.

"Not at all."

"What were they talking about? Has something happened?" Lady Todac pressed. There was, again, a long period of silence where the younger demon's expression remained impassive, the internal debate over whether or not to share the information concealed.

"The Elders have decided to reestablish the Guardian Tournament. It was decided at an emergency session today."

Lady Todac's body tensed, her mind flashing with memories of the Tournament Slaughter—the tragedy that had claimed her mate's life and had nearly killed Keito.

"How..." She swallowed hard. "How did the Elders get the approval of the rest of Council? After what happened last time..."

"They're desperate," Keito said. "Things are getting worse, and quickly. While the council forty years ago would never take this drastic action, this new generation wasn't alive when the slaughter happened. They don't remember…"

The two slipped into silence, both lost in memories of the previous Guardian Tournament, and the happy times before the tragedy—the times before their lives were shattered.

Lady Todac was startled out of her reminiscing when Keito bolted to his feet with a low growl. She barely had time to turn her head before two demon Protectors from the Dimension Protection Council stepped cautiously into the cave home, trying not to startle the on-guard former Guardian.

"Peace, Keito," one of the Protectors said, raising a hand. "Is that how you greet old friends?"

"What are you doing here?" he snarled. "And I would hardly call you a friend. I made it clear that I would never entertain the trivial matters of the Dimension Protection Council again. I suggest you leave, *now*."

"We have come to ask you to report to the Elders' Chambers tomorrow in the Middle Dimension at midday," the Protector explained, ignoring Keito's warning.

"Why?" he asked with a sinking feeling in his stomach.

"You're no longer unemployed," the other Protector said. "You have been called to serve in the Guardian Branch."

"*What?*" Keito snapped. "You cannot do that without my permission. According to the Guardian Code, I have the right—"

"We do not have the luxury of observing such courtesies," the first Protector interrupted. "You have been too busy hiding in this cave to realize that the realms are going to hell."

"They were going to hell when I was in service. And I am well aware of the state of things," Keito sneered. "But I am not interested in being some DPC attack dog. I've told you before. I'm *done*. Tell them to find some other demon who wants to be on their leash."

"Do you really think Council forgot how much you hate to be on a leash? You turn around and bite whoever tries to control you. But you have some incentive to be obedient this time. You are to be part of the council-sponsored team competing in the Guardian Tournament."

"You can't be serious…" Keito hissed. "They want *me* in the tournament? Do you even *remember* what happened last time?"

"We do," the first Protector said. "But this is the command of the Elders. You will be on this team, Keito. You do not have a choice."

"What are you going to do if I refuse?" Keito taunted, preparing for a fight.

The other Protector sprinted to Lady Todac, drawing his dagger as his fingers tangled in her hair, yanking her head back to expose her throat. The Protector knew he had to show no fear, though he was sure his hand was minutely shaking as he pressed the blade to her flesh. The Elders had instructed them to threaten Lady Todac if Keito was difficult, but the Protector knew Keito was a very dangerous demon, and if there was any weakness or hesitation in his actions, Keito would kill him.

The ex-Guardian froze, his expression controlled as he stared at the glinting dagger. His mind worked around every possible way he could get Lady Todac out of danger. Keito knew they would not kill her, but would take her captive, which was arguably worse than death. He also knew Lady Todac would not fight them, as the peace oath she had taken after her mate was murdered would prevent her from doing so. Even with the dagger against her jugular, she looked at peace, ready to go to the next life and be reunited with her mate.

Keito, however, was not willing to gamble with the well-being of the demon he saw as a second mother.

His eyes passing between the blade and the determined look of the Protector, Keito's muscles slowly relaxed.

"What is your answer, Keito?" the first Protector prompted. "You know how these sorts of negotiations often go."

"*Fine*," he sneered, "I'll go to the little pep-talk."

The Protectors smiled and one even dared to chuckle. He released Lady Todac but kept his dagger handy, knowing it would be suicide to be unarmed after pissing off the infamous Keito DeVero.

"We knew you would see it our way," he said with a smirk. "You better be there tomorrow or we have the authority to detain her until you cooperate. The rest of your group will be waiting for you at the portal in the Middle Dimension, including your dear friend, Hanyi. After all, we wouldn't want you to get lost. It has been a very long time since you've been to the compound."

They exited the cave, haughtily jeering at Keito, even knowing he could still hear them. Keito's fists tightened at his sides and he ground his teeth together, trembling as he refrained from attacking the Protectors.

"*Hanyi?*" he barely managed to say around his clenched teeth. "Why would they drag him into this, too? He shouldn't have to..."

"Keito..." Lady Todac whispered.

"Why is this happening *now?*"

"You don't have to do this for me," she said. "They cannot hurt me without angering you. They wouldn't dare—"

"No, they wouldn't kill you," he agreed. "But they would imprison you and maybe even torture you. You know there aren't any laws protecting demons. They'll do anything necessary to get me to cooperate…"

Keito lifted a hand to his head.

"Damn it…I can't go through this again…"

~∧~

It had been years since Hanyi Treneke had taken a human form, though it was impossible for him to determine if his discomfort was from the unfamiliar physical form, or if it was due to the Protectors ordering him back into service and back into the Guardian Tournament.

"Why does the council want *me* to participate?" he finally said, squinting against the bright fire of the Protector's torch. "I have not been a Guardian in decades. I'm out of shape and the realms have changed. I'm too old."

"You're not out of shape, Hanyi," one Protector assured. "I'm sure you never stopped training, even after you retired. You were born to be a Guardian."

"The years have not been kind to me."

"You're a Treneke Wolf," the other Protector said. "You've got a few decades left in you. You might not be at your peak, but you are still strong enough for the Guardian Branch."

"The *tournament*, though?" Hanyi asked skeptically. "What possessed them to bring that back? After what happened…" Hanyi closed his eyes. "I don't think I can walk into a stadium again."

"We understand this must be difficult but the Elders command this of you. We need you back in service, and this team needs you. You and Keito are essential."

"Keito, too?" Hanyi gasped, his eyes shooting wide.

"Yes, Keito as well," the first Protector affirmed. "The demon Protectors should be discussing this with him as we speak."

"How could you think…don't you understand? Keito…" He tried to find the right words. "Don't do this to him. If the Elders want me, then that should be enough. But don't do this to Keito. He deserves to live his life quietly, now. He's done more than enough for the realms."

"There is nothing we can do about it. The Protectors sent to him were told to do whatever necessary to secure his participation and compliance."

"What does that mean?" Hanyi asked.

"You know exactly what that means."

Hanyi rubbed his forehead, his expression conflicted and lined with pain. The Protectors shared a brief glance before one of them cleared his throat.

"Have you been in contact with Keito since he left?"

Hanyi's expression immediately hardened, becoming guarded and cold.

"Of course I have."

"Then you've discussed the Tournament Slaughter."

"What was there to discuss?" he said sharply. "We both saw our friends and family massacred. The nightmares speak for themselves."

The Protectors fell silent, their eyes turning to the forest ground.

"Are you willing to work with him again?" one said, raising his gaze.

"What is *that* supposed to mean?"

"Are you sure that you want to associate with Keito again?" the Protector clarified. "After everything that happened, can you still work with him or will it be too painful?"

"Keito has been, and always will be, a trusted friend. Whether or not either of us will be willing to work with *Council* again is the question you should be asking. You can't possibly comprehend what you are asking of us."

"If Keito participates, will you?"

"I don't think I'll have a choice. I'll have to do damage control. The more you piss Keito off, the more he's going to let you feel his anger."

"You will come, then? To the meeting tomorrow?"

Hanyi nodded reluctantly.

Satisfied, the Protectors walked back into the dark forest. Once sure they were out of earshot, the older Protector heaved a sigh, shaking his head.

"This is extremely foolish."

"The tournament?"

"The tournament, this special team…" He shook his head again. "But especially forcing these two back into service. It can only lead to bloodshed."

Hanyi had taken his time walking back to where his pack waited to hear why the Protectors had pulled their alpha away. He wandered through the trees, his head bent, trying to acclimate to the feeling of being on two legs again. Lost in painful memories and sharp anxiety about what he knew was coming, he was startled when he saw the wolves of his pack in front of him. He stood, staring blankly. The pack inched forward, their eyes worried as they studied his human form.

Dark understanding fell over the Treneke Wolf Tribe.

~/\~

Eclipse Retani sat in Elder Lunar's dimly-lit study, running his fingers through the long bangs of his nearly-black hair as he thought over the news of the Guardian Tournament.

"Do you think you are ready for something as big as this case?" she asked, sitting on the edge of her desk in front of him, expectant.

"Why did you decide to hold a tournament?" he asked. "Seems too risky. The realms are chaotic and you want to *distract* the Guardians by pitting them against each other for sport?"

"It's unorthodox, I know, but we are running out of options. Things are already out of hand. We have to gather everyone who could be responsible for the break in the seal and see what we can learn from there. We need to start producing answers, Eclipse, and you know how Guardians are. They're suspicious by nature, but with all the Guardians being killed, they'll be nervous about any Council investigation. The tournament will allow us to conduct covert investigations and learn more about the state of things." She slipped from her desk, walking to Eclipse and trailing her fingers over his shoulders. "Besides, you're my best Guardian. I need your help. The competition should not be difficult for a Guardian of your caliber."

Her fingers traced teasing patterns over his shoulders, causing him to smirk. His Elder had made passes at him for years, and he had long grown accustomed to the flirtation, now merely amused by her advances.

"Who would be on my team?"

"Dalton Teban, Mitoki Ecaep, Hanyi Treneke, and Keito DeVero."

"...you wanna run those names by me again?" he said, unable to stop the way his eyes shot wide. The Elder of the Darkness Realm laughed.

"I know that some of these names must be a shock—"

"Try *all* of them," he retorted. "I assume Dalton is leading the team?"

"He is your top-ranked Guardian. It's not nepotism from Elder Teban. He really is a phenomenal Guardian."

"I know. I've only spoken with him briefly during annual testing, but I have heard of his abilities. But...the others..."

"Keito and Hanyi, you mean?"

"Are they still alive?" he asked. "They're both...I mean, you realize they're *legends* in the Guardian Branch, right? They have commemorative statues. They're practically..." His hands motioned nonsensically, as if he could grab the words to express his surprise out of the air.

"It must be exciting for you," Elder Lunar said with a knowing grin.

"But...the tournament was the reason they quit."

"It was," she agreed. "But they want to help, particularly with the state of things. They are still as pure as Guardians come. They won't stand by and watch the realms split further."

"And Mitoki? I have to work with him every day?" Eclipse asked, his voice laced with something that Elder Lunar could not discern.

"I know he's young and he's from the Realm of Light, but try to play nice."

Mitoki Ecaep shoved the door open just enough to slip under the chain and into the deserted structure. He knew he did not need to sneak into the abandoned Guardian Tournament stadium, as he would be competing in one in two short months. But after hearing the news that he had been chosen to be on the council-sponsored team, he had become consumed with a sickening feeling he could not ignore no matter how he tried.

Worried about alerting anyone in the nearby office buildings to his presence, he waited for his eyes to adjust to the dark before moving forward, the small flashlight untouched in his pocket.

Having never been in a stadium before, he did not know what to make of the doors on either side of the hallway, but he was sure that the set of double doors at the far end would lead him into the main arena.

The screeching of rusted hinges set his teeth on edge as he pushed open the double doors. He remained still, listening for any noises that would tell him someone had heard the loud doors. Once he confirmed he was alone in the stadium, he explored further.

There were enough small windows along the top of the audience seats to let in the light of the full moon, allowing Mitoki to study the enormous arena. The seats had been eaten away by forty years of neglect, and graffiti adorned the wall encompassing the dirt arena, which had become home to broken bottles and discarded cigarette butts.

Despite the decrepit state of the abandoned stadium, the air was alive with energy.

Mitoki, as a touch-sensitive psychic—one able to spark visions with physical contact—felt the energy in the arena more acutely than a normal human. Pain, fear, and hatred surrounded him, circling, occasionally brushing his cheek like a passing, frozen breeze.

The nineteen-year-old Guardian kicked the bottle at his feet and watched it tumble across the dirt. After bouncing twice, Mitoki could see flames engulf the bottle and he had to blink several times to rid himself of the vision.

He crept a cautious gaze around the stadium as he took a few measured steps to the center of the arena. When training to become a Guardian, he learned what little information there was on the Tournament Slaughter. Over two thousand lives had been lost—most of them civilian. He knew that the stadium had been barricaded and burned, but there were no reports of who had committed the crime, or the reason for the carnage.

Standing in the middle of the arena, the negative energy consumed him. Even though the stadium in which he stood was not the one that had been attacked, the negative emotions surrounding the practice of the Guardian Tournament were enough to haunt the stadium and bombard his psyche.

Mitoki hesitated.

Before he could think better of his actions, he crouched and grabbed a handful of coarse dirt.

Almost immediately, the smell of smoke invaded his nostrils. He heard the crackling of flames as they ravaged the chairs and clothes of those in the stadium. Distant screams were drowned by the deafening cracks of the collapsing structure. The heat was stifling.

Mitoki carefully raised his eyes, not wanting to move fast in fear of breaking the vision, his fingers still gripped tightly around the dirt.

On the far side of the arena, silhouetted by flames, was a tall figure. He stood alone, surrounded by the hellish chaos while seeming unaffected by it. Mitoki could not see any defining features, but he could feel him watching the Guardian, preparing his attack.

Mitoki focused on the figure, trying to ignore the screaming and the negative energy as death consumed those from forty years previous. He wanted to see the perpetrator, but the more he focused on the silhouette, the more his head ached and the tighter his chest grew.

He began coughing, feeling a pressure on his ribs that he had never experienced before. His heart was pounding. The longer he looked at the man, the more frightened he became.

That was when he knew the enemy was extremely powerful—more powerful than anyone Mitoki had faced before.

The figure raised an arm, drawing Mitoki's attention away from his suffocation. With a single sweep of his hand, the fires around Mitoki extinguished, the heat and smell vanishing in an instant.

However, the figure had not extinguished the fire. He had broken through Mitoki's psychic vision to stand in front of the Guardian and make his presence known.

The dark figure smiled.

Terrified, realizing that the perpetrator of the Tournament Slaughter was standing in front of him, Mitoki drew his gun.

Before he could aim it, the figure vanished.

The cold air made the hair on the back of Mitoki's neck stand on end. Shivers ran up his spine like electricity and a cold laugh sounded at his ear.

"Soon enough."

And then, the oppressive energy was gone.

All the negative memories and dark feelings vanished, the dilapidated structure looking as sad and decrepit as any other abandoned building. Mitoki was frozen to the spot, his gun poised, his breath short, and his mind racing at the understanding that their enemy was already watching him, and undoubtedly, the other members of the soon-to-be Team Dalton.

There was a knock at Dalton Teban's front door late at night. A few moments later, Dalton opened the door to find his grandfather standing on the porch without the company of his security detail.

"Grandfather!" he gasped, ushering him inside rapidly and closing the door after glancing up and down the dark street to be sure no one had seen the Human Realm Elder. "What are you doing here? Where is your security?"

"I came to see you," he answered, ignoring the second question.

Dalton's wife walked in to the living room with her sleepy six-year-old daughter on her hip. The young girl was dressed in her pajamas, ready for bed, but when she saw her great-grandfather in the living room, she perked up.

"Grandpapa!" Theresa squealed.

She squirmed out of her mother's arms and ran to Elder Teban, who scooped her up lovingly.

"Grandfather, you really shouldn't be here. It's too dangerous on the streets these days for someone of your status," Dalton scolded.

"Do not use that tone with me, young man," he scolded, cuddling his great-granddaughter. "I have something very important to discuss with you and I wanted to do so in person."

"Grandfather," Dalton said, glancing at his wife and daughter, "we agreed that anything work-related was to be discussed anywhere but in my home."

"I know, and I apologize for breaking that arrangement," Elder Teban said. "But this is extremely urgent. I didn't get out of the emergency session until an hour ago and this is something that cannot wait."

"Theresa, come on. Time for bed," Frieda said, taking her daughter's hand and leading her upstairs as she complained about wanting to spend time with her great-grandfather. Dalton watched the two disappear out of earshot before turning back to his grandfather.

"What is so urgent? Has something else happened?"

"Council met today for an emergency session. We discussed the break in the seal that I told you about last week," Elder Teban started.

"How did they react?"

Elder Teban motioned for Dalton to sit and then took the seat opposite his grandson, explaining the proceedings of the emergency council meeting. Once Frieda had put Theresa to bed, she sat next to Dalton, holding his hand as she listened to them discuss the decision to start the Guardian Tournament and have Dalton lead a team of the best Guardians in the branch.

"I don't like this idea," Frieda said, her hand tightening around Dalton's. "It will make things more complicated. Wouldn't it be easier to hold investigations individually and narrow possible suspects? You're distracting the Guardians by using the tournament."

"Unfortunately, with the deaths of so many Guardians fresh in everyone's mind, we're worried about frightening the Guardians further. We would rather conduct investigations covertly within the tournament, where they can be distracted from the possibility that they might be investigated. It's more likely they will let their guard down."

"But the tournament is a drastic move," Dalton said. "How did you get Council to approve it? After the massacre, I'm surprised that they would be willing to give it the green light."

"Things are bad, Dalton, and they're getting worse," Elder Teban said. "The tournament is not the only drastic measure we've taken. The team you will be leading is going to be made of the best Guardians in each realm."

"So, Eclipse Retani, Mitoki Ecaep, Sanyai Tyien—" Dalton started listing the other top-ranked Guardians.

"No, not Sanyai."

"Who are you getting from the Demon Realm?"

"Keito DeVero."

Dalton could not stop his jaw from dropping.

"*Who?*"

"You heard right. Keito DeVero." He nodded. "I'm sure you know who that is."

"Of course I do," Dalton breathed. "And I'm sure you understand my shock and confusion. He retired."

"We unretired him," Elder Teban said simply. "He will be essential to your team. He and Hanyi know the tournament—"

"Hanyi Treneke?!" Dalton gasped. "*Both* of them?!"

"Yes, both of them," Elder Teban confirmed with a chuckle. "They know the tournament inside and out. They will help you with the technicalities and training, as well as keep you informed when things don't go as they should in the tournament. Their inside knowledge will be invaluable to you."

"But they haven't been seen in ages. How did you…"

"They want to help," he said. "They've been living as civilians and have been affected just like everyone else. When they heard of the tournament, they understood why we brought them out of retirement."

Dalton raised an eyebrow skeptically. "I find that difficult to believe."

"You might have some difficulty controlling Keito, but that is why we were sure to bring in Hanyi. Trust me, Dalton, you're going to need them."

He sighed and shook his head.

"I don't like this, Grandfather…" he said. "Something is very wrong with all of this. I can feel it."

"There is a meeting with everyone on your team tomorrow at midday. Your teammates will meet you in the Middle Dimension outside their respective portals. Pick them up tomorrow and bring them to my office."

Chapter Four

Dalton started early the following day to gather his new team for the meeting with the Elders. He had been unable to sleep the previous night, however, and was walking in a slight haze.

Once he had cleared the portal into the Middle Dimension, he hopped on the shuttle to go to the portal building for the Realm of Light, which was the next nearest portal in the city. When he descended the steps of the bus, he spotted Mitoki on a bench outside, his eyes distant on the ground, lost in thought. Dalton always forgot that Mitoki was quite young as he had only met the top-ranked Guardian from the Realm of Light on three occasions. Mitoki's demeanor exhibited maturity beyond his years—like many Guardians—but his face was still child-like, and his wide hazel eyes and blonde hair did nothing to harden his innocent appearance.

"Mitoki," Dalton called. Mitoki stood, taking his outstretched hand. "How are you? I haven't seen you since annual testing."

"I'm well, thank you," Mitoki said. "How about you?"

"Can't complain."

Mitoki could tell from his genuine smile and the light in his green eyes that Dalton was a down-to-earth Guardian. He knew that Dalton was the grandson of the head Elder, and that he had married and started a family young, as he was just approaching the age of thirty. Otherwise, Mitoki did not know much about the man who was about to become the leader of their team in the Guardian Tournament. He had never felt confident enough to approach the top-ranked Guardian outside of annual testing.

"I guess we better get going to the Beast Realm portal," Dalton declared, unsure what else to say to Mitoki. He mentally kicked himself for feeling so nervous. Since the age of fourteen, he had been risking his life as a Guardian, chasing down powerful murderers and those who had the power to be a threat to the five realms. But standing there with Mitoki, he was terrified to become the leader of a team of Guardians—particularly when two of those Guardians were the living legends Hanyi Treneke and Keito DeVero.

"Pretty strange, huh?" Mitoki said, walking with Dalton back to the shuttle. "Hanyi Treneke?"

"I know." Dalton barked a disbelieving laugh. "I never thought I'd get to meet him, let alone work with him."

"A lot of people have said he was very light-hearted when he was in service," Mitoki said. "Do you think he still is? I mean…after what happened?"

"Somehow, I doubt it."

Hanyi was not at all what the humans expected. The two recognized him from pictures, but he had never met them before, so when they approached, his sharp brown eyes looked them up and down briefly through the mussed strands of greying-brown hair that fell over his eyes.

"Dalton?" he asked, pointing to the top-ranked Guardian.

"Yes," Dalton said, finding his voice very thin as he stared at someone he had grown up idolizing. Hanyi looked younger than expected, but Dalton knew Hanyi was part of a pack of powerful wolves that lived impressively long lives. Despite knowing that, Dalton did not expect the wolf to look forty.

"I've heard a lot about you. It's great to meet you." Hanyi smiled broadly, shaking Dalton's hand. "It's great to meet the man behind the legend."

"Same here." Dalton beamed, eased by Hanyi's warm expression. "I mean…you're *Hanyi Treneke*."

"Oh, don't worry," Hanyi said. "I'm not as bad as everyone said. I actually did do a good job on occasion."

He shook Mitoki's hand as well.

"And you are?"

"Mitoki."

"Ah, the young one from the Realm of Light, of course. It's very impressive, accomplishing what you have at such a young age. You're going to have to help me out, though. I'm old and I don't have the energy I once had. You young ones are going to have to be patient with the old man, here."

The two younger Guardians could only nod in response, still nervous and star-struck. When five awkward, silent seconds had passed, Hanyi glanced around them.

"I guess we have to pick up…Eclipse now, right?"

"Yeah," Dalton affirmed, breaking out of his trance. He turned back to the shuttle stop only to see the bus pulling away from the curb. "I guess we're catching the next shuttle."

"How old are you two?" Hanyi asked, following Dalton as he stepped to the side of the shuttle sign.

"Twenty-nine."

"Nineteen."

"Yikes, I'm so old…" Hanyi laughed. "You two must be a little nervous about the tournament."

"A little," they both admitted.

"Understandable," he said. "But it's not as scary as you think. The anticipation is the worst part. Once you get in the ring, all the background anxieties fade away and you get caught up in the competition. It's not that scary."

"What about you? How do you feel about it? I mean…"

"After last time?" Hanyi said, surprising them with how easily he broached the subject. "It's going to be a little difficult, but I'll do my best. I won't let the team down."

Hanyi was so lighthearted that Dalton and Mitoki did not know how to react. They had expected someone who had seen such tragedy as a Guardian to be darker, quieter, and less willing to interact, but the wolf was so happy he seemed almost idiotic and his attitude broke the tension.

A few of the Guardians on the shuttle to the Realm of Darkness portals recognized Hanyi and whispered, pointing, though he seemed not to notice until Dalton mentioned the gossip.

"I can't wait to see how people react to seeing Keito again." Hanyi grinned devilishly.

Once they reached the towering building housing the many portals leading to the Realm of Darkness, Eclipse was walking out of the revolving doors, his eyes on his phone. When Dalton called to him, he shoved his hands into his pockets, his shaggy hair shielding his surprised hazel eyes at seeing Hanyi and Mitoki.

"Eclipse," Dalton said, extending his hand as they drew close.

"Dalton," he greeted back with a firm handshake. "Mitoki." He nodded curtly, extending his hand. Mitoki felt very nervous around Eclipse—he always had. Eclipse had a rough attitude and it was hard for others to get close to him. Even his appearance was unsettling as he was dressed entirely in black, though he clearly had no problem showing off his physique with the way the black shirt clung to him.

"Ooh, I bet you're quite the ladies' man," Hanyi said, also shaking hands with Eclipse. "Look at you. You definitely have the sexy-mysterious thing working for you."

Dalton tried not to smile, but he was happy that the older Guardian was not at all put off by Eclipse's appearance. Eclipse could not say anything for a few seconds before he chose to ignore the comment completely.

"It's nice to meet you, Hanyi," he said. "I'm Eclipse Retani."

"Nice to meet you," Hanyi said brightly. "How old are you?"

"Why do you keep asking?" Dalton laughed.

"I'm trying to see how many generations I am behind you."

"I'm twenty-seven."

"Okay…" Hanyi mused, pensive. "Well, at least I won't be the oldest."

"We have one hour before we have to be at the Elders' Chambers," Eclipse said, glancing at his wristwatch. "We just have to get Keito."

Hanyi scoffed and the humans turned, perplexed by the reaction.

"Oh, sorry, that wasn't supposed to be funny," the wolf said with a sheepish grin.

"Why did you laugh?"

Hanyi clapped to his hands together and rubbed them. "It's just time to get the bratty demon." He sighed before wincing playfully as he thought about his old partner. "I warn you, he can be *very* temperamental. Once you get to know him, he's not so bad. He just has to warm up to you."

The Guardians caught the next shuttle to the portal building for the Demon Realm, which was the smallest of the portal buildings, but when they stepped off the bus, Keito was not outside waiting for them.

"Figured as much," Hanyi grumbled. "Alright, come on."

"Where are you going?" Mitoki asked.

"I have a feeling that Keito is sulking about this whole thing. He's probably lost track of the time and avoiding coming here for as long as he can. We're going to go get him."

The building housing the portals to the Demon Realm was entirely empty apart from the three guards monitoring access. Dalton flashed his ID and then vouched for Hanyi as the other two humans were admitted upon showing their Guardian IDs. Dalton was about to ask which of the five portals they should take when Hanyi told him they all led to the same place.

"Are you sure we shouldn't wait for him here?" Mitoki asked.

"Why? You scared?" Eclipse jeered.

"No," he said. "I've been to the Demon Realm on assignment before. I just want to know *how* we're going to find him."

"I don't think he's far from the portals," Hanyi assured.

Dalton always found the ten seconds of black weightlessness disorienting when traversing the portals, but it was even more disorienting when traveling to the Demon Realm, since the one-room structure around the portals had a dirt floor and no sign of modern amenities.

The guards on the other side nodded to the four Guardians before turning away to resume their quiet conversation. Dalton looked around the ramshackle room, becoming worried when there was no sign of Keito.

"I don't know about this…" he said slowly.

"About what?" Hanyi asked, stepping to Dalton's side.

"I just…" Dalton did not know how to phrase what he was feeling about Keito's absence, but Hanyi nodded, understanding the silence.

"Don't worry, Keito's very loyal, and even though he seems like he's being flakey now, he's just throwing a small tantrum. He'll get over it."

The three humans blinked at the wolf incredulously.

"What?"

"Nothing, it's just…the way you talk about him…" Dalton said with a nervous laugh.

"Come on," Hanyi coaxed, pushing open the cloth and reed sheet covering the door and walking into the musky woods surrounding the structure. The humans were on edge instinctually, now in the ever-feared Demon Realm, trying not to recall every horrific story and legend they had heard about the ancient land. Hanyi seemed entirely unconcerned.

"Did you come here often with Keito?" Dalton asked.

"All the time," he said, looking at the paths they could take before turning right, the humans in tow. "Keito never moved to the Middle Dimension. He was born and raised in the Demon Realm. But you probably already knew that."

"We did," Eclipse said.

"I don't know the Demon Realm as well as he does, obviously, but I know that there is a clearing over there that he liked to pout in when he was trying to avoid something."

"*Pout?*" the humans said simultaneously.

"I'm saying all this now so that I don't say it when he's around," Hanyi said. "I'm just teasing, of course. Keito's just complicated. You have to learn that it is simply the way he is and don't take his weird habits personally."

The four reached the clearing Hanyi remembered, but there was still no sign of the demon. Hanyi huffed and shook his head as the others joined him in the center of the glade.

"I hate it when he does this…" He groaned loudly. "Come *on*, can't you be a good Guardian *once* in your life?"

"Waitin' for someone?" a voice called.

The Guardians turned to the man leaning against a tree behind them, tapping a dagger against his arm, his amused expression causing them to go on high alert. As the man stood straight and stepped forward, two others appeared from behind trees, a third swinging down from a branch.

"We mean no trouble," Hanyi said.

"No?" the first demon pressed, stalking closer as the Guardians moved together, preparing to defend themselves. "Because, you know, whenever humans come here, they're asking for trouble."

"And whenever *Guardians* come here," one woman added, smirking, "they *deserve* trouble."

"We are waiting for a demon Guardian," Dalton explained calmly, meeting eyes with each demon. "We will leave once he arrives."

"You think that the fact you're waiting for another Guardian will save you?" the first asked, drawing closer and raising the dagger between them, glaring. "Perhaps we should kill all five of you and shove your sorry corpses back through the portal. Send a message to those assholes in Council warning them to stop killing our kind."

"Use violence to prevent more violence?" another voice said on the edge of the clearing. "Bravo. With intellect like that, you'll be a lord in no time."

All eyes turned to the new demon who had appeared on the outer edge of the clearing. Everyone recognized him—the humans from pictures, and the other demons from reputation and his piercing golden eyes.

"What the hell are you doing here, Keito?" the leader of the small gang growled. "This doesn't concern you."

"I'm afraid it does concern me," he said, his step measured as he approached the confrontation. "Killing Guardians is against the law. I'm sure even someone of your level understands that."

"Of *my* level?" the demon scoffed, turning away from the Guardians to face the older demon. "Perhaps you have forgotten where you are, Keito. You are far from friendly territory. You have no power on DeVastes land."

Keito scoffed.

"You really believe that I have no power on the DeVastes land?" Keito turned to Hanyi, quirking an eyebrow. "I'm embarrassed for you that you're being terrorized by these idiotic baby demons."

The female demon let out a screech and launched at Keito, teeth bared, but the older demon stepped calmly out of the way.

The two others also attacked but he easily dodged, his expression stoic. When one of the younger demons swiped a dagger at Keito, the former Guardian grabbed his wrist and flipped the younger demon on his back, breaking his arm in the process. The female then attacked with her own knife, though Keito redirected the weapon and turned her, pressing the blade into her throat enough for her to feel blood trickle down her jugular.

The final demon hesitated, glancing between Keito and the leader of their small gang. The leader shook his head minutely.

"I thought so," Keito said, shoving the girl away and tossing the dagger to the ground. "Run home, kids."

Keito turned to the Guardians, jerking his head to the path, silently telling them to leave. The Guardian team began walking, the young demons shakily pulling themselves to their feet behind them.

The human Guardians were unable to keep themselves from turning to look back at Keito, surprised to be in such close proximity to the legendary Guardian. Because of the constant glancing, Mitoki saw when the leader of the young demons growled and turned his knife in his hands.

Mitoki opened his mouth to warn Keito, but the knife had already left the demon's hand, flying at Keito's back.

Keito turned, grabbing the knife and spinning once more to gain momentum before hurling the knife back. It lodged itself into the demon's arm with a sickening snap, the force pushing him to the ground.

"I told you to run home," Keito snarled. "Now go, before I decide to really do some damage."

He nodded for the Guardians to start walking once again.

When they could no longer hear the worried discussions of the younger demons, Keito playfully smacked Hanyi upside the head.

"Didn't I teach you *anything*?" he jeered.

Hanyi laughed, rubbing the back of his head.

"You know me. I'm a lover, not a fighter," he defended. "And besides," he punched Keito in the arm, "we wouldn't have had to come looking for you if you weren't off pouting and had just met us in the Middle Dimension like a good demon."

"I got a late start. I was not *pouting*," Keito grumbled, rolling his eyes.

"I thought you said you were going to stop teasing like that when he was around," Dalton chuckled, turning to Hanyi.

"I changed my mind."

Chapter Five

Dalton and the others remained silent, their footsteps echoing in the vast, marbled halls leading to the Elders' Chambers. The travel between the Demon Realm and the Dimension Protection Council Compound had been quiet and awkward. Even Hanyi had stopped trying to lighten the mood, finally hit with the gravity of their meeting with the Elders.

The guards led them through the corridors with stoic faces to the ornate, heavy doors. With a flourish of ceremony, they pushed open the doors and stepped to the side, allowing the Guardians in.

The newly-formed team approached the five Elders seated at the long table in the meeting room. The portraits of previous, steely-eyed Elders watched them approach and sit in the chairs placed opposite their respective Elder.

"Welcome, Guardians," Elder Teban greeted, his gaze passing over each of them as his smile caused his eyes to crinkle. "I am grateful that you came on such short notice. We all appreciate it." His eyes fell on Keito and then on Hanyi, scrutinizing the former Guardians. "I know that we have never formally met, but I was in Council before you both retired."

"I don't remember you," Keito said shortly.

"On to business," Elder Celeste cut in, worried that Elder Teban would aggravate the demon. "I'm afraid we don't have much time to discuss this. You know of the delicate situation within the Guardians and the realms. I'm sure that the Protectors also explained our reasons for hosting the Guardian Tournament."

"I'm afraid that they did not," Hanyi said. "I was only informed that I had been unretired and was being commanded to compete."

"I'm sure you have heard of the number of Guardian deaths recently," Elder Ari said. "Only a few days ago we had another Guardian snap, ranting about demon domination and killing eight Guardians before he was finally taken down."

"Was he a human?" Hanyi pressed.

"He was."

"Guardians have gone off the handle before," Keito said. "This one incident should not be enough to reenact the Guardian Tournament."

"It is not only one incident," Elder Celeste insisted. "Many Guardians are being killed, both by nervous Guardians and terrified civilians."

"And the situation is likely to get worse," Elder Teban added. "The Dimensional Holding Seal is fractured in two places. That explains the holes ripping open in the dimensional fabric and how demons are getting into other realms to kill humans."

"How many instances have there been of that?" Keito pressed.

"Twelve in the last year," Elder Teban said. "The death toll has been nearly fourteen thousand from those combined incidents."

"Don't exaggerate the numbers for your political agenda," Keito said. "There have been *eight* instances, and the death toll managed to just pass seven thousand across all three human-inhabited realms. And the Old Blood Lords have made examples of those demons."

"Your Old Blood Lords are bloodthirsty war mongers," Elder Lunar sneered. "If they *have* made examples of the criminals, that's one thing. But the people have seen the damage only a few demons are capable of, and it has sparked so much fear that they are murdering anyone even *suspected* of being a demon."

"Sounds like you do not have very good command over your subjects. That's hardly my concern," Keito noted.

"Keito," Hanyi whispered in warning.

"It's alright," Elder Teban assured Hanyi. "We are well-informed of Keito DeVero's infamous petulance. We were prepared to hear such infantile remarks."

"Infantile?"

"You have spent so long in isolation that you have not seen the severity of the current state of the realms," Elder Ari said. "The Dimensional Holding Seal has been *fractured*. Do you have any concept of what that means?"

"Elders," Dalton interjected, hoping to keep the meeting from turning into a confrontation, "about the fractured seal, what has Vestera Hizoku had to say about it?"

"I'm afraid he has not responded to our requests for aid," Elder Teban murmured, lowering his gaze.

Keito and Hanyi shared a silent look.

"Surely he would know that his seal had been broken," Mitoki added. "He likely knows the culprit, too."

"We do not know what he knows," Elder Celeste said, shaking her head. "He has been very silent."

The Guardians fell quiet, not sure what to make of the dragon lord's absence. While it was true that no one ever saw the dragon, everyone knew of his existence and power. To hear that he had abandoned them in their time of need was troubling.

"My Elders," Hanyi started, "how do you expect the Guardian Tournament to help you catch the person who broke the seal?"

"We do not expect it to be easy," Elder Teban admitted. "But we are quite confident that Guardians, perhaps a large group of Guardians, are responsible for, not only the break in the seal, but the unrest within our Guardians and the people of the realms."

"You're saying there is a leak of information?" Eclipse concluded. "That the people have heard rumor about the demons wanting to take over the realms?"

"There is no such plot among demons," Keito said.

"I'm not saying there is," Eclipse defended. "But if the people of the human-inhabited realms were to hear of such a plot, it could cause a violent and chaotic reaction. When we were on our way here, we were attacked by four young demons who wanted revenge for the demons that have been lynched. The more violence we allow to occur, the worse it will become. Soon, we won't be able to keep the people calm, nor the demons from seeking revenge."

"That is why we decided on the Guardian Tournament," Elder Teban said with a nod. "The people are fearing Guardians for various reasons. We have demons that work for the Guardian Branch, very powerful demons that could turn on us at any moment. And, considering the Guardian that killed the others two days ago was human, we have much to be concerned about in our human Guardians, as well. If we put the Guardians against one another, there is a possibility that these individuals will attempt recruitment, or even make a mistake and allow us to discover where each Guardian's loyalty lies."

"My Elders," Keito started, "I'm sure you are well-informed of the Tournament Slaughter. I'm sure you are also aware that a similar tactic was used regarding the tournament that year. Therefore, if you wish to repeat that incident, feel free to throw yourselves into the burning building as well. But if you think that I'm going to be a part of that madness again, you are sadly mistaken. I want no part of this."

"Keito, we are fully aware of what happened last tournament, and if you think that somehow disqualifies you from participating in this one, *you* are the one who is sadly mistaken," Elder Lunar said.

"Do not talk down to me," Keito warned. "You're just trying to use us as bait to draw out very dangerous individuals. I'm not going to be some worm on a hook. I quit the Guardians forty years ago and I fully intend to remain *out*."

"Keito," Elder Teban started, standing to lean over the table, his angry eyes focused on the demon, "need I remind you that this is partially *your* fault?"

"I would be *very* careful in choosing your next words," Keito warned, leaning forward.

"I think we all need to calm down and take a deep breath," Elder Renard said, raising his hands, preparing to leap between Elder Teban and Keito.

"You're telling me to calm down?" Keito snapped. "You search me out, unretire me—against the Guardian Code—and then you threatened the only person I have left after the Tournament Slaughter to force me to participate again, and I'm supposed to roll over and take it?"

"Keito, please," Elder Celeste pled. "If anyone is necessary on this team, it's you. You hold all the records in the Guardian Branch. You have solved more impossible cases than any other Guardian on record. You led your team to victory in the Guardian Tournament eight consecutive times. You are invaluable to this team."

"I left that life in the past," he said. "Now, I am choosing to walk away." Keito excused himself from the room.

Hanyi stood.

"I'll talk to him, Elders," he offered. "I'm sorry about this." He hurried after Keito.

"Hanyi," Elder Ari called. The wolf turned. "He *must* join this tournament. If any of you don't, the dimensions will be in danger. I know you understand that. Make sure Keito understands, as well."

Hanyi nodded once and left the meeting room.

"While I understand what you are hoping to accomplish with this tournament," Dalton started, "I must admit that using us as bait is not an aspect I'm entirely comfortable with."

"You must not think of it as us using you as bait," Elder Teban corrected. "We are sending you on covert investigations. You are meant to infiltrate the tournament and find those that would seek to destroy the council and the realms. We know that these are extremely dangerous people. The thought that anyone, or even a group of people, with the power break the seal set by the most powerful dragon alive is a terrifying prospect." He looked among the three human Guardians, his gaze pleading. "But I trust you. The Elders trust you. And we know that you will find the culprits. This is not only a matter of severe damage to the seal—this is a case of high treason. Someone is trying to dismantle the Dimension Protection Council and destroy all five realms."

"Keito!" Hanyi called, running after the demon. "Keito!!" He grabbed the demon's arm.

"Let me go!" Keito barked, rounding on Hanyi, his teeth bared. Others in the hall whirled around at the noise before scurrying away. They were not about to get mixed up with two Guardians who had been forced back into service.

"Just listen to me!" Hanyi demanded as Keito yanked his arm away. The demon did not leave, studying the floor tiles intently, shifting his weight between his feet as if preparing to run but willing to listen.

"Thank you," Hanyi said. "I know you're angry. I understand better than anyone. I don't want to leave my family for this circus the Elders are putting on again. But...what Elder Teban said is right. It is *our* fault this has to happen in the first place."

"Hanyi, don't do this to me."

"I'm not trying to blame you, Keito, you know that," he said. "I admit, I purposely stayed away from you these last few years, but I just...I couldn't bear the thought of how bad things have gotten and how it was our fault for not stopping it when this was our case." Hanyi motioned back to the doors of the Elders' Chambers. "These Guardians are *young*. They weren't even born when the slaughter happened. They don't know that this was already a case. Are you really going to let them figure everything out the hard way? If they do that, then it will just be a repeat of what happened to us."

"I can't..." Keito closed his eyes. "I can't do this again, Hanyi. I *can't*."

"Why can't you?"

"Can *you*?" he challenged. "Can you really go back to this assignment? Can you handle waking up every day and thinking about how this will likely end?"

"I've had to deal with the last forty years waking up and not knowing if we've already lost," Hanyi whispered. "I wake up every day thinking it's going to be the day I hear that he's succeeded. Compared to that, I'm willing to go back to this case."

The demon Guardian remained silent.

"Keito, let's *finish* this," Hanyi insisted. "If we leave these boys to handle it, they are going to die. And then we will have failed *again*. Could you bear that a second time?"

Keito sighed heavily, tilting his head back as if he was surrendering to death, too tired to fight.

"I don't know what you've been going through these last several years," Hanyi said. "I know I am in no position to ask this of you, but *please*."

"Hanyi, what you're asking me to do…" Keito's voice became choked and he had to take a moment to compose himself. "I want it to be over. I really do. But when I see this coming at me, it's like…like I know that this is just going to be another round in his game. His sick, twisted entertainment…" He stopped and swallowed hard. "Damn it, I don't know what else to do…"

Hanyi dropped his gaze. "He had to know this would pull us both back in," he muttered. "He's been planning this all along while we've turned a blind eye." He raised his hands in defeat. "And now he's trapped us. We can't ignore it anymore. We have to finish what we started."

Keito nodded. "I know."

~/\~

Keito and Hanyi reentered the Elders' Chambers slowly and the Elders' expectant gazes locked on the demon as the others of the soon-to-be Team Dalton turned.

"Alright," Keito agreed. "I'll play your game again."

"Thank you, Keito," Elder Teban said, bowing his head shallowly.

"I'm not doing it for you."

"I understand." Elder Teban lifted a folded paper from the stack in front of him. "We all agree?"

The Guardians glanced at one another and nodded, certain they had no idea to what they were agreeing.

"Perfect, then you should go meet your training master. She is a dragon living here in the Middle Dimension and she is an excellent trainer. We have contracted her to get you in shape for the tournament." Elder Teban handed the piece of paper to Dalton. "Here's her address. She's expecting you this afternoon."

Chapter Six

The journey to their new trainer's house was silent. Dalton could tell that Eclipse and Mitoki wanted to discuss the tournament and their new mission within the competition, but with Keito's irritated expression and Hanyi's nervous, downcast eyes, they did not feel right breaking the silence.

The newly-formed team took a tram and then a bus to the outskirts of the only city in the Middle Dimension. Homes of the council members faded into sprawling farm land stretching back into gently-rolling foothills. The human Guardians busied themselves watching each bus stop pass and counting down to the appointed stop scrawled on the scrap of paper Dalton held. With only an elderly couple left on the bus, there was nothing to distract them from the anxiety coiling around their ribs about meeting their new trainer so far in the middle of nowhere.

From their bus stop, the team trudged over hard-packed dirt roads, Dalton constantly checking the denoted address with the numbers painted on the stone posts delineating each farm. He finally stopped at the correct address and led the others up the path toward the front door of a small house nestled between a barn and what appeared to be a second, larger, domed-top barn.

Dalton tried not to let the others see how his hand trembled as he knocked.

An older woman answered the door. Her black hair was starting to grey, framing an angular, dark face punctuated with green eyes that scrutinized the Guardians with animal intensity—a common trait among dragons in their human forms. She was not especially short, but her stocky frame made her look even smaller as she barely reached the height of the Guardians' shoulders.

"You must be the Guardians the Elders sent," the woman noted after she had cast a sharp eye over each of them, her voice rough with age and wisdom.

"You must be Master Jikia," Dalton greeted, unable to completely hide the nervousness in his being.

"Well, come in, come in. Let's get to know each other. We have a lot of work to do."

They obeyed the order hesitantly, crowding in the foyer, unsure where to go. When Jikia had closed the door behind Keito, she led them to the back of the house and down a long, narrow hallway. She easily pushed open the heavy door and stepped down onto the dirt of the domed structure the Guardians had seen from outside.

The building was not a barn but an arena similar to the ones in the Guardian Tournament and the ones used in training young Guardians during their apprenticeships. Dalton could not help but smile thinly at the wave of nostalgia that washed over him when his shoes hit the hard-packed dirt and his eyes took in the cabinets lining the tall walls, no doubt filled with training equipment he had not used since his own apprenticeship.

"No doubt this is a familiar setting for all of you. And yes, you are back in training, boys. You're going to be spending a majority of your time in here in the next two months," Jikia explained. "I have rooms for you in the house, but that is only for sleeping. When you're not sleeping, eating, or on the toilet, you will be in here or helping me with farm chores," the dragon continued.

"This is a board and train?" Hanyi asked with a concerned laugh. "Oh...I'm going to need to go home and tell everyone I'll be gone for a while."

"Don't worry," she said. "Once we have a little chat, you all can run home and pack whatever you think you'll need. Though I expect all of you back before lights out so we can start training first thing tomorrow morning."

She motioned them closer and then gestured to the ground. She sat in the middle of the arena, waiting for the five Guardians to join her in a circle.

"I want to get to know each of you a little. Most of you I know by reputation, but that is only your work as a Guardian. I want to know where you come from, how long you've been a Guardian, your family...anything you're willing to share."

"Seems a bit personal..." Mitoki noted, wary.

"Maybe, but I'm the one that has to figure out the best way to train you and get you to work together as a team. You five did not have the luxury of picking your own teammates, so we're starting at square one." She raised her hands in a casual shrug. "So, I'll start. I am Guardian Training Master Jikia Topesca, but I ask you not to call me 'master.' I hate the title," she told them bluntly. "I am a dragon, true, but I have made my home here in the Middle Dimension and have been training Guardians for the past two hundred and twenty years. I've trained many gifted Guardians, but not any who have made it to the position of top-ranked, like you." She turned to Dalton. "And I will say, if what they say about you is true, Dalton, you are incredibly powerful for a human."

"I'm sure you've heard exaggerations," Dalton said with an uncomfortable chuckle. "But thank you for the praise."

"You've trained Guardians for the tournament before, then?" Eclipse prompted.

"Yes. I even had two teams become champions of the tournament," she said, glancing at Hanyi and Keito. "Until these two entered the tournament, that is."

Hanyi grinned.

"I don't recall ever meeting you formally, but I do remember you and some of your teams. I lost a few matches to several of the Guardians you trained."

"Liar," Jiki teased.

"No, really," Hanyi said. "They were impressive opponents. Although...I'm sorry to say, I was the weakest on my team."

"You were not," Keito said.

"Yes, I was. What team were you looking at?"

"*My* team, and you were not the weakest."

"No?" Hanyi challenged with an incredulous blink. "Who was worse? Jacob? Who lost three times the *entire* tournament? Hector, who never lost...*ever*? Who?"

"*Me*," Keito answered. "You kept a tally of how many fights you lost every season. You let that sit in the back of your mind and used it as a stick to beat yourself with. How many fights did you lose?"

"Twelve on my worst year..." Hanyi mumbled, looking at the ground as the humans smiled at the banter.

"Okay, twelve. Did you ever count how many times *I* lost? Do you remember my worst season?"

"In the tournament?"

Keito groaned and shot Hanyi an exasperated look.

"Well...that doesn't really count," Hanyi grumbled.

"Come on, say it. I already know the answer."

"So, you kept a tally, too!"

"Hanyi..."

"...twenty-three..." the wolf finally said.

Dalton and the other humans were surprised to hear that Keito had lost twenty-three fights in one season—particularly when he had been an eight-time champion of the Guardian Tournament.

"There we go," Keito declared.

"Yeah, well, that was because you never listened to any of us. 'No, Keito, you've fought four times and your intestines are falling out your side, let us take the last guy.' 'No, no, I can handle it.' That's *you*." Hanyi pointed accusingly at the oldest Guardian and the others laughed, some of the tension broken.

"I am not like that," Keito disagreed.

"Oh, yes, you are!" Hanyi cried. "You are, *completely* are!"

"Ignore him, he's a drama queen. He likes to exaggerate," Keito told the others with a playful roll of his eyes.

"I'm not exa—*hey!*"

"Okay, boys, we already know how well you two know each other. How about we agree that you're both right to some degree and come back to the present?"

"I'm *not* a drama queen…" Hanyi mumbled.

"Eclipse," Jikia addressed the quiet Guardian who had his eyes cast down despite the playful banter. He jumped, startled at the sudden address. "Are you alright?"

"Fine, just…a little worried about the tournament if two of the best Guardians in history *lost* some fights."

"There's no reason to be worried," Keito assured, shaking his head. "I still don't know how we were named the best Guardians in history. We're really not that great as Guardians."

"Speak for yourself," Hanyi quipped.

"There's no reason to be concerned. Individual losses in the tournament don't mean that much," Jikia seconded. "Who was your trainer? I know many trainers in the Darkness Realm."

"Master Feburn Genbuki. I've been his only student so you probably never met him." When he saw the confused looks from his new teammates, he shrugged. "He was my godfather before he was my trainer. When other trainers in the area didn't want to train me as a Guardian, he trained and got his license. But I'm still his only student."

"Did you live with him?" Jikia pressed. "What about your parents?"

"Both dead," Eclipse answered easily—it was a very common answer among Guardians. "When they died, Master Genbuki adopted my brother and me."

"Is your brother a Guardian, too?" Jikia asked.

"No," Eclipse said with a roll of his eyes. "He's the brainiac of the family. He runs his own research facility and always has his nose in a book or some complicated charts. I don't know. That was never for me. Being a Guardian was a clear path for me. I've been with the branch for almost fourteen years."

"Any hobbies? Wife?" their trainer prompted.

"No," he said, shrugging one shoulder. "I really don't have much of a life outside of work." He turned to Dalton, nodding. "But I do know Dalton has a wife and a daughter."

"Oh, trying to put the spotlight on me, huh?" Dalton teased.

"To be fair, *everyone* in the branch knows your daughter has you wrapped around her finger," Mitoki laughed.

"How old?" Hanyi asked.

"Six," Dalton answered, his face brightening. "I married young and we had Theresa not long afterward."

"That's not a path many Guardians take," Jikia noted. "But I guess you're a bit of a legacy in the branch, aren't you? Your grandfather is a council Elder and your father was a Guardian as well, wasn't he?"

Dalton nodded. "But I was just a baby when he was killed. He didn't raise me to be a Guardian or anything like that. It was just something I was drawn to, and for some reason was good at. I've been a Guardian for fifteen years already. It just flew by."

"When did you become top-ranked?" Keito asked.

"Only five years ago," he said with a shrug. "I think you hold the longest reign as top-ranked Guardian."

Keito cringed. "Reign? Yikes..."

"See, Keito? We're so old we're probably listed in textbooks only by our records," Hanyi teased. "Though I might just be a footnote after you and Hector."

"You and your brother hold a lot of records," Mitoki said. "Must have been tough, being the younger brother to the top-ranked beast Guardian of the time."

"I got a little jealous," Hanyi agreed. "I mean, Hector was incredible and I idolized him. But," he leaned over and put an arm around Keito's shoulders, pulling him into an unwilling hug, "*I* was the best friend and partner to the best Guardian in history, so I won."

"How long were you partnered? I didn't know Guardians partnered across realms," Dalton asked.

"Human Guardians don't, but demon and beast do," Keito clarified, lightly pushing Hanyi away. "And I was tethered to this one for nearly forty years."

Hanyi pressed a hand to his chest in mock hurt. "*Tethered*? I gave you the best years of my short life!"

"Short?" Mitoki repeated. "You're well over a hundred, aren't you?"

"Hey now," Hanyi laughed brokenly, "I wouldn't call a hundred and twenty *well over* one hundred. But yeah, even for a Treneke wolf, I am getting up there in years."

"What did you do after you quit?" Jikia asked. "Can't say I've seen many Guardians *quit*."

"Yeah..." Hanyi sighed, his face falling. "Well, I struggled with so-called civilian life after the Guardians, and...after the death of my brother in the Tournament Slaughter. But my surviving siblings kept me grounded and, eventually, I found a mate. I've got five pups, too. Though, they're not really pups anymore. They grow fast." Hanyi shook his head in disbelief as he looked among the three human Guardians. "I sound like such an old man. I've got five kids and the oldest is almost your age." He motioned to Mitoki. "Mind-boggling, really."

"You are the youngest on the team, Mitoki," Jikia said with a nod. "I'd wager you're among the youngest Guardians ever raised to top-ranked. That's impressive."

"Not really," Mitoki said. "The Realm of Light is generally pretty quiet. I'm just willing to travel for cases, so I rose in the ranks quickly."

"Another workaholic," Jikia said with an exasperated grin. "Don't forget to live a little while you're still young."

"Yeah, I've heard that a lot," Mitoki said. "I'm not a *complete* workaholic. I'm even engaged."

"Really?" Eclipse said, surprised.

"Yeah. We were going to get married in about four months, but now the date is up in the air until we learn more about the tournament and this assignment."

"Kinda young to be getting married..." Eclipse said under his breath.

"Guardians don't typically live long lives," Mitoki said with raised eyebrows. "I've always wanted a family of my own. And I love Rebecca. She's my biggest support. She's always helped pull me out of the dark headspace that comes with being a Guardian."

"I understand the feeling, Mitoki," Dalton said with a strong nod. "Congratulations."

"Thank you."

"Almost all of you actually have partners or children," Jikia mused with a pensive nod. "That's surprising to me. So many Guardians remain so devoted to the branch they don't form relationships." She turned her gaze to Keito, who clearly anticipated the attention was about to turn on him as he tensed and crossed his arms over his chest. "What about you? Did you settle down after you quit?"

"Not really," he said, his eyebrows going high. "I just...tried to disappear." He took a deep breath. "Truth be told, as a Guardian, I was a workaholic. I put blinders on and just did my job. So you all probably know just about everything about me."

"Yeah, as a *Guardian*," Hanyi said, rolling his eyes.

"Which has been a vast majority of my life."

"Do you mind if I ask how old you are?" Eclipse asked.

"Three hundred and twenty-six."

"And you were a Guardian for nearly that long?" Mitoki pressed.

"Not exactly. I got a late start. I didn't train as a child like humans. I joined when I was nearly forty. And from then until the Tournament Slaughter, I was a very active Guardian. But again, you probably already knew that."

"I had the honor of meeting your trainer often, Keito," Jikia said with a gentle smile. "Master Todac was a very wise and honorable demon."

"Yes, he was," Keito agreed, his voice barely above a whisper. "He and Hanyi's master, Master Linnel, were co-trainers of our team in the tournament, so I suspect you met them quite often."

"Yes, but when Team Keito began sweeping the tournament, your trainers had to be careful of jealous trainers. There was quite a bit of envy."

"I didn't realize the tournaments got political with the trainers," Dalton said.

"Near the end, it was a very cutthroat world to be part of," Jikia said. She took a moment to steady herself as she turned back to the two older Guardians. "I...I'm sorry the two of you must become part of this again. After surviving what you did, it can't have been easy to hear the news. But all the same, I'm sure you understand that they want you involved because the reinstatement of the tournament might motivate someone to attack the tournament and Council wants someone who would be able to spot the signs."

Keito winced and took a deep breath as Hanyi cleared his throat.

"We know," he whispered.

"Everything related to the tournament and the massacre has been a taboo subject for as long as I've been a Guardian," Dalton said. "I imagine it has to do with some embarrassment by the DPC about how the tournament got out of hand...but I'm sure it was also too painful to talk about."

"Keito, Hanyi," Jikia asked, "can you walk back into a stadium?"

"I truly don't know," Hanyi admitted. "I haven't been in one since the slaughter."

"The Protectors said that rules and security would be changed to try and prevent it from happening again," Mitoki said.

"There's no way you can prevent something like that," Keito said, his voice pained.

"I...don't want to bring up such painful memories, but you two were the only survivors," Dalton started cautiously. "Do you know what happened? How it started and how it got bad?"

Both Keito and Hanyi had dropped their gazes to the ground.

"Judging by what was left when the smoke cleared…" Jikia murmured, "I'm sure it was chaotic in there."

Hanyi swallowed hard, glancing up briefly, his mouth opening to speak though no sound came.

"The tournament had been getting bloody long before the massacre," Jikia continued, taking over for the silent older Guardians. "It was established as a final trial for Guardian trainees, testing their strength and power before they were inducted into the branch. But soon it became something of a sport. It didn't matter if the Guardians were just finishing up their training or seasoned and ranked at the top. That's why the DPC started forming teams and developed more complex rules for the tournament. As the tournament grew, the general public began to take an interest. The DPC saw it as a way to build a better public image for the Guardian Branch, so they started televising the tournament, making it a year-round competition with multiple rounds. Needless to say, it also brought in a lot of money for Council, and it just kept growing."

"I'm assuming the DPC eventually lost control of it," Mitoki said.

"Like a runaway train," Jikia affirmed. "Spectators would start betting pools, and Council never cracked down on the betting rings. As the competition grew and the stadiums were erected, well…" she sighed heavily, "you all know the magic Guardians are capable of. It was not uncommon for there to be audience casualties from rogue attacks. But even that didn't deter people. It was just part of the tournament. There were even souvenirs that could be bought by the audience celebrating that they had survived the Guardian Tournament that year."

"It wasn't just the audience," Hanyi added. "The whole affair was bloody."

"The tournament became rife with corruption," Jikia elaborated. "There are plenty of rules about conduct within the ring, but there was nothing stopping teams or trainers attacking each other *outside* the tournament, trying to get an edge on the competition."

"What was the prize for winning?" Mitoki asked incredulously.

"There was some monetary gain, but mostly it was for recognition. Those who won the tournament were ranked in the top percentile, which meant more respect within the branch."

"You have to understand something," Hanyi interjected quietly, his eyes still downcast. "Unless you were a spectacularly powerful Guardian, or you had been part of some high-profile, public missions, it was expected of you to compete. It was how you

45

advanced in the branch. If you *didn't* compete, you were often shunned by the other Guardians."

"So if it became ingrained in the Guardian Branch..." Eclipse murmured.

"*Too* ingrained," Jikia agreed. "Soon it was more about the tournament than about actually *protecting* the realms. And that last year..." Jikia hesitated. "There was something about that year. The tournament was the most brutal I had ever seen. My team lost in the second round but I watched the subsequent rounds, and even I was alarmed at how *bloody* it had become."

"What was so different about that year?"

"Things were bad that year. Like they are now," their new trainer answered. "Dimensional holes ripping open, corruption scandals leaking...everyone was consumed with this...panicked rage that just permeated the tournament." Jikia turned her gaze back to Hanyi and Keito. "And in the fifth round, the massacre happened."

She hesitated before speaking again. "Do...do either of you remember what started it?"

Hanyi paused, finally clearing his throat though he still did not lift his gaze.

"It—" He stopped. "I know that the first time *I* noticed something was wrong was when there was an extended break between fights. Two Guardians had died in the ring and the audience was baying for more blood, but the announcer said that the cameras had suddenly stopped working and they were trying to get them back up and running. I knew then that something was wrong. One or two cameras having a malfunction was explainable. All of them? Not so much."

"So someone sabotaged the cameras in order not to be seen when the massacre started," Jikia deduced somberly.

"Do you know who did it?" Dalton pressed as gently as his curiosity would allow.

Hanyi took a few moments to collect himself.

"We were working a case at that time. Our whole team. We were going after this guy but...we hit a dead end in the case. He took the opportunity of our unpreparedness at the tournament to strike back, and send a message to the Guardians and the council."

"Message?"

"That he had the power to do what he did," Hanyi clarified. "He...the stadium was barricaded, set on fire, and then everyone inside was slaughtered. There were flames everywhere. People were running and screaming but it was too chaotic and disorienting. They were being cut down left and right. It was…so systematic. So *precise…*"

"Stop," Keito said suddenly. "Please, stop. I can't…"

"Okay," Dalton said, his own anxiety mounting as he imagined the mayhem inside the stadium.

"I'm sure after what happened, there will be a lot more regulation on the tournament to prevent that from happening again, should anyone try to send the same message," Jikia said, her voice quiet, masking her own nerves.

"Then the tournament will be completely different?" Eclipse asked.

"No, I'm sure the mechanics of the tournament will remain the same," she said. "Six rounds, two sets per round, rounds every two months."

"And it's just…fighting?" Mitoki asked.

"There is a lot of strategy involved, but it is a fight at its core," she said. "In the first three rounds, the teams of five face off in the arena at the same time. This can lead to using group tactics for attacks, or everyone picking someone from the opposing team and dividing up to defeat the other team. It's about learning how to play your own strengths with the strengths of your teammates, and reading your opponents carefully. The first three rounds narrow the competition quickly. If a team is disjointed, they can easily be overwhelmed. In the fourth, fifth, and sixth rounds, it's one-on-one fights until a team has a majority of wins. You fight until your opponent surrenders or goes unconscious. Obviously, you're not allowed to kill in the ring, so conditions and restrictions can really help or hinder you in later rounds."

"Conditions?"

Jikia grinned. "Don't worry, we'll go over all the dos and don'ts for the matches themselves. You're not going to learn it all in one day."

"This…is a lot to take in," Dalton said, trying to mask his nerves.

"Well, be ready, because there is a lot more to learn," she said. "Like I said, first thing tomorrow we start training as a *team*. You've got to learn how to respond to each other by second nature. The five-on-five matches in the first three rounds can be chaotic, and we can't have the best Guardians in the branch eliminated in the first rounds. That would just be embarrassing."

"Yes, it would," Dalton agreed, laughing.

"So, best way to get better at fighting as a team is *communication*." Jikia shot a pointed glance at Keito as she said the word. "Alright? You got a problem? Talk it out. Remember, Dalton is the leader of this team so if there is some petty squabble between any of you, you go to him or come to me. Internal disputes in the team are going to be a hindrance to your ability to fight in the tournament. So, again, *communication.*"

The door to the dome opened and a young woman stepped inside. She paused when she caught sight of the Guardians, her haunting green eyes scanning the five men as she reached up to nervously stroke the tail of her long, braided black hair.

"Oh, there you are," Jikia greeted brightly.

"Sorry, that took longer than expected," she said.

"Guardians, this is my daughter, Tarrena," Jikia introduced. "Tarrena, these are the Guardians that the Elders sent over to train for the tournament."

"Nice to meet you." Tarrena smiled, becoming more at ease as she approached. "Actually, I have a lot of things to carry in. I could use some help." She eyed the Guardians expectantly. Jikia watched as all five stood.

"After you," Dalton said, following as Tarrena led the way out of the dome.

"Hanyi, I need to speak with you," Jikia called to the wolf. Hanyi returned to Jikia after brief hesitation. Jikia glanced over the wolf's shoulder to be certain the others were out of the dome before she spoke.

"I'm worried about Keito."

"How so?"

"In a lot of ways," she said. "Keito's participation in the tournament will draw a lot of attention, just like before. I worry that he might try to take charge of the team and undermine Dalton's authority."

"He would never intentionally do that," Hanyi assured with a chuckle. "Even when he *was* team leader he never liked giving orders."

"All the same, I don't want your knowledge of previous tournaments to make either of you go off on your own without consulting Dalton or myself."

"Understood," Hanyi said. "I'll be sure to keep Keito grounded as much as I can."

He began to turn away when she called his attention again.

"Also," she hesitated when he turned, "I...worry about his well-being. I don't think I realized the impact the massacre had on him. He's so different now..."

"Not really," Hanyi said. "Keito's always been moody. But...he takes the Tournament Slaughter as his personal failure. There's a lot of guilt wrapped up in this for both of us. And to be thrown into a team like this…it does feel a bit like we're dishonoring the memory of our previous teammates."

Jikia nodded contemplatively.

"Do you think you can work with these younger Guardians? Will it be too much?"

"Oh, I can work with them," Hanyi said easily. "I already like them. It's just going to take some time to get back into the mentality of it all, you know?"

"And Keito? Think he'll be able to handle this? The tournament? Working with a new team?"

Hanyi hesitated, pursing his lips in thought.

"I do."

"Really?"

"The thing is, as much as Keito is resisting right now, he knows he *has* to do this. Once he warms up to these boys, he'll be very loyal to the team. And believe me, Keito is the best ally anyone could ask for."

Chapter Seven

The first night staying at Jikia's had been restless for the Guardians. Once they had helped Jikia and Tarrena bring in the feed bags for the farm animals, they were granted a few hours to return home and grab what they needed. They returned to the Middle Dimension and each managed to get back to Jikia's before their appointed curfew.

But the dark quiet of the countryside provided no sleep. The day had been exhausting, but as their bodies longed for rest, their minds were alive with anxieties. Each could feel the anticipation down to their bones. They were about to enter a terrifying world and none of them knew how dangerous it would become.

Therefore, the five Guardians appeared uneasy and drowsy when they stepped out of their small rooms the following morning.

When they could find no sign of Jikia or Tarrena in the house or around the barn, Dalton suggested they go to the dome.

Dalton was the one who pushed open the heavy door to find the training dome submerged in darkness. All natural light from the high windows had been blocked and even the light spilling in from the doorway was not enough to penetrate the density of the shadows.

"She wasn't kidding when she said we were back in training," Dalton said. "I remember doing these kinds of exercises when I was twelve."

"Wasn't that long ago for you guys…" Hanyi teased.

Dalton cautiously descended the two steps until he felt the dirt under his shoes. The others fell silent, not wanting to break Dalton's concentration. Even standing still, Dalton could not hear anything, nor could his eyes adjust to the impenetrable darkness.

"Keito," he called. "Can you see or hear anything?"

"I can't see anything," he answered, joining Dalton in the dome. The other Guardians followed close behind, remaining clustered at the bottom of the stairs. "This is some sort of shadow spell. Our eyes are not going to adjust." He drew in a deep breath. "No unfamiliar scents."

"Someone breathing at our three o'clock," Hanyi added.

"And eight o'clock," Keito concurred. "My guess, Jikia and Tarrena."

As if in confirmation the door to the dome slammed shut, eliminating the last of the light. By second nature, the Guardians turned back-to-back, old training habits easily taking over. When they heard one of them take a step, they followed, their shoulders brushing, staying as close as possible without tripping over one another.

Eclipse did not hear the slicing of air that made Keito and Hanyi turn their heads, but he felt the fast-approaching danger and ducked out of the way.

"What happened?" Dalton asked, hearing the sudden movement and a soft clatter on the ground behind him.

"I think this is an ambush training," Eclipse said, standing straight.

"I hate these exercises…" Hanyi groaned.

The Guardians had stopped moving, their magic increasing their awareness. When the next dagger flew at Mitoki, Keito intercepted it, feeling along the edges of the weapon.

"Small blade," he announced. "Stay alert."

Almost immediately after Keito spoke, Dalton felt a dagger flying in his direction. Knowing he could not simply duck out of the way for fear of the blade embedding itself into one of his teammates, Dalton swept his hand in the direction of the approaching dagger, using his basic magic skills to knock the blade to the side, causing it to hit the dirt of the dome with a quiet skittering sound.

When the human Guardians had been younger and had been tested with such exercises before, there had been an objective, whether it was to find a hidden object in the dark while avoiding the attacks or to find the attacker and subdue him based on where the attacks were originating. But with Jikia, the attacks were coming from all angles and they were unsure if they were meant to split apart or stay together.

In the dark, they could only rely on their hearing and the extra awareness their magic skills provided to keep from being hurt by the incoming weapons. There was also the added danger of colliding with the other Guardians dodging their own attacks as the speed and frequency of the daggers increased around them. When they could, the Guardians would pick up fallen blades they had stumbled across and throw them back in the direction of incoming attacks, but their bigger concern was remaining unharmed and aware of their teammates' locations.

Eventually, the exercise forced the Guardians to break formation, and they had no choice but to focus only on their own physical safety as they were constantly moving or deflecting blades. Occasionally, they would hear something that sounded like a heavy bag hitting the ground, but the distraction of the sound proved too dangerous as Dalton and Eclipse both narrowly avoided very painful injury when they turned to the location of the sound. The hurried dodge had sent Dalton sprawling to the hard dirt of the dome, causing him to hiss in pain as he tried to regain his bearings before another dagger found him.

But the attacks had stopped.

The only sound for several seconds was the labored breaths of the Guardians.

The darkness around them pulled back fluidly, like fabric sliding away from them, allowing light to wash over the dome. It took their eyes a few moments to adjust as they all straightened and studied their surroundings, unsure if the test was over. There were small daggers scattered over the dirt, plain and dull, clearly meant for training, not for causing harm. Practice dummies had also been set up in various locations around the dome, and all of them had been struck with daggers, explaining the sounds that had occasionally distracted the Guardians.

There was no sign of Jikia or Tarrena.

Mitoki, Hanyi, and Keito holding daggers, the Guardians grouped together again, scanning the dome in silence, waiting for something.

Keito suddenly turned, throwing his dagger, causing the others to tense, not having heard the shift of someone's foot in that direction.

The dagger was knocked to the side before it could reach the wall and a laugh sounded.

"Very well done," Jikia said, her hand motioning to one side as she removed her cloaking spell. "Truly, I did not anticipate you would do that well."

"What is that supposed to mean?" Eclipse asked, slightly incensed.

"I just assumed that you boys had gotten lazy in your positions of power as the top-ranked Guardians. And I expected Keito and Hanyi to have lost some of their touch in retirement, but I am very happy to say I was mistaken."

Hanyi let out a long sigh, dropping his dagger and leaning on his knees, shaking his head.

"Don't be too sure about that," he said wryly. "I'm way out of practice."

"You did fine," Jikia said. "So well, in fact, that now I know where to start your training. This exercise was clearly too easy for you boys. I better intensify things."

Dalton shared a worried-but-bemused glance with the new members of his team.

The training itself was not easy, but their years of experience as Guardians in the field helped them learn quickly and sharpen skills from their early training days. Jikia was a tough master and did not coddle them, quick to point out their bad habits and how it was likely to get them injured in the tournament or even killed in the field. Soon, training for the tournament felt more like Jikia nitpicking their idiosyncrasies because they picked up on her training so rapidly that she had to find ways to keep the training difficult.

With the close quarters of them living together with the two dragons, the dynamics of Team Dalton made themselves known quickly. Everyone fell into a role.

Jikia was a tough trainer, but she was also willing to ask Keito for advice or techniques that she had seen him use in the past. While the Guardians were certain she was just as star-struck by Keito as everyone else, they did not know that she was also trying to get the demon Guardian to interact more with his new team. Jikia tried to keep the atmosphere during training light and engaging, considering the gravity of their mission within the tournament. But as a dragon, she struggled relating to the humans and came across as cold and distant, as was the case with most dragons.

Tarrena was much warmer and more approachable than her mother, and she took on the duty of being sure the Guardians stopped to eat and were comfortable in the house. She was quieter and more reserved, but whenever teased enough by the Guardians, she was able to fire back with her own sharp wit and was quick to challenge them to a spar if they wanted to test her, as she was certain she was more powerful than all the Guardians on Team Dalton, apart from Keito.

Dalton did struggle to take command of the team during their training, no matter how many times Jikia lectured him. Dalton was happier with discussion rather than orders, and while Eclipse and Mitoki already understood Dalton's managerial style, Keito and Hanyi struggled to follow his vague suggestions, and would often go their own way when it came to group training and practicing formations. Dalton told Jikia that he was happy to default to their experience, but she warned him that he needed to have a firmer hand with Keito and Hanyi, even if they were legends he idolized.

But Dalton was not the only one on the team that struggled to be direct. Mitoki was acutely aware of his position as the weakest one in the team. His health had always been delicate and he became winded far faster than the older Guardians. But he made up for any physical shortcomings with his quick reflexes and ability to think around any predicament. When sparring, even though the others were taller and stronger than him, he was able to win in about half of the spars.

Hanyi was quick to take Mitoki under his wing, stating that, as the former weakest member of a team, he had tricks he could teach the youngest Guardian. Everyone rapidly learned that these tricks were practical jokes and pranks on the other members of the team when they were not training.

Eclipse and Keito were the quiet ones of Team Dalton. Keito carried himself with a practiced calm that bespoke his age and experiences, while Eclipse was cold and standoffish, preferring to keep the others at arm's length. That was not something Hanyi was willing to accept. Before Jikia could even bring up Eclipse's coarse attitude, Hanyi had started jibing the quiet Guardian, sometimes irritating him to the point of anger—which would often dissipate into playful wrestling that helped the teammates learn each other's limits when it came to the banter.

While it was difficult for any of them to say they were close with the others on the team, by the time their training was coming to an end and the shadow of the Guardian Tournament began to loom in the near future, the five Guardians of Team Dalton were friends. They had learned when to back off from teasing and when to press each other about what was bothering them. The knowledge of how the tournament worked, why it had been disbanded, and the reason for its reinstatement seemed easier to handle as they learned how to work with one another and knew the others had their backs.

Even knowing they could rely on their new teammates, they could feel the danger fast approaching.

~∧~

Training had fallen into a predictable routine and as they waited for the official summon to their first round of the tournament, Jikia could see that Team Dalton was getting bored—the training was no longer challenging.

Therefore, when they walked into the dome after morning chores to see Jikia standing in the middle of the ring without the practice dummies, they were confused.

"I thought we were going to run ambush tactics again," Eclipse said as they approached.

"That was the original plan, but you boys are too comfortable in the routine. You're going to start getting sloppy," the dragon said, her lips quirking upward. "It will be any day that we get the letter calling us to the tournament. I can't have you slacking off now."

"So what are we going to do?" Dalton asked.

"Spar."

"Against each other?" Mitoki asked, his eyes going wide.

She nodded. "And unlike practicing attacks over and over, I want you boys to take this very seriously. Use your own skills and strengths to defeat your sparring partner."

"*How* serious?" Hanyi pressed. "How do we know we've defeated our sparring partner?"

"Well, I obviously want you to put your all into it," Jikia said. "But no cheap shots, no head injuries, and no forcing the other to pass out. Basically, when you want to stop the spar, admit defeat."

The Guardians turned to each other with varying degrees of discomfort. They had paired up to practice certain moves and attacks during training, but with the free rein Jikia had given them to spar, they were suddenly nervous about their own abilities and how they would compare.

"So, first spar," Jikia started with a decisive clap of her hands. "Dalton and Eclipse."

Jikia motioned for the other three to follow her as she stepped to the side of the dome, giving Eclipse and Dalton as much room in the training ring as possible.

Dalton could not help but smile nervously as he turned to face Eclipse. The younger man shook his head, shrugging nonchalantly.

"I guess…we just pretend we're in the tournament?"

"I guess."

Eclipse rolled his shoulders and bent his knees, his hands clenching and relaxing. Dalton took a deep breath, also preparing himself for the spar, mentally scolding himself for not taking closer account of Eclipse's fighting style during training.

"We're allowed to place bets, right?" Hanyi joked among those spectating.

"No," Jikia groaned with an exasperated laugh.

"Truly, they're so well-matched I wouldn't know who to put money on," Keito said.

"But are they strong enough for the tournament?" Jikia asked. "They both struggle with the team tactics so I'm sure their strength is one-on-one, which means these first three rounds will be difficult for them."

"I think only in this first round," Keito said. "I'm sure you understand that no matter how many lessons and tactics you put in their heads, once they're in the ring, it will all come down to instinct and the ability to react in the moment."

He caught Mitoki's questioning glance.

"Don't worry," he assured. "You will all do fine."

Dalton smiled at Eclipse as they both waited for the other to move first.

"I really don't know what to expect from you."

"One way to find out," Eclipse replied, a confident smirk painted over his features.

"Keito's always saying to let your opponent attack first."

"Well, one of us has to move," Eclipse teased. "And don't think I'll go easy on you just because you're my boss."

"I think the fact that I'm your boss will make you more motivated to beat me."

"Boys! Quit stalling!" Jikia barked.

Dalton turned to say something to their trainer but in the momentary distraction, Eclipse surged forward, lifting his fist for the first attack.

Despite the distraction, Dalton recovered quickly, rounding once to grab Eclipse's fist, yanking him forward and kicking the other Guardian's leg. Eclipse fell but before Dalton could release him, he grabbed the team leader's wrist and pulled him to the ground.

Dalton somersaulted away, getting to his feet as Eclipse jumped upright.

"Taking advantage of my distraction?"

"Clearly not enough," Eclipse said. "Still had your guard up."

"I didn't survive this long as a Guardian by being stupid."

Dalton took the initiative, his hand growing hot as he willed his energy into his palm, using magic to increase both his speed and the power of his punch. Eclipse matched him, meeting Dalton with his own magic-enhanced attacks.

Punches and swipes were blocked or redirected, their strength amplified by second-nature energy manipulation. It was clear they were not trying to land any hits for the purpose of winning the spar, but were, instead, trying to outsmart the other, taking advantage of any opening, laughing when their attack was thwarted.

"Are they *that* evenly matched?" Mitoki asked, surprised by the duration of the spar.

"They are but they're also just testing the other, trying to find any weaknesses," Jikia explained. "I'd rather they take this more seriously."

"They're afraid of seriously hurting one another," Hanyi said with a shrug. "Let them have fun with it. When they start to tire, one of them will make a mistake."

Once they had separated, struggling to catch their breaths after an extended volley of punches and blocks, Dalton expected Eclipse to hang back as before, assessing Dalton's stance and formulating another plan. But Dalton was ready and did not allow Eclipse time to catch his breath. He darted to the younger Guardian, startling Eclipse and allowing Dalton to land one hard punch to his gut—powerful enough to knock the wind out of him, but not enough to make him collapse.

Dalton's triumphant grin fell when he felt Eclipse grip his arm and pull him closer, lifting his head quickly so his head connected with Dalton's chin.

Pain radiated through Dalton, but before he could regain his senses, Eclipse threw him to the hard dirt and pinned him, trying to hide his wheezing and coughing as his diaphragm struggled to recover.

"Had enough?"

"Hell no."

Dalton twisted his body, lifting his legs to knee Eclipse as hard as he could in the back. Eclipse pitched forward, releasing Dalton so his hands would break his fall. Once freed, Dalton punched Eclipse in the side and used magic to flip the other Guardian onto his back. One more hard punch forced Eclipse's eyes to bulge and he motioned his hand across his neck in a signal for surrender.

Dalton let out a long breath and collapsed on the ground, cradling his jaw as he tried to catch his breath. Eclipse turned onto his side, coughing as he struggled to breathe once more.

"Well done, boys," Jikia complimented, walking forward with the others of the team. "Took some time to get you there but you finally took it seriously."

"You alright?" Keito asked with a half-concerned smile, offering a hand to Dalton.

"I think so..." he said once he was on his feet. Eclipse lightly pushed Mitoki's offered hand away as he stumbled upright.

"*Damn*," Eclipse wheezed. "Were you *trying* to break my ribs?"

"No," Dalton said. "But I was a little unnerved. Normally, one of those punches is enough to put someone on the ground."

"Unfortunately for you, my master is very fond of gut punches as well and doesn't hold back," Eclipse said, wincing as Jikia forced him to stand straight so she could assess his injuries.

"Wow…what happened to you two?" Tarrena asked with a laugh, entering the training dome.

"Just a little sparring," Hanyi answered. He grinned knowingly, motioning to the envelope in her hands. "Is that what I think it is?"

A thick silence settled over the Guardians as they caught sight of the letter. Even knowing their reason for training was to compete in the Guardian Tournament, seeing the envelope with the official wax seal of the Dimension Protection Council caused their reality to come into sharp focus.

Jikia took the letter from her daughter and opened it, the Guardians crowding behind her to read over her shoulder. Dalton expected the letter to radiate with power and foreboding, but instead the letter contained paragraph after paragraph of jargon concerning the first date of the tournament, travel requirements, bracketing, and dozens of other things he did not understand about placements and rotations.

All he understood for sure was that they were going to be competing in the Realm of Beasts for the first round and the date for the official start of the Guardian Tournament was only six days away.

Despite how fast his heart began beating, his blood had turned to ice in his veins.

"There it is," Jikia said, lifting the letter. "Stadium 4B, Realm of Beasts, six days."

"It's been so long since I've seen one of these," Hanyi said, plucking the letter out of Jikia's hands as his eyes scanned the words. "Oh…Keito, look. It's just like old times."

"Let's hope not," Keito droned.

"Oh, come on," the wolf whined as Keito took the letter, also scanning it. "We always had fun in the Beast Realm, remember?" Keito continued scanning the letter, clearly understanding more of the information than Dalton had. Hanyi huffed at being ignored. "You're no fun."

Keito smirked. "I'm heaps of fun."

He caught Dalton's uncertain gaze as the team leader looked between Keito and the letter. Silently, Keito offered the letter to Dalton.

Dalton tried to block out the conversation around him as he read the words on the paper, desperately trying to understand everything about the tournament. Seeing a lot of information he did not know caused his worry to spike. He was not sure how he was meant to conduct covert, internal investigations during the tournament when he did not completely understand the workings of that tournament.

"Dalton?" Jikia called his attention.

He looked up from the letter.

"Are you alright?"

"Yeah," he said, holding the letter out to her. She took it from his grasp.

"Not to worry, Dalton," she said. "A lot of this is for the trainers. I'll help you with anything you don't understand." She turned back. "Okay, enough stalling! You're still sparring. Mitoki, how about you and Hanyi?"

"Uh…" Mitoki hesitated, turning to look at the older Guardian, who was sporting an enormous, unnerving grin.

"Are you sure?" Dalton pressed. "No offense to Mitoki, but Hanyi's fought in these tournaments before. Mitoki hasn't. Doesn't Hanyi have a big advantage?"

"It will be good for Mitoki," Keito said. "Hanyi knows how to train for the tournament and he'll be a good test for Mitoki to see how he handles the power difference." Keito looked at Jikia. "To be honest, I'm surprised you didn't have all of them spar with *me*."

"You were often the practice dummy. I thought I would give you a break," their trainer teased. "Also, they won't face demons as often as they'll face humans and beasts." She nodded to Mitoki. "Alright, you two are up."

Dalton could see Mitoki wanting to protest, but the youngest of Team Dalton took a deep breath and turned to face Hanyi as the others stepped to the side.

"Hanyi," Keito called. "Go easy on the kid, okay?"

"I'll try, but you know me. After training with *you* so much, I don't really know how to hold back."

Mitoki let out a long sigh, taking only a moment to focus himself before he turned his full attention on Hanyi, ignoring the worried expressions on the sidelines.

When Mitoki assumed a defensive stance, Hanyi smiled and also prepared for the spar. As before, they waited for the other to make the first move. Hanyi made quick jerks forward to scare Mitoki and they continued to work, making the young Guardian flinch each time. Keito could not help but roll his eyes at the display.

Mitoki was the first to move, the magic in his fists sparking as he threw punches at Hanyi, who quickly dodged, clearly startled by the strength of the attacks, but unconcerned.

After a few dodges, Hanyi lifted his own fist, but Mitoki ducked low and launched forward, colliding with Hanyi and bringing them both to the ground.

As Mitoki was scrambling to get Hanyi restrained, he felt the older Guardian's body shift, morphing into the wolf the Guardian had only seen on occasion during training.

Knowing Hanyi now had very sharp teeth to use in their spar, Mitoki reached under Hanyi's head, grabbing hold of his ear and pulling, forcing the wolf's head to turn away from Mitoki's face as he growled and struggled to get out from under Mitoki. He snapped and snarled, but the younger Guardian was stronger than he looked and managed to keep Hanyi down for several long seconds.

Finally, Hanyi managed to squirm away and get to his feet, trying to run a distance that would give him the momentum for a proper tackle, but as he finished his first stride, sharp heat coiled around one of his back legs, slicing into his skin as the line of magic tightened. Growling, he turned and lunged at Mitoki, teeth bared, ignoring how Mitoki's broken concentration had freed him from the magic bind.

Turning his body, Mitoki wrapped an arm around Hanyi's neck and twisted, bringing them both to the ground heavily as Mitoki kicked one leg back to take Hanyi's hind legs out from under him.

With a whine that startled Mitoki enough to release him, Hanyi scrambled away once more.

"I'm done!" he snapped, shifting back into his human appearance as he retreated.

There was uncontrollable laughter from the bystanders. Keito was clutching his stomach as his laughing fit continued.

"If I'd known he'd be so hard for you, I would have told *him* to go easy on *you*!" Keito chortled. "Someone's out of practice!" Keito doubled over laughing. The others in the room were barely suppressing their own giggles, shocked at how quickly the spar had concluded.

"Shut up!" Hanyi snapped at the demon. "You are a demon! You stay strong as you age, but I'm *a lot* older!"

"Did you break a hip, old man?" the demon jibed.

"*No*, just a leg that never properly healed!" Hanyi retorted, his voice sharper than the others had ever heard before.

Keito went silent abruptly.

"Hanyi, if you were going easy on Mitoki to build morale, it's okay to admit it," Jikia said, sensing the shift in tension.

"Shit, Hanyi, I..." Keito's quiet voice surprised everyone. Hanyi turned his eyes to the ground, crossing his arms over his chest.

"No, I'm sorry..." he murmured.

"You never told me," Keito said.

"I wasn't about to bring it up."

"I'm...sorry, Hanyi, did I hurt you?" Mitoki asked, approaching the older Guardian, noting his tense shoulders. Hanyi took a deep breath, pursing his lips in a half-smile.

"No, you did very well," he said. "Just...sometimes old injuries flare up, and my broken leg from the Tournament Slaughter didn't heal properly."

The quiet that fell over the ring was heavy and cold.

"I didn't know you got a broken leg from that," Dalton said sheepishly.

"I should be thankful it was the worst injury I got out of that," Hanyi muttered. Only he noticed the way Keito's eyes darkened. "I didn't want to bring it up. I'm old, a lot older than you seem to realize. And as much as I would like to joke about my bad joints and aching bones...sometimes, they really do slow me down."

"Is there anything I can do?" Jikia asked. "I know a lot of healing spells that could probably fix your leg."

Hanyi's smile did not chase away the sadness in his eyes. "Thank you for the offer, but the injury is a part of who I am now. And besides, in my human form it hardly gives me any trouble. It's just when I move it wrong in my wolf form."

"I wish you had told me," Keito murmured, his eyes still on the ground.

"Hey," Hanyi started, walking over to the demon and placing a hand on his shoulder. "It's fine, okay? Yeah, I have some pain now and then, but it's only because you carried me out that I'm even *alive*." His expression brightened, the playful light coming back to his eyes. "So, what do you say, *old man*? Ready for your turn in the ring?"

"Yes, I think it's time we see you spar," Jikia agreed, happy some of the tension was now gone. "Who wants to spar against the demon?"

"I nominate the leader," Mitoki said, pushing Dalton forward.

"*Me*?"

"You're the leader. You go first."

"You feel up to that, Dalton?" Jikia asked.

"Um..." Dalton turned his gaze onto Keito, unable to completely mask his nerves. His mind had gone blank at the thought of sparring with the legendary Guardian.

"Don't worry, Dalton," Keito said. "I was the only demon on my team and I was often used as the practice dummy. You don't have to hold back on me, and I know how to keep my strength at a level you can manage."

"But the demons in the tournament will not be holding back," Eclipse said. "How strong are you in comparison to them?"

"Who's the current top-ranked demon Guardian?"

"Sanyai Tyien," Dalton answered. A knowing smile came over Keito's lips.

"She's tough," he said. "Her trainer was a real asshole. But she learned well because of it."

"You pushed her so hard," Hanyi laughed. "She couldn't decide if she wanted to quit or kill you."

"*You* trained her?"

"Only in her last years of apprenticeship, right before I retired," Keito affirmed. "If she's the top-ranked Guardian, I have an idea how strong the others are."

"And how strong are you in comparison?" Eclipse repeated.

"Let's just say I'm not too worried," Keito said with a mysterious smile. "So, Dalton?"

Dalton took another deep breath to calm his nerves.

"Okay," he agreed. "I sparred with Sanyai once a couple years ago. She really ran me ragged."

"Then it seems she took most of my lessons to heart," Keito said, motioning Dalton to follow him to the center of the training dome.

"Keito," Jikia called. "I've seen what you can do, so nothing fancy. Keep it simple."

"Don't underestimate me *that* much," Dalton lamented.

"Yeah, Dalton's surprisingly tough," Eclipse agreed, rubbing the dull ache in his abdomen.

"I feel like I should be insulted by the way you said that," the leader of the team said with a playful glare.

"Impressive as you may be, you've never fought against someone like Keito before," Hanyi said.

"What does that mean?"

"Most of the demons you fight in the realm are the younger ones that cause trouble because they are bored and think they are tougher than they really are," Keito explained. "You have *no* idea of the power some demons possess. I have fought with some of the strongest demons in the realm and I have learned techniques from them. So, in a way, yes, I am different from most demons you have faced."

"I'm sure there is truth to what you are saying, but I also know that you're trying to psyche me out."

Keito grinned. "Is it working?"

"I will be careful, but more than anything, I'm curious to see what you can really do."

"It will be a while before you can see that," Keito teased. "You're still a human. You can't handle my full strength."

"Not yet."

"Fine. Let's see if you are worthy of taking over my position as top-ranked Guardian." Keito turned to face Dalton as the human slid one foot back and raised his hands to defend, taking slow breaths as he prepared to fight the demon.

The two sparring Guardians were not the only ones who were tense. All eyes were locked on the two, feeling excitement course through them as they waited for one of them to move.

Dalton expected Keito to take a defensive stance, to take deep breaths and shift and stretch his muscles in preparation. But Keito stood casually opposite Dalton, his hands by his sides, waiting for his team leader to make the first move. But even though Keito did not move, Dalton saw the gradual change. Keito was always difficult to read, and the glints of emotion behind his golden eyes were often the only flicker that bespoke what he was feeling. The longer Dalton watched his stoic teammate, the darker Keito's eyes became, as though even the small, flittering emotions were draining out of him, leaving nothing but an empty shell.

Keito looked resigned to defeat—perhaps even death.

The stare became so unsettling that Dalton felt compelled to move. He leapt at the demon, but Keito stepped easily to the side. The human turned and tried to use his magic to give him greater speed, but the demon was far faster. Again, Keito dodged effortlessly. His eyes were still guarded, but Dalton could sense Keito analyzing him, calculating the precise moment Dalton would be weakest. Keito's hands remained at his sides. Apart from dodging the attacks, he barely moved.

"Why aren't you doing anything?" Dalton snapped.

Keito did not respond. When he ducked Dalton's fist, his fist connected with Dalton's stomach. Dalton circled away from the punch, knowing that Keito had barely used any power behind the attack, even though his ribs screamed in pain. He tried to jab his elbow at the back of Keito's head in retaliation. The demon dropped to the floor and kicked Dalton's feet out from under him when he was off-balance.

The team leader barely managed to catch himself on one hand, though his wrist bent awkwardly and he had to hide his cringe as he rolled into a crouch, facing Keito again.

Keito stood straight, allowing Dalton a moment to clamor to his feet.

"You are going to need to try some more sophisticated techniques," he said.

"Alright, then."

Dalton used as much magic as he was comfortable with to match pace with the demon. He threw punch after punch, following Keito with a leap forward every time the demon effortlessly dodged.

"That's not more sophisticated," Hanyi said with a roll of his eyes.

Dalton was forcing Keito to move in circles. He saw how the demon dodged and continued to make him dodge the same direction until they had completed three circles. He tried not to let his actions give away that he had a plan, but he could tell with how closely Keito was watching him that the demon knew Dalton was not throwing punches at random.

When Keito's foot slid over the same spot he had visited three times, Dalton dropped to a crouch, clutching a handful of dirt and throwing it at Keito. The demon flinched, allowing Dalton to somersault away.

Keito started after him for a counter-attack but stopped abruptly, turning his gaze to his leg. He tried to step again but his right ankle was caught in a tight magical binding cuff.

"A binding circle?" Keito asked in disbelief. "Using some old-school techniques."

"The old ones are often the best and the least-expected," Dalton agreed. "You can't move from that circle, and I can throw more than one energy attack at a time."

"Bring it on, kiddo," Keito challenged with a grin.

Hanyi blinked in surprise at Keito's behavior and then a gentle smile took over his face.

"Everything alright?" Jikia asked, noticing the expression.

"It's been a long time since I've seen Keito have fun in a spar," he said. "It's nice to see."

Dalton was focused, moving around Keito and throwing energy attacks as often as he could physically manage. Keito dodged with little difficulty. The attacks he could not dodge he attempted to reflect back, but when Dalton saw him preparing to counter-attack, he changed his direction and pattern, thwarting Keito's attempted counter.

Dalton was not going for an immediate victory. He was reading Keito, learning how his face and body language changed when he was preparing to attack. When he saw the slight narrowing of

Keito's eyes and the way his hands tensed, he searched for weaknesses in the demon's stance while keeping him preoccupied with simple attacks.

When he was sure Keito was not expecting it, Dalton darted to Keito's other side to exploit the small opening that had appeared in the demon's stance. Keito shifted his foot, dropping to a crouch to catch Dalton's wrist before he could land the attack, pulling him into the binding circle and whispering the spell that transferred the shackle to Dalton.

By the time Dalton felt the energy lock around his right ankle, Keito had circled out of range of the spell, grinning triumphantly.

"I thought I caught you with your guard down!"

"You did," Keito said. "I'm just quicker than you." The demon concentrated his energy into his palm for an attack. "Your turn."

Dalton became the one avoiding magical attacks barreling toward him. He was not as quick as Keito and it was harder for him to dodge with one leg firmly confined, but he managed, even throwing counter-attacks to control Keito's movements.

When Keito stepped close enough for Dalton to reach, he grabbed the demon's arm and tried to pull him into the binding circle. Keito turned and pulled Dalton's arm over his shoulder, straining the elbow as the binding circle fought to keep Dalton in position. Using his other hand, Dalton reached over Keito's other shoulder and grabbed at his own forearm, pulling Keito back with all his strength. They both fell to the ground with the demon in a chokehold.

Keito elbowed Dalton in the ribs, his grip loosening. Keito rolled away, smiling while he caught his breath.

"Not bad."

"Not done," Dalton said, grabbing the dagger that was always strapped to his calf, kicking Keito down with his free leg and pressing the blade to his teammate's neck, pushing a knee into the demon's diaphragm. "If this was a real fight, I would have done this."

Keito's hand pushed Dalton's shoulder, his legs hooking Dalton's extended leg, flipping them over so he was pinning the human down with the knife now directed at Dalton's neck.

"And if this was a real fight, I would have ended it like this."

"Okay, leg, *leg*. Still trapped," Dalton said quickly, cringing as he rapidly tapped Keito's arm. Keito let his leader up and Dalton twisted his leg back into a normal position the instant Keito broke the binding circle. Dalton flopped backward.

"Okay, I think...I should not fight any more today." Dalton said breathlessly. "Ow..."

Keito helped the human to his feet.

"I will say, Dalton, I'm very impressed," Keito said, handing the dagger back to its owner. "If you would let go of your fear a bit, you could really grow as a Guardian."

"What is that supposed to mean?" Dalton asked with a teasing glower.

"He's right," Jikia seconded. "You have a lot of power that's locked inside you. Some of it seems to come to the surface when you're battling opponents far stronger than you. You just can't reach it normally, likely due to your own fear of controlling such power."

"Well, if I can't control it, better keep it locked down."

"No, it's not," Keito disagreed. "I know a demon who repressed his powers out of fear and those powers grew so immense that they rose to the surface and hurt everyone around him because he didn't learn how to tap into it and control it."

"Don't sugar-coat it for him, Keito," Hanyi jeered.

"Besides," Mitoki added, seeing the pensive look on Dalton's face, "I'm sure that demons are radically different from humans when it comes to stuff like that."

"Perhaps. Demons are stronger naturally, after all," Jikia said, also concerned about the look on Dalton's face. She turned to Keito. "Which means you're still good for another spar. Who wants to fight the demon next?"

The two younger humans went quiet, both turning to Hanyi.

"What?" the wolf asked.

"What about you?"

"Me fight Keito? No, thank you," Hanyi said. "I had my ass kicked enough when I was training with him. I'm too old to match up to him now."

"Neither of you?" Jikia asked, pointing at the younger Guardians.

"Well..." Mitoki started hesitantly. "I'm...I don't want to."

"I think this is a good place to end today," Eclipse agreed. Keito hung his head, bemused by their reluctance to spar with him.

"Do you?" Jikia asked, her eyebrows high. "What if both of you were to fight him together?"

The two humans refused to look up, waiting to hear their trainer order them to spar. Instead, she sighed.

"Fine. Wash up for dinner."

Chapter Eight

The Guardians could hardly remember the early post-training dinners they had shared. As they had come to know one another conversation became easier, and it was the norm to joke about training. As usual, Hanyi was the one to initiate the jibing.

"Dalton, with the way you were punching Eclipse, I was sure you were trying to break his ribs," Hanyi laughed, his mouth full of food. "Is it now the norm to punch your subordinates while on assignment?" Small pieces of chicken were flying across the table as the wolf rambled on, gesticulating enthusiastically with his fork.

"Chew before you speak, Hanyi," Keito scolded.

"*Me*? Eclipse was the one who head-butted me and nearly broke my jaw!" Dalton protested, rubbing the bruised underside of his chin.

"You didn't give me any other options, boss," Eclipse said with a confident smirk. "I was taking the spar seriously, like our trainer instructed."

"Oh, sure, *that's* why you head-butt Dalton," Mitoki said. "Because Jikia told you to."

"Well, Mitoki, you also took the instruction to heart," Jikia said with a broad smile from the head of the table. "After all, you managed to defeat the eight-time tournament champion in record time."

Keito shot an amused glance at his former partner as the others pursed their lips against laughing.

"Hey!" Hanyi said, his glare softened by the enormous grin on his face. "It's not nice to pick on the elderly!"

"I have to ask," Mitoki started, "*were* you going easy on me?"

Hanyi hesitated, his cheeks puffed out with food.

"A little," he admitted. "But, if I'm being honest," he swallowed his food to speak clearly, "I *severely* underestimated you. You're just always so quiet and you don't really show your strength. So I thought I would tease you, and in my overconfidence, I was thrown off by how fast you attacked. Then I was scrambling to regain ground and I got sloppy, hence—" he smacked his leg. "So, yes. I did go easy on you, but I should have stepped up my game, too. By the time I realized my mistake, I was already hurt."

"Learn from the old man's mistakes," Keito said. "Never underestimate any opponent. In some cases, it's better to use overkill."

"I mean, I was hardly being *tactical,*" Mitoki said. "I was so afraid to fight you, I just sort of…panicked."

"Good," Jikia said with a strong nod. "Fear is a good thing and if you know how to channel it, it can really help you in the tournament, particularly if you do as Keito says and never underestimate who you are facing in the ring. When the demon Guardians come into the arena, you might not always have Keito to rely on."

"Keito?" Eclipse said, grabbing the demon's attention. "You're a hybrid demon, right?" Keito nodded. "Is that what makes you so powerful? You said you were powerful enough to win in a fight with any of the demon Guardians, but…I've seen Sanyai fight. She's tough as hell. Is it because you're a hybrid that you're so powerful?"

"Now that you mention it," Tarrena said, turning to the demon, who was obviously uncomfortable with being the topic of conversation, "you never mentioned what type of hybrid you are."

"You're a fox and a wolf mix, right?" Jikia asked. "I remember hearing a bit about your heritage during previous tournaments," she added, her face becoming pensive. "Your master said your fox lineage was really rare…a clan that I'm sure I will butcher the name of."

Keito shook his head. "It's fine," he said. "Most human documentation just translated it as Shadow Fox. Not many can pronounce the name."

"Which side?" Tarrena pressed.

"My mother's."

"Why is the Shadow Fox clan rare?" Mitoki asked. "I don't know anything about demon clans."

"Clans come and go," Keito said, his eyes still cast down to the table. "The political and tribal landscape of the Demon Realm is constantly changing. But my mother's clan was almost completely annihilated in a war a few centuries ago. Very few pureblood Shadow Foxes remain. The survivors were either sold into slavery or were integrated into other clans." Keito finally turned his gaze to Eclipse. "Almost always, hybrid demons are weaker than purebloods. My powers will never reach the heights of my mother's clan."

"Was your mother a pureblood?" Dalton asked. When Keito nodded, he continued. "What about your father? The wolf side?"

"…he was a pureblood, too," the demon answered. "But I try to ignore my paternal heritage as much as possible."

"Why?" Eclipse asked before he could think better of the question.

"My father was, in short, a horrible, bloodthirsty monster who never thought of anyone other than himself," Keito said, his voice filled with anger. "And my father's family is a purist clan, so they were quick to get rid of me, since I'm just a filthy hybrid to them."

"I didn't realize purist clans like that existed," Dalton said, surprised. Keito nodded strongly but, before he could elaborate, Jikia spoke.

"One of the oldest demon breeds is the Silver Wolf Clan, and they are purist to a fault," the dragon snarled. The Guardians glanced around the table, an instinctive shiver running down their spines from the rage in her voice.

"I'm sensing some tension in your voice," Hanyi said, trying to keep his tone light. "Not fond of Silver Wolf demons?"

"No," she said. "A Silver Wolf demon murdered my father and massacred most of my clan."

"...how long ago?" Keito asked, his eyes once again distant on the table as he waited for her answer.

"You already know who it was."

Keito took a moment before turning to Jikia, his eyes apologetic.

"I'm so sorry."

"Who are you talking about?" Eclipse asked, looking between the demon and the older dragon. Tarrena was silent, pushing her food around on her plate, waiting for her mother to explain.

Jikia shot a questioning glance at Keito, but it was obvious that the demon preferred the dragon to tell the other Guardians the information.

"I might be misinformed about the politics, so correct me if I'm wrong, Keito. Among Silver Wolf demons, there is a ruling family of sorts that holds an incredible amount of power, not just in the clan but in the entirety of the Demon Realm. One of the former rulers of the Silver Wolf Clan was a notorious murderer and he was the one who massacred my clan."

"Former ruler?" Dalton repeated. "So he's dead?"

"So they say," she said. "There's rumor that he's actually alive somewhere, hidden away, waiting for the right time to return and wreak havoc on the realms. There have been whispers of his return for centuries. Most devout followers believe his soul has been preserved somewhere and with the right rituals, he will be reborn and wage war on all five realms."

"Preserve his soul? Is that even possible?"

"With strong enough magic," Eclipse said with a nod.

"This demon had enough power to pull it off," Jikia said. "He was a bloodthirsty menace. He was responsible not only for killing my family, but I'd say...hundreds of thousands of humans and demons."

"How have we never heard of him?" Dalton gawked. He looked at Hanyi. "Did *you* know about this?"

The wolf nodded silently.

"If he used to be such a terror to the realms, I'm surprised we've never heard of him."

"Not much is known about demons," Jikia said. "So little is understood about their abilities, their culture, their history...or even where they came from—a creature not quite human, not quite beast." She turned to Keito, who was refusing to join the conversation. "I'm sure there is much humans are not told about those residing in the Demon Realm."

"And this mass-murdering demon even killed *dragons*?" Mitoki pressed. "Why did he go after your family?"

"I was not technically born, yet. I was still in-egg when our settlement was massacred, but from what I understand, he came to us looking for an artifact that would help him kill the leader of all dragons—Lord Vestera Hizoku."

"What artifact? And why would he want to kill Lord Hizoku? I don't even think that's possible..." Dalton added under his breath. "He's the most powerful dragon in the universe."

"I don't know what artifact," Jikia said. "We didn't have it. As for why, I think he was starting to realize that the death threats from Lord Vestera were serious. He was said to have killed over a hundred dragons from our small settlement in that one day. He tortured who he could for information but when they couldn't give him what he wanted, he killed them. Females and young were not spared, either. My mother escaped with me and a few others and we took refuge here in the Middle Dimension."

"Can a demon kill that many dragons?" Dalton asked, turning to Keito, his eyes wide in disbelief.

"*He* could," Keito said. "A few demons have the power to kill dragons with relative ease."

"Regardless, that bastard got what he deserved," Jikia sneered. "He was killed in his home very shortly afterward."

"How? I mean, if he could kill *dragons*..."

"After a battle, when he was tired and drained of most of his powers, his home was ambushed by thirty assassins—some demons, some Guardians. He was killed and torn apart to be sure he was not a threat," the older dragon said. "I'm sure Keito knows the story."

"I was a child when he was killed," Keito said. "You know as much as I do."

"What was his name?" Dalton pressed. "Maybe I've heard his name somewhere."

"Yokouro DeVastes."

"I've never heard of him." Mitoki said.

"He's one of the demons the DPC prefers to keep quiet about," Keito explained. "If word were to get out about demons as powerful as Yokouro, it would cause pandemonium among the humans."

"I feel like I might have heard the name, but it might have been from a demon Guardian," Eclipse said, his brow crinkled in thought. "And maybe only in passing...I can't remember. It sounds familiar."

"Possibly from a demon Guardian. There is not a demon alive who does not know his name," Keito said. "He's one of the demons that terrifies even demons."

"You do seem a bit reluctant to talk about him," Eclipse noted.

"I might have been young when he was killed, but I know how to tell a boogeyman story from a warning, and I know I would be a fool *not* to fear him."

"I suppose it's a comfort then to know that he's dead." Dalton turned to Jikia with an apologetic smile. "I am sorry for your loss. It must have been difficult losing your father before you even knew him."

"A feeling you are familiar with," Jikia noted. "Your father was a great Guardian, Dalton."

"Thank you."

"If you don't mind me asking," Keito started, "was he killed on assignment?"

"No, not exactly," he answered. "I was just a baby at the time, but I heard that a demon attacked him. I don't know if it was some sort of revenge, or just a demon acting on their hatred of Guardians. But that demon attacked our home. My mother and I survived but my father was killed."

"I'm sorry..."

"I guess I always hoped I'd find the demon who killed him," Dalton said. "As I grew up, I realized how unlikely that was, but I still think about trying to investigate and find out who killed him."

"Was that why you became a Guardian?" Tarrena asked.

Dalton pursed his lips. "No. Actually, my mother outright forbade me from becoming a Guardian." He bowed his head, taking a breath to speak before hesitating. Sighing, he said, "She...couldn't handle my father's death. And when she wasn't drowning her pain in alcohol, she was screaming at me about how I would never follow in my father's footsteps, since I was the reason he was so distracted during the attack and why he died."

Heavy silence fell over the table.

"I hope you don't believe that," Jikia said.

"It's not that I believe it or don't believe it," he said. "I don't remember any of it. And clearly I didn't really listen to her anyway. After she ran off, my grandfather was travelling too much to take care of a kid, so he dropped me off at Master Bowen's training center, and I became a Guardian just like my father." He smiled. "And I'm happy with my life. And I hope that, wherever she is, she found some help."

"You never saw her again?" Hanyi asked.

He shook his head. "And…I'm relieved. She…" He trailed off. "…No, I never saw her again."

"It seems like all of you grew up without much parental guidance," Jikia noted. "It's been a common trait among Guardians I've trained."

"My father was around," Hanyi interjected. "He was very supportive of my decision to be a Guardian."

"What about your mother?"

"She passed away when I was two," he admitted. "But we were a happy family. I guess I'm the odd one out in that regard."

"At least you all know where you came from," Mitoki muttered, hoping he said the statement quiet enough to be ignored.

"What do you mean?" Dalton pressed.

"I mean, I was just abandoned in front of the portals for the Realm of Light when I was an infant," Mitoki said. "I don't even know which realm I was born in."

"I had no idea…" Tarrena whispered, mortified.

"Have you tried looking it up?" Dalton asked.

"A few times," Mitoki said. "But…I think there's a part of me that's afraid of finding out. I only learned about the abandonment story a few years ago. I always knew my master adopted me, but I had no idea I had just been…*left*. I've been wondering if my parents left me or if they're looking for me…if maybe I had been taken from them. It just makes me wonder."

"Do you think it would help to know where you came from?" Eclipse asked, avoiding eye contact.

"Eclipse," Jikia scolded.

"I just mean does the question keep you up at night?" he corrected, still keeping his eyes low. "Do you spend hours pondering what happened to your parents?"

"…yeah, when I don't have anything to distract me." He looked over Eclipse's face, scrutinizing every pensive feature. "Do you know something about them?"

When the silence had extended far longer than anyone was comfortable with, Eclipse raised his head and turned to Mitoki.

"Not much."

"Wait, how could you know anything about it?" Hanyi asked.

"It's a weird coincidence."

"You know my parents?" Mitoki asked, his eyes wide and expectant.

"...*knew*. And only when I was a kid."

"They're dead?"

Eclipse nodded somberly, his gaze pointedly focused on his empty plate.

"Why didn't you say anything before?" Mitoki asked.

"Honestly, I didn't know that you didn't know," he said. "When you became top-ranked, someone told me that you had been adopted after you were found at the portals, and it reminded me of what happened when I was a kid. I did some digging and...turns out you were the infant I heard about."

"These five worlds are quite small, aren't they?" Hanyi said, trying to lighten the mood.

"It's a coincidence," Eclipse repeated. "You were born in the Darkness Realm. But...your parents are dead."

"How did they die?"

"Are you sure you want to know?"

"Well, you've opened this can of worms so...yeah," Mitoki said. "Actually...it's a bit of a relief to know they're not searching for me. That I wasn't taken from them."

"You weren't," Eclipse said. "It...it was a serial killer. He terrorized my, *our*, birth town for months. When I was about eight, the family down the street was killed. Turns out they had been receiving threats for weeks and, in desperation, they left you somewhere they thought would be safe, but were attacked and killed."

"Did they ever catch the killer?" Dalton asked.

"He was dealt with," Eclipse answered vaguely. "My parents were his final victims." He let out a long sigh. "Sorry, I probably shouldn't have told you all that."

"No, no," Mitoki said quickly. "It's fine."

"Are you alright?" Keito asked.

"I...am," he said, his expression thoughtful. "It sort of explains a lot, including why I became a Guardian. I always felt like I had something I had to solve." He turned to Eclipse. "Thank you for telling me."

"Are you just saying that?"

"No," he assured. "Really, thank you."

"So…everyone but me comes from a horribly dark home life?" Hanyi asked, trying to ease the tension.

"I always thought you were out of place in the branch," Keito teased.

"Your father passed away of old age?" Tarrena asked the wolf, hopeful for a change from the bloody stories of the other Guardians.

"Well…not…exactly."

Jikia raised a quizzical eyebrow.

"Illness," he clarified. "Um…he became delirious and dangerous to those around him. He struggled to distinguish reality from his nightmares. Pretty shortly after his first symptoms made themselves known, he was convinced everyone was conspiring to kill him. One day, when our old team came to the Beast Realm, he just attacked everyone who wasn't a wolf." Hanyi lowered his head. "At that point, the pack made a decision to do him a mercy and…let him go."

"…the pack killed him?" Jikia asked, her voice filled with understanding.

"It was a kindness at that point," Hanyi answered indirectly.

"There was a point during my father's illness that he was begging for death," Tarrena explained.

The Guardians fell silent, having wondered about Tarrena's father but never feeling comfortable enough to ask.

"He became very sick. Not uncommon for dragons. And near the end, there were discussions about the mercy we should show to end his suffering. But in the end, he passed in his sleep."

"I'm so sorry," Dalton whispered, bowing his head and averting his eyes from the dragons.

"Geez," Hanyi groaned. "This was the most depressing dinner conversation we've ever had."

A round of broken chuckles sounded.

"Maybe I should join the Guardians," Tarrena joked. "I'd certainly fit in."

"No offense to any of these brave men, but under no circumstances are you allowed to join the Guardians," Jikia told her daughter. Even though she was smiling, everyone at the table could feel the gravity of the command.

"Dragons aren't allowed to become Guardians, anyway," Hanyi said.

"Good thing, too," Keito seconded. "We'd all be out of the job."

"Speaking of your jobs," Jikia said, "you all should probably get some sleep. Let's pack up tomorrow morning and head for the Beast Realm."

Chapter Nine

Dalton felt as though he could not see, even though he could clearly make out the details in the panels of dark metal in front of him. He had no sense of where he was, the time of day, or if he should feel threatened or comforted by the large, metal door in front of him. There was a darkness around the locked door, but his foggy brain could not tell if the darkness was surrounding the door or emanating from behind it.

He assumed he took a step forward as the door seemed suddenly nearer.

He could not explain his need to see what was within.

The heavy door swung outward, and despite the heft of the metal, the hinges did not screech or groan. Dalton stepped inside, a pressure falling over his head that forced him to flinch, his eyes squinting as he tried to see what was inside the small room.

In one dark corner, under near-complete cover of shadows, a young boy hugged his knees tightly, his head bowed, his body trembling like a leaf in a harsh gale. His skin was dirty and bruised, his forearms scraped from what Dalton somehow understood to be tree bark. The boy's hair was matted, pulling at his scalp and aggravating the open cuts around his ears and forehead.

Dalton opened his mouth to call to the boy but no sound came. He tried again, but his voice was swallowed by the heaviness in the air and choked by the surrounding dark shadows.

With a startled jump, the boy looked up, but Dalton retreated immediately. The boy had no face, his features blurred and warped. The thundering of his heart echoed in his ears as he stared at the boy, frozen and confused.

When the faceless boy turned to the door as it opened once more, seeming not to notice Dalton at all, the Guardian realized what was happening.

He was dreaming.

The fogginess was not typical for his dreams, though. Therefore he knew that the faceless boy in the dark metal room was not a conjuring of his own mind. His powers were reaching out, seeking answers to the mission he had been assigned. He had had visions before on missions where he had been desperate for a break in the case, but as he watched the heavy metal door open again, granting entrance to another faceless man, Dalton felt worry creep into his gut that he was seeing something forbidden—something he was not ready to face.

The man at the door stepped inside, leaving another faceless, taller man looming in the open doorway. The boy backed further into the corner, shaking his head violently.

"It's alright," the man approaching him said, his voice jumbled and distorted, though Dalton somehow understood the words. "I'm not going to hurt you."

"That's what they all say," the boy whimpered, his voice just as muddled, though his terror was evident. "You're here to kill me, aren't you?"

"No, no," the man assured, crouching to the ground when he knew he could not get closer to the boy without scaring him. "I'm not here to kill you. I want to talk to you."

"Talk?" the boy scoffed. "That's bullshit."

"Watch your tone," the man in the doorway warned, his voice booming through the space and making Dalton's chest rattle from the power of his command. The boy also felt it, flinching away.

"He's fine. He's just scared," the other man said over his shoulder. He turned his faceless head back to the boy. "Do you know who I am?"

The boy shook his head again.

"I'm from the Dimension Protection Council," he said. "I'm someone who can help you."

"No one can help me!" the boy barked desperately. "You're going to take me away and kill me, right?! I've…I've…"

The boy's voice cracked, broken by the sobs that overtook him as he curled around his knees once more.

"Do you know what you've done?" the man from Council asked gently. "Do you understand what happened?"

"Please…" the boy whined. "Please, just get me out of here. I didn't know what I was doing! I swear! I didn't mean to!"

"But do you know what you did?"

The boy went quiet, slowly lifting his head as he sniffed back tears.

"I said the words…" he whispered. "I just went where he told me to go…and I said the words…and then there was all this screaming…and noise…"

"Why did you listen to him?" the man asked. "Why did you say those words?"

"…he promised me the pain would stop."

The man crouching in front of the boy let out a long sigh, hanging his head.

"And it didn't, did it?"

The boy shook his head once again.

77

"…are you going to kill me?"

"I'm not going to kill you, but you have done something terrible," the man said. "You broke Vestera's seal on the realms. You—"

"Where is he?!" the boy shrieked. "Please! I'll explain it to Vestera! I swear I didn't—"

"Listen to me," the man said, reaching a hand out to the boy though the child flinched away. "I believe you. I believe that you didn't know what you were doing. And I believe that you were manipulated into breaking that seal. But that does not mean you are not somewhat responsible."

The boy let out a pained whimper, hiding his head once more.

"You opened another dimension," the man continued. "And now I need your help to stop this before thousands more die."

Dalton felt himself drawing closer to the boy, focusing intently on his face, trying to see his features, to peer through time and see the boy who had unknowingly broken the seal on the realms. His mind was spinning with questions about how it was possible a child reciting a simple spell could fracture the powerful seal, or when the conversation he was witnessing had taken place. But above all that, he desperately wanted to know the identity of the boy.

He drew even closer, trying to solidify the blurry face into discernible features, his mind aching with the effort.

A weight fell on his shoulder, taking the shape of a hand. He whirled around, startled to see a face he did not recognize. He barely had time to take in the bright hazel eyes that seemed to look right through him before the hand yanked him forward, closer to the person who had invaded his dream.

Dalton bolted upright, gasping for breath as he blinked the sweat from his eyes. His body shook as his mind resurfaced to reality, looking around his small bedroom at Jikia's, searching for the hazel eyes he could still feel watching him.

"Good morn—oh, what happened to you?" Jikia said, her bright greeting turning into acute concern when she saw the way Dalton stumbled into the dome with dark bags under his eyes and a full cup of coffee in his hands.

"Did you sleep?" Eclipse asked with a raised eyebrow.

"I honestly don't know," Dalton grumbled, approaching Mitoki, Eclipse, Jikia, and Tarrena. "Where are Keito and Hanyi?"

"They were up early so they agreed to take care of the morning chores," Tarrena answered. "Are you okay?"

Dalton rubbed his eyes.

"It's a thing that happens sometimes."

"What?"

"I get these...not visions, but kinda visions?"

"...visions but not visions?" Mitoki repeated slowly.

"Of the future? Like premonitions?" Jikia pressed.

"No, more like...when I am feeling stuck on a case, I get to look at something that happened that's either related to the case or maybe the cause of the case..." Dalton shrugged. "I don't know. It's only happened a few times. I can't do it at will."

"And you had one of those visions last night?"

"I *think* so."

"About the tournament?" Jikia asked.

"No, um..." Dalton took a deep breath. "About the break in the seal."

"What did you see?" Eclipse prompted.

"I...I *think* I saw who did it...or, at least who performed the spell," he said. "It was really hard to discern features, or time, or really anything other than the conversation. It was just a kid."

"Impossible," Jikia said strongly. "A kid wouldn't have the power to break Vestera's seal. It's not possible."

"He said that he just said the words. That someone told him to say the words and then...I don't know, he just said something happened. He looked beat to hell, so I figure the spell must have been big."

"Yeah, but it's Vestera Hizoku, you know?" Eclipse said with a disbelieving chuckle. "The most powerful known entity in the realms. A spell just snapped his seal? Just like that?"

"I don't know, I didn't get a lot of detail. I'm just telling you what I heard," Dalton said, rubbing at the headache throbbing in his temple. "The man said that the boy had opened another dimension. And that now the boy needed to help Council stop...something before more people died."

"Opened a dimension?" Mitoki repeated, his eyebrows going high. "What does that mean?"

"Not a clue."

"And what did he want the boy to do?" Jikia pressed.

"I don't know, I woke up at that point," Dalton said, shivering. "Kinda felt like someone yanked me awake by my eyeballs." He pressed his fingers into his eyes again, groaning. "Still a bit shaken."

"Understandably."

The door to the dome opened and Keito and Hanyi stepped inside, walking toward the others, Hanyi taking a deep breath and opening his arms wide to greet them brightly.

"Hey, do either of you know about another dimension being opened somewhere?" Eclipse asked.

Hanyi deflated, his arms falling heavily to his sides.

"Oh, good morning to you, too," he grumbled.

Keito's step slowed as he approached, his face becoming concerned.

"What are you talking about?"

Dalton groaned when he saw the others turn to him expectantly.

"I had a dream last night. Seemed a bit like I was watching a conversation that happened in the past." Dalton explained the dream to the two older Guardians, who remained silent, their faces stoic as Dalton described everything he could remember around his splitting headache.

"You two know anything about this?" Jikia prompted when Dalton was finished.

Keito crossed his arms.

"When was the first time you heard about Vestera's seal being broken?" he asked.

"Um…two weeks or so before they announced the tournament," Dalton answered.

"Because the seal has been broken for centuries."

"*Centuries*?"

"No, no," Jikia protested. "Vestera would know if his seal had been broken. He wouldn't just *leave* it."

"He's known about it since the day it was broken," Keito said. "And from what I understand, he has to leave it because the damage is immense. He can't repair it. He has to recast the seal in its entirety."

"Wait, *you've* known about it for how long?" Mitoki asked.

"This was the case we were on during the last tournament," Hanyi said. "So we've known about it for several decades."

"And you didn't *say* anything?" Eclipse asked incredulously.

"We were ordered not to," Keito explained. "The more people knew about the break in the seal, the more panic would set in. The Elders tried to keep a lid on it for a long time." He shrugged. "I guess now they realize that the problem is too serious and that was why they told the rest of Council."

"So, this new dimension that opened…" Mitoki mused. "As far as I know, the only two realms outside these five are the Middle Dimension and the Dragon Realm."

"There are thousands of dimensions and realms all through the universe," Jikia said. "Whatever new dimension was opened…it could lead anywhere."

"Even the Dragon Realm?"

"No, the dragons would know if there was a sudden hole in the realm," Tarrena said. "It must be a realm close to this collective. But without knowing where the portal is or if Vestera has made any attempts to seal it…it's impossible to tell where it leads."

"What exactly was your mission when you were investigating this?" Dalton pressed. "Find the break? Investigate the damage?"

"Find who broke the seal and kill him," Keito said simply.

"And did you find him?"

"Yeah, we found him."

"But you didn't kill him."

Hanyi closed his eyes. "It was my fault. We should've—"

"No, Hanyi, it was not your fault," Keito interrupted. "It's difficult to explain, but things got *really* complicated. We thought we had an opening."

"But you didn't take the opening?"

"No, and as a result, he locked down a stadium and murdered everyone inside," Keito said. "Well, almost everyone."

The others fell silent, a million questions hanging in the air above them, though they were too nervous to voice them.

"So the one responsible for the Tournament Slaughter is also the one who broke the dimensional holding seal?" Mitoki finally said.

"Yes."

"And you know who it is?" Mitoki raised his hands in exasperation. "So *why* are we even wasting time with the tournament? Why don't we just go after this guy?"

"It's not that simple," Hanyi said gently.

"No, I'm pretty sure it is," he insisted. "We go to Council, we tell them we know—"

"The council already knows that this was our case," Keito interrupted. "The Elders already know what we know. But they also know that this guy we're after comes with a slew of complications I can't even begin to explain to you." He sighed. "I understand your frustration, probably more than you know. And to be frank, the reason I didn't want to come back to the Guardians is because I did not want to come back to this case with all the red tape and complications. This case has led to more death than any case I've ever been on before...and it probably will bring more death than you're prepared for."

"And you're just telling us *now*?" Eclipse snapped.

"I wish I could just tell you everything," Keito said. "Truly, I do."

"Then *tell* us."

"Eclipse," Hanyi interjected, "it's more than just this one guy, okay? He's got people everywhere. I'm sure he's got spies and lackeys deeply set in Council and even in the Guardian Branch. If we just run after him, all we'll do is force him to kill us, and he'll keep doing what he's doing. We need to dig deeper. We need to find the people he's got in the Guardian Branch and the DPC. We need to do more than just kill this guy. It's rooted deeper."

"He broke the seal centuries ago," Keito added. "And he's had time to get his fingers deep into the Dimension Protection Council."

"Then the investigations of the other Guardians under the pretense of the tournament is actually something we need to do...not just go after the one who broke the seal," Dalton concluded, nodding. "Do you know who works for him?"

"Maybe a few people but a lot has changed over the last forty years," Keito answered. "I'm learning with you. The only thing I know hasn't changed is how dangerous he is. There are things about him that you're not ready to hear, and you won't be until you come face-to-face with him. So, for now, we look for his influence, see who's loyal to him and who is trying to derail our investigation. And that means we go through the tournament and do what the Elders ordered us to do."

"And when will we actually go after the guy?" Eclipse asked sharply.

"We won't," Keito answered. "He'll make himself known when he wants us to play his game. And believe me, he's already watching us very closely."

Chapter Ten

Packing what they needed for the Beast Realm proved to be challenging as they also needed to haul sleeping bags, medical supplies, and anything they thought they would need for the tournament—which they could not even begin to guess. Hanyi and Keito assured them that they would need very little in the competition, as firearms were forbidden in the ring and most Guardians used magic rather than physical weapons. But the humans still felt the need to carry multiple daggers in their packs.

The Beast Realm was the most undeveloped realm, and Hanyi told the humans that the best accommodations offered were with his pack as he added several flourishes of promising to actually cook the meat they fed the humans and offering refreshing baths via a river. While Keito was clearly no stranger to roughing it, the humans were a little more hesitant. Dalton said he did not want to be an imposition on the wolf pack, but Hanyi said it would be safer to stick close to an established pack in case anyone tried any underhanded tactics seen in the previous tournaments.

As Jikia and Tarrena would be visiting family friends in the Beast Realm until the beginning of the tournament, Jikia insisted the Guardians haul two more large rucksacks full of healing herbs and bandages with them. Eclipse and Dalton offered to carry Jikia and Tarrena's smaller duffels while Keito was left to shoulder both larger, heavier bags.

He groaned as he hauled them over his shoulders once they were cleared for passage into the Realm of Beasts.

"Right back to how it was before," he grumbled. "Make the demon be the damn *pack mule*."

"Oh, don't act like it's too heavy, because I know it's not," Jikia retorted.

Dalton always felt a sense of awe when he visited the Realm of Beasts, and even with the tournament looming in his future and the heaviness of his mission weighing on his shoulders, he still felt lighter walking in the fresh air of the unspoiled landscape. Even though there was plenty to discuss during the hours of hiking, most of the time was spent in silence, admiring the rolling hills, towering trees, and lush valleys of the wilderness led by the grey-brown wolf that was clearly happy to be in his home realm.

The hours fell away with ease, and it was only when the humans began to sweat under the unrelenting sun as they climbed a rolling knoll of grass that Mitoki finally spoke up.

"Should we stop for a while?" he suggested.

"We're close," Kcito assured, nodding to Hanyi, who had stopped at the top of the hill, his nose high in the air. He let out a whine before lifting his head higher and howling, the haunting call floating along the gentle breeze that offered a small reprieve from the heat.

Shortly after Hanyi finished his howl, distant calls from other wolves could be heard. In an instant, Hanyi broke into a run down the other side of the hill, leaving the Guardians behind.

"Hanyi! Wait!" Dalton called, starting after him.

"Don't worry," Keito said with a smile, taking up the lead. "He's too excited to be home."

The group entered a sparse forest where the trees were smaller than the ones they had already traversed. It did not take them long to find the wolves whining excitedly around Hanyi. Dalton was surprised by the sheer size of the pack. Though it was difficult to count the exact number, as the wolves bounced and played in the elation of their alpha's return, he was certain there were well over thirty wolves in the Treneke Wolf Tribe. Keito stopped on the outskirts of the reunion, waiting for the other wolves to see them. When the first one caught sight of the Guardians and the two dragons, it did not take long for the others to stop their revelry and turn.

For a moment, Dalton was worried they were not welcome, as most of the wolves dropped their heads suspiciously and inched forward. But Hanyi padded ahead of them and shifted back into his human form.

"Hi, sorry," he said, his smile broad. "Um, welcome to my home," he motioned his arms around the trees.

"Is...everyone okay with us staying here?"

"What?" Hanyi turned to see what Dalton was staring at and then he started laughing. "Oh, yeah, don't worry about them. They're fine." He gestured with his hand as though urging them forward, but only a few wolves stepped up before their bodies shifted into a human appearance, dressed simply in clothes that seemed to match their coat colors. One was a woman with long, dark brown hair and steely eyes. She walked forward easily, passing Hanyi as she opened her arms.

"Keito."

"Xana," he greeted, hugging her.

"This is my mate, Xana," Hanyi introduced to the others.

"It's very nice to meet you," she said, breaking her hug with Keito as she offered her hand to Dalton.

"You as well," he said, surprised by the strength of her handshake.

"Hopefully he hasn't been acting too childish in my absence," Xana said, shaking hands with Eclipse and Mitoki as they each said their names in introduction.

"I was on my best behavior!" Hanyi said in mock hurt.

"It's very nice to meet you. I'm Jikia. This is my daughter Tarrena. We've been training these boys," Jikia introduced them, shaking Xana's hand.

"Then you got him to focus?" Xana asked, winking at them as Hanyi's mouth dropped open, his hand pressed over his chest as though in shock.

"We tried," Jikia played along.

Dalton ignored the playful banter, smiling at the two young girls clinging close to Hanyi's legs, looking over the strangers hesitantly. He could tell just by looking at them that they were Hanyi's children, the resemblance in their eyes being almost uncanny.

"I'm afraid a lot of the pack doesn't know how to do this," Xana said, returning to Hanyi's side as she motioned over her human body. "But we can translate, if needed."

"These two little ones are my youngest," Hanyi said, placing a hand on the two girls' heads. "Miatta and Ashani. My sons are all away for training, so I'm afraid you won't get a chance to meet them."

"Training?" Mitoki repeated.

"Everyone in my bloodline goes through basic training, similar to Guardian training, but not so intense," Hanyi explained. "We believe it's important that the alpha bloodline be able to take human form and interact with humans, just considering the human realms and the council." He ruffled his daughters' hair. "And these two little runts will be going next session."

"Dad!" they whined, squirming away from him.

"And I know I have other family lurking around here somewhere…" Hanyi groaned, turning around to look at the pack.

"Sorry we don't really have any place for you to sit down," Xana said. "Just set your bags there," she motioned to the ground. "We'll clear some space and make a fire pit."

"Anything we can help with?" Dalton offered.

"No, no, you've had a long hike to get here," she assured.

Hanyi growled, shifting down to his wolf form and trotting toward some other wolves, who had their tails down as they whined. Hanyi lowered his head, his growl becoming louder, though his tail was wagging slightly as he did so. He lunged forward, circling two of the other wolves and nipping at the backs of their legs, causing them to whine and leap forward, their bodies shifting and morphing into two identical men. Hanyi also began walking on two legs once more.

"You need the practice," he teased.

"For what reason?" one lamented.

"We're not in line to be alpha." the other seconded.

"And two legs are just…awkward."

"I don't know how humans stay balanced."

Hanyi rolled his eyes, motioning to the Guardians.

"You know Keito," he said. "This is Dalton, Eclipse, and Mitoki. And this is Jikia, our trainer, and her daughter, Tarrena." He motioned to the twins. "These are my older brothers, Hari and Haru."

"Nice to meet you," they said in unison.

"And…" Hanyi let out an exasperated huff as he turned around once more. "I swear, my family does not want to be social today…Where is Hana?"

"Over there," Ashani announced, pointing.

"Hey," Hari said, grabbing Hanyi's arm. "Cut her a break today, okay?"

"It was a bad morning," Haru added.

Hanyi's entire demeanor changed. Dalton had only seen Hanyi's smile fall when they discussed the previous Guardian Tournament. But there was no trace of his normal bright expression as he nodded.

"How bad?"

Xana stepped forward, gently resting her hand on his arm.

"You should probably talk to her."

He nodded and turned to the Guardians.

"Sorry, can you guys give me a few minutes?"

"Sure," Dalton said.

"Here," Xana said, stepping toward the Guardians and drawing their attention, "let's get a fire going and get you settled."

"Hanyi?" Jikia called. "Is it alright if we head out?"

"Of course," he said over his shoulder. "We'll meet you at the stadium."

"4B," she said. "Do you know where that is?"

"That's pretty far from here," Hanyi noted. "Do you want to meet at the stadium or somewhere else?"

"We'll just meet you at the stadium the morning of the tournament," she said. "Will you be alright without us around?"

"They're in good hands," Xana assured.

"Alright, you boys just take it easy. Save your strength," she instructed. "The tournament is in three days. Don't go getting into trouble before that."

The Guardians bid goodbye to the dragons as Hanyi shifted back into his wolf form, walking among the pack toward two wolves on the far side of the gathering. The humans tried not to be too curious, busying themselves with clearing some of the loose underbrush and picking the best spot for a fire circle. Occasionally Dalton would look over the lounging wolves of the Treneke Wolf Tribe, trying to spot his teammate. Since he was not used to seeing Hanyi in his wolf form, it took him a long time to finally recognize the other Guardian lying next to the two wolves he had approached. One of them was sleeping peacefully, the other was stiff in posture, its nose pressed close to the dirt as it rocked slowly from side to side. Occasionally, Hanyi would nudge the other wolf and it would jump. But otherwise, they remained still, communicating in a way the humans could not comprehend.

As the Guardians set to gathering rocks for their fire circle, Hari and Haru offered to hunt for a deer for their guests. The prospect of a hunt got many of the wolves excited, and soon, more than half the Treneke Wolf Tribe had slipped into the trees to hunt. Xana stayed with the Guardians, helping them clear places for their sleeping bags and taking their canteens to fill in the nearby stream.

When the Guardians had nothing left to distract themselves, they sat around the fire circle with Xana and Hanyi's daughters, who were both in their wolf forms, gnawing on some of the discarded twigs for the fire.

Dalton tried not to stare at his teammate, but could think of nothing else to distract him as he sat on his sleeping bag and waited for the wolf pack to return with a meal.

"So, Xana," he started, turning to her, "how long have you and Hanyi been together?"

"Getting close to thirty years now," she answered. "I did not officially become his mate until about seventeen years ago when I had our first son, but we started getting close about thirty years ago."

"So it was after he quit the Guardians."

Xana nodded, throwing a quick glance to Keito before dropping her eyes to the ground.

"It was difficult to get close to him after he quit the Guardians," she admitted. "He was...he had shut himself off from everyone. He went into this strange survival mode." She turned to him, her voice getting quiet. "But he didn't have a choice. He came back after the massacre and had no time to mourn what he had lost. Hector was dead and the pack needed a leader. He had a duty."

"Is the alpha in order of lineage?" Mitoki asked. "Because Hanyi said Hari and Haru were his *older* brothers. Shouldn't one of them have been in line?"

"Twins are rare in the Treneke Tribe," Xana said, an amused smile taking over her face. "And Hari and Haru are inseparable. They can't stand to be out of sight of one another, and it's not a good trait for a leader to be so dependent on his brother. They need to be able to make decisions on thier own. So Hanyi took over after Hector's death."

"And his other sibling?" Eclipse asked. "Hana?"

"The baby of the family, Hanyi's younger sister," Keito answered, jerking his head in the direction of Hanyi and the other wolf.

"She would never challenge Hanyi for the position," Xana said. "She...she likes to stay in the background."

"I'm sorry, I don't mean to pry," Eclipse said, sensing he had stumbled on a sensitive topic.

"Let's just say, Hanyi was really the only option," Xana said. "And he did the best he could. But Hector cast a big shadow, and even when he was gone, it was difficult for much of the pack to submit to Hanyi's control."

"I remember reading that Hector had a very impressive record as a Guardian," Mitoki mused. "So I can only assume that extended to his home life as well."

"Hector was something else," Keito agreed. "He was the kind that was just naturally good at everything he tried. It was like he never struggled to understand anything, whether that was an assignment, a person, it didn't matter. He just had that innate ability to complete whatever task was in front of him. And not just complete it, but excel at it."

"He also commanded a lot of respect in the tribe, just by the nature of his being," Xana added. "I remember it always seemed like Hanyi and Hector were competing in everything. And Hanyi would try and try, but Hector always outshone him."

"Sounds like that would cause some contention," Mitoki said.

"I always thought it would, but it never did," she said. "Hanyi idolized Hector, and Hector never bested Hanyi out of malice or pride. He just always managed to do so, and Hanyi took it in stride. They were exceptionally close, even with Hanyi feeling as though he was always hidden by Hector's shadow. With the twins' weird idiosyncrasies and Hana's struggles..." Xana shook her head. "It seemed like Hanyi and Hector could turn to each other more than they could turn to their other siblings."

"Is she…okay?" Dalton asked, nodding to the wolf that was now lying on her side, pressing her head to Hanyi's shoulder.

Xana turned her gaze to Keito, silently asking if he knew how much Hanyi would be comfortable with sharing. Keito nodded and turned to explain.

"She's alright, she's just always struggled," he said. "She was probably the most overshadowed in the family. There were complications with her birth and because of those complications, unfortunately, her mother passed away, and Hana seemed to have some difficulties keeping up with her brothers. Hanyi's never really explained the details to me, but she struggles with distinguishing her reality. She's even run off from the pack for long stretches of time, and once returned with a pup of her own, who was born deaf and she blamed herself for her daughter's hearing. The brothers have tried to do everything they can to protect her, but that doesn't always help."

"She feels like she drags the family down, even the whole pack at times," Xana added. "We all think she may have the same illness as their father, but it's difficult to know for sure. Needless to say, that also creates some anxiety in the family. Hanyi is worried that she will lose her grip on reality entirely and end up like his father."

"I'm so sorry to hear that," Dalton murmured.

"Yes, it is a struggle," she said. "Some days are more difficult than others. Unfortunately this morning was a bad morning for her. But it's good for her to have Hanyi just be with her. It calms her down. He has a very steady presence to him."

"Steady, but a bit weird," Keito teased.

"I was honestly worried he would not be able to go back to being a Guardian," she mused, her voice getting quiet. "It took a lot to get him back after the massacre. I was worried he would fall back into that darkness."

Dalton was about to assure Hanyi's mate that Hanyi was constantly joking around with them, but stopped when he saw the intense stare occurring between Keito and Xana over the fire circle. Even though there were bright flames licking at the twigs and branches between them, the air seemed to get colder the longer they stared. Keito finally took a deep breath, standing.

"Excuse me," he said, walking away from the group as the three humans looked hurriedly between one another, not sure if they should ask where he was going. Keito had disappeared among the trees before they could call him back. Confused, Dalton turned to Xana.

"Um…sorry, what just happened?" he asked.

"Nothing."

"That wasn't nothing."

She closed her eyes, pained. "I just know the kind of darkness that comes with this mission. I saw the devastation it inflicted last time. And I can't see him go through that again." She turned to Dalton. "He still has nightmares, you know? He never got to move past the massacre. He still lives in it almost every night. He was broken when he stumbled back here, but he had to pull himself together for his family. He had to immediately deal with Hana's nearly violent breakdown over Hector's death, then other wolves began challenging for territory and position, and he had to step in and be the alpha and pretend that his entire world hadn't just been shattered."

She glanced back in the direction Keito had gone.

"I do have a little resentment toward Keito, and I know it's unfounded, but he just disappeared on Hanyi for years after the massacre. The only other person who knows what Hanyi survived and he just left him to deal with it alone. I know Keito had to process it too, but I can never get that image out of my head of the way Hanyi looked when he came home. He's the strongest wolf I've ever known, and to see him like that was more than I could bear. And he had no support to get through that grief."

"Not true," Dalton corrected. "He had you."

Xana stopped, staring at Dalton for several long moments before dropping her head.

"I've done all I can for him, but I can't protect him from this," she said. "I love him more than anything, and I know that this whole thing is a lot harder for him than he's letting on. And as strong of an ally as Keito is, death follows him." She swallowed hard, her voice becoming tight. "Please, watch out for Hanyi. Don't let him get swallowed by this again. Help him stay afloat as much as you can."

"He's been the one doing that for us through most of training," Mitoki said gently. "He doesn't really like to talk about what happened or how he feels about it."

"And he never will," Xana said. "He'll never tell you he's in pain. But if you do see his pain, don't let him wallow in it. And don't let yourselves get swallowed up in this, either. I can't bear the thought of even more lives being destroyed by this bloody tournament."

Ashani and Maitta suddenly leapt up, seeing Hanyi stand and walk over to the fire circle. They dropped in a playful stance as he mirrored them, lightly nipping at them and playfully growling as he made his way to the Guardians and shifted back to human form.

"Sorry about that," he said with a broad smile, kissing Xana on the cheek as he sat next to her. "Thank you for keeping them company while the others went on a hunt." He looked around. "Where's Keito?"

"Um, he just kinda..." Eclipse jerked his thumb over his shoulder into the woods.

"Hmm," Hanyi hummed. "Well, he's a big demon. He can take care of himself. He'll wander back when he gets hungry." He glared playfully at Mitoki. "Are you guys bragging about how Mitoki beat me in sparring yesterday?"

Dalton let out a bark of laughter.

"Yes, we've been telling your mate all about how a nineteen-year-old kicked your ass."

Xana's response was to give Mitoki a thumbs up with a wink.

Hanyi began telling Xana about their stories from training, easily striking up light conversation that had the Guardians laughing and feeling more relaxed as the sky became painted in vibrant reds and oranges with the sunset. Just when the Guardians were starting to feel the hunger pains in their bellies, the hunting party returned, many with rabbits and large birds for those who had stayed behind while Hari carried a deer over his shoulders in human form, bringing it to the fire to prepare and cook for the Guardians.

It was when the sky had grown dark and dotted with millions of stars that the Guardians partook in the meal the wolves had prepared, though there was a lot of debate about when the meat was cooked through. The atmosphere had become light as they began eating and joking with the wolves, the conversation from earlier mostly forgotten.

As they were laughing about a silly story concerning one of Hanyi's earlier cases, Mitoki gasped in surprise and jumped.

"Damn it, Keito!" he snapped. "What are you doing *lurking* like that?"

The others spun to see the dark-haired demon leaning against a tree, nearly blending in with the shadows of the woods.

"Sorry, didn't mean to scare you," he said.

"I have some deer for you, *dear*," Hanyi said, holding up a flat stone with the cuts of meat he had set aside for the demon.

"Oh, thank you, I'm not particularly hungry," he said, appearing agitated as he looked around the pack of wolves. Every eye had turned to him, sensing his tension. "Hanyi, can I talk to you for a minute?"

"Sure…"

Hanyi stood and approached Keito, who took two steps further into the woods to whisper something to him. The Guardians could not hear what they were saying, but they could tell from the way the wolves' ears were trained on the two that they could make out the conversation.

"Is everything alright?" Mitoki asked. Dalton shrugged.

When a few growls sounded around the wolves at something Keito said, Hanyi turned to them with a growl of his own before turning back to the demon.

"I don't think everything's alright," Eclipse said.

"Hanyi?" Dalton called, causing him to jump to attention. "Everything okay?"

"Um…" Hanyi started, pursing his lips. "Keito said he saw some suspicious looking people in the woods. He thinks they might be scouters, but you never know."

"Scouters?"

"Other teams of Guardians coming to scope out the competition beforehand," Keito elaborated, his tone measured. "I doubt we're in any serious danger, but after the previous rounds of the tournament, I'm a little uneasy. It was not uncommon for other teams to try and attack favored teams outside the ring to get an advantage."

"What do we need to do?" Mitoki asked.

"Nothing. I'm going to keep watch tonight, maybe do some patrolling around the area," Keito said. "With the tensions between the Guardian Branch and everyone else right now, we just need to be careful."

"Do you want to take shifts?" Dalton suggested.

"No, I didn't even really want to worry you with it," Keito assured. "I'm probably just being paranoid. But I didn't want to just disappear all night without telling you. Didn't want you to worry."

"Oh…" Dalton could sense that Keito was lying. Something about the way he refused to meet their eyes and the way the wolves seemed to be tensing as if ready for a fight had him thinking there was a much larger threat looming. "I appreciate that."

"I'll keep watch for the night. You all should get some sleep. You're going to need all your strength for the tournament," Keito continued.

"Come get me if you find anyone," Hanyi said, though the statement felt hollow.

"I will."

Keito turned without another word and disappeared back into the woods.

"Did he seem off to you?" Mitoki asked.

"For *Keito*?" Hanyi joked. "Not really." He began laughing. "I should tell you about the time Keito disappeared for three days while on a case and we finally found him in the Guardian Branch archives with another demon Guardian. And let me tell you, they were *not* researching."

Hanyi easily distracted the humans from Keito's weird behavior, though it took the wolves longer to relax and cluster close to the fire. It was impossible to tell time, but Dalton knew hours had passed with Hanyi sharing two embarrassing stories about Keito being caught in compromising situations. Around the heat of the fire with full bellies, exhaustion began to settle into their bones. Hanyi saw their drooping eyelids and put out the fire, bidding them goodnight as they climbed into their sleeping bags, the noises of the woods lulling them to sleep.

Chapter Eleven

Dalton startled awake, sitting upright as he gulped in air greedily, his eyes scanning his surroundings. It took his frightened thoughts several long moments to settle and remind him that he was in the Realm of Beasts. Allowing his shoulders to relax as his heart eased its terrified pounding, Dalton tried to recall the moment when he felt the dream turn from pleasant weightlessness to suffocating pain. Even as his brain swam back to full consciousness, he could still acutely remember the radiating agony that had seized his muscles.

As he rubbed his eyes roughly, he decided it was best to assume the bizarre dream was actually a panic attack.

The sun was barely over the horizon, giving little light to the area where most of the wolves had settled again once they realized Dalton had merely had a nightmare. Dalton's sudden movements had not disturbed his teammates, as they were still curled tightly in their sleeping bags. Hanyi and Xana were curled together, their two daughters nearby. But the alpha's family was still separated from the rest of the pack, and Dalton understood why.

When struggling to fall asleep, Dalton had heard soft whining nearby and spotted Hanyi twitching and whimpering in his sleep, clearly experiencing the nightmares Xana had explained the previous day. It was not long before the wolf leapt upright, jumping away from his family as he looked around wildly, trying to orient himself. Patiently, Xana had stood, walked to him and guided him back to where he had been before, nudging him until they both fell asleep again.

Dalton knew all too well what it was like to be awoken by nightmares.

He tried not to dwell on concerns about what new nightmares would be with him while tracking down the one who broke the dimensional holding seal. He focused on relaxing his body as he stared up at the brightening sky, allowing the crisp forest air to fill his lungs.

As he was starting to drift to sleep once more, despite the light washing over the land, he heard the wolves stir. He sat up slowly, looking over the Treneke Wolf Tribe, seeing those who had woken were watching a familiar dark-haired demon walking closer to Hanyi. Dalton stared at him, confused yet amused by Keito's mischievous expression.

Keito crept behind Hanyi, crouching as close as he dared to get. Puckering his lips, he whistled quietly near Hanyi's head. The wolf's ear twitched and he growled in his sleep.

The sound woke the remaining wolves, who turned quickly to watch the demon whistle again at Hanyi, unable to mask his amusement as Hanyi lifted a lazy paw to swat at the noise. Dalton shook Eclipse and Mitoki awake, motioning for them to be quiet as they blinked the sleep from their eyes. As Keito whistled a third time, everyone had their eyes locked on the two oldest Guardians.

Hanyi growled again, his lip curling up to show his teeth.

"Wake up..." Keito crooned, trying to make his voice sound distant and airy.

Hanyi lifted his paw again in another half-serious swat. Maitta and Ashani were jumping excitedly, trying not to whimper in glee as they watched the silly antics. Xana had turned her head to watch, light dancing in her eyes.

"If you don't wake up, I'm going to bite you," Keito warned. "You have to run forty laps before breakfast...you need to wake up."

Dalton did not know if Hanyi was actually asleep, but he was enjoying the half-hearted growls and groans from his wolf teammate. He assumed Hanyi was feigning slumber, waiting to see what Keito would do and playing it up for those he knew were watching.

Keito lifted one hand, pointing his sharp nails at one another before grabbing Hanyi's ear.

He bolted awake, jumping away from Keito with a yelp. The pack began barking and whining excitedly as the humans laughed. Hanyi growled at the demon, though his tail was wagging as he squared off to him.

"I did not bite you," Keito corrected the wolf's accusation, flexing his fingers. Hanyi growled again, his teeth bared, his head going low as he shifted his shoulders. He leapt at the demon, tackling him and pushing him to the ground to stand on his chest, a malicious snarl on his face.

Just when the humans were worried the two were in a serious fight, Hanyi's tail began to wag and he licked Keito's face as the demon cringed in disgust.

"Hanyi!" he snapped, pushing the wolf away. "We had a rule about this! You don't lick me and I won't kill you!"

Hanyi stepped off Keito's chest and nodded triumphantly as he shifted into his human form.

"Serves you right!" he declared strongly.

"Hey, I could have actually bitten you like Hector used to," Keito said. "Come on, I saw you sleeping so deeply, I had to see if you still had your reflexes."

"My reflexes are fine, thank you. I've had children. They took over where you and Hector left off!" the wolf laughed. Keito stood, wiping the saliva from his face, grimacing.

"You know, Hanyi, you could have just *told* me how you felt. After all the time we've spent together, we shouldn't have this kind of unresolved tension between us."

"Oh, you wish," Hanyi leered. "You think you're so irresistible."

"…I am, though."

"Well, the illusion was shattered for me long ago," Hanyi said. "I know how truly boring you are under that beautiful face and those alluring eyes."

"Oh, stop, Hanyi, you're making me blush."

Hanyi turned to Dalton and the others, shaking his head. "Do you see what I had to put up with for decades? It's a miracle my sanity is still intact."

Eclipse's expression turned skeptical and Hanyi's face fell.

"What?"

"Nothing."

"Hell of a way to say good morning, Keito," Mitoki laughed, untangling his legs from his sleeping bag and stretching.

"Hopefully that's not your standard good morning," Dalton agreed.

"Don't like your ear grabbed?" Keito asked.

"It's not my favorite."

Eclipse rolled his eyes. "Did you find anyone when you were patrolling last night?" he asked the demon Guardian.

"Yes, actually," Keito said. "But we're not under attack. It was just another team of Guardians who got a little lost. I ended up escorting them about eight miles west to where they had their camp. After that I just spent some time scanning the area, seeing if there were any other Guardian teams nearby so I could scope out the competition."

"See anyone?"

"No," he admitted.

"Well, I hope you got some sleep, too," Dalton said. "We need you rested for the tournament. Remember, we don't know what we're doing," he motioned to Eclipse and Mitoki. "We're going to need all the help we can get."

"I got some sleep," the demon assured.

"You know," Hanyi started thoughtfully, "it might not be a bad idea to give you a taste of what you'll be experiencing in a few days."

"We shouldn't spar. Jikia said to take it easy," Mitoki said.

"No, not spar. We should go to the stadium today. Take a look around, give you a feel for what you're going to see."

"That's not a bad idea," Keito agreed.

"I would like to see a stadium," Dalton said. "I've never been in the one in my own city, so it would be nice to get a feel for the layout of the place." He hesitated. "Are you two going to be alright?"

Keito and Hanyi shared a glance, understanding the weight of the question.

"I don't know," Hanyi finally said. "I haven't set foot inside a stadium since...well, I would rather know how difficult it is for me *now* than find out the day of the tournament."

"Are we even allowed inside, yet?" Eclipse asked.

"Technically no, but it's not as if they lock the door or anything." Hanyi shrugged. "If we get caught we'll just say sorry and that we didn't know. The worst they can do is kick us out of the building."

"If you are both okay with going to the stadium, I think we should," Dalton said.

The Guardians dressed in fresh clothes as Hanyi's daughters darted off into the woods to gather berries for them to eat for breakfast. Keito stripped down, but rather than change into new clothes, he set some clothes in a pile on a rock and then walked into the woods.

"Keito?" Dalton asked, becoming worried about the demon's propensity for disappearing into the woods mysteriously.

"Oh, don't worry, he just doesn't want you to see him shift."

"Shift?" the humans asked simultaneously.

"Into his animal form."

"Why is he doing that?" Mitoki asked, only realizing in that moment that all through training they had never seen Keito's animal form. Even though it was well known that all demons also had an animal form they could take, it was a very rare occurrence.

"Because Stadium 4B is far away," Hanyi said. "Keito will get us there faster than if we just walk, since dimension hopping is illegal here."

"It's illegal everywhere," Dalton said, his eyebrows high. "And are you saying that we're going to ride Keito to the stadium?"

"Yep."

"I'm...not sure I'm comfortable with that," Eclipse said.

"Why not?" Hanyi asked. "It's just like riding a horse. Except bigger."

"I've never ridden a horse, either."

Hanyi sighed, his head rolling back in exasperation.

"You want to spend the entire day walking to the stadium? And then we have to walk all the way back. It's not a one-day trip on foot. Trust me, this is best."

"Maybe, but it's weird. Keito—"

As if on cue, Keito stepped out of the woods, startling the members of Team Dalton once more. Dalton had only seen pictures and videos of demons in their animal forms—never with his own eyes. He barely stood at the height of Keito's knee, and even though Keito was a fox and wolf hybrid, he did not look like either. His body was thin and lanky, appearing like a distorted imagining of a canine animal. His black fur was streaked with silver strands and his eyes remained the same intense golden, though they appeared even more menacing when accompanied with the glinting claws and bright white teeth.

Keito was slow as he moved closer, sensing the unease in the wolves and the surprise in his teammates. He lowered himself to his belly, turning his head to the humans as Hanyi easily approached Keito, grabbing the stack of clothes he had set aside.

"*It's alright,*" he assured telepathically to the others, startling them out of their staring. "*This is a good way to travel long distances in places where there aren't any cars.*"

"Are you sure?" Dalton pressed, taking a hesitant step closer. Keito bowed his head as Hanyi easily climbed up on Keito's back, smiling at the others.

"Well? Come on," he urged.

Dalton was the next to climb onto the demon's back, trying not to pull at the soft fur as he sat himself behind Hanyi.

"How do I not fall off?"

Hanyi leaned forward and grabbed a handful of Keito's fur, glancing over his shoulder at Dalton.

"Hang on tight."

"Are you sure you can carry us all, Keito?" Mitoki asked, being the last one to pull himself onto Keito's back. The demon turned his head to look at the youngest of the team and they could all feel his incredulity.

"Hell, Keito could probably carry all of us in *human* form," Hanyi said.

The Guardians were hesitant to grab Keito's fur in fear of hurting him, but when he stood, jarring them, they quickly tightened their grip, struggling to keep their balance. Keito started at a walk, allowing the humans to get used to the pace as he picked his path through the forest. When he cleared the tree line, stepping onto a grassy knoll, his pace quickened, gradually becoming a full run. The others of the team had to lower themselves and hold on tighter to keep the wind out of their faces and remain seated. Dalton's muscles were starting to cramp with the effort of not falling when Keito finally slowed, carefully breaking out of his run so his passengers would not fall.

When Keito stopped moving, the others straightened wincing and whining as their strained muscles tried to relax.

"We made it," Hanyi announced over his shoulder with a broad grin.

The humans glared at the wolf before turning their gaze to their surroundings, nearly falling once more when Keito lowered himself to his belly again.

Dalton had been aware of tournament stadiums in several of the cities he had visited and he knew that there was one in his own city that he hardly noticed when driving his daughter to her soccer practices. After the tournament had been disbanded, the stadiums were shut down and most of them fell into disrepair. A few across the realms had been changed to museums dedicated to the Guardian Branch, but a majority were left abandoned. Dalton had always thought of the stadium in his city just as another graffitied edifice waiting for its turn to be demolished.

The stadium before him, however, stood alone in a large field, proud and tall. The domed structure was lined with gargoyles of great beasts, topping stone pillars that appeared old but well-maintained.

"Whoa..." Mitoki breathed, his eyes studying the stadium as the team stepped away from Keito. "I have one of these in my city, but it's in really bad shape. This one..."

"Has been refurbished," Hanyi assured. "And this is a smaller stadium. The ones in the human realms are much larger. After the slaughter, a lot of beasts tried to destroy these stadiums to dispel the negative energy."

There was a crunching, popping sound that caused the Guardians to look at Keito, seeing his fur retract into his skin as he writhed his body, morphing back into the human appearance they recognized. Mitoki's eyes were wide in horror by the time Keito stood on two legs again.

"Sorry," Keito said, taking the clothes Hanyi offered him and dressing. "It's not a pleasant transformation to watch."

"Look at how much work they put into rebuilding this…" Hanyi said, unfazed by Keito's shift. "They even replaced the statues."

"That's worrisome," Keito noted, pulling on his shirt.

"Why?"

"I thought that this tournament was just a pretense to investigate the Guardians and council members that might be involved with the corruption and breaking the seal. But the DPC is throwing a lot of money into rebuilding these stadiums…as if they want to start using them regularly again."

"They can be used for other purposes," Dalton suggested, trying not to show how unsettled he was by Keito's observation. "It could be a training dome for apprentices, or even a shelter for Guardians when they're stationed in other realms. A big building like this has its uses."

"I suppose," Keito said, clearly unconvinced. "Well, let's take a look inside. See if anything has changed."

"Yeah…" Hanyi muttered, his step a little more hesitant than Keito's as he looked over the stadium. Even though the humans of Team Dalton were eager to see the inside for themselves, they also made a note to keep watch over their teammates.

Keito led them to the first door he saw marked "Participants Only" and tried the handle. Unlocked, the door opened on well-oiled hinges, granting them access to a dark hallway. Keito stepped aside, holding the door open for the others.

"I don't think anyone is here," he said. "But we should still keep an eye out for guards or technicians setting up for the tournament."

"I think that even if we're caught, we're probably fine," Dalton assured. "I am top-ranked Guardian after all. I can probably come up with some excuse for us to be here if they try to kick us out."

"Might as well use the position if you have it," Hanyi agreed with a nod. "Right, Keito?" The others could hear an inside joke between the two older Guardians, but Keito just narrowed his eyes at Hanyi as he closed the door, cutting off the only light in the dark hallway.

"Got your ass out of trouble often enough," Keito said, orbing some magic in his palm to act as a light.

As they walked through the hall, each following Keito's example to use their magic for a light source, they noted the four doors, two on each side and each marked with a different number. Near the end of the hallway where a set of double doors stood, there were two notice boards with various posted papers.

"Where do these doors lead?" Eclipse asked, motioning to the doors on either side of the hall.

"They're the team rooms," Hanyi answered. "They're something like locker rooms for the teams competing. There are some medical supplies, some chairs, a table, a medical bed. It's up to the team if they want to stay in these rooms between their fights, but most teams prefer to be in the team box where they can watch the competition."

"We have one of these rooms?" Mitoki asked.

"Not in this hall," Keito said, looking over the notices on the bulletin board. "Looks like we're in The Corner. Hall D, room one."

"Lucky us," Hanyi said. He smiled at the others. "It's considered good luck if you get put into one of the team rooms in Hall D. Some silly tournament superstition, but The Corner is considered lucky."

"The Corner?" Dalton repeated.

"There's only two team rooms in Hall D, where there's four in all the others," Keito elaborated. "Means you only see one of the competing teams before you enter the ring, so you don't psyche yourself out as much being around even more nervous energy." He backed away from the bulletin board. "It's a good thing we came here today, actually. Apparently, there is a pre-tournament check tomorrow."

"I thought it was weird we hadn't been called to one," Hanyi mused, leaning close to Keito to look over the schedule on the board.

"So we have to be here tomorrow?" Dalton asked.

"Every tournament season, Council is supposed to call the teams in to check them for eligibility in the tournament. Guardians who have more than five cites against them are disqualified, anyone who seems volatile or too dangerous is also disqualified. We don't have to worry because we're a council-sponsored team, but we still have to be here."

"Why?"

Keito pointed at himself. "Because you have a demon on the team. I need to get tested before each round."

Before the others could ask Keito about the different treatment the demon Guardians received, Keito opened one of the heavy, double doors, causing light to flood into the hallway and making the humans hiss as their eyes struggled to adjust.

Dalton felt the anxiety claw at his stomach. The lights in the enormous domed ceiling were off, but the windows that lined the top of the immense structure allowed in plenty of light. He followed Keito and Hanyi over the hard-packed dirt past the sloping walls of the audience stands and into the ring. There were a few tables set up to one side that Dalton assumed were for the pre-tournament check, but otherwise there was nothing in the ring with them. A wall just barely taller than Dalton surrounded the ring, interrupted by several indents where three steps led up to a swinging door leading into what Dalton guessed were the team boxes. There were four larger halls out of the ring, evenly spaced and marked with a large A, B, C, and D above the double doors leading to the other hallways. The audience seats seemed to stretch on forever, the sheer enormity of the structure accented by how empty it was as they entered the ring.

"Here's the arena," Hanyi announced, holding out his arms wide as he turned in a circle, his voice reverberating off the empty audience seats. "It's obviously a lot bigger than the one we've been training in, but basically the same thing. Those little staircases lead to the team boxes where we can watch the other teams compete if we don't want to spend that time in the team room."

"What do you suggest? Team box or team room?" Mitoki asked.

"I always thought it was best to be in the team box and size up the competition, but it does depend on the day and how long the fights last. Sometimes it's best to rest in the quiet of the team room."

"Up there," Keito added, pointing to a large glass window above the hallway marked A, "is the VIP Box. The Tournament Board watches from there and makes all judgment calls and assessments for fouls or challenges to the announcer. You'll never actually *see* them, but they're always watching. They pass down their word to the announcer in the ring."

Hanyi walked slowly, his eyes passing over the audience seats. The others followed suit, turning away to study the stadium. Dalton could not help but wonder how incredible it was to see all the seats full of cheering spectators as the Guardians sparred for sport. He had seen some recorded fights of previous Guardian Tournaments, but the cameras had never been focused on the sheer size of the audience.

Keito saw something that caused him to stray further from the group, walking to one collection of team boxes.

Dalton walked over to Hanyi.

"How are you holding up?" he asked.

The wolf turned, nodding as his eyes moved over the stadium yet again.

"It's a bit surreal," he admitted. "But I'm...surprisingly okay."

"Are you sure?"

"Yeah," he said. "I don't know, it's almost like muscle memory. I'm just going through everything I went through before every tournament season. Weirdly, it doesn't feel any different."

Eclipse and Mitoki also approached.

"This really was a big production, wasn't it?" Mitoki said, awestruck.

"It really was," Hanyi agreed.

"Dalton," Keito called from his place close to the wall. Everyone walked to him, seeing the worried expression on his face. "The Elders said that only Guardians and council members had anything to do with this tournament, right?"

"Right."

"No one in the realms was to know about it?"

"No."

"So why are there brand new cameras?"

Keito motioned to the large black camera mounted on an oscillating arm, the capped lens pointed into the ring.

"Maybe it's for internal record," Eclipse suggested. "They're recording the fights so that if they see something suspicious they have a video to look back on."

"Those look suspiciously similar to what they used to use," Hanyi noted, eyeing the camera warily.

"No, they wouldn't broadcast it," Dalton said strongly. "The Elders know how dangerous this is. They wouldn't draw attention to it."

"They are completely rebuilding these stadiums," Mitoki reminded him. "And it seems like they're following the same formula as previous tournaments, considering Hanyi's feeling the same as he did at the beginning of every tournament season."

"The Guardian Tournament used to make the DPC a lot of money," Keito added.

"The Elders stated they wouldn't," Dalton insisted.

"...unless this isn't the Elders," Eclipse said, looking over the camera. "What if this is one of those in Council that helped with breaking the seal? What if they're trying to broadcast this and get the people to watch? They might be trying to get civilians involved so that it becomes *more* dangerous and we get distracted."

"That would certainly match up with previous tactics," Hanyi agreed.

As Dalton was about to say he could make some calls to others in the Dimension Protection Council, a boom resonated through the building. Keito turned to the source of the noise just in time to see the double doors for Hall B open. Nearly a dozen wolves rushed into the ring, surrounding Team Dalton with teeth bared and deep growls resonating through their bodies.

"What's happening?" Dalton asked, preparing for a fight.

"You're trespassing," a voice said as one of the wolves near the front stood, shifting into her human form, her clothes plain and black as she crossed her muscular arms over her chest, her glare intensified by the fine wrinkles around her eyes. "We're the guards of this stadium."

"The hell you're the guards," Hanyi sneered, stepping forward. "Raina, what are you doing here?"

"We *are* the guards, Hanyi," she insisted. "This is Opalon territory. We were hired to protect the stadium from any misguided attempts to destroy it before the tournament starts."

"You're doing a shit job," Keito said. "We just walked right in."

Raina turned her gaze onto Keito, an unimpressed smirk crossing her face.

"Keito DeVero," she greeted, looking him over coldly. "You're not at all what I was expecting. I thought you'd be bigger."

"Raina," Hanyi interjected, taking another step forward to confront her, his voice dark, "this is not your territory."

"Oh, I guess you didn't hear that Ludin relinquished," she said. "This is my territory now. And I'm so thrilled I caught a Treneke trespassing."

"This building is owned by the Dimension Protection Council, and we are all Guardians," Dalton said. "It may be on your territory, but once we entered the doors, we were on DPC land."

"You wish, human," Raina sneered. "The DPC thinks they can just open our land to anyone who wants to traipse in here and desecrate it? Our land is older than your pathetic council, and that means that this is still my land."

"If you want to make this about us, then you better tell your lackeys to back off from the rest of my team," Hanyi warned, his voice becoming gravelly. "You don't want to turn this into a war, Raina."

"What if I do?" she challenged.

Hanyi growled, his eyes beginning to shine as his body tensed. The others of Team Dalton prepared for a fight as the wolves surrounding them also lowered their heads, snarling in warning.

Raina leaned even closer.

"I'll come for the Treneke Tribe next, Hanyi."

"The hell you will."

"You've been on borrowed time anyway, old man," she said. "You can't sustain the Treneke Tribe. You're no Hector."

The humans could almost feel the mocking laughter from the rival wolf pack. Keito growled himself, though he refrained from speaking.

"It would have been far more beneficial if he had taken me as his mate when offered," Raina said, never breaking eye contact with Hanyi. "We could have combined the Opalon and Treneke into the most powerful pack this land has ever known."

"The Treneke Tribe is already the most powerful pack the land has ever known." He leaned even closer. "And you weren't his type."

"You're getting old and slow, Hanyi," Raina said. "So why don't we make a little wager, in the spirit of your return to the Guardian Tournament?"

"I'm not one to gamble."

"My daughter Taniya is a Guardian, and she's going to be competing in this very stadium with other pureblood Opalon wolves. I say it's time the next leaders of the Opalon show you their true strength. Should they defeat you, you consider relinquishing to my pack."

"Not that they stand any chance at defeating me, but why would I agree to that?" Hanyi asked incredulously, his eyebrows high. "I won't relinquish to you, Raina. If you want to try for the Treneke territory, you will put yourself at war."

"The Trenekes are not as strong as they once were. And your pups are still very young. They could hardly take over after your death at their age."

"Am I dying anytime soon?" Hanyi quipped.

"I think that's entirely up to you."

His eyes narrowed. "Is that a threat?"

Raina's expression turned cold. She lifted one finger, pointing it at his face. He stared at it, flinching when she prodded his cheek. Her finger traced the skin under his eye, over the bridge of his nose, and under his other eye.

"What do you think?"

Hanyi moved so fast the humans did not see him shift into his wolf form, lunging at Raina with a ferocious snarl. Chaos took hold as the other wolves lunged forward, some at the other Guardians and others at Hanyi. Keito began to retaliate when a booming voice shattered their eardrums.

"That is enough!"

The woman standing near the microphone at the announcer's stand watched coldly as the wolves separated, startled by the stranger's sudden appearance.

"Raina, what the hell is going on?" the woman asked, standing straight and clicking off the microphone as she made her way to the ring.

The female wolf shifted back into her human form.

"These Guardians were trespassing," she accused. "I was telling them to leave when they got violent."

"Is that so?" the woman said, walking across the hard-packed dirt. "Well, the team that supposedly got violent appears to be Team Dalton, which means they have clearance to be here and you have no right to threaten them."

"Ma'am—"

"And furthermore, if you were guarding the building properly, no one should have ever gained access to begin with." She looked over the wolves, unimpressed with the dark looks many were giving her. "We hired you to do a job, not make illegal bets among teams."

"That's not what happened."

"I heard what you said, Raina," she said. "Now, you and your pack return to your jobs."

Raina turned to Hanyi, her eyes filled with a rage, but she obeyed, returning to her wolf form and leaving through the ajar door she had entered.

"As for you," the woman said, "I'm sure you came here to see what safety measures are put in place, but we can go over all those tomorrow before the pre-tournament check."

"Yes, of course," Dalton agreed.

"And Hanyi," she said, turning to the older Guardian, "betting rings will not be tolerated in this season of the tournament. I hope you understand that."

"I understand."

She looked at Keito, holding eye contact with him for the time it took her to turn around.

"Please see yourselves out. We have a lot to set up for tomorrow."

"We should go," Mitoki agreed. "Are you alright, Hanyi?"

"Fine," he said. "Pissed, but fine." He nodded back in the direction they had come. "Let's get back to the pack."

Chapter Twelve

When they returned to the Treneke Wolf Tribe, Xana was orchestrating everything to be sure the Guardians had an earlier supper than the previous night. But after greeting his mate, Hanyi pulled her and his brothers aside, explaining the threat Raina had made at the stadium.

As they were discussing how to be sure Raina was not a threat to the pack, Dalton turned to Keito.

"Hey, what happened back there?"

"Pack politics," Keito answered. "There's no ruling class in the Beast Realm, but in many areas there are groups of animals that have dominion over territory, even if there are other beasts within it. The Treneke Tribe is easily the most powerful collective in this area. But it seems that the Opalon are growing in strength."

"So did she threaten to kill him or go to war with him?" Eclipse pressed.

"Seems like a little of both."

"Did other teams threaten each other like that in the tournament before?" Mitoki asked.

"Near the end, it became very common to run into other teams outside the arena and it often came to violence. This tournament brings out a lot of the worst in Guardians."

"So much for the peacemakers we're supposed to be," Mitoki grumbled.

"The Guardians aren't peacemakers," Dalton said, lowering his eyes to the ground. "I can see how the tournament was a way for the Guardian Branch to build rapport with the people. It's one thing to hear about the Guardians, to see the work they do when a crisis happens, but when those powers are put on display for entertainment, suddenly it's more fascinating than scary. And nearly all Guardians in the branch became Guardians because they had no other choice, because everything in their childhood funneled them in this direction, so I can see how violence would be common outside the stadiums. Guardians are some of the most poorly-adjusted people in the realms."

The humans chuckled lightly, their eyes downcast.

"Then you stick all of them in a tournament where they can flex their power, and yes, things can get very ugly very quickly," Keito concluded. "Not to mention all the corruption that is also playing a part in this particular tournament."

"Definitely not what I thought my assignments would look like when I first joined the Guardians," Eclipse muttered. "I always thought it would be heroics and saving people...most of the time it's killing. And every year I come to the understanding that, one day, I won't be fast enough, and I'll become another body for another Guardian to investigate." He sighed, turning his gaze to Keito. "Did you ever think you would retire?"

"No," he said simply. "I actually wanted the job to kill me. I guess until it almost did, that is."

Hanyi sighed heavily as he approached, sitting next to Keito and shaking his head.

"Everything alright?" Mitoki asked mechanically.

"I honestly don't know," he said. He turned to Keito, opening his mouth to say something before he stopped, exasperated. "I'm trying to reason with myself that all of that in the stadium was just to get under my skin. And it's *irritating* me because it's *working*."

"You're the eight-time champion," Dalton reminded him. "No way the other pack can beat you in the tournament. And it's five-on-five anyway, so we'll be able to help you."

"There are some instances where it can be made a one-on-one fight, but you're right," Hanyi agreed. "It's not even just the tournament. Whether or not I win or lose in the ring, I'm worried Raina will attack the pack." He hesitated a moment, once again starting to speak before he stopped. "Honestly, sometimes I miss worrying only about cases and tournament seasons. There's too much nuance outside the branch."

"I thought you enjoyed civilian life after you retired," Mitoki said.

"Many parts of it, I did," he agreed. "But even when you step outside the Guardian Branch, you're never really out. The perspective you gain once you leave...it can be harder than the job itself. Without being able to put those blinders on and focus on the work, there's too much time for me to replay my past mistakes and come up with hypotheticals about how things could have been different in previous cases. I can't tell you the hours I've spent trying to figure out what I could have done to stop the Tournament Slaughter."

"...there was nothing we could have done, Hanyi," Keito muttered. "I've done the same thing for the last forty years. And the truth is, he was set on sending us that message. We couldn't have stopped it."

"I guess I never really thought about retiring, either," Dalton said. "I know I need to put some thought to it, since I want to see my daughter grow up and have a family of her own one day…but I do worry about that perspective you gain once you leave the branch." He shook his head. "But I enjoy being a Guardian. I went on this case when I was fifteen where a family had been abducted by a cult that was sacrificing people to perform some pretty intense blood magic. It was the first case I really did on my own, and when I saved them…there's no better feeling than realizing that these powers we have and the training we endure as kids is all worth it to save people."

"I'm the same way," Eclipse agreed. "I was sixteen when I had that case that made me realize that being a Guardian was my calling."

"Keito," Mitoki started, "you became a Guardian when you were much older. Why did you join?"

"Anything was better than the life I was living before the Guardians," he said. "I was without purpose in life and I was living just to survive. But when I realized my inside knowledge of the darker corners of the Demon Realm could be very beneficial as a Guardian, I figured it was a good way to use my knowledge and abilities for the betterment of the realms."

"And you did," Dalton agreed. "You're a legend in the Guardian Branch."

"And yet, my legacy is also of the one who quit the day after the massacre of thousands." He turned to Hanyi. "You should take that threat from Raina seriously."

"Yeah…I think I will."

"Wait, why?"

"Because she more or less confirmed that she has allegiance to the same monster behind the Tournament Slaughter," Keito said. "Which means he's already making moves against us."

Keito's vague declaration had the Guardians demanding explanations that their older teammates were refusing to give. They wanted to know how she had shown allegiance to the one they were hunting, what sort of danger they were in from Raina and her pack, and how they could prepare for whatever fight they would find themselves in. But Keito and Hanyi both insisted that it was more important they stay focused on the first round of the Guardian Tournament, and that they would explain everything once the anticipation of the fights was over. Keito said that it was too easy to get caught up in the background threats that the tournament would catch them off-guard, and he did not want them distracted.

The argument was getting very heated when Xana brought over cooked rabbit for the Guardians, breaking their concentration on the heated debate and plunging them into tense silence as they ate pensively.

Due to his own anxiety about the possibility of an attack from the one responsible for the Tournament Slaughter, Dalton felt himself startle at a noise behind him. He turned to look, ready to laugh off his jump as nothing more than one of the wolves returning from a patrol in the darkened woods. But as he turned, he was certain he had not heard the noise at all, but something had caught his attention, something that tickled at the edge of his awareness. He stared into the shadows of the trees, straining, trying to see or hear what had caught his attention, but it was far too subtle, like the ghosting whisper of air being displaced from lungs.

Once he felt he could almost make out a shape behind a nearby tree, the sound was gone, leaving only an insistent pull in his ribs, calling him into the trees.

Dalton turned to the others of his team, who were too lost in their own thoughts to notice his unsettled expression. He studied Keito, wondering if he had heard the noise, but he seemed unaware. He could not help but wonder if that eased his mind or made him more concerned about the gradual pull he felt to go into the woods.

"The wolves are going to keep watch tonight," Hanyi said suddenly, causing Dalton to jump to attention. "We should try and get some sleep. They'll wake us if anything happens."

"Are you sure?" Mitoki asked. "We could also take shifts keeping watch."

"Don't know how much help we'll be since we don't know what to be watching *for*," Eclipse grumbled, glaring at Keito and Hanyi. Keito shook his head.

"The wolves will be fine keeping watch. We all need to rest and save our strength for the tournament. Once we're done with the first set, we can start worrying about Raina and her threats."

Mitoki and Eclipse appeared ready to launch into another argument with the older Guardians about sharing information when Dalton stood, stretching, trying to discreetly scan the trees behind him. His movement caught the attention of the others.

"Where are you going?" Mitoki asked.

"Nature calls," he lied, walking into the woods.

He walked until he was out of sight of the fire, the dim glow behind him hardly lighting his path as he continued. He was unsure how he knew where to go, or how to describe the feeling he was following, but he could not stop his feet from passing over the dirt and twigs of the forest floor. He felt compelled, but not frightened.

The thickets and underbrush made it difficult to tread quietly. His awareness was able to pick out flickers of movement around the tree trunks, causing him to stop and scan his surroundings, wary of how dark and quiet the woods had become. He crouched to grab the dagger strapped to his leg, keeping it close to his thigh as he continued following the eerie feeling.

The pull became stronger, curling around his ribs so tightly he was worried they would break. He forced his breathing to remain steady and slow, fighting against the instinctive panic he felt rising inside him.

Another flicker of movement halted his pace.

"I know someone's here," he whispered, his fingers tightening on the handle of his dagger. "Why don't you show yourself?"

The sound of wind could be heard through the trees, though Dalton's clothes did not rustle.

"Will you attack me if I do?" a distorted voice asked, moving around Dalton, bouncing among the shadows in the forest.

"That depends. Are you going to attack me?"

"No, Dalton Teban. I am not your enemy."

"I'm finding that difficult to believe," Dalton said. "You might have led me into a trap."

"You could have refused to follow my call," the voice said. Dalton had to force his eyes closed. He desperately wanted to continue scanning the trees, but he also knew he had to reach past what his senses were telling him to find the owner of the voice. "You are in danger, Dalton. I can help you."

"And why should I trust you?" he asked the surrounding woods. "For all I know, you are actually the one threatening to attack, the one manipulating the tournament, trying to lure me out here to kill me or size me up."

"No, your enemy already knows everything he needs to know about you," the voice said. "He has been watching you for years. Long before he orchestrated the tournament. The problem is you know nothing about him."

"I'd rather hear about it from my teammates than a mysterious voice in the woods," Dalton sneered. He could feel a stabbing in his left temple, but kept his eyes tightly shut. He was starting to get a sense of where the entity was, and he turned his attention to his left.

"Even they do not know everything," the voice said. "This is bigger than it was before. There are forces more powerful than you can comprehend at work, but whether you like it or not, you're in the middle of it. Soon, you'll start to see the true danger of your enemy, and it may overwhelm you, but don't let it break you. You have very powerful allies, Dalton. And they're watching out for you, even if you can't see them."

Dalton felt an electric current pass through his left wrist.

"Like you?"

Dalton's hand, glowing with his magic, reached out and took hold of the shadow he knew would be there, hovering over his shoulder. The apparition began to writhe, but the voice that sounded did not appear distressed.

"I am watching over you, Dalton. I always have. But there are those far more powerful than I behind you. You must complete what your older teammates could not. You must succeed where they failed. Trust your instincts, follow your gut, and know that you have unseen allies."

Dalton tried to pull the entity closer, feeling something solid behind the shadow, his mind flashing with the images of a person, though he could not make out their shape or features.

"Don't fear your power, Dalton. It will be what saves you."

The shadow began to slip through his fingers even as he tried to tighten his grip. He hissed in pain when the edges of the entity sliced through his skin, leaving several shallow cuts along his palm and fingers.

In an instant, the woods returned to normal, the pull around Dalton's ribs vanishing as his head whipped around, searching for the owner of the voice once more.

Instead, a hand took his shoulder. He turned on his heel, lifting his fist to punch whatever had startled him, but stopped short when he saw Keito behind him. The demon seemed startled by Dalton's apparent fear, but his expression was also filled with understanding.

"Come on," he said, jerking his head back in the direction of the Treneke Tribe. Dalton lowered his fist, his muscles gradually relaxing as he scanned his surroundings one more time. He then followed Keito's guiding hand back through the trees, too busy trying to make sense of the bizarre encounter to see Keito look behind him, confused but unconcerned about the presence he felt among the trees.

Having slept uneasily, the members of Team Dalton struggled to drag themselves out of sleep in order to get to the stadium in time for the pre-tournament check. Dalton and Keito said nothing about their encounter in the woods and the others did not bother to ask, feeling a tension in the air none of them could adequately explain.

Keito was once again the mode of transportation to Stadium 4B. The Guardians were greeted by a committee of people checking the rosters to be sure that all teams were present at the correct stadium.

When Team Dalton appeared at the back of the line, the teams in front of them immediately took notice and the whispering began.

There had been rumors going around about the council-sponsored team, but most of the Guardians did not believe that Hanyi Treneke and Keito DeVero were, once again, actively working. Upon seeing the two legendary Guardians with the three top-ranked human Guardians, the others could not help themselves from pointing and staring.

An attendant walking down the line noticed Team Dalton and quickly ushered them inside, insisting the Tournament Board wanted to see them before the check. They followed him to greet the woman they had seen the previous day, named Angela. She showed Team Dalton around the stadium, explaining the various security systems and safety precautions they had put in place for the return of the Guardian Tournament. Dalton was impressed at the measures, both magical and otherwise, put in place, but when he saw the way Keito and Hanyi appeared disinterested, he came to the grim understanding that even the increased security measures were not enough to stop those they were pursuing.

When Angela had shown Dalton everything the stadium had in place, she brought them to the ring and led them to one of the tables, asking them to check in while they waited for the rest of the Guardian teams to arrive. Keito helped Dalton fill in the parts of the paperwork he did not understand and they all signed their names, agreeing that no one had coerced them into the tournament and they were competing of their own will. Keito was far more hesitant to sign the paper than the others, but he still put his name in the appropriate box.

Once their Guardian IDs were scanned and logged, they were motioned to the ring, where a few other teams were standing, patiently waiting for further instruction.

"When you got your IDs reissued, did the Elders say you had to complete an annual quota again?" Dalton asked, glancing at Hanyi and Keito.

"Yes."

"But the quota is the minimum, right?" Mitoki asked. "Since you retired, your past case count should have been cleared."

"No," Keito said. "They based it off the year before retiring."

"How many cases do you have to complete this year, then?" Dalton asked worriedly.

"Seventy-three."

"Only forty-two for me," Hanyi said.

"That's more than *I* have," Eclipse said, surprised. "I think Dalton has fifty."

"Fifty-six," Dalton clarified.

"You had to complete all that while also competing in the tournament?" Eclipse gawked.

"There's two months between each round," Keito said with a disinterested shrug. "There's time to take cases."

"*Seventy-three,* though?" Mitoki asked, his eyebrows high. "That's insane. Did you always have to complete that much?"

"A few years before I retired, I was completing upwards of a hundred cases a year for my quota. After three years of that, I finally told the Elders I could not handle the workload while also being top-ranked and they dropped me to seventy."

"That is still ridiculous," Dalton said.

"Keeps me out of trouble," Keito said, though his tone was forced.

They turned as another Guardian team entered the ring, keeping close together and finding a spot to stand. No one mingled. A few Guardians would look at one another and nod in greeting, but they did not feel comfortable being social in the circumstances, knowing they were all rivals in the Guardian Tournament. When a group of young Guardians walked in glaring daggers at Hanyi, Dalton knew that they were the young wolves of the Opalon Wolf Pack. Hanyi kept eye contact with them until they looked away.

As more teams appeared, the atmosphere went from uncomfortable to serious. The Guardians began scoping out the other teams, trying to spot weaknesses and strategize how they could win against the different teams. They remained in their respective groups as the committee gathered near the tables, going over the final information with the few straggling teams. Most Guardians scrutinized Team Dalton with varying degrees of concern. Dalton was not sure if it was because they were the top-ranked Guardians and, therefore, presented more of a challenge, or if it was because Hanyi and Keito were in the ring.

He assumed it was both.

Keito and Hanyi were scanning the teams with expert eyes. Mitoki stood close to Hanyi, trying to discern what it was that Hanyi was looking for in the competitors. Eclipse was doing the same, trying to see what traits caught the attention of the older Guardians.

"Including me, there are two demons in this set," Keito informed the others. "I think I know him by rumor, but I don't know much about him."

Dalton tried to spot the other demon Guardian, but not every demon had a discerning feature like Keito's unusual eye color.

"Dalton," he said, "do you know the female team over there?" He pointed to a team across the ring. The women were clearly related, their hair pulled back from their eyes, which were hardened with experience as Guardians.

"Those are the Carlsons. All sisters, all elementals."

"Those are the Carlsons? I've never seen them before," Eclipse mused, surprised.

"An entire family of elementals, they might be the most challenging team in this set," Hanyi noted.

Dalton was about to agree and explain the power he had seen in the Carlsons during Annual Guardian Testing when a shudder ran through his body, halting his words in his throat. He turned to the opening doors of Hall A and saw the final Guardian team step into the ring. They walked with confidence as they strode to the committee tables to finalize their paperwork. Dalton felt an icy dread seep into his stomach, a feeling that grew in intensity when the sharp eyes of the team leader met his gaze.

"Make that four demons…" Keito corrected.

"I don't recognize them," Eclipse said, also consumed with the same unease. "*Any* of them."

"Me neither," Dalton and Mitoki seconded.

As the team left the committee tables, the team leader broke away from his group, confidently approaching Team Dalton. Everyone else in the ring fell silent, watching as the Guardian broke the unspoken rule of staying with their own teams.

He stopped in front of Dalton and extended a hand, though Dalton felt disgusted by the mere sight of his offered hand.

"Dalton Teban," he greeted. "I've heard so much about you. It's an honor to meet you."

Even though everything in his body told him not to, Dalton shook his hand.

"Thank you," he mumbled.

"Kyan," the man told him. "Kyan Tallah, from the Realm of Darkness."

"I don't recall seeing you at Guardian Testing," Eclipse said.

"I don't really stand out in a crowd," Kyan said. "And you see so many Guardians during annual testing, I'm not surprised I didn't make an impression."

"I find it hard to believe you don't make an impression," Keito said, his voice dark as he stared down the Guardian. Kyan turned, his mouth quirking in a smirk.

"Well, well," he started, "if it isn't Keito the Wandering Child."

"Don't call me that," Keito warned. Dalton had never heard the nickname before and was surprised by how angrily Keito responded. Kyan did not offer an apology, turning back to the others, scanning the members of Team Dalton with an approving nod.

"Team Dalton…" he mused. "You're going to be quite the challenge, aren't you?"

"You should go back to your own team," Hanyi warned him.

"Guardians!" Angela called, walking toward the middle of the ring. Kyan grinned at Dalton, bowing his head shallowly.

"I'll see you in the ring, Dalton."

Kyan returned to his team as Angela waited for him to take his place.

"Alright, listen up!" she started. "Lucky for all of you, you don't need to read over any more paperwork today. We know that you all received a rule booklet when you registered for the tournament and we assume that you have already read through the rules. If you haven't, you better get on that. Ignorance of the rules will not help you in any rulings against you or your team."

She glanced down at her clipboard, running her finger down the list of announcements.

"I'm sure all of you know about what happened in the last tournament, so you are all aware of how dangerous these fights can become. If you see or hear anything suspicious, you are to report it to the Tournament Board immediately. We are not taking any chances with safety this year and it is expected of all Guardians to actively keep watch for any dangers that could lead to a similar tragedy.

"Also, I would like to address a very important issue. This announcement is being made across all realms to those participating in the Guardian Tournament. The Tournament Board knows that you are all very aware of this team over here," she motioned to Team Dalton. "Yes, we know that Keito DeVero and Hanyi Treneke are considered to be legends in the branch, but they are Guardians participating in this tournament just like you. As for those of you from the Human, Darkness, and Light Realms, your bosses are also on this team. In no way will your position or job be threatened by competing against Dalton, Eclipse, and Mitoki. In this ring, no one has rank over anyone else. You are all at the same level. Do not hold back because you are worried about upsetting your bosses. They do not have the power to demote or retire you due to your actions in the ring."

She went through a long list of managerial announcements, telling each team their team box and team room numbers and then detailing emergency exit procedures should something occur in the building.

Finally, the Guardians were informed about conduct in the ring and reminded of the most important rules in the rule book. Dalton and his team had spent extensive time during their training with Jikia reviewing the rules, but Dalton was sure that all the Guardians knew the most important rule in the Guardian Tournament was that no one was to be killed in the ring.

They were told the tournament would begin the following morning and they were expected to be at the stadium an hour and a half beforehand to check in with the Tournament Board.

When the announcements had concluded, all teams without a demon Guardian were dismissed.

"What exactly do they test the demon Guardians for?" Dalton asked, turning to Keito as the other teams began to file out while the Tournament Board prepared for their tests.

"It's actually very stupid," Keito said with a heavy sigh. "Council doesn't trust demons. They test to be sure our energy levels aren't too high to compete with humans and that we have all the appropriate power limiters. It's basically the same thing that gets checked during annual testing. But I'm sure that, considering the massacre, they will be stricter with demons now. I'll probably get an extensive lecture about how my conduct in the ring can threaten my position as a Guardian."

"Wait, but they just said—"

"Yeah, they mean for everyone except the demons," Keito interrupted Mitoki. "Council likes to keep all the demons in the Guardian Branch on a tight leash."

"But that's against the Guardian Code," Dalton said. "All demons Guardians have been through testing and taken the oath, just like all human and beast Guardians. I thought there was a faith clause in the Guardian Code between the DPC and the demon Guardians."

"Oh, so I'm not the only one who's noticed that discrepancy," Keito grumbled. "When it comes to us, what Council says is radically different from what Council *does*. They like having demon Guardians around when they need demon power and strength, but demons are expendable. And believe me, it does not sit well with those back in the Demon Realm. The DPC is lucky the demons haven't gotten fed up with them already."

"Keito DeVero?" Angela called. "We're ready for you."

Chapter Thirteen

Keito opened his eyes as soon as he could see the light of the rising sun behind his eyelids. He stood, stretching as he glanced around the wolf pack. Nearly all the wolves were awake, some struggling with the sudden change in their normal schedule and sleeping heavily. Those who were awake turned to him, some wary and some disinterested.

He knew he was less welcome to the Treneke Wolf Tribe than the human Guardians. The history he shared with Hanyi created a lot of tension between the wolves and the demon. Keito bowed his head to the wolves and turned, walking into the forest.

He moved slowly, allowing his mind to wander with the rhythm of his feet. He followed a deer path until he cleared the trees and came upon a meadow with a babbling brook. Closing his eyes, he took a deep breath, his nose filling with the scents around him, his mind drinking in the resulting tender euphoria that made his head go light.

But even the feeling of peace the calm, beautiful morning brought him could not chase away the anxiety sitting heavy in his chest.

It was not the anxiety he felt at the beginning of previous tournament seasons, nor was it the worry that they would be attacked. It was a resigned apprehension, knowing that once they were in the tournament stadium, the human Guardians would be locked into an assignment that they were entirely unprepared to handle.

He splashed his face with the water from the brook, taking measured breaths to keep his worry in check.

Sitting heavily in the tall grass, he bowed his head and tried to clear his mind. He thought back to Dalton's encounter in the woods. And though he had heard Dalton speaking to something, he had not heard the voice that had prompted the younger Guardian's responses. He felt an energy around the woods, but it was not the hot, angry energy he knew to be their enemy. It was somehow familiar, and yet too distant to discern.

Keito had spent much of the night sitting against the base of a tree, his eyes closed in deep meditation as he tried to center himself, both for the tournament and to search for how close their foe lurked.

But even as he tried to focus, invasive thoughts of a radiant smile and large dark eyes continued to distract him. As the tournament had drawn closer he had been thinking of her often, forcing himself only to remember her bright expression and the sound of her laugh, rather than the way he had lost her in the hellish inferno of the Tournament Slaughter. His heart still ached for her and tears threatened to come to his eyes as he imagined her sitting next to him, teasing him about how she would be happy to spar with him if he needed to improve his skills before the start of the tournament. He could almost see how she would lean against his shoulder, the early morning light kissing her dark skin.

Pleasant memories hurt more than painful ones. Thinking about how blissfully happy and content they had been in those years before the massacre, how he had finally started to see a direction his life could take, a future, something he had never imagined for himself, he began to see his own arrogance. He had known from the beginning that he was never destined for such comforts.

But it was nice to imagine.

He reveled in the fantasy of her head on his shoulder, taking in the beauty of the stream in front of them as the sun rose higher into the sky. He could even imagine the fallen members of his previous team coming out of the forest, teasing them about sneaking off as they sat with them, excitedly talking about the new tournament season. Hanyi and Hector would place a silly bet with one another as they had each year, and Jacob would complain to Sadee that they needed more human friends and to stop hanging around rambunctious animals and a moody demon all the time.

And for those brief moments that Keito imagined them, he was transported to that time where those closest to him were by his side, not just memories.

Rustling grass broke the illusion and Keito turned over his shoulder, spotting four figures walking slowly toward him.

"Morning," Hanyi greeted with a forced smile.

"Morning," he repeated, turning to the human Guardians. "How are you feeling this morning?"

"Anxious," Dalton said. "You?"

"Same."

Hanyi sat in the grass with Keito, letting out a long breath as he looked over the landscape in front of him.

"Beautiful day, though."

The humans also situated themselves in the grass, drinking in the sight of the wildflowers, running water, and distant mountains.

Each was lost in thought, running through hypotheticals, worries, and fears of what was to come that day. Even as the vast nature around them tried to calm their nerves, they all knew that day was the beginning of a difficult mission, and their participation in the tournament was meant to be a challenge to the one trying to destroy the realms.

They were entering a war.

~∧~

When they entered the clearing around the stadium, they lingered near the edge to give Keito a chance to shift back into his human form and dress. As they tried not to be unnerved by how much larger the stadium appeared that day, Jikia called to them, having been waiting for them at the doors to Hall A.

"Good morning," she greeted.

"Morning," they mumbled with varying enthusiasm.

"Did you sleep well last night?"

"Not really," Dalton answered for all of them.

"That's to be expected," she said, nodding to Tarrena, who extended full canteens of cold water to them. "Drink some water. It will help. Also, I want to apologize that I wasn't here for the pre-tournament check yesterday. I assumed that you didn't need to be here because you're sponsored by Council, but I heard you were here anyway."

"They still needed to check me," Keito answered indirectly. "Red tape and all that."

"Did everything go alright?" she asked, sending a pointed look in Keito's direction.

"Give me some credit," he groaned. "I've only been overly tested just because I'm a demon for a majority of my life. I know how to not upset humans."

"Do you, though?" Hanyi challenged with a grin.

"It went fine. Seemed like most of the other Guardians were just as lost as we were," Dalton said. "Everyone mostly kept to themselves and just stared at one another."

"You have no reason to be nervous. I don't think you boys will have any trouble with the competition," Jikia assured.

"Tarrena?" Eclipse asked, seeing the way the younger dragon was staring at the backs of several people lined up along the side of the stadium. "What's wrong?"

They followed her line of sight to the people chatting lightly as they leaned against the stone walls of the building, smiling brightly.

"More Guardians?" Mitoki suggested.

"Guardians should only be coming through Hall A," Hanyi noted, his tone dark.

"Council?"

"Audience members," Keito corrected.

"No," Dalton insisted. "They must be family members of Council, or even of the Guardians."

Another large group of humans walked along the line, being ushered by a man in a bright orange vest.

"This way! This way!" he called excitedly. "Everyone please have your tickets ready. They're going to open the doors in about twenty minutes."

Dalton's blood ran cold.

"...how?" Eclipse hissed.

"It must have leaked somehow," Tarrena said.

"And Council immediately began printing tickets," Keito added.

Dalton broke away from his team, walking toward the man organizing the group of twenty humans in the back of the line.

"Excuse me," he called, trying not to let his panic turn to anger. "Excuse me, sorry. Um, are you bringing tourists to see the tournament?"

"It's the only type of tourism this realm allows," the man said with a laugh.

"And do you work for the Tournament Board?"

"No, no, I work for G-Tours. We sell season passes for the Guardian Tournament and then organize the travel to all the realms for our clients. The first round of the new Guardian Tournament has made business boom like you wouldn't believe. We sold out of all our package deals within a week. It's incredible!"

"You do realize this is an extremely dangerous event, right?"

"That's biggest reason to see it," he insisted. "Guardians, Council's elite policing force, battling each other, it's thrilling. That's what people want to see."

Dalton was about to snap at the man that he needed to get his tour group away from the stadium, that it was too dangerous for civilians to be near such an event, but a hand took his elbow.

"Come on," Keito said, gently pulling Dalton away.

"Wait, I recognize you from somewhere," a younger man said, pointing at Keito.

The demon did not respond, ducking his head as he continued to guide Dalton away.

"Keito, they could be *killed*."

"I know."

"We should stop this before they even get into the building! Tell them all to get out of here!"

"It's no use now, Dalton," Keito said. "Council has sold tickets, businesses have popped up to sell packages, this is exactly how it worked before. I told you, this tournament makes Council a lot of money."

"And what about civilian safety?" Eclipse challenged as Keito finally released Dalton's arm.

"Well, the force fields around the ring are new, so maybe those will keep rogue attacks from harming the audience," Keito said. "Otherwise, we just do what we can knowing that we have a lot of innocents around us."

"And how are we supposed to do *our* job when we're constantly worried about another massacre?" Mitoki snapped.

"You let *me* worry about that part," Keito said. "I know what to look for. Hanyi and I will keep an eye on the bigger picture problems for now. What *you* need to do," he lifted a hand to stop Dalton from going on another rant, "is learn the tournament. Focus on the fights, the mechanics, how the audience responds, learn how this event is run."

"He's right, Dalton," Jikia said. "A full audience certainly adds another complication we were not expecting. But think about it. If other Guardians are also distracted by a full audience, it gives you a better opportunity to monitor them and run your own investigations."

"It also gives this monster and whoever works for him more opportunities to kill," Eclipse added.

"He wouldn't waste his time picking off audience members," Hanyi said. "He's not looking to kill without reason. He's all about the message, the theatrics of it all."

"And we've given him even more potential victims," Dalton said.

"Team Dalton," a voice called from the doorway of Hall A, waving them over.

"I don't like this," Dalton muttered, but his feet moved toward the attendant, allowing him to lead the Guardians and their trainers to a table where they signed in and were taken to their team room.

"Oh, we're in the Corner," Jikia said, nodding. "That's good luck."

The Guardians did not comment.

The team room was sparse and dark, the lights barely cutting through the monochromatic grey of everything within. Keito placed the bag of medical supplies they had brought on the table and sighed heavily.

"There has to be some way to get the audience out of here," Eclipse said.

"I can try and make a call to Council, ask my grandfather what the hell he's thinking."

"It's too late, Dalton," Jikia insisted. "I know it's frightening and it adds a huge complication, but you can't take back the knowledge from the people that this tournament is taking place. And if you did, that's also going to tip off the Guardians you are trying to investigate them and they will become more suspicious of some internal plot. As worrying as this is, we have to let this go."

"Keito..." Dalton turned to the demon, hoping that the older Guardian could ease his fears.

"...I never expected Council to follow through with their claim that the people would not know of this tournament," he said. His gaze turned apologetic. "I'm sorry, Dalton. I knew this would happen. When I saw those cameras the other day, it confirmed for me that Council is bringing back the entire tournament."

"So what do we do?" Mitoki pressed. "Yeah, having an audience as a distraction might allow us to investigate better, but it also gives anyone loyal to this guy and his cause a chance to sneak in under our noses."

"Every single person in this stadium could be working for him," Eclipse said, his eyes falling to the floor as the enormity of the situation settled on his shoulders.

"Keito, you have to give me something to go on," Dalton said. "This just got a lot bigger."

Keito hesitated, turning to Hanyi.

"I...can't, Dalton," he said. "You're too worked up as it is. I'd rather have you focus on the tournament and let me worry about the other stuff."

"I can't!" Dalton burst, interrupting Keito. He lifted his hands in defeat. "I can't not worry about it."

A thick silence filled the team room. Dalton finally ground his teeth together and turned to Jikia.

"Is there a phone somewhere here that might let me get a call out to the Elders?"

"Yeah, in the administrative office," Jikia answered. "Come on, I'll take you."

Dalton could feel the eyes of his teammates on his back as he left the room and followed Jikia through twisting, dark tunnels under the filling audience stands to Hall A, where one large office was filled with people monitoring the cameras around the stadium, barking orders at one another as they tried to prepare everything for the fights.

Jikia knocked on one door in the room and a flustered looking man answered.

"Yes?"

"I'm Master Jikia Topesca of Team Dalton," she introduced. "This is Guardian Dalton Teban. He would like to make a call to the DPC compound."

"Fine, but make it quick," the man said, stepping aside and pointing to a phone in the corner attached to a large box that Dalton did not recognize, though he figured it was a device that connected to the Middle Dimension.

Dalton picked up the phone, dialing the number for his grandfather's cell phone—a number he rarely called unless there was an emergency.

After three long, shrill beeps, his grandfather's voice came through the receiver.

"Elder Teban."

"It's Dalton," he said. "How long have you known that there would be a full audience to the Guardian Tournament?"

The silence that followed his question was answer enough.

"Dalton, we had no choice. The information was leaked and the realms demanded to know what was happening. The best damage control we could do was open the tournament to spectators."

"And you didn't think to tell me about this?"

"I didn't want you distracted."

"I'm getting a little sick of hearing that," Dalton said sharply. "A full audience will distract me, Grandfather. How am I supposed to keep these people safe?"

"You're the top-ranked Guardian in the branch, Dalton," Elder Teban said. "There is a reason I assigned this case to you. You have great instincts about this. You just have to trust them."

"How can I trust anything? How can I even trust *you* if you didn't tell me that this would be happening?"

"…I didn't want you to try and stop the tournament," Elder Teban said begrudgingly. "I knew that if you found out about the audience and the broadcast, you would do everything you could to stop the tournament."

"Keito told me we're likely hunting the same person who massacred an entire stadium," Dalton snapped. "Why wouldn't *you* want to stop it?"

"Things are bad, Dalton," Elder Teban retorted. "They're really bad. And as much of a gamble as it is, I need the people of the realms to focus on something, something that *isn't* all the distrust within the DPC. I know it's not ideal, but the Guardian Tournament will keep the people's attention focused. We have to use what we can and right now, this is our best option."

"...you're baiting him, aren't you?"

Again, silence answered him.

"The tournament will be starting soon," Elder Teban said. "You should take some time and center yourself." Dalton closed his eyes, clenching his teeth against the angry words threatening to bubble out of him. "Good luck, Dalton."

Chapter Fourteen

Dalton and the others spent their time in relative silence as they waited for the tournament to begin. Dalton felt his anxiety and anger rising with every sound in the stadium as their team room rattled from the dull thundering of the audience filing to their seats following the announcement that the first match would start in five minutes.

But the moment he stepped out of the double doors and into the bright lights of the ring, the roar of the crowd drowned out all his thoughts. He could only scan the audience seats in awe as the spectators cheered and screamed in excitement, bellowing encouragements to the teams as they filed into the ring. Jikia and Tarrena silently walked to their team box, also warily eyeing the crowd.

Even though a crushing weight settled on the shoulders of the Guardians in Team Dalton, they stood tall as they met the other teams in the middle of the ring, focusing only on the moment.

"Ladies and gentlemen, welcome to the Guardian Tournament!" a female announcer called from the corner of one of the stands. A round of cheers shattered the Guardians' eardrums. "My name is Tecca and I will be your announcer today. Again, welcome to the first round of the Guardian Tournament here in the refurbished 4B Stadium!"

The cheers remained deafening.

"Before we get started, in light of recent events, we ask that you take this moment to locate the two nearest exits to your seat, which are marked with overhead lights. In the event of an emergency, tournament staff will guide you from the building to a gathering area outside. We ask that you follow all instructions from the tournament staff and exit in a calm and orderly fashion in the event of an emergency."

"That should ease everyone's minds," Hanyi noted sarcastically.

"Now, without further ado, give it up for the ten teams of Guardians in the ring!"

The stadium almost shuddered with the intensity of the applause. The demons and animals in the stadium cringed as their sensitive hearing was bombarded. The Guardians scanned the crowds, studying the faces they could make out, surprised to see a few hand-painted signs and banners cheering on their preferred team—Dalton tried not to notice that most of the signs were for his team.

"Each team was assigned a number on the roster when they checked in and then were paired off in brackets. The first of these brackets will be decided by a random dice roll and the matches will proceed from there in chronological order. Please turn your attention to the screen for the Tournament Board's results." Tecca motioned to the black screen mounted below the glass of the VIP Box. Yellow words flashed across the screen.

RESULT OF THE DIE ROLL: 4.

"As the result is four, the first match will be Team Quilic versus Team Jeanette!" Tecca announced. "All other teams, please exit the arena to your assigned team boxes. Team Quilic, Team Jeanette, please step to the center of the ring."

Dalton let out a long sigh as he turned with the others of his team to leave the ring, his chest reverberating with the excited hollering of the audience. Hanyi closed the team box door behind them as they sat on the open bench, watching the two Guardian teams in the ring. Dalton tried not to notice the mechanical whirring of the nearby cameras, or the way they panned over the Guardians, displaying their faces on the large screens above each section of the audience, enlarging the view for those seated in the higher rows.

"Please state any conditions you have for the fight," Tecca said to the two teams in the ring. Dalton barely recalled his knowledge of conditions with his mind swimming in anxiety, but he was sure that most Guardians would forego restricting magic attacks or limiting whether animals could fight in their natural forms. None of the Guardian teams knew each other well enough to properly use the conditions to their advantage. "Please remember that all animal form requests for demon Guardians and conditions on weapons must be approved by the Tournament Board. All weapons apart from firearms are permitted within the ring unless expressly restricted in match conditions."

"No conditions," both team leaders stated.

"Very well, then begin!"

A mechanical bell chimed once, and before Dalton could recover from the excited shouts of the audience, his attention was drawn to Team Jeanette, where one of the younger Carlson sisters had unleashed her powers, causing the air in the stadium to grow heavy with condensation. The other sisters also began immediate attacks as the large cats of Team Quilic dropped to their animal forms, dodging a spiral of fire that separated them so each could face one of the Carlson sisters.

One sister was tackled by the cougar of the opposing team, and though she pressed her burning hand to the animal's chest to push him away, his strength held. One of the other sisters, reached a hand out, vines rapidly growing from under her sleeve and coiling around the cougar's torso, pulling him to the ground long enough to free her teammate. However, she quickly became distracted as the leader of the team, a lion, ran toward her, forcing her to grow more vines from her other sleeve to bind him before he could tackle her.

The magic in the ring filled the air with static, which added to the excited energy of the audience. Dalton could also feel it. With each summoning of an element, or magical binding attack from the animals, the air sparked and made his hair stand on end.

The movements in the ring were difficult to keep up with as Team Dalton was always flicking their eyes between the ten participants in the match, watching as some broke away to help free their teammates or tackle one of the elemental Guardians. Dalton even found himself turning his gaze to the large screen across from their team box to watch the fight in better detail through the camera.

"Watch Team Jeanette," Hanyi told his leader. "The other team doesn't stand a chance."

The crowd stood and cheered as one of the younger Carlson sisters successfully encased the jaguar of Team Quilic in a large orb of water. No matter how he slashed at the sides of the orb, he was unable to break free and when his movement began to slow, the sister dispelled the water, soaking the hard dirt as she ran to the other Guardian, knocking him to the ground and kneeling on his side as she demanded his surrender.

As she secured a surrender from the jaguar, Quilic had taken an opening to gnaw through some of the vines restraining his teammates, dodging fire attacks that nearly singed him. He was soon too focused on Jeanette's fire to realize he had jumped too close, allowing one of the sisters to grow new vines, completely encasing him in the pulsing tendrils.

Dalton began to strategize how to avoid the vines in his own fight with Team Jeanette, turning away from the screen to the action in the ring. Instead, his gaze caught a dark face across from him. Kyan smiled, the expression chilling, bringing Dalton's attention entirely on the unnerving Guardian. He could feel Kyan challenging him, taunting him, laughing at him through his cold, lifeless eyes.

"Team Jeanette is the winner following a complete forfeit from Team Quilic!" Tecca announced excitedly, her voice over the loudspeaker breaking Dalton's staring contest with Kyan. The Guardians of Team Quilic were encased in cocoons of rock and rubble that were bound tightly by vines. Only the heads of Team Quilic were visible as they struggled to free themselves. The

Carlson sisters broke down the cocoons, helping the opposing team to their feet as they changed into their human forms, shaking hands with the sisters in a show of good sportsmanship.

"There will be a fifteen minute rest period until the next match as the ring is cleaned and cleared," the announcer stated. "The next match will begin in fifteen minutes."

The crowd immediately broke out into mumbles as the audience conversed about the short but exciting match that had played out before them.

"Do any of you recognize that Guardian over there?" Jikia asked Team Dalton, nodding across the ring to where Kyan had continued staring, unblinking, at Dalton. Dalton sighed.

"We saw him yesterday at the pre-tournament check," he answered. "He tried to intimidate us. Bit of a creep."

"Jikia? Are you alright?" Mitoki asked. Dalton turned, seeing that their trainer was standing at the edge of the team box, her hands gripping the wood of the front wall so tightly her knuckles were turning white. Her body shuddered as she shook her head.

"There's...something dark with him..." she choked. "There's dark energy looming over him...it's so powerful I can barely breathe." She shakily released the wall and began to stumble backward. Mitoki immediately went to help her, though once his hands took hers, he felt the same heavy energy envelop him, the psychic powers of his mind opening, allowing him to see a mass of darkness lurking behind Kyan and the others of his team, shadows enveloping him like pulsing, distorted arms.

He released her hand as soon as she sat on the bench next to him, trying to hide his own shaking.

"Are we in immediate danger?" Dalton asked, turning to Keito.

"No," he assured.

"Are you certain?"

"Absolutely."

Eclipse took a deep breath, closing his eyes as he straightened his shoulders. His own awareness allowed him to scan the audience, circling around the stadium before looking at the other Guardians in their team boxes, feeling as though he was unable to see some of them despite taking note of their presence.

"That's...weird," he mumbled.

"What?"

"I just did a quick scan of the stadium and there are some people that are *here*, I can sense them, I can see them but...they're not *here*." He turned his confused gaze across the ring to Kyan and his team. "Like their bodies are here but they're just husks."

"Like they're possessed," Mitoki seconded, nodding toward the opposing team.

"All of them?" Dalton asked, forcing himself not to look directly at Kyan as he studied the other four members of the opposing team.

"I think so."

"A multiple-person possession, that's…that's an enormous amount of power. I don't know if I've ever heard of someone with that amount of power and control," Dalton said.

"Oh man, are you in for some cruel shocks through this assignment," Hanyi tried to say lightly.

"There are some powerful spells that could make multiple-person mind control possible," Eclipse corrected. "It does seem like he's not there at all, but…he's still functioning and responding like normal. Him and his team. They're looking around, blinking, fidgeting…" He shook his head. "If they were just husks they wouldn't be so animated."

"So, are they under mind control or are they powerful and in alignment with whoever it is we're hunting down?" Mitoki asked.

"I honestly don't know."

"…I don't think they're Guardians," Dalton said. "None of us recognized him, but I can assure you that if that kind of energy came up to me at Guardian Testing, I would remember it. So would any of you."

"Then he either faked his Guardian documentation to get into the tournament, or the Tournament Board let him in anyway because *they're* working for the enemy," Mitoki deduced. "Or both, even."

"The demon on Team Felton did not recognize the two demons on Kyan's team," Keito added. "He did not know their names, what type of demons they were, who their Old Blood Lord is, nothing." Keito shook his head. "Demon Guardians make it their business to know about other demon Guardians. Politics can get complicated if you don't know to which land each demon pledges loyalty."

"I would think that demons would be more resistant to mind control," Tarrena said. "Unless they're the ones controlling the humans on that team."

"I'm going to assume that the person we're hunting, the one who massacred everyone at the tournament, is a demon," Dalton said, indirectly asking Keito.

"Yes, he is."

"So those two demons could be loyal to him and are controlling the others," Tarrena said.

"No, they're just like the humans," Eclipse said. "There's something looming behind them. Something controlling them."

"I don't recall him having this kind of influence before," Hanyi said. He turned to Keito. "I could see him forging papers and bribing or intimidating the Tournament Board, but mind control…was he able to do it this flawlessly before?"

"No," Keito said, his expression growing dark. "Something tells me he has called in some help."

Hanyi's face drained of color as he closed his eyes. He sat heavily on the bench, rubbing his hands over his face.

"What? What's wrong?" Dalton demanded.

"The type of control he's using over that team is called a draining bewitchment," Keito explained. "And it tells me that since the Tournament Slaughter, he has been very busy training and making himself stronger. That was not something he could do before, at least not to this extent."

"I've never heard of a draining bewitchment," Eclipse said.

"That doesn't surprise me. It's a very delicate practice. A bewitchment of this level more-or-less makes the bewitched individual an extension of the caster. I assume it is like inhabiting multiple bodies at the same time. Because of that, the bewitched person's aura and energy are drained from their bodies and become part of the caster's power. It serves to strengthen them."

"Won't that eventually kill Kyan and his team?" Dalton asked.

"It's already too late," the demon said. "They're dead."

"That is a horrible spell," Mitoki said. "How do we stop it?"

"We can't. The thing about draining bewitchments is that they can't be bewitched without consent. They have to invite the spell."

"Kyan *willingly* let himself be possessed like that? Does he know that it will kill him?"

"I would assume so."

"Who would allow themselves to be manipulated and killed like that?"

"This demon is very persuasive and manipulative," Hanyi explained. "And clearly he's become even more powerful in the forty years following the Tournament Slaughter."

"The break period is over." Tecca's voice sounded over the loudspeaker, startling Team Dalton. "The next match will be Team Meca versus Team Reley. Will those teams please make their way to the center of the ring?"

The two teams followed the order, stepping out of their team boxes and meeting in the now-clean ring.

"Please state any conditions you have for the fight."

131

"All animals in their natural forms," one human stated. When Tecca told them, the beast Guardians shifted and when no further conditions were stated, she called the match to begin. The audience erupted into excited hollering as the Guardians leapt at one another. The fight was long and brutal with neither team willing to surrender, leading to larger and more serious injuries. Dalton was becoming concerned for the safety of the ten Guardians in the ring, but the audience was cheering themselves hoarse. Every punch or bite landed caused an immediate round of yelling that resulted in the energy around the stadium swelling with excitement.

Finally, Team Meca surrendered, leaving the heavily injured Team Reley to limp to their team room for treatment, clearly exhausted and concerned about having to fight again.

"I'm still confused about this whole thing with Kyan," Mitoki said once both teams had exited the arena and the audience had quieted enough that he could be heard by his teammates. "Considering that we're also investigating the corruption in the DPC, I supposed it makes sense that he has enough contacts to fake Guardian employment and get the Tournament Board to let in this fake team. But if he's got his fingers that deep in Council and he's broken the seal on the realms, why doesn't he just take over? He seems like he would have the power to overthrow Council, so why hasn't he tried it already?"

"Because he's smart enough to know that he could never get away with it, not without the proper support," Keito said. "He's been working for decades, maybe even longer to get the support he currently has, and as the realms have dipped into further distrust and violence, his grip gets a little tighter. He's taking his time."

"About two years ago, the Elders sent me a report in strict confidence saying they suspected a possible coup brewing within the Dimension Protection Council. There was a lot of sensitive information leaked, but they weren't sure which branches were involved, though they expected several. I looked through the Guardian Branch when they told me about it but nothing really came of my findings," Dalton said. "Now I have to wonder if the information even reached them."

"That was two years ago?"

"Yeah, I wasn't supposed to say anything, but…"

"Ooh, telling secrets," Hanyi sang.

"But seems like even if the information had reached them, it probably wouldn't have done much good," Dalton concluded, unable to stop his small smile at Hanyi's teasing. "Seems like this has been going on since long before I was born."

With the end of the break period came the announcement Dalton had been dreading.

"The next match will be Team Dalton versus Team Felton. Please make your way to the center of the ring."

Trying to ignore the twisting of his gut and the worried jumble of his thoughts, Dalton led his team out of the team box and walked to the center of the ring. Even before they reached the center, the cheering had turned into a constant roar, making it difficult for Dalton to hear even the announcer.

"Please state any conditions you have for the match. Now that two demons have entered the ring, exclusive fights are permitted between them. Such fights will take place separate from the rest of the team and will count as a partial surrender from the losing team."

"I don't know if the mutt is really worth the effort," the opposing demon said with a condescending smirk. "And I don't trust the infamous Wandering Child to play fair."

"I would be more worried about *you* not fighting fair," Keito retorted. "Because we both know it would only be due to cheap tricks that you could win against me." As the opposing demon scoffed, Keito turned to Dalton. "It's your call."

"I say no," Felton, the leader of the opposing team, said. "Let's just make this one match, clean and simple."

"I have no problems with that," Dalton agreed.

"Are there any other conditions for the fight?" Tecca pressed. When both team leaders shook their heads, she called for the fight to commence.

The other demon lunged at Keito and the scuffle between the two quickly moved to one side of the ring, most of the cameras following their fight as the other eight Guardians squared. The two beast Guardians on Team Felton shifted into their animal forms, Hanyi jumping forward to challenge the bear in his own wolf form while the cougar leapt at Eclipse, claws extended and teeth bared. Felton's hand began to glow and spark with magic as he ran at Dalton, his fist raised. Dalton channeled his own magic into his hands, dodging the attack before throwing an orb of his energy at his opponent, though it missed its mark. Mitoki went on the defensive with the final Guardian of the team, studying his moves, trying to find an opening for a counterattack.

Their bigger anxieties forgotten, and the roar of the crowd a constant in their ears, Team Dalton focused on the match.

Eclipse was unable to escape the claws that dug deep into his flesh when the cougar fell heavily on his chest. When the beast Guardian opened his mouth and went for Eclipse's neck, the human dodged, lifting his shoulder just enough to get his arm on the other side of the cougar's neck. Magic bolstering his strength, he wrapped his arm around the cougar's neck and flipped them ungracefully, his skin ripping open with the movement of the animal's claws. In a short wrestle, Eclipse pressed his body weight down on the thrashing cougar, his fingers digging into the animal's thick hide as he used his magic to bind the animal tightly, tendrils of energy erupting from his fingers to coil around the other Guardian.

Eclipse's other hand pressed into the cougar's neck, another thick magical binding choking the animal.

"Surrender," Eclipse ordered through grit teeth.

The cougar's response was to turn its head and sink teeth into Eclipse's arm. His concentration broken, he reeled backward, blood erupting from the punctures in his arm as the binding magic dissipated, leaving the animal free to attack Eclipse once more.

While Eclipse began wrestling with the cougar again, Hanyi was clawing at the bear, biting at the thick fur that protected the far larger animal. Every time the bear would swipe, Hanyi would dodge and attack from another angle, annoying the lumbering bear more than harming him.

Hanyi finally startled his opponent enough to make an opening for himself where he tackled the other beast, knocking him to the ground. As fast as possible, Hanyi clamped his teeth around the underside of the bear's neck, pushing his snout as deep into the thick fur as possible to try and maintain hold on the larger animal's throat. Once he felt the thick cords under the fur, he held firmly, but carefully. He had to fight his instinct to clamp his teeth as tightly as possible to secure the kill.

The bear threw even more violent attacks when he realized the wolf was trying to strangle him. The movements caused his muscles to strain as oxygen was denied. He became dizzy, stumbling as Hanyi held on tightly, his paws clawing at what they could reach of the other Guardian. When the bear's balance failed him, Hanyi leapt away to avoid being crushed as the other Guardian crumpled heavily to the dirt. There, he remained still apart from his rasping breaths. Hanyi cautiously moved closer to confirm the other Guardian was unconscious before turning his attention to helping his teammates.

Dalton was punching at Felton, who was retaliating in turn, both of them using magic to dodge faster and put more power behind their attacks. Felton was too fast for Dalton to land a good hit and he was struggling to dodge his opponent's rapid jabs.

When Dalton saw Felton look away for a split second to assess his teammates, he took the opportunity to fake a punch to the face only to hit him hard in gut. Felton curled around the fist with a groan of pain, though his hands wrapped around Dalton's arm and pulled him closer, kicking his legs out from under him.

They both tumbled to the ground, Dalton trying to keep a sense of himself in the brief confusion. Pain radiated through his chest as Felton landed a punch, but it lacked the power of a proper stance as they both struggled to get to their feet again. Dalton was upright first and moved to deliver another punch when Felton ducked his head and leapt at Dalton's torso, putting him back on the ground and knocking the wind out of both of them. His lungs desperately trying to take in oxygen, Dalton pulled himself to his feet, turning his eyes on Felton who seemed to be struggling to do the same.

Seeing his opponent's shaking legs, Dalton knew he was getting close to a victory.

He leapt at the other Guardian again, throwing harder punches, desperate to land a final hit. Felton dodged and then retaliated, though his moves were becoming sloppy as he, too, became desperate to finish the match.

A misstep from Dalton allowed Felton to land a hit to Dalton's gut, but rather than grab Felton's arm and pull them both to the dirt again, he grabbed the other Guardian's shoulder and moved into the punch, his head connecting with Felton's jaw.

With an agonized cry of pain, the other Guardian fell backward and Dalton lost his footing, his head spinning from the force of the impact. Sliding back along the dirt, he watched to be sure Felton stayed down.

"Stealing my moves there, boss," Eclipse said with a broken chuckle, offering his unbloodied arm to Dalton and helping him to his feet.

"I'll be sure to give you credit in any post-match interviews," Dalton said, groaning as he rubbed his head. "You alright?" he nodded to the bloodied arm and the gashes showing through his torn shirt. When Eclipse nodded that he was fine, they both turned to Mitoki, who was still confidently dodging his opponent, even as Hanyi stalked closer, looking for an opening to help the youngest of Team Dalton.

"Why aren't you *doing* anything?!" his opponent huffed angrily, throwing another heavy fist toward Mitoki's face. The younger Guardian moved easily out of the way and turned on his heel, leading his opponent in another direction. Blinded by rage at being unable to land a hit, the older man followed. Mitoki allowed him to swing twice more at his head before he dropped to a crouch, dodging another angry swipe and grabbing the dagger from his leg. He lunged forward from his lowered position, slashing a deep wound in his opponent's thigh before kicking the larger man's legs and forcing him to fall heavily.

Before his opponent could recover, Mitoki leapt on the man's back, using his knees to pin down the man's arm and shoulder before yanking his head back and pressing the dagger to his throat.

"Surrender."

The man hesitated, his nostrils flared and his teeth grinding together as he glared back at Mitoki. Upon seeing movement in his periphery, he turned his focus to the wolf stalking forward, growling with his head lowered. Eclipse and Dalton also stepped forward.

"I wouldn't try it," Mitoki warned, the sharp blade pressing a little deeper into the soft flesh of his neck. "Your odds don't look good."

With great reluctance, the other Guardian nodded and Mitoki released him.

Keito and the other demon were still wrestling to one side of the ring, and if the audience's screeching excitement was anything to judge by, the match was thrilling.

"Should we interfere with that, or…"

"Nope," Hanyi said, standing back on two legs. "Let the demons duke it out. We just need to stay out of their way."

The fight between the demons was brutal with claws and sharpened teeth leaving large gashes and gaping bite marks in each of them. But they were not deterred, scraping and scratching at each other viciously, trying to gain just enough ground on the other to force them into submission.

The other demon thought he had Keito pinned firmly against the wall surrounding the ring, but Keito kicked one leg back between his, striking his heel on the back of the other demon's knee before grabbing the back of his head and angrily slamming it into the wall, stunning him long enough for Keito to circle away.

The other demon growled, his eyes closed tightly in pain as he pressed a hand over his throbbing temple.

"Not bad, mutt."

"You should learn to be more respectful to your elders," Keito said. "Even if I surrender to you now, my team still wins."

"But you won't do that," the younger demon said.

"No, because you are going to send a message to the other demon Guardians for me."

"And what message is that?"

"That I'm back, and I won't tolerate any idealist political bullshit to permeate through the Guardian Branch."

The other demon laughed. "Is that what you think will happen?" He shook his head. "You're too late, old man. You already know what's coming."

"Do *you*?"

"Revolution."

"Is that what you think he'll do? He will *destroy* everything. He wants to rip apart everything that's been built between the five realms. How can you think that will be better?"

"That's better than being treated like a mad dog, only let loose when your master wants you to kill something before they put you down when you're no longer controllable." The other demon shook his head. "You should know better than anyone. If the humans won't see us as equals, won't treat us better than some fascination or abomination, then we have to remind them that they're insignificant little specks in the universe compared to us. And Yokouro will do that for us."

"It doesn't have to be only one or the other," Keito snarled. "We can coexist."

"Now who's spouting idealist political bullshit, Keito?" the younger demon asked. "You may think fondly of humans, but I can assure you they don't feel the same about you. And you know it."

"I refuse to prove them right," Keito said.

He lunged forward, his hand closing around the younger demon's neck as he pinned him to the ground, his hand covering his opponent's nose and mouth with bruising force.

"Surrender," he ordered. "The match is over."

The other demon stared at Keito, assessing the severity of his expression before nodding. Keito released him, standing and offering a hand. The other demon ignored the presented help.

"The war is beginning, Keito," he said, pulling himself upright. "I suggest you figure out which side you're on."

As the demon began walking toward his teammates, meeting up with those who were still conscious, Keito walked back to his own team, knowing from the relieved looks on their faces that they had not heard the conversation between the two demons.

"The winner is Team Dalton!" Tecca called into the thunderous applause that shook the stadium. "Obviously," she added under her breath.

Chapter Fifteen

"The next match will be Team Kyan versus Team Siante. Will those teams please come to the center of the ring?"

Team Dalton perked up, turning their attention to the ring, abruptly ending their light conversations about how the first match in the tournament was not as difficult as they anticipated. Dalton's gaze locked on Kyan as he led his team to the ring to meet with Team Siante and the superior look in Kyan's eyes made Dalton's blood turn to ice.

"Please state any conditions."

Both team leaders shook their heads, so Tecca called the match to start.

The ten combatants launched at each other in a flurry of fists and magic as the audience regained their voices to rattle the stadium walls yet again.

Dalton was startled at how quickly the fight became brutal. It was difficult to discern each Guardian in the ring, but he did realize that while Team Siante was landing every attack, Team Kyan seemed unaffected, retaliating in kind whenever they could land a hit, though they did not appear to be taking the match seriously.

The infuriated opposing team attacked more viciously, but that only served to tire them, their punches seeming to cause no pain and their magic not even singeing the skin of Team Kyan.

Desperate to feel as though he was gaining some ground in the match, Siante reached out with a magical binding spell, the streaks of bright energy shooting toward Kyan at terrifying speed. Kyan stopped moving, allowing the magic to wrap around his wrists, smiling when he saw the satisfaction on Siante's face.

Before the other Guardian could prepare another magic attack, Kyan yanked on the binding spell, pulling Siante forward at a stumble and giving Kyan the opportunity to kick the other man hard in the ribs. His eyes bulged and his mouth dropped open as the oxygen was painfully forced from his lungs. He collapsed to the ground, holding his abdomen, feeling the sharp edges of three broken ribs.

Kyan smirked, watching as the magic bindings around his wrists dissipated with the broken concentration.

"Still want more?" His tone dripped with contempt. Siante ground his teeth together, staggering to his feet and delivering the hardest punch he could muster to Kyan's jaw. Fueled by adrenaline and panic, he tackled Kyan, wrestling with him around the pain of his ribs.

Three of Kyan's men had defeated their opponents—two unconscious and one struggling to remain upright after his painful surrender. The fourth member of Team Siante was displaying incredible resilience against the two demons that constantly tore at him, their enhanced speed and strength disorienting. Dalton was reminded of predators toying with wounded prey.

When the fourth member finally fell to the ground with four large gashes over his left shoulder, one of the demons began laughing mockingly.

"This is just pathetic."

"You better just surrender," the other suggested, leaning down to the Guardian on the ground. "Save yourself the pain."

"Yes...I...surrender," the man stuttered, backing away from the looming demons. With a triumphant nod, the twin demons turned away, spectating the wrestling between their team leader and Siante.

Siante refused to relinquish. He kicked and punched at Kyan with all his might, his eyes bright with what Dalton figured was a mixture of desperation and rage. Kyan allowed the other Guardian to pin him down, kick and punch at him, but when Siante straddled his torso and began raining punches on his face, Kyan sat upright, wrapping his arms around the other's torso and pushing him to the ground, shoving Siante's face into the hard dirt as he hooked the Guardian's arm. With a sharp jolt, Siante's bone snapped.

"I surrender!" Sainte howled in pain.

"And with that painful end, the winner is Team Kyan. Uh, can we get a medical team in here?" Tecca asked. "They did some damage."

Mitoki's eyes were wide, his face paling a few shades.

"They didn't even seem to flinch at most of those attacks," he noted.

"They are basically walking corpses," Hanyi reminded him. "I doubt they feel any pain."

"And that's what we're up against?" Eclipse said.

"They'll do worse to us if we give them the chance," Keito said. "I have a feeling they are here just to test our strength, to give our enemy a chance to see who Council has sent in response to his threat."

"Again, there will be a fifteen-minute break before the next match," Tecca said, stuttering a little as she worriedly watched the medical team collect the injured and unconscious members of Team Siante.

"That was a brutal fight," Tarrena whispered.

"That's closer to what I remember from the previous tournaments," Jikia said.

Dalton was trapped in a staring contest with Kyan as he returned to his team box, his face permanently painted with the arrogant smile that made Dalton's hair stand on end. He felt as though, even from across the ring, Kyan could hear every word they were saying about him and his grin just confirmed that he was only the first in many opponents they would face as they tracked down their foe.

The fifteen minutes between fights passed incredibly fast as Team Dalton half-heartedly tried to strategize how to take down Kyan and his team, too worried to develop a solid plan. Their attention was brought back to the ring when Team Taniya was called to fight Team Kraymon. The wolves of the Opalon Pack were facing off against another team comprised of only beast Guardians.

The match was one of brute strength and instinct as the animals scraped and clawed and bit at one another, their eyes wild and their snarls drowned out by the roaring of the enthralled audience. As the match dragged on, Dalton began flinching at every attack, worried about the Guardians killing each other, as neither team seemed to be backing down.

But once the wolves got the bear on the opposing team to surrender, they worked as a team to defeat the others and limped away victorious.

"At least they'll be tired if we face them next," Hanyi murmured.

"You don't think they could actually defeat us, do you?" Eclipse asked skeptically.

"No," he said. "But we don't need another team draining us of energy before we meet Kyan and his team in the ring."

After another break, Team Jeanette and Team Reley were called to fight. Team Reley was still heavily injured from their first match, and with the Carlsons' impressive control over elemental magic, they defeated Team Reley with ease.

"The waiting is brutal," Dalton groaned, sitting back in his seat and rolling his neck.

"Wait until later rounds," Hanyi teased. "When you have to sit around through long matches, fight, and then sit around for more long matches."

"The waiting is a part of the competition," Keito agreed with a nod. "And it can be the thing that breaks a Guardian team if they lose their focus during the breaks."

Dalton did not have to wait long. The next match was Team Dalton versus Team Jeanette. As they walked out to meet the Carlson sisters in the ring, Dalton found himself smiling at Jeanette, mirroring her nervous expression.

"Hey, boss," Jeanette greeted.

"Jeanette," he responded, nodding to the other sisters. "It's going to feel strange fighting you like this."

"It will be embarrassing when we kick your ass, Dalton," one of the younger sisters said with a smirk. Dalton chuckled, the others behind him grinning as a small amount of tension left the ten Guardians in the ring.

"Teams, please state your conditions."

"Sorry, Hanyi, but after last time, we've decided that beast Guardians need to stay in their human form," Jeanette said. "Hanyi Treneke is not allowed to take his wolf form," she repeated louder for the announcer.

"Hanyi Treneke must remain in his human form. Are there any other conditions?" Tecca prompted. "Team Dalton?"

Dalton shook his head. "None."

"Then you may begin!"

Dalton was not surprised that each sister focused on one member of his team, as that had been their tactic in previous matches, but he was startled at how *fast* Jeanette launched at him, bright flames sparking around the black gloves on her forearms. He dodged but felt the heat of the fire near his shoulder. When Jeanette turned to follow him, he misstepped, having to angle his body as he fell to roll into her approach. As she turned once again, his leg connected with hers, bringing her to the ground as the fire around her arms dissipated.

Dalton tried to grab her arms and restrain her before she regained her bearings, but as his fingers closed around her left wrist, the flames returned, singeing his palm.

As he backed away, he grabbed the dagger at his calf and crouched defensively, smiling. Jeanette also smiled, the flames growing over her arms as she rolled her shoulders, preparing to attack Dalton once again.

Eclipse had managed to push the youngest Carlson sister, the one able to grow vines from the seeds she kept on her, to one side of the ring. When the vines snaked out from under her sleeves, he was able to dodge freely without worrying about where his teammates were fighting.

He did notice that the youngest Carlson sister seemed to be acting desperate to encase him in the vines as she had with her previous opponents. Her expression was nearly frantic as she followed after his every dodge, the thick, coiling vines lurching forward like snakes with every step they took. He was soon focusing more on his opponent, trying to figure out the expression on her face, rather than taking note of where the vines lay.

The stalks had grown so long as they had chased Eclipse around that he tripped over a larger vine behind him and fell to his back. The younger Guardian took the opportunity, breaking the vines from her wrists as she leapt at Eclipse, pinning his arms down as another type of vine coiled from under her sleeves. As Eclipse began struggling with her, he felt the sharp slicing of the thorns. As the vines thickened, so did the thorns, digging deeper into his skin as the tendrils snaked down his arms.

"Surrender!" she grunted, struggling to keep him on the ground even as both of them began bleeding from the swelling hooks.

Eclipse could feel the shaking of her arms and noticed her strength quickly fading. Exhausted from her previous matches, the younger Guardian was struggling to overpower him. He pushed against her, trying to ignore the thorns and using his magic to push harder against her straining muscles. She grit her teeth, trying to keep Eclipse down despite knowing she was in no shape to be fighting against one of the best Guardians in the branch.

With a flex of his magic, the vines encasing both their arms split and fell away, allowing Eclipse to flip their positions and pin down the youngest Carlson sister.

"You're exhausted," he said, his tone gentle.

"Don't patronize me, Eclipse."

"I'm not, I just know that when you get tired, you're more likely to get hurt," he said. "Surrender."

"As a Guardian, my enemies won't give me a chance to surrender," she spat. Eclipse could hardly help himself from feeling a twinge of pain in his chest, seeing just how young his opponent was as she repeated what she had likely heard during every training session she had ever had.

"Then it's a good thing I'm not an enemy," he said, easily pushing her hands back down when she started fighting again. "Surrender."

She was breathing heavily, looking around to see the state of her sisters, all of whom were exhausted from the prior matches. Not wanting to be the first to surrender, she willed her power to grow more vines.

Dark sparks of energy bit into her wrists as Eclipse's magic retaliated.

"Surrender," Eclipse repeated, his tone even.

She ground her teeth together and the older Guardian could see the gears in her mind turning as she tried to come up with another means of winning the match. Finally, she let out a long sigh and closed her eyes.

"Can you at least make it look good?" she asked, a nervous grin pulling at the sides of her mouth.

Eclipse smiled and nodded.

He eased his grip on her wrists and she pushed herself upright, shoving him in the chest, though Eclipse could feel her trembling. He fell back harder than needed and easily dodged some slow punches as she launched at him. He grabbed one of her wrists, pulled her to the ground, and rolled them so she was face down on the dirt. He lifted his other hand, his magic surrounding his entire arm in a dark fog.

"Surrender!" he demanded.

She stared at his hand and then at him and nodded, quietly thanking him as he released her and helped her to her feet.

On the other side of the ring, Dalton was becoming frustrated in his match with Jeanette. She was chasing him around the ring, throwing punches and trying to trip him with magic attacks that he was barely able to avoid. He could not get close enough to her to knock her down and she did not give him enough time to concentrate on a magic attack that would actually do any damage to his opponent.

As he turned to spin away from another fiery punch, he noticed Hanyi helping his opponent to her feet, securing the second surrender from the sisters. Dalton was struggling so much with fighting Jeanette he tried to tell himself it was because the two of them had always gotten along and he did not want to fight her—but he knew he was lying to himself. He had underestimated her and was now scrambling to form a plan.

"Getting a bit tired, Dalton?" Jeanette taunted.

"I'm sure you are as well," he said, dodging another punch as he tried to nick her shoulder with his dagger, though he missed. "You've fought twice already. You must be getting tired."

"Fire can keep going as long as there is something to feed it," Jeanette reminded him. "I've still got plenty in me to defeat you."

Something about the statement gave Dalton pause as decades-old lessons began to resurface in his brain about magical classifications and the different types of elemental manipulations.

When Jeanette launched at him again, he turned his attention to her arms, watching the way the fire surrounded her gloves.

A pained cry nearby distracted both Dalton and Jeanette and the cheering of the audience was coupled with the collective gasps of the stunned crowd. Even as Dalton saw the way Jeanette's younger sister, who had been fighting Mitoki, clutched at her slightly distorted leg, the audience only cheered louder.

Coughing and spluttering, water dripping from his head and face from the dispelled magic, Mitoki turned to his opponent.

"Do you surrender?" he coughed.

She nodded, gritting her teeth against the pain of her broken ankle. Mitoki struggled to get to his feet, Hanyi rushing to help as Eclipse and the two other Carlson sisters that had surrendered immediately tended to the injured Guardian.

Taking advantage of his distraction, Jeanette lunged at Dalton and tried to tackle him. He stumbled, but managed to stay upright as he turned his attention back to his opponent.

"Keep your head in the fight," she told him.

Dalton was about to protest when Jeanette began furiously punching at him again, the flames threatening to burn his face as he dodged. Stunned at the sudden brutality—she had never aimed for his face before—Dalton tried to flee. Jeanette was after him, emboldened by the cheering of the audience behind her.

Taking a chance and preparing himself for the pain, Dalton turned toward her, crouched low to the ground, and lunged forward, his arms wrapping around her waist as he tackled her. He felt the pain at the back of his neck and on his shoulder as she grabbed at him but soon both were gasping for breath as they hit the hard dirt. Dalton grabbed the top of one of Jeanette's long black gloves and pulled, yanking it away from her skin as she struggled to fight him off.

Once the glove was free, Jeanette's other hand pushed Dalton hard in the side.

Searing pain shot through him and made his vision go white. He let out a startled yell though it was drowned out by the thrilled whooping of the audience. The bellowed encouragements for both Dalton and Jeanette combined into a resonating roar that made it even harder for Dalton to gain his bearings.

Fighting against his instinct to move away, Dalton turned into the hand burning against his ribcage and grabbed her wrist, once again clawing at the glove and yanking it off as Jeanette let out a screech and tried to wrench her hand back.

The glove slid from her skin and the burning stopped in an instant.

Dalton let out a small breath of relief, but then quickly rolled away from Jeanette, grinding his teeth against the agony of his disturbed burns. When he got to his feet, Jeanette shook her head.

"That's not fair! You knew I had a Dragon Ring!"

"I swear, I didn't," he gasped, being sure to keep a firm hold on both of her gloves to keep her from reclaiming the item that sparked fire for her to control. "I just guessed."

"You process my paperwork every year! You had to know!"

"I didn't," he insisted. "Otherwise, I would have removed it before you had a chance to do this," he motioned abstractly to his side. "Or I would have just asked you to remove it in the conditions for the match."

Jeanette was breathing hard, though Dalton did not know if it was due to exhaustion or anger.

"You swear you didn't know?"

"I swear."

Jeanette's shoulders dropped.

"Then…I concede." She shook her head, running a hand over her face. "I'm exhausted."

"I'm sure you are," Dalton said, impressed.

She glanced around the ring, seeing Mitoki, Hanyi, and Keito step forward, ready to tend to their team leader. When he noticed the way she searched the ring for the youngest of her sisters, Mitoki spoke up.

"Eclipse took her to Hall A for treatment for her ankle," he said.

"Come on," one of her sisters said, motioning for Jeanette to follow her.

"And with that, the win goes to Team Dalton!" Tecca announced. The exhilarated cheering of the audience drowned out Jeanette congratulating Dalton and thanking him for a good fight, but he nodded and shook her hand, understanding what she had tried to say.

Keito helped Dalton to the team box where Jikia was already prepared to take care of the burns to Dalton's side.

"I'm really glad we didn't fight them first," Hanyi said, raising his eyebrows. "We might have actually been in trouble."

"Are you alright, Mitoki?" Tarrena asked, seeing the drawn look on the youngest's face.

"I just feel bad about her ankle," he said. "I didn't mean for that to happen. I could tell she was getting desperate and sloppy and I tried to tell her to just surrender, but she didn't listen."

"Injury is going to be common, and it's not just scrapes and bruises. Broken bones are bound to happen," Hanyi said. "You can't blame yourself. You didn't go in there with the intention of causing severe harm."

"I still feel bad."

"She'll be alright," Tarrena assured. "The emergency medical team is equipped to handle her injury. I'm sure they even have a healer on call that can heal her broken ankle."

"Exactly," Hanyi agreed. "You have no reason to feel bad. Right, Dalton—*gah!*" Hanyi shied away and squirmed to the other side of the team box when he saw the extensive burn on Dalton's side as Jikia cut away the shirt to see the damage.

"You were saying about the medical team?" Dalton asked, flinching as the burned fabric pulled at his skin.

"Hate to tell you, but they won't see you unless sanctioned by the Tournament Board," Keito said, also looking over the burn. "The medics only see teams that have been eliminated unless the Tournament Board calls for a medical examination."

"Wait, he's supposed to fight like this?"

"That's what I'm here for," Jikia said. "I can heal the worst of this, but not all of it," she told Dalton, holding her hand close to the wound as gentle streams of blue energy floated toward Dalton's burns. "I can't use up all my healing energy when you still have fights ahead, just in case."

"Then the tournament sees the medical team as an unfair advantage to teams that are continuing to fight?" Mitoki pressed.

"The waiting is part of the tournament," Keito repeated.

"The exhaustion and the wounds from the previous fights are meant to help even the fights as we get closer to the final match," Hanyi elaborated, holding up his hand to keep himself from seeing Dalton's injuries. "Having a healer that can just magically make the injuries disappear is a bit antithetical. Trainers can tend to their team, but the medical team is reserved for severe injuries or disqualified teams."

"Uh, Dalton," Eclipse said, approaching the team box from the ring as he returned from Hall A. Dalton looked up at him, trying not to cringe at the stabbing needles of pain that came with healing energy. "Your abs are up on the big screen."

Dalton turned his gaze to the screen across from him and saw that a nearby camera had focused on him, displaying the wound for everyone to see, though the reactions of the audience proved that most spectators hardly noticed the wound.

"Ah, yes," Keito said, rolling his eyes. "Forgot they did that."

He stood and turned his back to Dalton, stepping in the way of the camera to block most of the view of his team leader, though the crowd was clearly displeased. As some began to boo at Keito, Tarrena turned away from Mitoki's wounds and stood in front of Keito, glaring at the camera, her bright green eyes glinting as they began to take on their dragon shape.

The sounds of displeasure quickly ceased, though many began teasing Tarrena about protecting her "boyfriend" from gawking eyes.

"That's the best I can do," Jikia said, pulling her hand away as Dalton turned to look at the mostly-healed burn. "Let's see...I have some gauze here that we can bandage around that. I've got the self-adhesive, the cloth, the pink ones..."

Hanyi's head whirled around.

"What?"

Jikia smiled. "What? You want some pink bandages?"

"Um, of *course* I do."

Jikia lifted the roll of pink bandages out of the medical supply case and Hanyi's entire face lit up.

"It's my color!"

"You can't even *see* the color pink," Keito noted.

"Don't care. I know I look damn good in pink." Hanyi turned when he heard Eclipse give an exasperated groan. "But maybe we should save them for Eclipse. I think the pink bandages would best suit him."

"No thank you," he grumbled.

"Oh, come on. It would match your skin tone!"

"What does that even mean?"

"I dunno, but I've heard people say it. Besides, black and pink look good together, right? Most of your wardrobe is black. Time to add a splash of color!"

"Wolf...I swear..."

"What do you have against the color pink?"

"Nothing! Why am I even having the conversation with you?"

"Because I need to know if I'm getting you something pink for your birthday. When is your birthday, anyway?"

"Down, boy," Keito laughed, placing a hand on Hanyi's head.

"Oh, come on, it could be a whole theme!" he whined. "I'll get everyone something pink for their birthday!"

"Are you doped up on painkillers or something?" Tarrena asked.

"No, he's just like this," Keito said. "And leave me out of the pink gift-giving. You may not know what it means, but I do know that pink *doesn't* match my skin tone."

"At least you're willing to play along with my antics," Hanyi said, throwing an exaggerated pout in Eclipse's direction.

"Do you still want the pink bandages? They're actually in here as a joke," Jikia asked.

"Yep!" Hanyi stuck out his arm, eager.

As Hanyi tried to get Jikia to bandage him before Dalton, Tarrena turned her attention to the bleeding gashes in Eclipse's arms.

"Let me clean those," she said, pulling her own tray of first aid items closer as she sat on the bench next to him. "Don't worry, I won't use the pink bandages."

"I don't have an issue with pink, it's just…" Eclipse cast a quick glance at Hanyi, "don't you think he's being a little too relaxed about all this?"

Tarrena shook her head. "He's just trying to lighten the mood. Break the tension and all that. It's important to relax a little during this very stressful event." She grinned. "And you know he picks on you so much because he gets a rise out of you, right?"

Eclipse sighed. "It's fine. He seems to enjoy needling me."

"It does seem to be your dynamic," she said as she dabbed antiseptic on the wounds. "I saw what you did during that fight," she said, keeping her eyes low. "Playing up the fight at the end for show."

"Reputation is important for Guardians," he said. "She's young with a bunch of powerful sisters. Thought I would give her a little confidence boost."

"That was very kind," Tarrena said, flicking her gaze up to meet Eclipse's before quickly turning away and grabbing some bandages. "You put on quite the tough guy act, don't you?"

Eclipse could not help but laugh lightly.

"Don't tell anyone."

Keito turned to Hanyi, who wagged his eyebrows at the demon before nodding as he threw one more glance at Eclipse and Tarrena, laughing to himself and turning to check on Dalton once more.

It seemed that only seconds had passed after Jikia and Tarrena put away their bandages that Tecca spoke into the microphone.

"May I have your attention please? The semi-final match will be Team Dalton versus Team Taniya! Will those teams please step into the ring?"

"Two in a row?" Eclipse lamented, getting to his feet.

"And if we win this fight, we'll be fighting Kyan's team afterward," Keito added.

"Well, that's great," Dalton said with an irritated huff.

"No doubt that was on purpose," Hanyi said. "I have a feeling this will happen to us a lot."

Dalton was slightly unnerved by the glaring coming from Team Taniya, but much of the malice was diminished by the heavy bandages and the limping of two members of the team.

Dalton slowed his step, motioning Keito and Mitoki forward as he turned to Hanyi.

"How do you want to handle this?" he asked.

"They're all going to try and gang up on me, I think," Hanyi said. "Pack tactics, work together to take me down. But they're injured. I say, if that's what they do, let them attack me and then each of you grab a wolf and pin them down until they give up. They're hurt. I doubt they'll put up much of a fight."

"Are you sure?"

"I'll try and get Taniya isolated and fight her, put on a show for her mother and all, but otherwise, yeah," Hanyi said. "I think that's how we should play this."

Dalton nodded and caught up to the others in the center of the ring.

"Please state any conditions you have for the match," Tecca told them.

"The wolf, Hanyi, in his animal form," Taniya said, almost interrupting the announcer.

"Hanyi must fight the match in his animal form," Tecca repeated. "Any other conditions?"

Dalton straightened, struck with an idea.

"Taniya must also fight in her wolf form," he called. "But everyone else on her team must fight in their human forms."

The horrified looks on the other wolves almost made Dalton smile. He threw a glance at Hanyi and saw the wolf nod in approval. Taniya let out a long growl as she glared at Dalton.

"You think that will make it harder for us to win?" she snarled.

"I don't think you have a chance at winning," Dalton said honestly. "You're too injured and too tired. But I also don't think this match is about my team versus your team."

"You're correct about that," she snapped, glaring at Hanyi.

"Are there any other conditions for the match?" Tecca prompted. When both Taniya and Dalton shook their heads, she called the fight to begin.

Dalton hurriedly stepped out of the way as Taniya shifted into her wolf form and lunged at Hanyi. The wolves moved away from the other Guardians, clawing, biting, growling, and tearing at one another viciously, seemingly with no care about the rules of the tournament.

The others in Team Dalton circled the remaining Guardians.

Taniya had pulled away from Hanyi, lowering her head and growling, though it was almost impossible to hear over the roar of the audience. She gnashed her teeth at Hanyi, rocking her shoulders in preparation for the fight, her hackles raised.

"What are you doing, Taniya?" Hanyi asked.

"I'm challenging you, old man."

"You're not even an alpha, yet. You cannot challenge me," Hanyi replied. *"What I want to know is why you, a Guardian and a wolf from the proud Opalon Pack, would sink so low as to show your bellies to a psychopathic mass murderer."*

Taniya launched at Hanyi, grabbing at the thick fur around his neck, though he turned his head, his bared teeth connecting with her snout and startling her enough to back away, squaring up for another attack.

"Is that what you think?" she snarled.

"I know you're working for Yokouro," Hanyi said strongly.

"And what are you going to do about it?"

"Don't you see what he's doing?!" he snapped.

"He's taking the initiative," she retorted. *"He wants to eliminate the humans. Our lives can return to the peace and balance our land once knew, before they showed up and put us into this council where we have to appear like them just to appease them! Just so that we can stand up to them when they invade our land and try to rip it apart and build whatever they call a society!"* She began stalking around him, her head low. *"You're just as bad as the humans, Hanyi. Not only do you call them friends and want to bow to the rulings of the human-run circus of a council, you actually <u>enforce</u> those rulings. You, a Guardian, when you should be fighting for our land, not for the council."*

"You're a Guardian, too!" Hanyi barked. *"You work for Council."*

"No! I work for Yokouro," she growled. *"I only became a Guardian after he said he needed more people on the inside, more creatures ready to tear apart the regime of humans."*

Hanyi's snarling slowed.

"*He's played you,*" he warned. "*He's playing your whole pack. He's a demon, he's not a wolf.*"

"*Demons understand the devastation humans can create, perhaps more than we can. And he's right. The humans have to fall.*"

"*You became a Guardian because of him?*"

"*We all did,*" she said, moving her head back to signify the rest of her team.

"*He didn't want you to be a Guardian to tear apart things from the inside,*" Hanyi said with a disbelieving laugh. "*Sure, if you did, it would help him. But he only targeted your pack because it's the closest rival of the Trenekes. It's not because you're special, or loyal, or stronger...it's only because he can use the Opalon Pack to get to me. It has nothing to do with you or your pack. It's because of me.*"

"*He doesn't care about you!*" she screeched. "*You're an old, beaten-down, has-been! He's looking to the future!*"

"*Yes, he is,*" Hanyi agreed. "*He knew he was going to put together a Guardian Tournament. He knew that I would be called to participate in it. And he knew that the Guardians Council sent to oppose him would come to the Realm of Beasts, allowing him to play those moronic little games he loves so much. That's why he encouraged you to become a Guardian, that's why he's helped the Opalon Pack get stronger, and that's why you're in this tournament. Not because of anything you've done or any grand plans for the future he wants to see. But because he's using you to toy with me, and once you've outlived your use, he'll dispose of you as he's done to countless others.*"

Taniya leapt at Hanyi again with no intention of backing down. The two scraped and bit and snarled, but it was clear that Taniya was far too tired to put up a real fight and it was not long before Hanyi ducked under Taniya and clamped his jaws around her throat, pinning her as his teeth clenched on her windpipe. She struggled, her claws scraping at Hanyi, but she could feel her head going light and she whispered her defeat in a panic.

Hanyi backed away, shaking before shifting back into human form.

Taniya growled at him as he approached her.

"With Taniya's surrender, Team Dalton walks away victorious again!" Tecca called, understanding that Hanyi's shift meant he had defeated the other wolf.

Slowly, Taniya resumed her own human appearance, glancing at the wounded, exhausted members of her team. She glared at Hanyi.

"Don't think this is over."

As she returned to her team, Dalton and the others approached Hanyi.

"That was a fast fight," Dalton said with a forced smile.

"She was too tired to do any damage," Hanyi said.

"Are you alright?" Keito asked.

"Yeah…" He glanced at the other wolves as they exited the ring. "But I think we should really be on our guard after that."

"We will be," Eclipse agreed.

"The Tournament Board wishes for me to announce that because Team Dalton will be fighting three times in a row, the Board has granted a twenty-minute rest period before the start of the final match."

"Good," Dalton groaned, rubbing his irritated burn wound as his team trudged to their team box tiredly.

Chapter Sixteen

As the brief fight with Taniya's heavily-injured team did not leave any fresh wounds on the members of Team Dalton, bandages only needed to be checked before the Guardians sat amid the hungry hum of the audience, feeling the minutes tick by too quickly and yet not fast enough.

Dalton closed his eyes and tried to tune out the noise, feeling his heart picking up pace as the anxious energy permeated through his skin. He did his best to meditate, trying to ignore the cold stare he could feel from Team Kyan across the ring.

Rather than become tired and bored in the twenty minutes between the matches, the crowd seemed to become more invigorated, the chattering turning into a constant white noise that seemed to escalate in volume to a near-deafening din. When Dalton opened his eyes from his attempted meditation, he saw his own face on the large screen above the audience, a nearby camera panning over the members of Team Dalton. It was in that moment that Dalton remembered the tournaments were broadcast to the realms live, and that the twenty-minute wait was probably filled with chatter from commentators across the different realms predicting how the final match in that stadium would end.

When he turned to look at his teammates, he saw Mitoki's leg bouncing anxiously, Eclipse sitting with his arms crossed tightly over his chest as he scanned the stadium, and Hanyi and Keito both scanning Team Kyan with dark expressions.

"How are we going to approach this?" he asked quietly. Even though he knew it was hard to hear him over the crowd, the other four turned, agitated. "That team has two demons and all five of them are being controlled as basically corpse puppets. How are we going to defeat them?"

Dalton's eyes fell on Keito as Eclipse and Hanyi also turned to the demon. Keito took a deep breath, looking at Kyan before shrugging.

"I don't know," he said honestly. "As horrible as this sounds, we might have to actually kill them."

"...but they're already dead."

"I mean don't treat this like a spar but like a case. Hit vital points, do some damage. Since they're already dead, we can't be disqualified for killing them. And even if we could, our enemy wouldn't let us get kicked out this early in the tournament. It's not his style."

"Then why send the team to us at all?"

"As a gauge," Hanyi answered. "This will be your first run-in with any of his men. He's going to see what you're made of."

"Which now that I think about it..." Keito muttered, his expression becoming concerned. "I don't think this team is meant to fight us as much as toy with us." His gaze fell to the floor in thought. "He's all about the message, the drama...he doesn't want to kill us or overpower us, not yet."

"He'll try to convince us that what he's doing is right?" Mitoki guessed. "We've had a lot of training in dealing with that, though."

"And he's had a lot of practice in manipulation," Hanyi warned. "Say this team is really just to toy with us and see what the humans are about," he said, speaking to Keito, "what about the two demons?"

Keito looked up again, glancing over the twin demons across the ring as he shrugged.

"My guess is they're for me," he said. "But if they *aren't*..." He hesitated. "Don't let them attack you together. They will rip you to shreds."

"So, do we have a plan?" Eclipse asked.

Dalton rubbed his forehead. "*No.*"

"You're not really giving us much to go on," Eclipse said, glaring at the two oldest Guardians on the team.

"I'm just as blind as you are," Keito said, holding his hands up peacefully. "Just because I was after him before does not mean I can predict what he'll do or what he'll send his men to do."

"Are there any conditions we can ask for?" Mitoki suggested. "Anything that might tip things in our favor?"

"If you told me a way to break the draining bewitchment, I can try," Eclipse said. "I'm familiar with most bewitchments. I can probably do the counter spell."

"I don't know how it's done," the demon said.

"I don't like going in blind," Dalton said. "Not with this team. It was clear they didn't take their last match seriously. We don't know what they can do."

"Maybe instead of making a plan for how to deal with them, we make a plan for how to watch out for each other," Mitoki suggested. "Let's be honest, even if Keito takes on one of the two demons, it will take all of us working together to take down the other."

"If we're lucky," Hanyi said.

"But if we can't focus on the other demon because of the three other members of the team, then we need to eliminate them as a threat first."

"Good point."

"Keito, think you stand a chance against those demons?" Mitoki asked.

Keito nodded slowly, once again glancing at the opposing team.

"I think so," he said. "But if I end up against both of them, stay clear because I will not be paying attention to where you are."

"If we let Keito handle the demons, we can all team up and eliminate the other three," Eclipse added. "Dalton, you distract Kyan and then Hanyi, Mitoki, and I will gang up on the other two and get rid of them. Then we'll help you take down Kyan."

"And if we think we can, we'll help Keito after that," Dalton added. "Okay, so we watch out for one another and just eliminate each threat as we can."

With a decisive nod, the other members of Team Dalton agreed.

Both Jikia and Tarrena remained quiet as the Guardians spent their final minutes of the rest period gathering their remaining strength and mentally preparing for the fight ahead. They continued to share concerned looks, trying not to let the Guardians know how worried they were for them.

"Alright, everyone!" Tecca called. The audience tried to silence, but the excitement at realizing she was about to announce the start of the final match was too palpable. People were standing in their seats, screaming loudly to get the match started, bellowing for their preferred team to triumph.

"The finals of the first set of Round One of the Guardian Tournament are about to begin here in the 4B Stadium!"

The competing Guardians felt the reverberating cheers in their chests, rattling their bones.

"The final match will be Team Dalton versus Team Kyan. Guardians, please enter the ring."

With a final calming breath, Dalton led his nervous team into the ring.

The chanting of various names became a muddled cacophony that shook the hard dirt of the arena. As Dalton drew closer to the smirking Kyan, he felt the weight of every innocent life in that stadium that remained ignorant to the bigger dangers surrounding the tournament.

He stopped in the middle of the ring a few paces away from Kyan, his heart beating angrily against his ribs.

Kyan's smirk widened. "We're finally here," he said, his cold voice slicing through the noise of the crowd to drip like acid in Dalton's ears. "About time, wouldn't you agree?"

"Please state any conditions you have for this match. Once again, exclusive fights between demon Guardians are allowed to ensure the safety of the humans on each team."

Kyan huffed. "Where's the fun in that?" He turned over his shoulder to the announcer. "I request a five-on-five match, but the demons are to fight in their animal forms."

Dalton felt his stomach twist as he turned to look at Keito. Keito turned to the announcer.

"If the Tournament Board approves that condition, my own will be that both demons on Team Kyan will be my opponents and only my opponents in order to ensure the safety of the humans on our teams."

"Keito—"

"Remember, just stay out of my way. I won't be watching where you are," Keito said, interrupting Dalton.

"Can you take them both on at the same time in animal form?" Mitoki asked.

"I stand a better chance than you trying to take down a wolf demon in animal form," he responded.

"They might not approve the condition though," Eclipse said.

"Oh, they will," Keito assured, motioning to the crowd baying for blood.

Tecca had to start her sentence three times as the audience continued to drown her out.

"As with all conditions concerning demons in their animal forms, the Tournament Board must approve the condition. If it is approved, Keito DeVero will be the exclusive opponent of the Lucali twins of Team Kyan."

Dalton was certain his heart was going to leap out of his throat as he waited among the fevered roaring of the audience for the ruling of the Tournament Board. The twin demons shook their heads, tutting.

"Bold, mutt."

"You really believe you can take us both on at the same time?"

Keito smirked, shifting his shoulders to square up to the two demons.

"I've faced bigger and far more powerful demons," he said. "You forget who I am."

"No, we know exactly who you are, Wandering Child."

Keito's lip curled lip curling to expose his teeth. Before he could respond, a chime sounded through the speakers of the stadium, causing a hush to fall over the audience as they waited for the official announcement.

"The Tournament Board has decided to allow Keito DeVero and the Lucali twins into their animal forms for the match. As per Keito DeVero's request, the demons are only to fight one another."

The second half of Angela's statement was drowned out by another deafening cry as the audience anxiously awaited what they were sure would be a thrilling fight to behold.

Kyan quirked an eyebrow at Dalton.

"Anything else you want to add?"

Dalton wanted to say something, to come up with some condition that would give him an edge on Kyan, but as he stared into the dark, lifeless eyes, his mind seized up, and rather than speak, he shook his head.

"If there are no more conditions, you may begin the match!"

Dalton was about to lunge at Kyan in a weird haze of panic when a hand on his arm yanked him to the side. The Lucali twins ran at Keito, shifting into their animal forms mid-sprint amidst the roar of the audience. Keito had turned to sprint to the other side of the ring, bringing the demons away from his teammates as he, too, popped and writhed into his animal form.

The two wolf demons were both larger than Keito and Dalton became concerned that the ring would not be large enough to contain the three demons. Such concerns did not seem to plague the audience as they screamed themselves hoarse, ignoring the other Guardians as they watched the demons scrape and roar at one another, often moving too fast to be seen as anything other than black and grey blurs.

"Dalton!" Hanyi barked, reminding him to stop watching Keito and follow their plan. He rounded on Kyan, expecting his opponent to have taken advantage of his distraction, but the other team leader was standing calmly where he had met Dalton in the ring, waiting.

Dalton felt sparks dance over his skin as he let his magic surge forward, strengthening him.

"Well, Dalton?"

"Thought you would have attacked me when my back was turned," Dalton said, taking a careful step forward.

Kyan rolled his eyes. "What type of Guardian do you take me for?"

"The fake kind."

He laughed. "I was a Guardian, Dalton. When you were about eleven years old."

"Is that when you decided to let some demon drain you of your life?" Dalton snapped.

"Ah, so Keito spotted the draining bewitchment. Damn, I thought for sure he wouldn't know that one." Kyan clicked his tongue to the roof of his mouth. "Oh well." He turned over his shoulder to see that Eclipse, Hanyi, and Mitoki had brought one of his teammates to their knees, Hanyi clamping his teeth around the man's throat as Eclipse and Mitoki held him down, demanding his surrender. The final teammate was already unconscious on the ground.

"Are we going to fight?" Dalton sneered, taking another careful step forward, never allowing his magic to diminish, prepared at any moment to defend or attack.

"That depends entirely on you, Dalton."

"This is a fighting tournament. It's what we're supposed to do."

"Yeah, but you don't really care about the tournament," Kyan noted. "I mean, you sailed through the competition with no problems. You are the best of the best after all. You're really here because of people like me."

A pained roar caused Dalton and Kyan to turn, seeing Keito angrily biting at one of the other demons that had him securely pinned to the wall of the arena. While Dalton wanted to watch and be sure of Keito's well-being, he took advantage of the distraction to leap at Kyan, landing a hard punch to his face.

Kyan remained upright, stepping back two paces as he lifted a hand to his jaw.

Dalton did not give him time to regain his bearings. He continued to throw punches, pushing his opponent backward as he tried to bring him to the ground. His vision tunneled, focused only on where Kyan was moving and where he could land another hard punch. When he saw Kyan stumble, he took the opening to extract his dagger and slash the other man's chest.

No blood came from the wound, leaving a slit through the shirt and skin that gaped whenever Kyan moved.

Horrified, Dalton hesitated and his opponent smirked.

Turning on his heel, he kicked Dalton in the stomach, sending hot agony through his abdomen as he fell to the hard dirt.

He tried to focus on Kyan around the blinding pain, but Eclipse intervened, punching Kyan in the face and pushing him away from Dalton as Mitoki tried to help the team leader up.

"Are you alright?"

He tried to gasp for air, his battered diaphragm struggling to function. He nodded tightly, watching Eclipse fight Kyan as the leader of the opposing team dodged, uninterested in his new challenger, watching Dalton at every opportunity.

A yip from Hanyi was immediately followed by Mitoki yanking Dalton out of the way as the thundering paws of the demons drew closer, forcing the others to one side as Keito chased one of the twins, snarling angrily. While trying to get out of the way, Eclipse lost his focus and Kyan punched him hard in the jaw, forcing him to the ground.

"Come on, boys," Kyan taunted. "Take me down, just like you did those two." He motioned to his unconscious teammates. "The sooner you deal with me, the sooner you can help Keito with them."

Dalton stepped forward. "Were you sent here just to see what kind of challenge we posed?"

"I suppose," he said. "But I'm not just watching you, Dalton. You are, of course, the star of the show, but I'm also watching everything going on inside this stadium." He motioned to the stands. "Seeing how people will react to the new tournament, see how the Guardian Branch has changed. You must understand, there was a reason my master waited so long to start another tournament. He had to make sure most of the Guardians who were alive in the time of the Tournament Slaughter were dead or out of the picture. Otherwise, no one would have allowed it back."

"And what does your *master* gain with the tournament?" Eclipse spat. "More people to lock in a building and kill?"

"No, that's paltry to him." He pointed at the Guardians with both hands. "He gets you."

"Your master can break the seal on the realms, and he's interested in three human Guardians?" Mitoki asked skeptically.

"Sure is," Kyan answered. "You have to look at it from the bigger perspective. Every doomed civilization should have a chance to defend itself, and you boys are the realms' defenders."

"What does that even mean?"

"You don't know anything about demons, do you?" Kyan asked. "It's okay. I didn't, either. Demons aren't just a random species that populates a realm next to ours. They're gods."

"...*really?*" Eclipse asked, clearly unconvinced.

"Think about it. Human in appearance, mannerisms, language, but with powers our tiny brains can't possibly understand. And, on top of that, with animal forms and tendencies that are of the same species known to humans. They are gods made from the combination of all our worlds, and they're here to pass judgment on humanity."

Dalton, Mitoki, and Eclipse were staring at Kyan, unsure how to respond. They turned to one another, sharing their concern and confusion, wondering if Kyan could hear the absurdity of the declaration.

"You can't really believe that."

"Oh, I do," he said strongly. "I've *seen* it." Kyan's smile grew. "You boys have no idea who you're facing. My master is more powerful than all Guardians in the Guardian Branch *combined*. And he's nowhere near the power of some other demons. How would you feel if I told you that there are demons that even the all-powerful dragon Lord Vestera Hizoku cannot hope to defeat, but can only pray to keep them contained?" He quirked an eyebrow. "Would you believe they are gods then?"

"Even if what you're saying *was* true," Mitoki started, "demons are meant to live in coexistence with humans. They don't exist to pass judgment. And this demon that you serve would rather see all humans wiped out of existence than coexist with the other realms."

"Of course he would," Kyan said. "And he should. Humans do nothing but spoil and destroy. You should ask your demon teammate about some of the atrocities humans have committed against demons, and not even just lynching or killing them. I'm talking about the true horrors humans have done to demons. It's time humans face their judgment."

Dalton leapt forward and began attacking once more, Eclipse and Mitoki quickly following as Hanyi kept a careful eye on Keito and the other demons.

"You're just delaying the inevitable," Kyan cackled, dodging punches, kicks, and dagger swipes, leading the Guardians further into the middle of the ring. "Once he destroys what Council considers its finest defenders, my master will lead the charge against humanity and he'll annihilate anyone that stands in his way."

"You think setting fire to a locked building and killing thousands because he *can* is a noble cause?"

"And a necessary one."

"Murder is never justifiable," Dalton insisted, lodging the dagger into Kyan's side, though the other man merely chortled and circled off the blade, leaving another gaping, bloodless wound.

"Be careful, Dalton," he warned. "You forget that you're a murderer, too. And you justify it in your mind as preserving the peace." He laughed loudly, ducking a kick from Mitoki to grab the younger Guardian's leg and swing him into both Eclipse and Dalton, sending the three into an ungraceful heap on the dirt. "And if you think you're anything better than the council's personal murder squad, *you're* the delusional one."

They untangled themselves and struggled to their feet as Kyan looked them over.

"You know, I'm sure my master would be willing to talk with the three of you, get you to see his point of view."

"We're not interested," Eclipse sneered.

"Besides," Dalton added, "we know that you're under the draining bewitchment and that you're already dead. Which means we're not even talking to the real Kyan right now. We're talking directly to his *master*." Dalton readied his dagger. "You've given me your pitch, and here's my answer."

He started at Kyan, forcing him to take a step backward. Mitoki and Eclipse both sprinted forward, each trying to take Kyan's legs out from under him, though he easily dodged. But while focusing on the two younger Guardians, Dalton had surged forward and struck the hilt of his dagger across Kyan's face.

Mitoki then kicked Kyan's leg hard enough to hear a faint crunch as the magically enhanced attack broke his bone. Though he showed no pain, he crumpled to the ground, unable to balance his bodyweight. Eclipse wrapped an arm around Kyan's neck as he fell to a crouch and yanked him violently, finally bringing Kyan to the ground.

Dalton leapt on him, holding the hilt of his dagger tight as he repeatedly punched Kyan's face, unable to tell if his shaking was due to exhaustion, anger, or fear. His opponent's face seemed to shift and distort with each strike, shaping like hard clay under Dalton's force.

Finally, Dalton yanked Kyan up by the collar of his shirt, panting and nearly growling through his teeth.

"I'm coming for you, you son of a bitch."

Kyan's eyes rolled behind fluttering eyelids. Dalton was about to release him when his eyes snapped open once more and focused on Dalton. They were no longer the dark brown, lifeless eyes of Kyan. Bright, powerful, golden eyes stared back at him. Dalton knew precisely who he was looking at—the demon he was chasing.

"*Good.*"

Kyan's body went limp and his eyes slid shut.

"Dalton has defeated Kyan," Tecca announced, "but Team Dalton still needs one more surrender to win the match."

Dalton stared at Kyan's still, chalky face for several moments, catching his breath, the bright gold color of the eyes that had peered through his opponent seared into his mind. Eclipse's hand on his shoulder finally convinced him to release Kyan.

"You okay?"

He could only nod, the words stuck in his throat. He stood straight, his knuckles burning and his fingers cramping around his dagger. It took considerable effort for him to will his fingers to release the weapon.

As he started to feel his muscles relax, the stadium came back into focus. The thunderous crowd hardly seemed to notice the other four members of Team Dalton, focused on the impressive battle of creatures inside the ring. The cameras were focusing on the three demons from every angle, zooming in whenever the combatants were still enough to be caught on camera.

"How's he doing?" Dalton asked, walking over to Hanyi.

The wolf stood upright, shifting back into his human form.

"He's taking a beating."

"How do we help?"

"Do you see the *size* of those guys?" Hanyi gawked. "We're just staying out of the way at this point."

"We have to do something," Eclipse insisted.

"We can't," he insisted. "The conditions were that Keito would take on these two demons alone."

"And what if he can't?" Dalton pressed. "If Keito surrenders, the demons have to fight us, right? To get the majority of surrenders?"

Hanyi lifted his hands, making gesticulations as though trying to grab words out of the air. "I mean, I *guess*."

Dalton turned back to the fight, watching one of the grey, lanky wolf-like creatures leap onto Keito's back, his teeth sinking into the thick fur around Keito's neck. Keito turned, wildly snapping his jaws back at the other demon, finally flipping them both over and landing on top of the wolf. Squirming away from the loosened bite, Keito turned his head and sunk his teeth deep into the throat of the other demon. For a moment, Dalton was certain blood was erupting from the demon's neck and he became terrified that Keito would be disqualified for killing in the ring. But the darkness he saw around Keito's teeth rose into the air like smoke, dissipating with lingering sparks.

Before the magic could do any more damage, the other demon leapt over his brother and collided with Keito. Keito held on to the demon's neck as he was pushed away, tripping the other brother and eventually disorienting all three demons.

The heavy, sparking magic from Keito only seemed to invigorate the audience as they began shouting obscenities at the demons, too lost in the spectacle of the fight to worry about the danger to the combatants.

"He's lost a lot of blood," Mitoki noted, glancing around the ring at the thick pools of crimson that were soaking into the hard-packed dirt.

"Keito's tough as hell," Hanyi said. "Just trust him. He'll win."

"You sure?" Eclipse asked, wincing when he saw Keito be violently thrown by his back leg toward the middle of the ring.

"…mostly."

Keito struggled to get to his feet, and before he was fully upright, the two wolf demons were on him once more. As one of them tried to get his teeth around Keito's throat, he pushed his paws into his opponent's belly, pushing the larger demon back just enough to duck his head and, once again, lock his jaws around the other demon's throat.

The dark red-purple magic from Keito's teeth was far more visible to the other members of Team Dalton now that the battle was closer to the center of the ring. Dalton could make out the gashes and bite marks amid the torn fur of the two grey wolf demons, but as with Kyan, there was no blood. Instead, Keito's magic seemed to funnel into the large gashes and punctures, attacking from the inside.

As the other brother tried to stop Keito's attack once again, Keito bit harder and jerked his head sharply to the side. The tearing of fur and flesh could not be heard over the cheering, but Dalton saw the flap of skin that Keito had nearly removed from the other demon's neck. As Keito's first opponent stumbled, collapsing to the ground, eyes rolling wildly, the other let out an ear-shattering roar that did not resemble any animal Dalton had heard before.

Keito was, once again, pinned to the ground by the second demon. Tired, he struggled to get in a position to attack the other brother in the same way.

"One of the Lucali twins has passed out. That means that Team Dalton now has the majority of surrenders!" Tecca announced. "The match—"

She let out a startled cry when she saw the other wolf demon grab a mouthful of Keito's fur and fling him across the ring. The other Guardians scrambled out of the way as their teammate fell heavily to the dirt and rolled twice.

Barely hiding his shaking muscles, Keito rolled to his feet and began running at the charging wolf demon, neither of them slowing as they drew closer.

The impact was an audible boom that had everyone in the stadium wincing. The two slid in a tangled mess along the dirt before Keito managed to roll the other demon onto his back, avoid the snapping jaws, and clamp his teeth furiously around his opponent's neck, the magic fog diving into the openings in the other demon's flesh.

Straining with the effort to keep his opponent down, Keito bit harder, determined to finish the fight.

He released the other demon, who turned onto his side, straining to get to his feet before letting out a quiet whine and collapsing.

The elation and excitement of the audience drew attention away from Keito's bleeding wounds, and the way the unconscious demons popped and contorted down to a human form on the dry dirt of the arena.

"The winner of the first set of Round One of the Guardian Tournament in Stadium 4B is Team Dalton!" Tecca declared.

Chapter Seventeen

There was movement all around the stadium. The audience was on their feet, cheering until they were hoarse. Tecca was trying to make final announcements, though no one paid her heed. The medical team that had been waiting to tend to Team Kyan rushed in to cover the unconscious, naked demon Guardians and tend to the others of the defeated team. Jikia and Tarrena ran across the bloodied dirt toward the Guardians, both grinning broadly.

"You did it!" Tarrena cried, throwing her arms around Dalton and hugging him tightly. He stumbled back into Eclipse, exhaustion beginning to settle into his bones as he tried to regain his senses.

"Ow..." Dalton laughed, hugging her back despite the pain that his brain was starting to notice again.

She released Dalton from his hug and immediately wrapped her arms around Eclipse, hugging each Guardian in celebration.

"You did very well," Jikia agreed, hugging Dalton a bit gentler than her daughter. "But I knew you would."

"Thank you," Dalton said, taking deep breaths as though he had been hardly breathing the entire day.

"Team Dalton," a man asked as he approached, his bright red armband showing he was part of the medical team. "Do you need our assistance?"

Dalton scanned his team, his eyes finally resting on Keito, who was still standing in his animal form nearby, his coat occasionally shuddering as his own exhaustion became apparent.

"I think Keito's the only one seriously injured," he noted. "Keito? Do you want to go with the medical team?"

Keito shook his head.

"Are you sure?" the medic asked, noting with apparent alarm the extent of Keito's wounds.

Again, Keito shook his head.

The medic turned away, grumbling something about demons as he returned to the others of the medical team.

"Are you sure, Keito?" Mitoki asked. "You've lost a lot of blood."

"*It looks worse than it actually is*," Keito communicated to them telepathically.

"Oh really?" Jikia challenged, narrowing her eyes at him. "If that's the case, go back to your human form."

The demon hesitated.

"Right. Let's see how bad it is," she prompted again, motioning for Keito to move closer.

He shook his head, sitting on his haunches.

"The cameras are still rolling. I am not changing back."

"Everyone saw you shift into your animal form. I know it's not the most pleasant thing—"

"I will be naked upon reverting to my human form, and I don't need the cameras broadcasting everything to all the realms."

"Oh." Tarrena was unable to think of a more coherent response.

"So...now what?" Eclipse asked, looking around at the crowd as they began shuffling and gathering their belongings to leave. "Do we just...leave?"

"You can if you want," Jikia said. "I need to go meet with the Tournament Board to get your rankings and all the boring advancement paperwork, but you boys can head back to the pack if you want. Hanyi, are they still where we first met with them?"

"Yep," Hanyi said with a nod. "We can wait around for you, if you want. Keito, are you our mode of transportation?"

He nodded his head.

"No, you boys go ahead and head back," Jikia assured. "I don't know how long this will take."

"Do I need to be there, too?" Dalton asked.

"No, I'm the registered trainer of the team. This is technically my job," she said. "You can join me if you want, but I'm sure you're ready to get out of this stadium."

"Yeah," Dalton said with a broken laugh. "Are you sure?"

"Go ahead and go," she assured, squeezing Dalton's arm reassuringly. "You've earned the rest."

"It feels weird to just leave, doesn't it?" Mitoki said. "All that, and now...we just walk away."

"We'll be back in a few days. Not to this stadium but to 1B Stadium, for the second set," Tarrena reminded them. "The good news is there are only five matches that time."

"Only..." Dalton repeated with a chuckle.

"I always found the night after a round to be weird," Hanyi agreed. "All this excitement and adrenaline and then we just go someplace quiet, nurse our wounds, and fall into a coma. It's a very extreme change from the tournament itself. It can be jarring."

"Well, you boys should head out before the audience starts gathering at the exit to fawn over the champions of the first set," Jikia teased. "Because they will."

"Oh, yeah, we're outta here," Dalton agreed happily. "See you in a little bit?"

"I'll meet you back at the pack. I know where to go," she said, motioning for Tarrena to follow her as they walked across the ring toward Hall A.

"Keito, are you *sure* you don't need some sort of medical attention?" Dalton asked one final time.

"Once we get back to the pack, I'll work on healing myself. I promise, I'm alright."

"And how do you plan to get out of the door?" Eclipse asked, motioning to the double doors leading to their team room that were obviously way too small for him.

"Just block my bare ass from the cameras, please."

The Guardians hurried to gather their belongings while Keito searched for spare clothes in the locker room only to find there were none. Crowding around their demon teammate, they made their way to the exit of Hall D. There were crowds of spectators excitedly chatting about the fights they had just witnessed, but they did not immediately notice Team Dalton exiting the stadium.

Keito's body popped and shifted back into the animal form, and the strange movement caught the attention of those closest to the exit.

"Move, move, move, move," Hanyi urged, nearly shoving the humans away from the exit as Keito lowered himself to his belly to allow the Guardians to climb onto his back. Dalton scrambled to move faster as those who had seen them began calling that they had spotted the winning Guardians.

As audience members began swarming closer, security and attendants to the tournament also rushed forward to protect the exhausted participants.

Once the other four Guardians were seated and gripping onto Keito's thick fur, the demon managed to slip away from the worst of the crowd and run across the clearing into the trees, leaving the stadium and the adoring fans behind.

As they got further away from the stadium, a surreal feeling began pervading Dalton's mind. Even so shortly after the tournament, the matches and anxiety he felt seemed like distant memories. The only parts of the tournament that remained clear were Kyan's words and the way his eyes changed to the chilling, golden stare.

It was late afternoon when the Guardians returned to the Treneke Wolf Tribe. The wolves woke from their lounging naps and greeted them excitedly, being careful not to nudge the Guardians too hard for fear of aggravating their wounds.

With Keito's blood staining their ripped clothes from the travel back, the Guardians gathered new clothes and followed Hanyi's lead to a hot spring in a rocky section of the forest not far from the pack.

Knowing they would destroy their clothes, they piled them together before easing into one of the warm pools of the hot spring. Mitoki waited until the other Guardians had stripped down before disappearing behind a tree to do the same, hissing as he none-too-gingerly sank up to his neck in the steaming water.

"You okay?" Hanyi asked, laughing.

"Fine," he said shortly, being sure to remain completely submerged. "Just a little self-conscious."

"As long as you're not hiding any wounds from us that need tending," Keito said, leaning back on one of the rocks as he relaxed in the hot water.

"Oh, yeah, like you're one to talk," Hanyi scoffed, playfully flicking some water at Keito.

"I'm wondering something," Dalton said, also situating himself on a rock along the edge of the pool as he soaked in the almost-too-hot water. "Why does Keito return to human form naked and you have clothes when you go back to your human form?" He pointed at Hanyi.

"Oh, that's part of the training we have," Hanyi answered. "Beasts only take on human appearances in order to communicate with humans and since the first contact we ever have with humans is when humans are clothed, we learn to take on an appearance with clothes as well."

"How? And why can't Keito do that?"

"My fur retracts," Keito said. "His spell detaches his fur to create clothes."

"Wait, your clothing is basically your detached fur?!" Eclipse exclaimed. "That's disgusting!"

"Just for that, I'm going to take every opportunity to throw my shirt at your face," Hanyi said with a smirk. "You only have yourselves to blame. Humans insist on wearing clothing for *some* reason. I'm just trying to be polite and adapt to customs."

"Dalton, you okay?" Mitoki asked, noting the distant look on the team leader's face.

"Huh? Oh, yeah," he said quickly. "Just kinda lost in thought. Tired, and all."

Even he knew his words were not convincing.

"What did he say to you?" Keito asked.

"What?"

"Kyan. What did he say to you during your match?"

"A lot of stuff, I guess," Dalton said. "A lot of stuff I've heard before from criminals like mass murderers or those who sacrifice people for blood magic. Humans are bad, must be judged...but I don't know. This felt different."

"Like not only did he believe it but he could *do* it," Mitoki agreed, his gaze falling to the water.

"He said that demons were gods meant to bring judgment upon humans," Eclipse added.

Keito barked a loud laugh.

"Oh really? If that were the case, believe me, it would have happened long before this. That's an extremist belief in the Demon Realm, one that demons cling to when they hear about the oppression of demons or crimes committed against demons."

"Like lynching?"

"...yeah, like lynching," Keito agreed.

"What else?" Dalton pressed. "Kyan said humans have done worse than lynching demons. What else do demons think we do to them?"

Keito opened his mouth, but hesitated.

"There's no need to concern yourself with—"

"Keito."

He let out a defeated sigh.

"When it comes to us, it seems like humans don't just want to *kill* demons. They don't just want to eliminate us. But because we're powerful and humans are afraid of us, they...try to beat us down before killing us."

The three human Guardians did not try to dispute the statement.

"I don't think that humans are innately evil, which is another part of the extremist beliefs of the Demon Realm," Keito said when the silence had grown heavy. "And even though I've seen what humans do when they're afraid of a demon, and I've had my own experiences as a demon trying to interact with humans, I still think there is a way for demons to coexist with humanity."

"Even though humans do horrible things to demons?" Mitoki pressed.

"Humans do horrible things to *each other*," Hanyi said. "But they also do a lot of good for each other."

"This is a dangerous train of thought to follow," Keito said. "Questioning humanity's capacity for good and evil. As Guardians, we're more likely to see the evil side of humanity, and not just humans, but demons and beasts as well. It's easy to be caught up in thinking that there's no hope for anyone and that it would be easier if this psychotic demon came in and destroyed everything. But you have to remember the number of Guardians, *good* Guardians, and doctors, and officers, and philanthropists and people who do *good* for the realms. Just because the darkness in people casts a long shadow doesn't mean there's no good left in the world."

"It's easier to look at the shadow than the light," Hanyi agreed, his tone quiet.

"...you've had a lot of time to think about this," Dalton said.

Keito nodded. "I grew up around a lot of extremist beliefs in the Demon Realm. And yet, I'd much rather protect humans than destroy them."

"He also said that Guardians were no better than the Council's professional murder squad," Eclipse said. "And that we're nothing more than that."

Keito let out a long sigh. "I can't say I disagree there. We murder for the purposes of keeping the Council in power and the realms in the best peace we can achieve." It was Keito's turn to drop his gaze to the water. "But with the corruption setting deeper and deeper into Council, it does make you wonder if they use the Guardian Branch just to eliminate any possible opposition."

"That would actually explain why this demon is trying to destroy everything from the inside. He likely wouldn't have any other way to attack Council without the Guardians being sent to disrupt any attempt he made," Mitoki mused.

"The way the tournament spiraled away from Council's control also speaks to just how deep his influence is seated," Eclipse added.

"And if the Guardians are too busy fighting each other during the tournament, breeding distrust and competition within the branch, we can't really organize to work against him." Dalton shook his head. "A professional murdering squad set on murdering each other."

"Hopefully not," Keito said. "As I said, the darkness in people casts a long shadow. But there is still a lot of good. If we can find a way to bring this demon down and uproot his corruption, I'm sure there will be a lot of Guardians supporting us as we do so."

"...I hope so," Dalton murmured.

The Guardians decided to walk back to the Treneke Tribe when their eyelids became almost too heavy to keep open. They trudged back through the woods with their exhausted brains trying to think through what Kyan had said, though it only caused their unease to increase.

"Ah-ah!" Jikia snapped when Mitoki began crawling into his sleeping bag. "Get over here. Everyone's getting their wounds redressed."

Jikia and Tarrena tried to work quickly to get the Guardians tended to so they could get some sleep, but Xana was also intent on getting them to eat something before they collapsed into bed.

Dalton's mind was racing, wanting to turn over every piece of information he had gleaned from the tournament, but his body was crying for sleep, and before he could even tell the others goodnight, he was fast asleep, despite the unease in his chest.

Chapter Eighteen

Dalton was aware of the hard surface pressing into his back and the imposing darkness that surrounded him. He was not sure if his eyes were open or closed but he somehow understood the bounds of the space encompassing him. He was still, his limbs heavy and cold, his skin prickling in a way that made him question if insects were crawling all over him.

Without moving, the space around him became bigger, his own frailty and weakness radiating through him like an ache deep in his bones. The prickling of his skin turned into scratching as the darkness began to claw at him with dozens of sharp, angry hands.

"If you only could see what I see..."

"Let me explain! I can explain!"

"If you kill me, you're just as evil as you think I am!"

The words jumbled together, filling his ears with a barrage of pointed hisses and screams. Even as the sentences snaked around one another and became a singular noise, he saw the faces as they spoke, pleading with Dalton, staring at him in a way that he still could hardly stomach. Dalton had learned to push down the pain at seeing the dead—it was a reality he faced with every case—but he had never been able to handle the realization in someone's eyes as they looked at Dalton and saw their murderer.

The hands grabbed and scraped at him, their sharp fingers like razors flaying his skin though no blood trickled from the wounds.

Instead, the weight of the cold shadows pulled him down further, the hard surface against his back cracking and giving way as he was dragged through the darkness, the breath squeezed from his lungs, the pressure in his skull threatening to push his eyes from their sockets.

And in an instant he was face down on another cold, slippery surface, the weight gone.

His body gradually oriented itself, allowing him to get to his feet and look around. There was nothing around him, but he knew he was confined, trapped in some enclosure of shadows and heaviness.

His feet slid over the glassy surface upon which he stood, shimmering and reflective despite the lack of light.

Dalton slid his left foot forward, expecting the same hands to reach up and grab at his ankles, dragging him to even darker depths.

But the heaviness came from all around him, not just from below. Even within his chest, the mass of darkness threatened to break his ribs.

"So this is considered a nightmare to you."

Dalton turned, expecting to see someone behind him, but he was still alone. The voice rattled his skull but not because of volume. The power behind the voice was enough to make him feel smaller, as though no matter how fast or far he ran, he could never reach the edges of his prison.

"Very interesting…"

Dalton recognized the voice, but only from the edges of a dream, as though his mind knew he *should* know the owner of the voice, but he still could not recall the man's face.

"I'm dreaming."

"Of course you are."

"Then you're just a part of my mind."

"No, Dalton," the chilling voice contradicted. "The hands dragging you to the darker recesses of your mind, *that* was all conjured by you. I am just a spectator."

"I'm dreaming…"

"It's the only way I can communicate with you right now. Others won't let me get closer to you."

"Are you the entity from the woods?" Dalton asked, even though he already knew the answer.

"No…who is this entity in the woods?"

"…I don't know."

"In the habit of talking to specters, Dalton?"

Dalton closed his eyes, though it made no difference in what he was able to see.

"You're him. The demon that's behind all this."

A rumbling chuckle sent chills up Dalton's spine.

"I suppose you could say that, but this has roots that are even older than me. And I am old, Dalton."

"I won't let you get under my skin."

"Oh, but I'm already there," the demon taunted. "And you know it."

"I need to wake up."

"Seems what Kyan said struck a nerve, didn't it?"

"I *need* to wake up…"

"You're so much more honest when you're asleep, though. You let the pain and guilt consume you. You allow yourself to remember those you have killed—"

"Wake *up*."

"—and you revel in the masochistic agony of questioning your position as a Guardian. As one of the defenders of the peace." The voice laughed again.

"Wake up, damn it!"

"But down here, in the quietest, most reflective parts of your mind, you know the truth, don't you? You need that pain. Because as long as you feel the guilt, you can ignore the rush of power you felt when their blood dripped off your fingers."

"Enough!"

"Don't you see?" The voice drew closer, a cold rush of power encroaching on the skin of his back as the voice nestled at the base of his neck to whisper. "We're not so different. I'm just more honest."

Dalton whirled around, ready to fight whatever was behind him. But all he saw were bright golden eyes staring back at him.

He jolted awake, sitting upright with such speed the wolves around him jumped in surprise, watching as he turned around and slid backward across his sleeping bag, his eyes frantic in the trees for those same unnerving eyes. A cold sweat over his skin caused him to shiver as his chest heaved with shaky breaths.

"Dalton?"

He jumped and turned, spotting Hanyi's worried face.

"Are you alright?"

As his thoughts swam to the surface, allowing him to remember where he was and who he was with, he let out a long breath and closed his eyes, rubbing his face.

"Sorry…"

"Bad dream?"

"Yeah."

Hanyi nodded in understanding. "There's some rabbit stew Jikia and Tarrena have been cooking for us. Are you hungry?"

He nodded, untangling his ankles from his sleeping bag and turning over to stand when every muscle in his body protested the movement. The agonized groan that escaped his lips had Hanyi grinning.

"Yeah," he said knowingly. "Welcome to the Guardian Tournament."

"I thought I was in decent shape…" Dalton grumbled, struggling to coordinate his sore muscles to stand. As he tried to get to his feet, his body gave out and he fell heavily on the still-sleeping Mitoki.

"Ow!" Mitoki yelped, pushing Dalton and punching him weakly in the back. "What the hell are you *doing*?!"

"Sorry," he said, grimacing as he attempted to stand once again.

With a sympathetic smile, Keito offered a hand to Dalton, helping him up.

"Once you have something to eat, we should all go on a walk, work out the worst of the stiffness," he suggested.

"That sounds *awful*," Dalton whined as he tried to bend his legs to walk, still hunched over. "This is pathetic…"

"It's normal," Hanyi said from his seated position on a log near the fire circle. "Why do you think I didn't help you up? I can hardly move, too." He leaned back to look at Mitoki, who was easing himself into a sitting position, his face pinched in pain. "How're you doing over there, Mitoki?"

"I feel like I've been hit by a bus," he lamented, placing a hand over his eyes as his head began to pound violently.

"How do you know what *that* feels like?" the wolf laughed.

"What the hell is going on?" Eclipse mumbled, wincing as he became aware of his own sore muscles upon waking.

"Good morning, sunshine!" Hanyi greeted brightly.

"Morning, *cupcake*," Eclipse growled through gritted teeth.

"I have a new pet name!" Hanyi beamed.

"Why do I see three of you?" Eclipse groaned.

"Well, well, look who's finally up," Jikia greeted, walking through the trees to join them once again, Tarrena behind her, both carrying a basket filled with cuttings from a plant none of them recognized. "How's everyone feeling?"

The collective groans were answer enough.

"I thought so."

"Hey, just remember, you won the first set," Tarrena said, setting her basket down. "Hard to believe you're one of the finalists of round one with you griping and whining like that."

"You get in the ring next time," Mitoki challenged.

"You've got a few days of rest," Jikia assured. "I've got some things to help with redressing wounds and to ease the pain. As soon as you boys feel up to it, you should go on a walk, stretch out a bit."

"Again, that sounds awful," Dalton said, sitting heavily next to Hanyi.

"Can't be limping when you walk into the finals," Jikia said. "I'm sure even as we speak, the post-set news coverage is talking all about Team Dalton."

"What do you mean?"

"The news stations all across the realms are going to be tearing apart the matches from yesterday across all realms. It's how the tournament coverage fills the time between sets."

Dalton's face drained of color.

"Dalton, are you okay?"

"For some reason it didn't occur to me until *just now* that my wife probably watched all that yesterday."

Eclipse closed his eyes.

"Oh, no, I hope no one in my family watched, either," he said.

"I didn't think about that," Mitoki muttered. "Damn it, I don't want Rebecca watching the tournament."

"Doubt you can stop any of them from watching," Hanyi said. "They're going to want to be sure you're all doing okay."

"Hopefully Frieda's not letting Theresa watch any of it," Dalton said strongly.

"I doubt she would," Tarrena said. "But it's probably something you should all discuss with your families when you go home."

"I don't have to worry about that," Hanyi said. "No TV here."

"Same," Keito agreed. "And give your families some credit. I'm sure if they felt too overwhelmed seeing the fights, they would just wait for the announcement of the winners of each stadium to be sure you advanced."

The human Guardians did not seem appeased by the statement.

Dalton admittedly felt better after some stew and the strange herb concoction Jikia forced them all to drink. When Keito suggested they go on a walk for some light exercise and stretching, he felt as though he could manage the activity.

The Guardians started slowly through the trees, allowing their legs to find a rhythm around the soreness. A gentle breeze invigorated them as they came upon the nearby creek and filled their canteens before walking along the babbling water, enjoying the sounds of the woods.

Even though Dalton felt a weight in his chest and his head still buzzed from his nightmare, he felt calmer as they walked among the trees. His mind meandered from thought to thought, never fully grasping any concept before moving onto the next, allowing him to slip into a semi-meditative state.

He stopped to look over the stream, Eclipse and Mitoki passing him, lost in their own thoughts. Keito was slower to walk past him, but followed the younger Guardians, keeping them in sight. Hanyi stopped with Dalton, also looking over the water.

Dalton closed his eyes and took a deep breath, stretching, hardly feeling the soreness. There were a thousand things weighing on his mind but he tried to let them float away with the running water, only allowing the overwhelming nature of his thoughts overtake him for a second before he took in another deep breath of the clean forest air.

When he turned to continue on his walk, he jumped, surprised.

"Hanyi," he said. "Sorry, I think I zoned out for a while."

"That's okay," Hanyi said. "I do it all the time."

Dalton laughed, rubbing his face. "Where are the others?"

"Just ahead." Hanyi jerked his head back, turning and walking with Dalton along the narrow deer path they had been following. "Dalton, are you okay? You seemed a little distant yesterday, and just...with everything going on, I want to make sure you're okay."

"I don't know," he said, turning his eyes to watch his feet over the path. "I wasn't really expecting Kyan to get under my skin like that. During the match, it was easy to just dismiss what he was saying. But later...I don't know, I couldn't stop thinking about it. And then the nightmare."

"Yeah, seemed like a bad one."

"...something you get too, huh?"

Hanyi shrugged.

"Comes with the job, I suppose."

"I've had nightmares ever since I joined the Guardians. But lately, my dreams seem heavier."

"This case will do that to you."

"I'm starting to understand how difficult it must have been for you and Keito to come back to this," he murmured, refusing to meet eyes with Hanyi. "This is getting to me already and I've barely started investigating this demon. You two have been living with him over your head for decades." He chuckled brokenly. "I guess I should be the one asking you if you're okay."

Hanyi pursed his lips in an attempted smile.

"If I'm being really honest, Dalton, no. I'm not okay. But if I was really okay with going back on this case after everything, then there would be something *horribly* wrong with my sanity," he laughed. The levity died as Hanyi looked everywhere but at Dalton. "But I'm doing the best I can."

"I really appreciate you coming back to this case, Hanyi," he said. "I don't know what I would do without you or Keito. Even if you won't exactly tell us anything."

"We just don't want you to make the same mistakes we did," Hanyi said. "We lost a lot of people to this demon. *A lot*. And I would rather come back to this shit-show of a case than bring that kind of pain on you." His voice became tight with tears. "And I never want you to lay awake at night wondering why you survived when the others didn't." He swallowed hard. "It should have been me dead in that massacre. I was the one who hesitated. *I* was the one that convinced everyone else on the team that we should wait. It was my—"

"Hanyi, you can't wallow in that," Dalton interrupted, stepping in front of the wolf to stop him. "You heard Keito. There was nothing you could have done."

"He's only saying that to make me feel better."

"No, I don't think he is," he insisted. "Okay, say this demon pulls the same thing again. Say I survive what you did and I blamed myself for what happened. Would *you* tell *me* that it was my fault?"

"No."

"So why do you blame yourself?" he pressed. "You didn't lock the stadium down. You didn't set the fire. You didn't kill everyone inside. That was this demon, and even if you had made different decisions, something tells me he would have gotten his message across anyway."

Hanyi closed his eyes.

"I can't imagine what you've survived, Hanyi. And the fact that you're smiling and joking with us every day still amazes me. I know I can't take away the pain you feel at coming back to this case, but I want to also help you through it, the way you're helping the rest of us. If you want to blame yourself, I can't stop you no matter how hard I try. But I do want you to know that it was no accident you survived the massacre. You're stronger than you give yourself credit for and now you can bring this son of a bitch down for good."

Hanyi stared at Dalton, the ambient sounds filling the silence between them. He lowered his head and cleared his throat.

"Thank you, Dalton," he said. "And we are going to take this son of a bitch down."

"Damn right we are."

Hanyi grinned. "I like this little bonding moment we're having."

"I'm glad you're feeling better."

"You know what would make me feel even better?" Hanyi asked, raising an eyebrow. "A belly rub."

"I am not rubbing your belly even if you go into wolf form," Dalton chuckled, turning away and starting up the path again.

"Oh, come on," Hanyi whined, jogging after him. "One little belly rub. I won't tell anyone."

"Nope."

Hanyi shifted down into his wolf form, running in front of Dalton before dramatically dropping to his side and exposing his belly.

"Not happening," Dalton laughed, stepping over the wolf and picking up his pace on the trail. Again, Hanyi ran in front of him and collapsed, his tongue hanging out of his mouth and a laugh playing in his eyes. "Hanyi!"

Hanyi quickly got to his feet and dropped his shoulders to the ground, staring at Dalton for a long second before whipping around and running along the path. Dalton chuckled, shaking his head as he jogged to catch up.

Chapter Nineteen

Only ten minutes previous, the woods had appeared inviting and filled with adventure. But now that they were out of sight of their camp, the five men were hesitant to continue the impromptu trip through the trees.

"Derek, this isn't a good idea," one finally called to the man in front of the group.

"Oh, come on, camp's not that far away. We're safe," Derek said, rolling his eyes, tired of hearing the growing protestations behind him. "How often are we going to be allowed into this realm? We should take advantage of it."

"We should have at least told someone we were going," the youngest man in the group grumbled.

"Then they would have tried to stop us," another reminded him.

"Man, Chris, you see the size of these trees?" Derek laughed, looking up into the boughs. "You know, if the Beast Realm would just loosen up a bit, they would see how much money they could make from the human realms. We could fell these big trees, pay top price for them, and *still* make a profit on the amount of lumber." He pat the bark of the nearest tree. "How big do you think this forest is?"

"Dream on," the man behind him said, shaking his head. "Just because they opened tourism for the tournament doesn't mean they'll entertain business ventures."

"Brian's right," Chris said. "Bunch of dumb animals…"

The group continued their walk through the woods, griping about being unable to make a profit on the old growth within the forest. The further they walked, the colder the air became, morning dew lingering in the shade of the trees, giving an almost misty quality to the ground.

"Alright, that's enough, we should head back. We're going to get in trouble and banned from the rest of the tournament season, or something," the youngest insisted, shivering as the temperature seemed to drop a few more degrees.

"Nate, they're not going to ban us from watching the tournament," Brian said with a condescending laugh. "You have any idea the small fortune we dropped on these packages? You're lucky you're even here, since you're just the intern."

"We're building company trust, Nate," Derek added, stopping at the trunk of an even larger tree. "In fact…" He reached into his jacket pocket, extracting a sharp utility knife and sliding the blade open. "I say we leave our mark. Prove that we were here and we were here together."

"What do you mean?" Nate asked worriedly.

Derek tapped his knife against the nearest tree.

"We're going to carve our initials in this tree," he said, smiling as he stepped closer and began etching into the bark.

"No, stop. Come on, this is why the Beast Realm doesn't want human tourists."

"It's one tree in a forest of thousands," Brian said. "Damn, you are such a pathetic wimp. Just put your damn initials on the tree." He shoved Nate forward as Derek continued to carve.

"No, we signed—"

"We paid a lot of money to be here," Chris reminded him. "And I'm not going to sit around a camp for two more days waiting for something to happen until the finals of the tournament."

"But—"

"Shut up and do it," Derek ordered, slapping the knife into his hands and pushing hard on his shoulder, nearly sending him face-first into the tree trunk.

As Nate hesitantly followed orders, the final man, Peter, spotted something in the trees and began walking toward it. The white, lumpy mass was barely visible through the tree trunks and foliage, but as he moved closer, he started to notice just how *large* it was.

"Whoa...come check this out," he called, immediately distracting the others from carving.

It took the others a few seconds walking closer to see what had caught Peter's attention, but once they spotted it, they eagerly moved closer.

As soon as they were able to make out what was in the trees, their pace slowed and astounded smiles took over their faces.

"Holy shit..."

A mound of sun-bleached bones stood among the trees, surrounded by a circle of fallen tree trunks, each of which had been worn out in the middle to grant entrance to the pile of bones. Skulls and ribs twisted together around leg bones and antlers decorated with vertebrae that had tumbled down the pile of bones.

"What the hell is this?" Brian gawked, walking closer as he reached for his phone to take a picture. "No way a bunch of dumb animals did this."

"Who else could it be?" Derek retorted, also taking pictures with his phone as he approached one of the worn-away sections in the nearest rotting tree trunk. "This must be some sort of sacrificial alter or something. This is insane..."

"Maybe we should just get out of here," Nate murmured, his stomach twisting at the sight of the bones in the cold forest.

"God, you *wimp*," Chris barked, grabbing Nate's arm. "Just for that..."

"No, let me go!"

Nate struggled to get free of Chris' grip as he was dragged to the log and pulled through the worn section of bark to stand in front of the bones.

"Worried they're going to leap to life and get you?" Derek chided. "They're just bones. Nothing dangerous."

"I just don't think we should be caught snooping around here. What if it's some kind of religious site?"

"Well, *clearly* it is," Peter laughed, joining the others in the circle of logs and looking over the pile, his eyes bright with fascination. "Wonder if it's just deer and stuff in here. Think there are any humans?"

"Yeah, this is where they throw the corpses of humans who trespass," Brian said, leering at Nate.

"That's it. I'm out of here."

"No, you're not," Chris insisted, holding him back. "Come on, let's each take a picture in front of the bone pile. And Nate, I swear, you complain one more time, we will throw you into this bone pile."

Nate begrudgingly took his picture first and then was quick to take the cameras and phones of his colleagues, wanting to get their pictures taken as rapidly as possible so they could leave.

"This is some of the weirdest shit I've ever seen," Derek said.

"Why do you think they do it? Pile all the bones up like that?"

"Should the Mount of Marconian begin to tumble, as will the mighty mountains of mud and stone," a voice said behind them, causing the humans to turn to the dark figure shrouded in a cloak standing on one of the logs, his hidden face turned to the five humans. "And should the blood dry on the bones and become part of the cracked earth, the rivers will diminish and turn to barren silt. And with every season the Mount is not fed, the herds will flee and bellies will ache around their emptiness."

"W-what?"

"Or so the wolf packs of this area believe."

The figure stepped easily off the log, landing softly on the dirt, his unhurried step bringing him closer to the humans at a menacing glide.

"Who the hell are you?"

"A tourist, like yourself," he said.

"You're not a monk of this...weird death temple?"

The figure scoffed, the sound running up their spines like icy fingers.

"Oh, no, not even close. I don't believe that this pile of bones controls the seasons or migration patterns of the prey animals. But it certainly is a sight to behold, isn't it?"

"How-how do you know about this?"

"I make it my business to know as much as possible," the figure said, turning away from the bone pile to look at the humans. "I'm surprised to see humans this far away from the designated camps. Looking for a little adventure?"

"We didn't mean any harm," Nate stuttered, his entire body shaking. "We're going back now."

"Why?" the shrouded figure asked. "Don't you want to take more pictures of this macabre work of primitive animal art?"

"No…no, I think we'll just go now," Peter said, starting to back away from the figure, sensing fast-approaching danger.

"Take out your cameras. Take another picture."

"No, we understand," Derek said, also backing away, his body shaking. "We shouldn't be here. We'll go back now."

"Yeah, we-we get the message."

"Ooh, you were close, but not quite," the figure said. "See, this isn't about teaching you a lesson. It's about sending a message."

"Right, yeah, we get it," Derek babbled. "We shouldn't be sneaking off to places we're not allowed."

The figure groaned and the humans knew he was rolling his eyes.

"Look, buddy, we don't want any trouble," Chris said, raising his hands. "And you're outnumbered anyway. There are Guardians all around here."

The figure tilted his head to the side and the five men could feel the cold smile hidden under the cloak. "Not close enough to hear you scream for help."

~∧~

The overcast sky had Team Dalton feeling lethargic and they were more than happy to doze in and out of sleep with the Treneke Tribe, despite feeling more rested than the previous day.

Dalton was beginning to worry about an approaching thunderstorm as the air grew hot and his hair stood on end. He was about to ask if they should find shelter somewhere when a distant wolf howl startled everyone. The wolves perked up, their ears locking on the sound as Hanyi immediately fell into wolf form, standing tall, listening to the howl. When the howl sounded once more, Hanyi lifted his head and joined in the call, causing the entire tribe to lift their heads and join in. The sound was both haunting and deafening, and it filled Dalton with dread.

"What's going on?" he asked.

"I don't know," Keito said. "But it doesn't sound good."

The howling slowly trailed off and the pack remained silent for several minutes, occasionally whimpering as they kept their attention focused in the direction of the call. A few minutes later, the sound returned, but closer. Hanyi howled in response, though the call was much shorter.

It was not long after the short howl that another wolf appeared in the trees, moving slowly, his head and tail low as he approached the Treneke Wolf Tribe. As Hanyi walked cautiously over to him, he lowered himself to his belly and crawled forward, tilting his head and wagging his tail to show he was not a threat.

With him still on the ground, a long silence took hold of the forest. Dalton wanted to ask what was going on, seeing the agitated twitching of the other wolves, but he was too afraid to break the tense silence.

His own anxiety was mounting when Hanyi turned around and quickly stood on two feet, his face pale and his eyes wide.

"Hanyi? What's wrong?" Mitoki asked.

"Uh...there-there was an attack."

"An attack?"

"On some of the human tourists here for the tournament," he said, licking his lips nervously. "We have to go. Now."

Keito was instantly on his feet, starting toward Hanyi. The humans also scrambled upright, joining the wolf. Keito stopped and turned around, jogging to Jikia and Tarrena.

"In light of everything, I think it would be best if you stay here and protect the pack if needed," he said.

"Understood," Jikia agreed. "Go."

He ran to catch up with the other Guardians.

Despite the lingering soreness and lethargic energy of the day, the Guardians were able to keep up a steady jog through the forest for quite some time, following Hanyi, their minds racing with possibilities about what they would encounter when they came across the crime scene. Even though Hanyi had not specifically said that the tourists had been killed, he knew from the horrified look on his teammate's face to expect a bloody scene.

Even knowing that, he was not prepared to see five humans splayed out on a pile of discarded animal bones, their blood staining the mound of white, their expressions locked in unimaginable horror as their glassy eyes stared up into the trees, a line of blood drawn across their face under one eye, over the bridge of their nose, and under the other eye.

A team of Guardian Forensics was already taking account of the scene, taking pictures within the demarcated crime scene. Dalton could see further back in the trees a line of black-clad security personnel securing the area to be sure no one curious enough got too close.

Dalton was also surprised to see a familiar face within the crime scene boundary.

"Elder Ari," he called, ducking under the barrier to join him. He approached the Elder slowly, unable to tear his eyes away from the macabre scene before him.

"Dalton," the Beast Realm Elder greeted. "I didn't know you were in this area."

"Not nearby, but we heard about this," Dalton said, motioning to the pile of bones. "What is this place?"

"The Mount of Marconian," Hanyi answered. "It's an old, *old* site that is considered somewhat sacred to the wolf packs of the area."

"Including yours?"

"No," Hanyi answered. "This is outside of my territory." Hanyi's eyes also could not leave the heap of bones. "It's a ritual site, I suppose. Some wolves believe that the great wolf Marconian, a bit of an ancestral legend, died in this spot but his spirit was still hungry, still needed to hunt. So wolves would bring kills here to feed his spirit, and they believed that if the ever broke the ritual and Marconian's spirit was not appeased, the herds would migrate far away and the rivers would dry up and a bunch of other disasters would happen that would force the wolves to leave their home or starve."

"You don't think that a wolf pack did this, do you?" Eclipse asked. "Like a way to warn off human tourists during the tournament?"

"No," Keito said.

"There is demon energy all over this area," Dalton said. "What is that mark on their faces?"

"The killer's calling card," Elder Ari said with a heavy sigh. "Or a scare tactic. That used to be the mark of a very infamous demon known for killing without reason."

"I think we can drop the act, Elder," Keito growled, glaring.

"We don't know for sure that he's returned."

"You brought back the Guardian Tournament," the demon snapped. "Of course he's returned. You're baiting him, and we know that we're the bait."

Dalton also fixed Elder Ari with a hard glare.

"This is the same demon that Keito and his team were after before, isn't it?"

"It doesn't make sense," Elder Ari insisted, motioning to the humans on the pile. "Why would he do this?"

"To send a message," Hanyi said, raising his hands in exasperation. "It's what he *does*."

"He does seem to be answering your challenge," Mitoki agreed. "And you allowed the tournament to be open to the public, giving him a chance to do things like this."

"But why just these five? Why here? Why not go after the entire camp? It's right over there." Elder Ari motioned abstractly. "This is too small for him."

"Elder!" one member of the forensics team called, jogging over with a phone in his hand. "I've found something."

Team Dalton gathered close to the Elder, not daring to touch the phone as the gloved forensics member pressed the screen of the phone to play the video.

At first, the video only showed the ground, the image shaking and jarring violently.

"—we get it," a voice said through the recording. "We shouldn't be sneaking off to places we're not allowed."

A distant, irritated groan could be heard in response.

"Look, buddy," a second voice added. "We don't want any trouble. And you're outnumbered anyway. There are Guardians all around here."

"Not close enough to hear you scream for help."

The voice sent a violent shudder through Dalton's body as his eyes shot wide. He recognized the voice.

Before he could say anything, terrified screaming sounded and the camera moved, swinging over the ground as the man holding it tried to run. However, the camera suddenly flew into the air, showing flashes of the overcast sky before falling to the ground, the lens pointed up into the trees. A hand scrambled for it as a blood-curdling scream sounded amid bellows to be released and to leave them alone.

The phone was picked up once more and turned onto the bone pile.

In sharp contrast to the white bones stood a figure cloaked in black, holding one of the men up by his throat as two others tried to run away. The one being strangled began to turn red, his face contorting as the life was squeezed from him.

"Come on! Go!" one man whimpered, bumping into the man holding the camera. The image moved rapidly again, but in only a few seconds, the panicked breathing once again gave way to screams. The camera fell to the ground and was dragged through the dirt and fallen pine needles, distorting the screaming of the men.

Those crowded around the phone were beginning to shy away from the sounds of the men being choked and dragged. The distant gurgling was also a sound the Guardians understood, as they could see from where they stood that all five men had had their throats cut. The man holding the camera let out a terrified cry as he was dragged along the ground. He was hoisted up by the cloaked figure, the phone clutched to his chest to capture the murderer.

At first, all they could see was the black fabric draped over his chest. But as the man was shoved onto the pile of bones, the figure's attention turned to the phone.

"Recording, are we?" his dark voice asked, a smile lacing the question.

The man could only whimper in response.

"You're braver than your colleagues," the figure said. "Realize that this is nothing personal. You didn't do anything to deserve this. You were just the ones that happened to wander too close to the monster."

The man holding the phone began panting, panicked as the camera jumped with his trembling.

The figure lifted one hand, removing his glove slowly, deliberately, finger-by-finger until he revealed the pale skin of his hand, marred by pitch black designs that swirled over his clawed fingers.

He wiggled his fingers at the camera before snatching the device from the man's hand and tossing it aside. It landed in the dirt, leaving only a black screen as the backdrop for the man's final screams.

Silence took over the recording, broken only by the soft footsteps of the demon walking around the area and the hollow clacking of bones as they were shifted under the weight of the bodies.

"The phone ran out of space after another fifteen minutes," the man said, stopping the video. "No pictures of his face, unfortunately."

187

Elder Ari appeared troubled. Dalton was about to comment that he had heard the menacing voice in his nightmare, but was, once again, interrupted by Keito's abrupt turn to leave the crime scene.

"Keito?" Hanyi called.

Once outside the boundary, Keito pressed his head into the bark of a nearby tree, his shoulders shaking almost violently. With a shout, he lifted his fist and punched the tree, causing it to groan and partially splinter.

"Keito!" Dalton snapped, startled by the sudden outburst. "What is it?!"

The demon's fist connected with the tree three more times before the trunk gave way and split, causing the boughs to fall heavily to the ground as the trunk groaned and dropped to the forest floor, colliding with four other trees on the descent.

The demon stood next to the splintered stump, breathing hard, his bloodied fists quivering.

"He has a physical form…"

"What?" Dalton asked.

Keito turned, returning to the group with his eyes glaring angrily at the ground.

"He has a physical form now," he repeated sharply. "That's what he wanted to show us." He imitated the short wave of the demon's fingers. "He was showing off. He's been training these past decades to get stronger. I thought the Tournament Slaughter would have exhausted him, but it turns out, I've just been blind to how much stronger he's gotten."

"What are you talking about, Keito?" Eclipse asked. "A physical form? Was he an incorporeal entity before?"

"Something like that," Hanyi answered, his face even paler once he realized what had set off Keito. "He did do all this himself, with his *hands*. He didn't order someone else. He didn't possess another…*he* did it."

"How did I let it get this far?" Keito hissed.

"That doesn't matter," Dalton said, trying to keep his voice steady. "We know now. And, if he's got a physical body, we can kill him."

"It's not that simple," the demon whispered. He rubbed his hands over his face. "He's going to dance circles around us. Lead us on trails and do everything he can to destroy us, not just physically, but mentally. And now, he's even stronger than he was forty years ago." He motioned to the phone. "Who knows what else he can do now."

"Keito, how could you not know that he was getting stronger?" Elder Ari growled. "He's a demon. Surely you had to know *something*."

"He knows I'm trying to kill him. You think any of his followers would just walk up to me and offer information?" Keito snapped. "And I tried to take him down before." Keito began stalking toward Elder Ari. "I did everything I could, and the Elders *didn't listen*! I tried to warn you about this!"

"Keito, take a breath," Mitoki said, trying to gently push Keito away from Elder Ari.

"Why am I even pleading my case to you?" he asked. "Why would I think that you would listen to me now?"

Elder Ari did not respond, his expression impassive as he stared at the demon.

"Elder," Dalton started, "this demon is clearly dangerous."

"Aren't they all," Elder Ari said, glaring at Keito. The demon took a step forward but Hanyi immediately pushed him back.

"Let it go," he said strongly.

Startled at the sudden hostility toward Keito, Dalton hesitated before continuing.

"What I'm trying to say is that perhaps we need to take a different approach. This was Keito's case during the last tournament and that ended with a horrific massacre. Perhaps disbanding the tournament—"

"Your grandfather said you were throwing a fit about that," Elder Ari interrupted. "Listen to me, *all* of you. We did not intend for the tournament to be a public spectacle again."

Keito scoffed, rolling his eyes.

"But now it is," Elder Ari continued, his tone cold. "And we've decided that it will serve as an appropriate distraction for the people of the realms. It will keep the attention off the search for this demon."

"It will also distract *us* from searching for him," Dalton said. "How is this beneficial for anyone?"

The forensics officer backed away from the confrontation, turning to the bone heap that was causing an uneasy feeling to grip his insides. As he stepped closer, he thought he saw the pile of bones slowly expand before contracting, a soft rattle sounding from deep within the mound. He stopped in his tracks, his blood turning cold.

"Dalton, the information leaked. We had to control it somehow," Elder Ari defended.

"You should have controlled it differently."

"What are you going to do when the information about this demon reaches the people?" Hanyi challenged. "How are you going to control it then?"

"*If* it leaks, which we're trying to keep from happening, we will use his criminal record against humans to pressure the higher powers of the Demon Realm to turn him over to the DPC for proper legal proceedings."

Keito began laughing in disbelief, shaking his head as Elder Ari continued to speak.

"Are you an idiot?!" he snapped. "He's an Old Blood Lord, you *can't* bring him in for legal proceedings. You *know* this!"

"Wait, what?" Mitoki asked, looking between Elder Ari and Keito. "Is that true? You can't try him?"

"We could," Elder Ari insisted, though he was speaking only to Keito.

"*How*?" Keito challenged. "Not only are Old Blood Lords protected from most DPC rulings, he has extremely powerful allies at his disposal." Keito's entire demeanor changed, a dark glower taking over his features. "What are you going to do when he calls on them?"

"Um…Guardian Teban?" the forensics officer called over his shoulder.

"One second," Dalton said, holding up a hand. "Elder Ari, you better explain what your plan is here, because I'm not seeing one other than throw me and my team at him and *see* what happens. And it sounds like there's more politics involved than you've—"

"Guardian Teban!" the forensics officer yelled, catching their attention. "Something's moving in there!"

All eyes fell on the bones and the five bodies stretched out atop them. The other members of the forensics team backed away from the bones, hearing rattling within.

"What the hell…" Eclipse whispered, approaching the logs surrounding the pile of bones.

"It looks like…it's *breathing*," Mitoki said.

"Get away from there," Dalton ordered, motioning the forensics team away from the bodies and bones. "Elder Ari, stay behind us."

"What the hell is happening, Keito?" Hanyi asked.

"I have no idea."

As the five Guardians inched closer, excited yipping sounded around the bone pile. Wolves darted out from behind trees, snarling and gnashing their teeth at all those around the crime scene.

"Opalon Pack!" Hanyi announced before dropping down to his wolf form and baring his teeth at the encroaching wolves.

"We protect the Elder and the forensics team," Dalton declared. "Raina, this is a bad time to cross paths with us. We will kill you if you attack." He cast his eyes over the menacing wolves, not able to discern which one was the alpha female of the pack.

Team Dalton began backing away from the bone pile, doing their best to shield Elder Ari and the others from the Opalon Wolf Pack.

"You wouldn't dare attack your own Elder," Mitoki challenged. "The assassination of a Council Elder is grounds for immediate execution."

Still, the wolves stalked forward.

Dalton heard the popping and snapping that came with Keito's transformation into his animal form and soon the demon had jumped forward, putting himself between the wolves and the humans, his head low as he snarled.

The Opalon Pack retreated a few steps.

Then, the pile of bones moved again.

Creaking and clattering as the bones struck one another, the mound heaved, bones scattering down the sides to cover the bodies of the human victims, leaving only their heads exposed as ribs skittered down to encase the corpses as the mass of bones undulated.

The humans watched in horror as the bones twisted together to form a gnarled leg, another appearing shortly after. The bones stretched up to resemble a ridged spine as another clacking collection of discarded bones congealed together to create a terrifying visage that resembled several animals, its head twisted to the side on a thin neck.

The head wobbled as it moved from side to side, bones moving as it opened its mouth, a cacophony of sharp clicks shattering their eardrums before the front foot of the bone beast fell upon the earth with enough force to rattle the fallen trunks surrounding it.

As Dalton stared in stunned panic, the Opalon wolves leapt forward to attack.

Keito leapt over the attacking wolves to slam his bodyweight into the moving bones. The creature hardly flinched, its head swinging to retaliate, though Keito was far faster.

While the other Guardians were more concerned with the creature, the sudden ambush of wolves from the Opalon Pack forced them to focus on keeping the forensics team and Elder Ari safe. Dalton grabbed his dagger and shoved one of the leaping wolves back when a hot, sparking wave of magic washed over him. Eclipse had his fist raised to his shoulder, his magic arching over them in a protective barrier.

"I won't be able to hold this for long. We need a plan."

"Anyone have a gun?"

The blank, worried looks that followed the question told Dalton everything.

"How are none of you armed?!"

"How are *you* not armed?!" one of the forensics officers retorted.

"The security staff has guns," Elder Ari said, motioning in the distance.

"I can send up a signal, draw their attention," Mitoki suggested.

"As well as the attention of anyone else nearby," Eclipse reminded him.

"Have a better idea?!"

Keito hit the ground hard as the beast knocked him away. While most of the wolves were surrounding the barrier containing the humans, when they saw Keito fall, many ran to him, biting and scratching at him wherever they could reach.

One of the wolves leapt at Eclipse's shield. The power of the protection spell flung the wolf away violently, but Eclipse still flinched.

Dalton turned to the terrified forensic staff, their eyes flicking between the circling wolves and the bone beast that had taken a step away from the surrounding logs, loose vertebrae and teeth falling in its wake as it lumbered closer to the fight.

"Stay close to us and close together. If you run, these wolves will follow. Stand your ground. Mitoki, send up a signal as soon as Eclipse drops the shield and we'll do what we can until the security detail reaches us."

Eclipse staggered as he lowered the shield, but Mitoki immediately raised his hand, bright white sparks shooting high into the air to alert whoever was nearby that they needed help.

The Guardians did not have time to orient themselves in the battle before the Opalon wolves surged forward. Those on the forensics team bellowed and stood together, trying to make the wolves back off. Elder Ari had shifted into his lion form, growling menacingly and swiping at any wolf that drew too close.

Dalton was tackled by two wolves, knocking him to the ground where one immediately tried to tear at his jugular. He lifted an arm to protect himself, the teeth of the wolf sinking into his flesh. He pressed his other hand to the wolf's chest and with a sharp burst of magic, he sliced deep into the animal.

The second wolf was far more hesitant to attack once she saw Dalton shove her limp pack mate to the side and get to his feet.

Mitoki was protecting the forensics team, his hands almost impossible to see beyond the magic encasing them. Whenever a wolf tried to attack the cluster of humans, Mitoki would push them back so violently the wolves were left bleeding and limping from thousands of sharp needles of magic. Eclipse was fighting alongside the Elder, being sure most of the wolves were stopped if they tried to attack him from behind. Hanyi was lunging at the opposing wolves, going on the offensive and pushing back those he crossed paths with, blood dripping from his mouth.

When the wolves had stopped attacking him to focus on the other members of Team Dalton, Keito was able to turn his attention back to the bone beast. The clacking that followed every movement put his teeth on edge and every time he touched the creature he could feel the biting cold that seemed to radiate from it. But no matter how much he bit at it or tried to tackle it, it seemed unfazed, clumsily staggering forward and trying to retaliate despite its slow pace.

When Keito heard gunshots and shouting, he turned away from the beast to see the security detail for Elder Ari running through the trees to join the fray. The wolves began yipping and retreating, taking a moment to strategize how to attack with the armed men surrounding the Guardians.

A heavy, cold weight hit Keito in the side, knocking him to the ground before encasing his torso. The bones that made up the creature's hand pressed into his ribs, pushing him harder and harder into the dirt. Gunshots sounded and chips of bones rained over Keito as the guns were finally turned on the creature.

The bone beast turned its tilted head slowly, the rattling of cracking skeletons emanating from within as it growled. Keito struggled to breathe, writhing against the weight of the creature.

The wolves had encircled the security detail that surrounded the forensics team and Elder Ari, leaping forward in bold attacks whenever they noticed attention had been turned to the bone beast.

The beast released Keito, shambling toward the collection of humans, the bullets striking its dense body with no effect. Keito watched it move, trying to spot any weakness. It did not bleed. It did not feel pain. He had no idea how they could defeat it.

Thunder rolled overhead. Dalton shuddered as air grew colder the closer the creature drew. The volley of gunfire abated and the group began to retreat. Seeing the fear, the surviving wolves began closing in once again.

Keito got to his feet unsteadily, his heart falling when he saw that the nearby humans had also seen Mitoki's signal, hiding behind trees as many of them pointed their phones at the confrontation.

"Any ideas, Dalton?" Mitoki asked, retreating another step, trying not to trip on anyone else.

"No. You?"

"It's slow. Maybe we can outrun it," Eclipse noted.

"And lead it where? And what about the wolves?" one of the forensics team asked, fear causing his voice to tremble.

Keito put himself between the beast and the humans once more, his entire body emanating with magic as he lunged forward, finally pushing the beast backward. The first droplets of a rainstorm began to fall and another round of thunder passed overhead.

As Keito dodged the limbs of the beast, his ears picked up on something in the distance. The wolves also turned their heads, looking up into the darkening clouds.

When Dalton followed their line of sight he saw a dark shadow rapidly moving closer.

The bone beast turned its attention to the sky, rattling and clacking, the bones fluttering like hackles being raised in anger.

The black dragon landed heavily as near the battle as it could without harming the humans, though many trees still fell in its wake. The beast pushed Keito to the side once more, turning its attention to the much larger creature. With an angry roar, fire erupted from the dragon's mouth, igniting dried pine needles and dead leaves. The wolves yipped and began to retreat, knowing they stood no chance against the dragon. The fire charred sections of bone as the beast stalked forward. But the dragon did not let up, stepping forward, wings spread, fire consuming everything around it.

Hanyi was chasing off remaining wolves as the rain began to steadily fall. Keito limped closer to the group of humans, wary of the fire and ready to attack the beast when the dragon stopped its attack.

The rain came down harder, interfering with the dragon's flame and forcing it to stop.

The beast undulated and clacked as it rocked back and forth, seeming to study the dragon through the many empty eye sockets of the skulls over its body. The dragon growled, lowering its head and taking a few steps forward. Keito also snarled, moving closer and challenging the beast once again.

As the remaining wolves of the Opalon Pack cried and howled, disappearing into the forest as the rain began to beat down on them, the beast turned to follow. Both the dragon and Keito rushed after it, the unnerving clacking of bones piercing everyone's ears as it lumbered clumsily into the trees.

The dragon stopped its pursuit, shrinking to the form of a familiar young woman. She ran to Team Dalton and the others as Keito chased away a few straggling wolves.

"I saw your signal. Are you alright?" Tarrena asked, looking over everyone.

"Thanks to you," Dalton said with a relieved sigh, blinking against the increasing downpour, watching the water slowly extinguish the flames. "Shit, if you hadn't shown up..." He could not even imagine what would have happened.

Tarrena looked over the forensics team, Elder Ari, the security detail, the humans filming from the trees, and Keito, who limped back to the group. She jerked her thumb in the direction of the bone beast.

"So what the *hell* was that?!"

Dalton shook his head, wide-eyed.

"I have no idea..."

Chapter Twenty

The Guardians moved through the next hours by muscle memory. Even as Tarrena tried to get them to tell her more about the confrontation, the murders, and the bone beast, they knew they had other things to deal with before discussing the event with her.

As Dalton tried to get Elder Ari and the forensics team to the nearby camp of tourists, he noticed the humans hiding among the trees with their phones pointed at the group. Anger and dread filled him in equal measure, but he pushed the feelings to the side and immediately began damage control—as he had been taught to do as a Guardian.

He and the security detail made sure all the humans were accounted for and then led everyone back to the camp, fighting against the torrential rain that came down in thick sheets, threatening to slice through them.

Keito remained in his animal form, taking up the back of the group and watching for any further attack. The security detail mostly surrounded Elder Ari, though a few flanked the rest of the group as they trudged through the brush to the camp.

There was a collection of a few dozen tents set up in a field near the river. No one was outside waiting for them, but nervous family members and others who had fled from the confrontation were gathered in the openings to the tents, watching.

Dalton, Eclipse, and Mitoki easily began directing people, asking Tarrena to check over anyone with injuries and demanding to see those who had organized the trip. Eclipse made sure that everyone was accounted for—apart from the five murdered men— while Mitoki and Dalton helped everyone to their tents, asking them to delete any pictures or recordings they had taken on their phones. A few times they were tempted to take the devices to be certain that evidence of the bone beast would not be leaked, but they knew they had no legal reason to do so.

Hanyi made sure the Elder and forensics team were safely put into one of the larger tents to dry off and collect themselves. The security detail stood watch over the tent as Keito checked the surrounding area to be sure they had not been followed and were not in immediate danger of attack.

The Guardians moved in a haze, going about what they knew they needed to do while their thoughts were clouded with the terrifying visage of the bone beast.

Finally, Dalton, Eclipse, and Mitoki joined Hanyi in the tent with Elder Ari and the forensics team.

"Elder Ari, we should get you back to the Middle Dimension as soon as possible," Dalton said mechanically, too tired to think of any other course of action. The Elder looked up at him, opening and closing his mouth a few times as he shook his head.

"I…don't know what that was."

Dalton sighed heavily, sitting in front of the Elder and rubbing his face, only noticing how cold and wet he was when pain radiated through him at the touch of his frozen hands.

"Elder Ari," he started, "this demon is not playing around, okay? He's not going to only focus on the tournament, and the tournament is not going to keep anyone safe."

"…no one is safe," one of the forensics officers said. "Did you *see* that thing?!"

"We have an incredibly dangerous enemy on our hands, Elder Ari," Mitoki said. "We need more information to go on if you want us to go after him."

The lion shook his head.

"Keito was right," he breathed. "We were all blind to how much stronger he had become. How did he get so strong so quickly?"

"Where is Keito?" Eclipse asked.

"Oh, probably waiting for someone to bring him some clothes or something," Hanyi said, jumping up and leaving the tent.

Elder Ari let out a defeated sigh.

"Is there any way to bring this demon before Council as a criminal?" Dalton asked. "Are we trying to capture him? Or are we trying to kill him?"

"…you can't kill him."

"So we're trying to capture him."

"We can't try him, either," Elder Ari added.

"Are you suggesting we do *nothing*?" Eclipse gawked.

"This demon is already dead," Elder Ari said. "We killed him centuries ago."

"We? The Council?"

"It was decided that it was too dangerous to have him alive," Elder Ari explained. "The Council Elders at the time worked with Vestera Hizoku to kill him. It was only later that we learned he had heard about the planned attack and performed some forbidden blood magic to maintain his soul, even when his body was dismembered."

"That's why he didn't have a physical form before," Mitoki deduced. "Then the physical form we saw in the video was the result of more dark magic."

"Almost deep magic," Eclipse corrected. "Sacrificial-type blood magic."

"How do we make sure he's killed for good?" Dalton asked.

"…I truly don't know," Elder Ari said. "He's got friends in high places, *very* high places. It's why he could not be tried before and why he was assassinated rather than imprisoned. His position as an Old Blood Lord made everything too complicated."

"What's an Old Blood Lord?" Mitoki pressed as Keito and Hanyi entered the tent, Keito with a towel wrapped around his waist.

"One of the rulers of the Demon Realm," Keito answered. "The highest rung on the social ladder in our society."

"How was he able to do that, Keito?" Elder Ari asked, his gaze cold and dark as he stared the demon down. "I've never heard of him doing something like that."

"Neither have I," Keito said. "It's not really his style. But I think it was for the attention, for the show. He knew that there were humans nearby who would be curious enough to investigate. He's answering your challenge."

"He's so much stronger than before…"

Keito nodded.

"Do you think he'll attack this camp? Or us again?"

"Normally, I would say no," Keito said. "But after all that," he motioned to the outside of the tent, "I'm not sure what to expect from him."

"It does seem too early for him to make such a dramatic move," Hanyi agreed. "He liked to build things to a fever pitch. Countdowns, hidden clues, anything that made you feel the anticipation of what was to come without knowing what he would do. He's a showman. He makes everything a big production."

"I don't think he would use that…*creature* to attack the tournament," Keito mused. "And perhaps he will focus his attention more on us than the civilians."

"Do you really think so?" Dalton asked. He did not like the idea of having such a dangerous, unpredictable demon after him but it was preferable to tracking him down through a sea of bodies. He also vividly remembered Kyan say that Dalton was "the star of the show."

"I do," Keito said. "Council-sponsored team, sent his own team to size us up, made sure that his attack happened near a wolf territory which would assure Hanyi would hear about it…" He swallowed hard, his eyes lowering to his feet. "Plus, two of his old toys are in his sights again."

Hanyi also dropped his head, his eyes closing.

"Dalton," Elder Ari said, leaning forward, "I truly did not think something of this magnitude would happen. I did not expect this demon to be so strong. And…" He trailed off, seeing the darkness that had taken over Dalton's eyes. "You know I can't let you walk away from this case, though. Any of you. We have to find some way to contain him and destroy him, and if we can focus his attention somewhere, maybe we can find an opening."

Dalton wanted to snap at Elder Ari. He wanted to scream at him that the Elders already knew the demon and had misled him into being bait to draw the demon out of the shadows. He wanted to convince the Elder to stop the tournament and focus the entire Guardian Branch on bringing the demon to justice.

But something stopped him. Something about the way Elder Ari was staring at him and something about the way the Elder was handling the entire situation felt wrong. He knew that even if he pleaded his case a thousand times, the Elder would not budge.

As he bit his tongue almost hard enough to draw blood, the tent flap opened and one of the organizers of the camp leaned inside.

"I'm terribly sorry to disturb you," he said. "If there is a convoy returning to the Middle Dimension today, I ask that three of our members go with you. They are…badly shaken."

Dalton closed his eyes, suppressing the anger and frustration he felt churning in his gut. He nodded.

"Of course."

~⋀~

By the time the Guardians saw off Elder Ari and the three humans that wanted to return home early, Dalton felt the exhaustion deep in his bones. The rain had not let up and night was quickly descending. The members of Team Dalton did not speak as Keito took them back to the Treneke Tribe. The wolves had moved further into the dense trees to escape the rain and Jikia had set up a tent for them, which Dalton was thrilled to see.

"I was so worried about you," Jikia said, hugging each of them as they walked toward the tent. "I've got some hot stew for you and bandages if you need it…" Her words slowed as she looked over the drawn faces. "What happened?"

Tarrena approached her mother, gently touching her temple as Jikia's eyes shot wide.

"…what the hell was *that* thing?"

"We don't know," Mitoki said tiredly, ducking into the tent to search for his bag. Eclipse and Dalton did the same. Xana walked

199

on two legs into the tent to join them, immediately hugging Hanyi tight. Two smaller wolves lingered close to the opening of the tent, unsure if they should greet their father or give him space.

"Are you alright?" Xana asked.

Hanyi nodded, his eyes still downcast.

Jikia watched helplessly as the silent, tired Guardians grabbed dry clothes and sat heavily on their sleeping bags, their movements slow, as though dragging the weight of the world. Xana ran her hand over the side of Hanyi's face, trying to meet his gaze though he would not lift his head.

"You boys need to eat," Jikia insisted, grabbing some of the travel bowls she had in her pack and going to a covered pot in the corner of the tent. Even though she heard no response, she ladled the stew and shoved the bowls into their hands. Mitoki stared into the bowl for a few moments before setting it aside and dropping his head into his hands. Eclipse also stared at the bowl, making no moves to eat. Dalton refused to take his portion entirely, as did Hanyi. Keito took the offered stew, but also set it aside immediately.

"...I don't know how to help you right now," she whispered.

"There's nothing you can do, Jikia," Dalton said. "Thank you, though."

Tarrena crouched next to Mitoki, placing a hand on his shoulder.

"Hey, are you okay?"

Mitoki shrugged her hand away, dropping his hands to his lap as he stared blankly ahead. She turned to Eclipse, seeing the same vacant expression on his face. She sat next to him, rubbing his shoulder gently as he forced a tired smile in her direction.

"Dalton," Jikia started, crouching in front of him, "if you have to back out of the tournament to go after this demon, then back out of the tournament."

"I don't think I can."

"Of course you can."

He shook his head. "I think that if I were to try, this demon would focus his attacks on the tournament to lure me back. Seems like he'll herd me in the direction he wants me to go."

"All the more reason *not* to go that direction."

"It might be the only way I can get to him," Dalton said.

Jikia huffed. "How are you going to have the energy to fight this demon when you are wearing yourself down through the tournament? I can barely sense any aura around you. You are *drained.* The tournament, then this attack, and the Round One Finals the day after tomorrow—"

"I *know,* Jikia," Dalton snapped. "I know."

"You're going to kill yourself at this pace," the dragon insisted. "And you're no good to anyone dead."

The pattering of rain on the canvas roof of the tent filled the silence between the Guardians.

Hanyi finally turned around to look at Dalton, Xana's hand still holding his shoulder tightly.

"What do you want to do, Dalton?"

Dalton had assumed the same catatonic stare, sitting on his sleeping bag, his soaked and bloody clothes in a pile on the floor next to him, his body shivering as it tried to warm.

"Nothing," he said. He closed his eyes. "For now, we sleep. Tomorrow, we rest. And after the finals, we figure out how we're going to kill this demon. We're not going to leave the people of the realms at his mercy."

Even though the two younger humans were overwhelmed by the magnitude of their assignment, they nodded in firm agreement. Keito stepped outside the tent, the rain not as harsh under the thicker tree canopy.

"Then at least *eat* something," Jikia insisted, grabbing one of the discarded bowls of stew and shoving it into Dalton's hands.

Xana gently took Hanyi's face in her hands, turning him back to face her.

"You don't have to do this," she whispered.

He forced a smile, one hand taking hers. He did not offer any other response. Xana let out a long sigh before kissing Hanyi and stepping out of the tent.

When she saw Keito, her anger flared.

"It's your fault he's being dragged back into this, you know," she snarled, storming over to the demon. "It's because of *you,* because *you* need a damn *handler* that Hanyi has to shoulder this again."

Keito retreated a step from Xana, bowing his head.

"I know," he whispered. "I'm sorry, Xana. If I could have spared him—"

"You *can't?!*" she snapped. "I doubt this psycho wants Hanyi. It's *you* he's after!"

"I would have argued for him to remain in retirement but he insisted—"

"Of *course* he insisted! That's what he does! He's loyal to a fault and you know that! You should have been a better friend to him and kept him out of this!"

"Xana," Hanyi called, stepping out into the rain as the others in the tent leaned forward to listen. "Don't take this out on him. It's not his fault."

"Isn't it?" she growled. She stepped in front of her mate, taking his face once more. "I won't let you destroy yourself out of some twisted sense of duty."

"That's not what's happening," Hanyi insisted.

"Yes, it *is*."

"Xana, come on." He glanced around them at the wolves listening to the argument and the Guardians trying not to be intrusive while still eavesdropping. "Let's go somewhere else and talk about this."

"No, they should hear what this case did to you before!" Xana snapped. "It destroyed you, Hanyi. *He* destroyed you." She pointed sharply at Keito. "He put you in the path of this monster, and I will not let you follow him again."

"Xana." His voice was firmer, his eyes narrowing. "Let's go somewhere else and talk about this."

She growled, but before she could protest again, Hanyi dropped to his wolf form and nudged her leg. Reluctantly, she followed suit, the two padding into the trees away from the nervous pack and the overwhelmed Guardians.

Keito leaned his back against a nearby tree, hanging his head.

"Keito?"

The demon looked up, meeting eyes with Dalton.

"I'm sorry, Dalton," he said. "It's my fault this is happening. I should have finished this forty years ago." He swallowed hard. "And I'm sorry that you have to pay for my mistakes."

He turned away, walking in the opposite direction of Hanyi and Xana as he, too, disappeared into the trees.

Dalton reclined on his sleeping bag, staring up at the tent, allowing his overactive mind to wander as it needed. He knew that he could not allow his uncertainty and doubt take hold of him for too long. He fully intended to hunt down the demon taunting them and destroy him before he had a chance to devastate more even lives.

~∧~

Hanyi knew that leaving the Treneke Tribe in such an anxious state was a dangerous move. He was already struggling to prove that he was strong enough to have the role of alpha in the pack, particularly at his advanced age. Prioritizing the Guardians over the well-being of the pack would be tolerated to a point. But with the threat of a very dangerous and notorious demon looming, the patience of the wolf pack was wearing thin.

Still, Hanyi could not stand to see Xana in pain.

When they reached the nearby brook, swollen with the rain, Xana stopped and turned to her mate.

"Hanyi, please, walk away from this."

"You know I can't do that," he said gently.

"Why do you care about the orders of the Elders or Council? After everything that's been happening? Everything that happened in the last tournament?"

"It's not about the Elders or Council," he insisted. *"It's not even about Keito."*

"I find that hard to believe," she said. *"The only reason you agreed was because you knew Keito would need to be handled. You were always trailing behind him picking up the pieces. You did it with Hector and you do it with Keito."*

"That's not fair."

"No, it's not fair," she agreed. *"But it's true."* She gently nudged him with her nose. *"I love you, Hanyi. I want to protect you. But I can only do that as much as you'll allow me. And you taking on this mission...I can already see what it's doing to you. And I can't understand why you would want to put yourself through this again."*

"I'm doing it for me," he said. *"You said I can't let this darkness take over again, but it never left me. You know it never left. And it never will. I don't know that I want it to. I can't just turn my back on this. It has haunted me for decades, and it will haunt me until the day I die."*

"But why do you have to be in the middle of it?" she asked. *"You could have acted as an informant. Let Keito and the others go off and fight him. You didn't have to be on the front line."*

"I can't give you an answer you'll understand, Xana."

She went quiet, staring at him for a long time while the rain eased its onslaught.

"You know, I remember when we first sent Tsaym to training," she said, thinking back to the day their oldest pup left the pack to train as all Trenekes in the leader's bloodline did. *"He asked me if he was training to be a Guardian like you. I told him if he wanted to, he could, but you said that you didn't want him wrapped up in the politics of the Guardians. And once he left, I asked if you missed*

the Guardians, and you told me you were done with the council for good."

He dropped his head.

"*And even then I didn't believe you,*" she said. "*But as time passed and things stayed relatively quiet, I thought that, perhaps, you had started to shed the weight of the Guardians. But now that I see you picking that burden back up and trying to shoulder it again...I can hardly stand that I saw this coming and I'm still desperate to get you to walk away.*"

He leaned forward, pressing his head to her neck.

"*How bad do you think this is going to get?*" she whispered.

"*It's going to get bad.*"

"*Worse than before?*"

"*...I'm afraid so.*"

She turned her head, pushing it against his chest.

"*I can feel your heart on this, Hanyi,*" she breathed, pushing even harder against him. "*So no matter how bad it gets...I love you. I'm not keen on your self-destructive habits, but I love you and I believe in you.*"

Hanyi pushed back against her as he rested his head against her neck.

Chapter Twenty-One

Raina had been disoriented and confused for nearly the entire night. She had heard the howling and yipping of her wounded pack mates all around her, but only managed to find nine members of the formerly large wolf pack among the trees, many of them on the muddied forest floor, just as confused as their alpha.

As the night progressed and the sky grew dark, the remaining storm clouds blocking the moonlight, Raina and her pack had been surrounded by the spine-tingling clacking of the beast from the Mount of Marconian. But no matter how they searched in the dark, they could not find the monstrous creature.

It was not until the clattering sounds began to fade that Raina felt her senses begin to return. She could smell the blood in the air under the thick scent of rain. She knew the static causing her fur to stand on end was not from the storm, but from the magic of a nearby powerful being.

Rather than run from the sound of bones crunching together, she followed it, leading her wounded, disheveled pack out of the forest and into the plains, chasing the noise of the bone beast.

Even in the dark, Raina could see the structure drawing closer, though she was nearly in front of its crumbling edifice before she recognized it. The long-abandoned building had been erected as a Council Hall for the Realm of Beasts when the Dimension Protection Council had first been established. When the beasts rebelled against the modernization of their world and attacked all man-made buildings, the hall had been abandoned. There were at least a dozen such structures that had succumbed to nature, growing thick with foliage and crumbling with age.

The abandoned hall in front of Raina was half-eroded away, large blocks of stone trailing to one side as though the entire building had slid across the plains. The windows were gone and grass and shrubs had rooted in every feasible opening.

But there was a gentle, glowing light from within.

She proceeded cautiously, barely hearing the gentle rattle of the bone beast around the back of the building.

As she limped to the decayed wall, she saw the creature collapsed to the ground, slowly heaving in rattling breaths. A fire in front of the beast illuminated three figures, each clothed in heavy black robes, though only one had his hood drawn over his face. The three seemed to be in deep conversation when they turned to the wolves.

"Raina," the hooded figure greeted, his tone cold. "I am surprised you have the audacity to show yourself."

She flinched from the words but she could not stop herself from moving closer.

"*I tried, Master Yokouro,*" she said. "*The Elder had security detail. They were armed.*"

"I did not ask for excuses," Yokouro said, moving around the fire to approach the wolves. "You barely put a scratch on those Guardians and you outnumbered them three-to-one."

"*It was difficult, Master,*" she whined, shying away from him. She turned to the pile of breathing bones. "*Its presence was too potent. It hurt to move.*"

"You told me you were stronger than the Treneke wolves. I told you if you could damage or eliminate any of those Guardians, I would give you the loyalty of the Treneke Tribe. But you were chased off by some gunshots and a bad feeling like a base animal. Certainly not a trait the Treneke Tribe would find appealing in a leader."

"*Give me time to regroup,*" Raina insisted. "*Send me after the Treneke Tribe without the help of this monster.*" She jerked her head to the bone beast. "*I can defeat Hanyi and take over the Treneke Tribe.*"

"That's what *you* want, not what I want," Yokouro said. "What I ordered you to do was maim or kill the Guardians. I couldn't care less what happens to the Treneke wolves."

"*I can do it.*"

"No, you can't," he said. "You've proven that to me already."

"*Please, Master, give me another chance.*"

"Your second chance was that I didn't kill you myself once you fled the battle," Yokouro said. "If you had stayed out of my sight, I would have let you live. Instead you came back groveling with pathetic excuses. You've wasted your second chance."

The demon swung his hand in front of him, bright spears of magic erupting from his fingertips to strike the wolves. Some were killed outright. Others whined and cried as the magic embedded in their bodies, piercing them from the inside until they, too, went still.

Yokouro sighed, turning back to the two with him.

"Bit unfair to give them a task you knew they would fail," the demon with dark hair noted. "And with such personalized incentives."

"I am not responsible for her ego being too large to tell her when she's out of her depth," Yokouro said. He turned to the other demon, who had been mostly silent during their entire meeting. "You're disappointed in me."

"No."

"Well, *I* am disappointed." He motioned back to the creature he had formed. "This lumbering beast was nothing more than a scary thing to look at. It moved slower than a glacier."

"I told you you weren't strong enough, yet," the lighter-haired demon said. "Puppeteering takes power, concentration, and patience, all three of which you are currently lacking."

Yokouro growled, looking over the bones, studying the way it throbbed with the pulsing magic that held it together.

"It doesn't think. It doesn't react. And it takes too long to act on my commands. What am I doing wrong?"

"You created it, Yokouro," the dark-haired demon reminded him. "If it's lacking something, you have to figure out what it needs."

"The mutt demon couldn't put a dent on it, the dragon's fire did start to destroy the magical binds, but it didn't deter it," he mused.

"Are you planning on using that to fight the Guardians?" the dark-haired demon asked, raising a skeptical eyebrow. "They can easily outrun it, and you will tire before they are threatened by it."

"I performed the spell as you instructed," Yokouro said, rounding on the two demons. "Is it really that I do not have enough power to puppet it? How can that be possible? I'm one of the strongest demons in existence."

"You do not have enough power to puppet something that needs so much attention to keep it together," the light-haired demon told him. "It's bone. And five weak human bodies with barely enough blood and flesh to fuel the binding hex."

"Why use that against the Guardians at all?" the other demon pressed. "You showed them what you're capable of. I'm sure that scared them plenty."

"No, these ones are different," Yokouro said, a smile in his voice. "It's not just about scaring them, it's about pushing them."

"We talked about this, Yokouro. You have to—"

"I know, I know," the hooded demon groaned. "But I watched them. I saw the way they pushed through their fear. I can feel their resolve. So I need to find a way to break it." He turned back to the heap of bones. "I need to see just how far they'll go in a fight against me. Which is why I want this heap of worthless bone to pose a real challenge. I want to see what they do without their mutt demon and when they're facing something much bigger and more powerful. I need to know if they would put their own lives on the line to strike the killing blow." He turned back to the other demons. "Once I know that, I will know how hard I need to work to break that fighting spirit."

The other two shared a look across the fire before turning their gazes back to Yokouro.

"So," Yokouro motioned his hand over the bones with a small flourish of his fingers, "why don't you give it some pizzazz?"

The lighter-haired demon sighed, walking to the beast, his eyes scanning the structures that had formed to give the creature shape. He then turned to the ten dead wolves in the grass next to the bone beast.

Closing his eyes, the demon took a deep breath and then placed a hand on one of the skulls on the head of the beast.

The cold energy that surrounded the creature vanished in an instant, a wave of heat radiating outward as the bones gave a mighty jolt. The clacking and rattling became a constant hum, the bones vibrating until one of the legs extended and landed over a few of the dead wolves. With a skittering sound that echoed off the ruins of the building, bones circled the carcasses, passing them up the legs into the torso of the creature. Each limb reached out to the wolves, eventually collecting all of them, creating a glowing, red mass in the center of the bones. It thrummed and pulsed, a deep beat that preceded a shudder of rattling bone.

The light-haired demon removed his hand, looking over the reformed beast that had now taken on the shape of a wolf, though still formed from the twisting bones of other animals, the humans that had awoken it encased in ribs like a collar around the creature.

Yokouro smiled from beneath his hood as the bone beast shook its head, far more animated than before.

"Perfect."

~/\~

Elder Demetrius Renard of the Demon Realm had to focus intently on not rolling his eyes as he listened to Elder Ari complain once again about nearly being killed by a moving pile of bones.

"You don't understand!" Elder Ari barked at the other four Elders. "He's *much* stronger than we thought."

"He made a pile of bones move. That's hardly out of the scope of things he is capable of," Elder Celeste noted, also irritated with the beast Elder's rambling.

"He didn't just *move* a pile of bones, he turned the pile of bones into a *monster*. What part of that are you not getting?!"

"Syrus, calm down," Elder Teban groaned.

"No, you were not there! You didn't see it!"

"I said calm down," Elder Teban snapped, leaning back in his chair. The Elders' Chambers echoed far too much as it was, and he was already nursing a headache. While he understood that Elder Ari was concerned about the apparent increase in power displayed, he was in no mood to join in on the panic. "What exactly do you want us to do about it?"

"We need to reconsider things," Elder Ari stated.

"Are you insane?" Elder Lunar said. "The realms and the other branches are already teetering on the brink of all-out rebellion and you want to make us look like we're just grasping at straws?"

"We *are!*"

"The people don't need to know that!"

"What would you suggest we do?" Elder Celeste demanded. "This whole bone incident was one isolated thing in the Realm of Beasts. It's hardly cause for inter-realmal panic and we don't need to facilitate that by taking drastic action."

"Some of the tourists *recorded* it."

"So you said," Elder Teban said. "I called Lucas in to search through everything he can and see if anyone has uploaded a video of this bone creature."

"And if they have?" Elder Ari challenged. "There were plenty of people who witnessed it, plenty who can corroborate what they saw."

"People will shut up for the right amount of money," Elder Teban said shortly.

"And then we just have to hope that no one hears about the hush money," Elder Ari sneered.

"That's hardly the worst way we could handle this situation," Elder Lunar said.

The door to the Elders' Chambers opened. Since it was already so late at night and the building was mostly-deserted, they all knew it could only be Lucas Bex, the head of Council Intelligence.

"Well?" Elder Teban prompted, motioning him closer before he had a chance to completely enter the room. He rushed forward, reeking of cigarettes and barely containing his shaking.

"It appears a video was found uploaded in the Realm of Humans, Elder Teban," Lucas said, turning his tablet around to display the video. The Elders crowded around the screen to watch the short, shaky video of the confrontation. Elder Ari scoffed.

"I will be accepting your apologies now."

"How widespread is it?" Elder Teban asked.

"Considering it's only been public for a few hours, far," he answered. "I'm seeing it pop up on all the continents of the Human Realm. It will only be a matter of time before we see it in the Realm of Light and the Darkness Realm."

Elder Celeste replayed the video, pointing.

"The creature moves pretty slow," she noted. "We could say it's an animatronic of some kind. It doesn't move like a living creature."

"That's because it was made out of the bones of dead things," Elder Ari grumbled.

"Do you want me to scrub it, Elder Teban?" Lucas asked. "No guarantee I can get all of it, but I can try."

"No, Lucas," he said. "There are likely others that will start popping up from other sources as the first round of the tournament comes to a close." He turned to Elder Celeste. "If we lean into the animatronic angle, we could actually direct this in our favor."

"That we staged it as a publicity stunt?" Elder Lunar asked with a knowing smirk. "That we were creating more excitement around the Guardian Tournament?"

Elder Teban nodded strongly.

"We'll turn this unfortunate encounter to our favor. This will get more eyes on the Guardian Tournament and away from investigations. If we get ahead of this, people will be more willing to accept that we always knew this was going to happen." He tapped the tablet screen before passing it back to Lucas. "Get your teams on putting together information framing this as a planned publicity stunt. Now. Before it becomes more widespread."

"Yes, sir."

As Lucas hurried away, Elder Teban stood.

"Go home, Syrus. Get some sleep. And when you come back tomorrow, I don't your head muddled in idiotic panic. Understand?"

The Elders dispersed, Elder Teban giving Elder Renard a pointed glare when the demon Elder walked back toward his office rather than leave the council compound. But Elder Renard ignored the cold look.

He trudged back to his office, finding it difficult to think and even harder to breathe. The dark corridors of the Council Hall seemed to grow smaller as he approached his office door.

Once he had shut himself inside, he sighed heavily, leaning against his desk. He hated how foggy his thoughts felt and how dulled his senses had become. He knew he was far older than nearly every demon in Council, but his body felt weaker than he had ever known before.

As he rubbed his tired eyes and straightened, he spotted an envelope on his desk, the red wax seal proudly situated on the back of the expensive stationary.

He froze.

With a shaking hand, he took the envelope and broke the seal, deliberately taking his time to extract the letter and unfold it. He recognized the penmanship immediately.

Demetrius,

I hope this letter finds you well. I have tried on several occasions to seek audience with the Elders and have been consistently and succinctly denied. It is clear to me that I am not welcome within the Dimension Protection Council Compound, so I do hope that my messenger is able to deliver this letter to you.

I am appalled at the audacity the council has shown at re-enacting the Guardian Tournament without consulting me first. Not only does this put Guardians and members of the council in danger, opening the tournament for spectators leaves too much room for error for me to continue to ignore.

As I am fully aware of the distrust within the realms, I understand the way that Council chose to handle the information leaking to the public. However, had you consulted me when you were planning to reinstate the Guardian Tournament, I would have warned you of the dangers of coaxing Yokouro out of the shadows once again.

While you seemed certain that coercing Keito DeVero would lure him to the Guardian Tournament, it is in fact Dalton Teban's involvement that has spurred Yokouro into action. I do not know if Council is aware, but the two are tied by fate to confront one another. But Dalton is not ready for such a foe and knows nothing of the destiny they share. Now that you have placed Dalton in Yokouro's line of sight, there is nothing that can stop what has been set in motion. Yokouro will do everything in his power to get Dalton to face him in battle, and the result of that battle could spell destruction for all five worlds.

Yokouro has been training, and even in the last two weeks, there has been more activity with the Kage Lords' territory than I've seen in decades. I'm sure I do not need to warn you of the devastation those two can bring if Yokouro orders them to his side. I have done what I can to aid you with containing the Kage Lords, but as you are aware, even I cannot control what they decide to do.

I do not understand why Council seems so opposed to my guidance on this matter. While I can make conjectures about the beliefs of the Elders, I am confident that you, as the Elder of the Demon Realm, are often overrun by your human colleagues, so even if you were to warn them of the impending danger, they would not fully understand. My powers can only do so much, Demetrius. If this continues on the current, destructive trajectory, the only aid I will be able to offer is to remove the Dimension Protection Council from power and take control of all five realms.

Whatever path you choose, I hope you are prepared for the consequences.

Sincerely,
Lord Vestera Hizoku
Head Chair of Demon Council
Dragon of the Third Generation, Heir to the Throne of Chaos

Elder Renard's hands were shaking even more violently by the time he reached the intricate signature of the powerful dragon. Each word struck him deeper and deeper as he realized that the most powerful demons in the Demon Realm were beginning to stir to action once again.

He dropped the letter to the desk and cradled his head in his hands, trying to think around the pounding of his head.

Chapter Twenty-Two

"Welcome, everyone, to the Round One Finals of the Guardian Tournament in the Realm of Beasts! My name is Tecca and I will be your announcer today!"

"We get the same annoying girl?" Mitoki lamented, though the others could hardly hear him griping over the thunderous applause of the audience.

There were only six teams in the ring that Tecca had to introduce, each team having been the winner of the first set of fights in each of the stadiums around the Beast Realm. The crowd occupying the stands of the much-larger 1B Stadium were far more raucous, displaying their loyalties to the various teams by how loud they cheered when the team was introduced. Dalton tried not to notice how loud the audience cheered for his team, or the glowers that fell across the faces of the other teams when they heard the blatant favoritism.

"Again, before we get this round started, the Tournament Board would like me to remind you to take a moment to locate the two nearest exits to your seat. All exits are marked with overhead lights and tournament staff will escort you from the stadium to a gathering area outside in the event of an emergency."

Many members of the audience were bellowing at the announcer to get on with the round and stop wasting time. As other voices joined in, the excited energy in the stadium became nearly electric.

"The first bracket will be decided by the roll of a dice based on the registered numbers of the teams and will proceed in chronological order following the first match," Tecca said, speaking a little faster than necessary to appease the audience. "Please turn your attention to the screen for the results of the die roll."

The audience refused to quiet, stomping their feet excitedly as the result was displayed.

"Based on the result of the die roll, the first match will be Team Randall versus Team Dalton. All other teams, please exit the ring to your team boxes."

As Dalton and Randall led their teams to meet in the center of the ring, Dalton turned to Keito.

"You said there was only one other demon this time?" he asked.

"Not on this team," Keito assured, motioning to the team box where Team Ikanul sat. "But there are beast Guardians on this team."

"Are there any conditions for the match?" Tecca asked the two teams.

"All Guardians on both teams must fight in human form," Dalton said. Before they had been called to the ring for the start of the finals, all members of Team Dalton agreed on the condition, worried about getting seriously hurt or exhausted by the sharp teeth and claws of beast Guardians before they started tracking down their demon enemy.

While Randall did not look pleased by Team Dalton's condition, he did not offer any protestation.

"Are there any other conditions?"

Both team leaders shook their heads and Tecca called the match to commence.

Even though all five members of Team Randall tried to gang up on Dalton by lunging at him at the same time, Keito was quick to yank two of them away from his team leader, tossing one in Hanyi's direction before taking on his own opponent. Eclipse and Mitoki managed to wrestle away another opponent while Dalton dodged and retaliated against the remaining two members of Team Randall. While normally Dalton would have considered the two Guardians weak opponents, he was still exhausted from the encounter with the bone beast and therefore struggled with the two-on-one fight, losing focus when one of them managed to land a hit.

Randall pulled out a dagger, smiling when he saw the way Dalton eyed the blade warily.

"What? Worried I might make you bleed a little?" he taunted.

"Bet you never *really* had to work on a case, did you?" the other Guardian said.

"What does *that* mean?"

"You're Elder Teban's grandson," Randall laughed. "Nepotism has been following you your entire life."

"Oh, is that what it is?" Dalton said, fighting the urge to roll his eyes. "My grandfather likes to put me on cases that will likely kill me because of nepotism."

"Don't play dumb," Randall sneered. "We saw what happened the other day. We were there." He scoffed, circling Dalton with his dagger prepared to fight. "Of course it's Dalton Teban and his team defending Elder Ari against that stupid enchanted bone creature. Humans may not be able to spot a hex puppeting, but a Guardian can spot that in an instant."

"Nice publicity stunt," the other man snapped.

Dalton could only stare at the two Guardians circling him, surprised not only by the anger in their voices, but their conjectures about what had happened at the Mount of Marconian. Before he could stop himself, he laughed.

"See? Even you realize it's ridiculous!"

Randall launched at Dalton again, taking Dalton's reaction as proof that the confrontation had been staged. The other Guardian on Team Randall was also about to attack Dalton when a hand caught the back of his neck and pulled him back. Keito leaned over his shoulder, smiling at the younger Guardian.

"Hi."

He punched the other Guardian in the stomach, feeling the way he curled around the attack, stunned by the strength despite the fact it was nowhere near Keito's potential.

Hanyi was struggling to remain in human form, as per the conditions of the match, which also made it harder for him to effectively pin his opponent down to force a surrender. As he was delivering punches, hoping one would finally make the other beast Guardian falter, Eclipse and Mitoki were wrestling with another beast Guardian who was much stronger than he looked. However, the two continued to get in each other's way, getting more frustrated with each other than the Guardian bearing up to their blundered attacks.

Dalton was able to avoid Randall's attack better once he did not have to worry about the secondary opponent, and it did not take long for him to knock the dagger out of the other Guardian's hand, kick his legs out from under him, and press his own dagger to Randall's throat.

"Ready to surrender?"

"Not even close."

Randall struggled with the dagger, though he noted Keito coming closer to the scuffle, ready to help his team leader. Randall and his team had struggled in the first set of matches and he had barely recovered enough strength to arrive to the final matches on time that morning. Therefore, seeing the demon Guardian waiting to jump in made it harder for him to struggle.

He did manage to get the dagger away from Dalton's hands but as he turned to jab at Dalton, a foot fell on his wrist, pinning the weapon to the dirt.

He looked up at Keito.

"Why don't you call it a day here? You seem a bit tired."

"Screw you," Randall grumbled, trying to pull his hand free from the demon's weight, his other hand hitting weakly at Keito's ankle. The demon sighed, crossing his arms over his chest.

"I'll wait."

Randall weakly struck Keito's leg a few more times before turning his attention back to Dalton, who was watching his struggle with mild amusement. When Randall clumsily swung his free arm at Dalton's face, he caught the younger Guardian's wrist and then delivered a quick punch to Randall's cheek.

His eyes fluttered and he slipped unconscious.

Hanyi had knocked out his opponent and Eclipse had managed to put the final member of Team Randall in a chokehold.

"Tap when you surrender," he repeated, squeezing his arm around the other Guardian's neck. As Eclipse's opponent caught sight of the waiting members of Team Dalton, he nodded tightly and rapidly tapped Eclipse's arm.

Once released, he gasped for air, holding his neck as the color gradually returned to his face.

"And with that, Team Dalton wins the first match!" Tecca announced. The audience cheered in a feverish euphoria, screaming out disparaging remarks to the other team as they celebrated the strength of Team Dalton.

The only conscious member of Team Randall looked among the faces in the stands before turning his disgusted glare to Dalton.

"Because, of course, the shining star of the Guardian Tournament will always win," he snarled at Dalton as he passed, pushing away one of the medical team that had come to collect the unconscious Guardians in the ring.

The words resonated through Dalton's gut. Keito placed a hand on Dalton's shoulder and began leading him back to the team box.

"Come on."

Eclipse pushed Mitoki hard in the shoulder.

"What the hell? Why did you keep going for his legs?"

"I was trying to put him on the ground!" Mitoki defended.

"I didn't want him on the ground. I wanted to get behind him and you kept turning him!"

"Hey, hey, boys," Hanyi said, stepping between them and holding his hands out to stop them from arguing. "You won."

"It wouldn't have been so difficult if I had just done it alone," Eclipse said.

"Oh, excuse me. I'll leave you to tackle the behemoth alone next time."

"Hey, come on, we're a team," Hanyi said with a light laugh. "We're like family. Just hug it out and agree to do better next time, okay?"

Both human Guardians groaned and marched to the team box, leaving Hanyi to trail behind, pouting playfully.

Dalton's eyes were downcast as he stepped into the team box.

"Why so down?" Jikia asked. "You did well, considering how drained you all are."

"He said that the whole thing with the bone creature was a publicity stunt," he said. "That it was to make *me* look better, somehow."

"That's just jealousy," Hanyi assured. "Trust me, it happens a lot."

"You should have asked him why he didn't jump in to help if he was there," Keito said. Dalton let out a soft snort, one side of his mouth curving upwards in a tired smile.

"Yeah, I should have."

"It's okay to feel in a funk, Dalton," Tarrena assured. "You're exhausted and the last few days have shaken everyone up."

"I know," he said. "I guess I'm still processing everything. I feel like I have to pick apart every word to be sure I know what someone is really saying. Everything feels like it has more weight now."

He sat on the bench in the team box, trying to tune out the din of the audience as the break between matches passed slowly. Team Dalton was hardly injured, leaving them to spend most of the break in silence, studying the remaining teams around the ring and searching the audience for anyone that seemed out of place, though it was impossible to know for sure in the mass of excited faces.

"I've noticed there's no one like Kyan in the finals," Mitoki said. "No creepy draining bewitchment or anything."

"I noticed that, too." Dalton said. "So, the question is, do you think any of the Guardians here are loyal to him? And not because of weird mind control?"

"I don't know," Hanyi said, glancing over the faces of the Guardians. "But the demon on Team Ikanul is staring at you, Keito."

"I've been trying to ignore it," Keito said.

"Do you know him?"

"He looks sort of familiar, but no, I don't think I do," he said. "But since most demons do know *me*, he's probably got some grudge against me and that's why he's staring."

"You make friends wherever you go, don't you?" Hanyi teased.

"What kind of grudge?"

"Oh, who knows," Keito said, shrugging nonchalantly. "I've made enemies over the years."

"You're awfully casual about it," Jikia noted.

"It's just a part of my normal life at this point."

Dalton also studied the other demon, wondering if he had any ties with the demon they were pursuing. He did not sense the same cold malice he felt with Kyan, nor did his skin prickle with dread as it had upon seeing the crime scene at the bone pile. He was sure that the other demon Guardian was not a serious threat, and his own worry eased at ignoring the way the demon was staring startled him. His mind had already accepted that he could only focus on the larger threats and petty squabbles between Guardians was not his concern.

Logically he knew it *was* his concern, as part of his job as top-ranked Guardian was to manage internal feuds, but a Guardian's damaged pride seemed so inconsequential compared to everything else occurring around the tournament.

The sentiment that he was the main attraction to the Guardian Tournament sat uneasily in the pit of his stomach. He knew that his case had far-reaching repercussions and that he had been entrusted with the perilous mission of hunting down and destroying a very dangerous demon. But within the framework of the Guardian Tournament, it was clear that he was a favorite that was expected to win the entire event. The audience cheered louder whenever his name was announced, or whenever any members of his team appeared on the larger screens.

He could feel Kyan's words creeping back through his brain. The demon was watching the entire tournament. He had orchestrated things so that the tournament would be brought back into practice, waiting until those who could remember the tragedy of the massacre could no longer speak against its use. He had wanted the tournament to be a show, a dramatic backdrop for his plan—whatever that was.

But as Kyan had said, Dalton was the star, the main event that the demon was watching within the tournament, even as he studied public reactions and listened to the roar of the crowd. He was focused on Dalton.

Dalton's hands began to shake and a cold sweat broke out over his body. He turned to look behind him and the audience seated closest screamed in excitement when he spotted them. They waved, yelled encouragements, cheered at him with such intensity he could only smile awkwardly back and turn around, his heart pounding.

He was being watched. The audience was watching his every move. The other Guardians were watching him. And a very powerful demon that was untouchable to Council was watching him.

As he listened to the crowd behind him and saw his face appear on the screens again, he started to realize that people were not just watching him, they were *depending* on him.

The weight of the realization was almost too much for him to bear.

Chapter Twenty-Three

Dalton tried not to let his panic consume him as Team Myat fought Team Levete. Dalton hardly watched the battle, finding that the constant movement and cheering of the audience only added to his apprehension. His eyes remained on the floor as he counted his breathing and tried to remind himself that he promised not to worry about his mission until after the finals of the tournament.

When Team Ikanul fought Team Merek in a long, brutal battle, the audience became so invested in the fight Dalton was worried they would rush into the ring themselves to join the battle. Rather than keep his attention on the fight, Dalton was constantly looking back to the crowd, his already-agitated state making him more aware of each voice screaming at the Guardians in the ring.

Even when Team Ikanul defeated Team Merek and the tournament entered the standard ten-minute break, Dalton felt his pulse thudding in his ears.

He was brought back to the present by a hand on his back. Eclipse was looking him over, squeezing his shoulder.

"Hey, we need you to come back to the tournament," he said. "I don't know where you are, but we need you here."

He nodded quickly.

"You're right, you're right." He inhaled deeply, closing his eyes. "I'm here. Just got a little overwhelmed with everything."

"That's fine," Eclipse assured. "Just remember that whatever part of this is overwhelming you, you're not alone in the fight. We've got your back."

Eclipse's hand on his shoulder as well as the understanding eyes of everyone in the team box helped Dalton ground himself as he looked among his teammates and the dragons sitting with them.

"Thank you," he murmured. "I...think I needed to hear that."

He was able to spend the remaining break time centering himself and preparing for their next match, remembering their strategy and knowing he had to play the tournament to the strengths of his team.

"The next match will be Team Dalton versus Team Myat!" Tecca announced once the rest period was over. "Teams, please enter the ring."

Dalton straightened his shoulders and walked with his head up as he approached Team Myat in the center of the ring. He had taken note of the beast Guardian team in their previous fight, but he had not been able to watch long enough to see how easily they had won, so he was unsure how his tired team would fare.

"Are there any conditions for the match?"

"All animals must fight in their animal forms," Myat said immediately, cutting off Dalton before he had a chance to state his own condition.

"Well, there goes that plan," Mitoki groaned.

Dalton turned to Keito, silently asking if there was anything they could ask for in the conditions, but the demon remained silent, unsure what to suggest.

"Are there any other conditions?"

Dalton reluctantly shook his head.

The instant Tecca gave the cue to start the match, the five beast Guardians of Team Myat dropped down and lunged at Dalton.

Dalton was immediately surrounded by claws and teeth. He could not see what animals had surrounded him or even hear the shocked responses of the audience around the gnashing of teeth and deep growls. He thought he heard his teammates struggling to remove the beasts from atop their team leader, but he could not be certain.

He toppled to the ground, his arms raised, his legs kicking at whatever he could. Searing hot gashes were torn open across his skin and instinctive panic gripped his body. A primal part of him was begging him to surrender, that if he did not forfeit he would be killed.

But he remembered that the match was a spar, and despite everything in his body telling him he was moments from death, the beasts were not trying to kill him, only scare him into surrendering.

He curled into a ball, tucking his head as he took a deep breath, concentrating around the pain to collect his magic into a single shockwave that pushed everyone away from him, the magic hitting the force field around the ring and dissipating as the audience watched the sparking magic fizzle out before their eyes.

Once Team Dalton recovered from the shockwave, they leapt on the nearest animal, eager to keep the opposing Guardians away from their injured team leader.

Dalton slowly pulled himself to his feet, noting the tattered remains of his shirt becoming saturated with blood from the gaping slashes of claw marks and bites on his body. The pain was sharp and hot behind his eyes, making it difficult for him to concentrate on what was going on around him. He saw and heard the struggles nearby, but could not discern which of his teammates was fighting which animal.

It was only when he counted four animals in the ring that he realized something was wrong.

There was one Guardian missing.

Dalton began searching frantically for the fifth member of Team Myat, but there were no unconscious Guardians yet, and even when he looked up into the air, he did not see another animal waiting to attack.

As he spun around, dizzy and worried, the cheering of the audience became pointed, several people screaming at Dalton to look down.

Dalton did turn his attention downward, but not at the urging of the audience. A new sharp pain made itself known at his chest. He glanced down to see a large brown bat within his shirt, biting hard at his chest.

He let out a stunned yelp and tried to grab at the bat, though it flew from his chest, becoming tangled in the ripped confines of Dalton's shirt. His wings began beating rapidly against Dalton's chest and neck. He had to flinch away, blindly reaching for the bat as it tried to free itself. While the two Guardians were becoming frantic in the predicament, the audience could not help but laugh at the ridiculous spectacle.

The others of Dalton's team began walking away from their own fights, cut and bruised, but victorious. Even they were confused by Dalton's predicament.

Dalton began smacking at his shirt, hitting his own chest and only striking his opponent half of the time.

When he finally got hold of one of the bat's wings, the animal wiggled and writhed until it freed itself of Dalton's shirt. He then shifted into human form, Dalton holding one of his arms, and punched Dalton with his other hand.

Stunned and more than a little annoyed, Dalton huffed and swung at the Guardian in front of him, but as his fist sailed through the air. The Guardian had returned to bat form and flown away from Dalton's grasp.

"Get *back* here!" Dalton barked, jumping up in an attempt to grab the bat.

"Actually, in accordance with the conditions set by Team Myat—" Tecca began to announce.

Dalton ignored her, chasing after the bat as it flew rapidly around him. The bat dropped low to the ground and Dalton managed to push his hand onto his opponent's body, pinning the bat to the dirt.

"Got you!"

The beast Guardian shifted into his human form again, kicking Dalton hard in the legs and bringing the human to the ground.

"Damn it!" Dalton snapped as the now-released bat began flying once more.

"Since Team Myat stated in their conditions that all animals—"

"Get back here, you son of a bitch!" Dalton barked, chasing after the bat once more, ignoring Tecca and the growing laughter in the crowd.

"Would you like some help?" Mitoki asked, trying not to laugh at the determined look on Dalton's face.

"No! I've got this!"

Keito smiled, giving Dalton a thumbs-up. "Go get 'im."

Dalton managed, once again to grab the bat from the air, immediately pulling the bat to his chest and laying atop the animal on the ground, pinning him.

"Hey! Stop the fight!" Tecca barked. She ignored the booing and nasty words from the crowd as she gave Team Dalton an exasperated look. "Because Team Myat specified in their conditions that all animals were to fight in their animal forms, Taullam is disqualified for fighting in contradiction to those conditions."

Dalton's body jolted as the beast Guardian once again took a human form, angrily pushing Dalton off his back.

"Get off of me," he grumbled, getting to his feet to dust off.

"And with the final disqualification, the win goes to Team Dalton!"

Dalton also got up from the ground, wobbling a little as he tried to dust off what was left of his clothes without aggravating the cuts that covered his body.

"How're you doing there, boss?" Eclipse asked, looking over Dalton's wounds, trying to laugh off how nervous he was about the extent of the injuries.

"I kinda hate that I won that on a technicality," Dalton panted. He leaned on his knees. "I also hate that that's the *second* time today I was jumped by five Guardians at once!"

Eclipse brought Dalton back to the team box, supporting him as he limped gingerly out of the ring. As he guided him up the stairs he made a worried joke about Dalton's injuries being serious enough to warrant a visit to the medical team.

"If he sees the medical team he might be disqualified from this last match," Jikia warned.

"I'm alright," Dalton assured. "You can heal me up a bit, can't you?"

"I can close the worst of your cuts, but I can't replace all the blood you've lost."

"Not to mention the rest of you have a lot of cuts yourself," Tarrena noted, turning Eclipse's arm to study a heavily-bleeding gash. She hovered her hand over the wound, her healing energy transferring in blue tendrils of magic. "I don't know that we can heal all these and whatever you obtain in this last match..."

"I'm not badly hurt," Hanyi said.

"Neither am I," Keito seconded.

"Dalton definitely got the worst of it," Mitoki agreed. "Focus on him. This next team has the demon Guardian, so we should try to avoid having any of us disqualified due to injury."

"I can deal with the demon," Keito assured.

"With the way he's been glaring at you, we can't be too careful," the youngest said.

"There are ways to make the match one-on-one," Hanyi suggested. "And you can always request the two demons fight separately so that he's not a wild card in the match."

"I don't feel comfortable letting Dalton fight in this condition," Jikia said, moving her hand away from another large wound she had managed to mostly-heal. "Remember, it's not just the tournament you have to deal with."

"I think I'm alright to fight," Eclipse said, standing to block Dalton from the view of the cameras as they, once again, focused on his disheveled state.

"I think I'm alright, too," Mitoki said.

"Have you seen those claw marks across your leg?" Tarrena grumbled.

"In the end, Dalton, you have to make the call," Hanyi said. "How do you feel? Do you want to fight?"

"Not really," Dalton said. He winced as more sharp needles of healing energy stitched his skin together. "I honestly don't know what to do. I think, as long as I don't have to worry about that demon, or the tiger Guardian on his team, I'll be alright. Their last fight was long, so they're probably tired as well."

"That's true," Jikia said, clearly debating with herself about whether she wanted to let Dalton walk into the ring again.

The Guardians exchanged uncertain glances, waiting for someone to make a decision.

"How would you have handled this, Keito? With your team?" Dalton asked, finally turning to the demon for advice.

"...I would request a separate fight between Ikunal and myself," he said. "And then I would have told you to take on the weakest member of the opposing team while the others dealt with the rest. But it would have been a gamble for me, too."

"How can we make this a one-on-one match?" Mitoki pressed.

"We'd have to get the medical team to declare Dalton ineligible to finish the match. It wouldn't harm our advancement in the tournament, but it does impact rankings," Hanyi said. "Which impacts how we're bracketed in subsequent rounds."

"I think I only caught about half of that," Dalton groaned, rubbing his temple.

"I can watch Dalton's back in the match if you can take care of the demon," Eclipse told Keito. "Sorry, Jikia, I don't remember most of the things you told us about ranking and bracketing, but I don't think we should show any form of weakness right now."

The team trainer ground her teeth together, finally nodding reluctantly.

"I hate that I see your logic, but you're right."

"Then I'll request a separate match between Keito and Ikanul," Dalton said. "And will that happen first or last?"

"First."

"Good, that will give me some more time to rest before we face the rest of the team."

Keito looked across the ring at Ikanul, seeing that he was also locked in heated discussion with his own teammates, who were heavily bandaged and also quite exhausted from their previous match. He imagined that the conversation was progressing similarly in their team box.

"May I have your attention please?" Tecca started into her microphone. "The ten-minute rest period is over, which means it is now time to move on to the final match of Round One of the Guardian Tournament!"

Her own excitement was bolstered by the hollering of the audience.

"The final match is Team Dalton versus Team Ikanul. Guardians, please meet at the center of the ring."

Chanting and rhythmic stomping feet filled the stadium as the ten Guardians approached one another. They could feel the excitement of the crowd swimming around them in thick, static energy as the cameras all rotated to focus on the final two teams.

"Guardians, are there any conditions for the match?" Tecca asked, her voice trembling with barely-contained delight. "Now that two demons have entered the ring, exclusive fights between demons are permitted to ensure the safety of the human Guardians."

Keito smiled, shrugging one shoulder

"Why not?" he said. "What do you say? One-on-one? You've been eyeing me this entire time."

Ikanul barked a laugh.

"Sure you want to face me in one-on-one?" he challenged. "You must be tired, considering all your extracurricular activities."

"I feel just fine."

"Of course you do," Ikanul said. "You're Keito DeVero, after all. You're always fine somehow."

Dalton did not miss the minimal way Keito's expression fell at the odd weight in the statement.

"Guardians?" Tecca asked.

Dalton turned to Keito for confirmation, and when his demon teammate nodded, he raised his voice.

"I agree to have the demons fight in an exclusive match first," he said.

Ikanul raised his voice as well.

"Why make it that boring?" he asked. "If Keito really is feeling up to it, why don't we make this a Martyr Match and bet it all?"

The audience, who had been waiting with bated breath to hear if the demons were going to fight on their own, began murmuring in confusion, not understanding the condition.

"Translation?" Dalton asked Hanyi.

"A Martyr Match is a type of one-on-one match," he said. "One representative from each team will fight and whoever wins that match wins for their whole team."

"Then that's good for us," Dalton said. Deciding to ignore the worried look on Hanyi's face, he turned to Ikanul.

"A match between you and Keito that will determine the winner of this round?" Dalton asked.

"Such a condition must first be approved by the Tournament Board. If the challenge of a Martyr Match is accepted by both the Tournament Board and Keito DeVero, the exclusive fight between these two will determine who walks away the winner of Round One of the Guardian Tournament."

As the audience listened to Tecca's explanation, their fervor escalated. They were screaming at the Guardians, the announcer, and the glass of the VIP Box to approve the match, thrilled by the mere idea of such a high-stakes fight.

The soft chime of the announcement system immediately silenced the crowd as a man spoke from the VIP Box.

"The Tournament Board has decided to approve the challenge of a Martyr Match between Ikanul Zahl and Keito DeVero."

Tecca was nearly shaking in excitement as she turned back to Keito, yelling into the microphone as the audience erupted in noise.

"Keito DeVero, do you accept the challenge?"

Keito turned to Dalton.

"Are you okay with this?"

"Is there any chance you're actually going to lose?" Dalton asked.

"Always a small chance," Keito said.

"I'm willing to take the risk. If nothing else, it will give us all more time to focus on other things."

Keito laughed quietly and nodded.

"I accept."

The other Guardians had to strain to hear Tecca telling them to leave the ring for the start of the Martyr Match. Dalton stumbled a bit on his way back and Hanyi had to help him climb the stairs into the team box as his head became light from the long trek to the center of the ring and back. He sat heavily next to Jikia, trying to get the world to stop spinning around him.

"So what do you think?" Eclipse asked, sitting next to Dalton with a sigh. "Ten minutes and we can leave?"

The others laughed lightly, though Hanyi only barely mustered a smile.

"You don't think he's actually in danger of losing, do you?" Tarrena pressed, seeing the hesitant look.

"No, not really. Keito's likely much stronger than Ikanul," Hanyi said. "It just surprises me that he was so willing to bet his team's progress in the tournament on a one-on-one fight with *the* Keito DeVero. It seems strange to me."

"Ego can blind a lot of people," Mitoki agreed. "But Keito will knock him down a few pegs."

"Maybe."

"Well, now you're starting to worry me," Dalton said.

"It's just like Keito said. The politics between demons can get very complicated, and Keito has made a lot of enemies in his years. I just worry that this demon will know how to strike the right nerve."

"Are there any conditions for the Martyr Match?" Tecca asked.

"Can you think of anything, Wandering Child?"

"Do not call me that," Keito growled.

"Why not?"

"Because that's not who I am anymore."

"Not what I've heard," Ikanul said, raising a skeptical eyebrow.

"Do you have anything you want to limit during our fight, Ikanul?" Keito prompted, his expression becoming cold.

"No."

"Me neither."

"Remember, you are *not* allowed in your animal forms unless you expressly ask for the condition," Tecca said.

"That won't be necessary. Two legs is just fine," Ikanul said.

"If there are no conditions, you may begin!"

Ikanul moved first, sprinting forward at Keito with his claws poised for a swipe at the older demon's face. Keito easily dodged, leading Ikanul around the ring as he watched the way the demon moved, trying to spot any glaring weaknesses in his form.

To the audience, the demons were moving extremely fast, the cameras struggling to follow them. But Keito was hardly struggling to run from the other demon. He began to wonder why the other Guardian was moving so slowly.

He turned, going on the offensive and beginning his own chase.

"Are you trying to drag this out?" he asked, swiping at the younger demon though Ikanul dodged.

"No, not necessarily."

Keito retreated, slowing with the other Guardian until they were standing to one side of the ring, staring at one another.

"What do you want from me?" Keito asked.

Ikanul tilted his head to the side, opening his mouth slowly.

"I have been wondering for decades what it would be like to stand in front of you," he said. "But you are not what I expected."

"Who is your Old Blood Lord?"

"I don't have one," Ikanul answered. "I was raised in the Middle Dimension after my family lost their title and were forced to flee in disgrace. All because of some *kid*."

The audience was becoming impatient with the two Guardians standing still in the ring, yelling at them to continue the fight and making it impossible for anyone else to hear their conversation.

Keito's eyes widened.

"You can't be Prevek's son, you're too young."

"His grandson," Ikanul corrected. "Then you do remember him."

"Of course I do."

"Is it true, then? That you killed him?"

"...not directly."

"But you were the cause."

"Unfortunately, yes. And it is something I live with every day," Keito said. "But this is not the time or place to bring about a family grudge. I tried to warn your grandfather to stay away from me—"

"I don't want to hear your excuses!" Ikanul snapped. "I don't care." He shook his head. "What you did…it forced me to become a Guardian."

"Just to find and confront me?"

"Because I had no other way to exist!" he barked. "What else can a refugee demon do but submit to the control of Council? I couldn't return to the realm. I'd be a defector. A human-sympathist."

"Then you stand behind this extremist movement brewing behind the tournament?"

"Where else *can* I stand?!" Ikanul growled, lunging forward. "I don't understand how you can oppose him! You, of all demons, should be on his side. Why aren't you?!"

The younger demon began attacking with earnest, bringing the audience back up to a fever pitch of excitement as the blurring shapes dashed over the dirt, finally landing attacks and causing the other to bleed or stumble.

"Because I don't believe in what he's trying to do," Keito said when he pinned the younger Guardian against the wall of the ring. "And I can tell that you don't believe in him, either."

"You don't know what I believe!"

Ikanul's head collided with Keito's face, stunning him long enough for the other demon to wrestle him to the ground, scratching and biting at him, his deep growl causing Keito to reflexively bare his teeth.

"I can see that you're struggling," Keito said. "Listen to me," he gasped, pushing back on the younger demon as Ikanul's hands closed around his throat. "If he was really advocating for better treatment of demons, why was everyone so quick to turn on him? How could other demons in the realm support his assassination if he was working for the equal treatment of demons?"

Ikanul shook his head, his hands beginning to shake.

"I don't know what to do, Keito…"

"Be better than he is," Keito choked, straining as his claws cut into his opponent's wrists, pushing the hands away from his throat. "Your grandfather was killed because of Yokouro. Yes, I was there, but it was because of the fear and confusion he created that your grandfather was murdered. And if he gains any more ground, things will get much worse for demons. He's not trying to make things better for us. He's trying to bring us all under *his* control."

Better able to breathe, Keito twisted his torso and struck the back of his fist against Ikanul's cheek. He flipped the younger demon to the ground, pinning him.

"I understand your fear," he said. "It's easier to follow him, but I know you can feel that it's not the right thing to do. You're a good soul, like your grandfather was. Don't sully his memory by allying with the demon that caused his destruction."

With an angry shout and a flex of magic, Ikanul threw Keito backward, rounding on him and charging forward, claws and teeth bared, roaring angrily. Keito retreated, nodding.

"That's fine," he said. "Take out your frustration here. Think about everything he's taken from you and your family. Get the anger out of your system."

Dalton became worried that the fight had taken a dangerous turn for Keito. The younger demon was roaring and growling, his movements sharp and pointed, drawing blood from Keito on more than one occasion while Keito barely retaliated. The audience drank it all in, excitement thrumming through their bodies even though they could hardly make out the details of the fight between the demons.

But Keito could feel the emotional shaking of the younger demon's arms and knew that he was not in danger.

When Ikanul faked a retreat, Keito following him, he changed direction and tackled Keito to the ground, both of them rolling several times before coming to a stop with Keito straining to pin him down.

Keito spared a glance at the stands and smiled.

"Wanna give them a show?"

Breathless and shaking, Ikanul grinned.

"Let's see if you live up to your reputation."

In an instant, both demons were up once more, feeding off the cheering of the crowd as they sparred. As the younger demon began to tire, they came to the silent understanding of who would win their match, but Ikanul continued the spar until he could not push the older demon away.

Keito rolled him, wrapping an arm around his neck and locking his legs around him.

"Had enough?" he asked.

As the roar of the audience threatened to shatter their eardrums, Ikanul struggled half-heartedly and finally tapped Keito's arm in defeat.

The excited cries from the stands rattled the stadium, creating a high-pitch whining feedback on the speakers as Tecca loudly announced Team Dalton the winners of the first round of the Guardian Tournament.

Chapter Twenty-Four

Leaving the stadium was a far more dramatic ordeal than any member of Team Dalton was prepared to handle. As Keito and Ikanul shook hands and parted, the other members of each team entered the ring to meet them, only able to nod and smile in acknowledgement as the nearly-riotous celebrations in the stands made hearing each other impossible.

Even after they were officially called the winners of the round in a short closing ceremony discussing the next round of the tournament, Dalton and the others agreed to wait for Jikia and Tarrena in their team room as they met with the Tournament Board. Dalton was very weak on his feet and was happy to rest in the relative quiet of the small room while they gathered their things.

"Hard to believe that it's just...done. Round one is over," Mitoki said.

"Don't worry, we still have five more to get through," Eclipse said.

"No need to bring down the mood," Hanyi whined. "Enjoy your victory. It was well-earned."

"I feel like I'm going to need to sleep for a week to recover," Eclipse groaned. "Even on difficult cases, I don't know that I've ever pushed my endurance to this extent."

"That's why the tournament was believed to make Guardians stronger," Keito said. "But it's also the reason there are two months between rounds. The break is necessary."

"How're you holding up, Dalton?" Mitoki asked, noting the way he held his head in his hands.

"I just want to wash up, change my clothes, and get some sleep," he said. "I'm really starting to feel the blood loss."

"You know, they really should have extra sets of clothes in these team rooms," Hanyi noted, shaking his head in disappointment.

"We'll just have to start packing emergency clothes with our bandages," Mitoki joked. "I have my jacket Dalton, if you want it. It probably won't fit you, but I still have a mostly-intact shirt."

"The same can't be said for the rest of your clothes," Dalton laughed, pointing at the shredded fabric on the outside of his right thigh. "Thank you for the offer, but I'm alright."

"Next round, pack more clothes," Mitoki said with a strong nod.

When the dragons collected them from the team room, they trudged through the dark hallway to the exit, the adrenaline almost completely gone, leaving only room for bone-wracking fatigue.

But the outside of the stadium was crowded with excited audience members and tournament staff. The tourists let out thrilled cries as they surged forward, fighting against the interlocked arms of the staff to reach for Team Dalton. Stunned and unsure how to react, Dalton moved forward at Jikia's gentle guidance, looking among the flushed faces around him.

"Guardian Teban!" one man called, leaning forward with his camera extended. "How does it feel to win the first round of the new Guardian Tournament?!"

"Were you at all worried that you might not win this round?!" a woman called, thrusting her own camera forward, the badge reading PRESS on her chest telling Dalton why there were so many cameras directed at him.

"It must be difficult to face your own subordinates in the Guardian Branch in such a brutal fighting sport. Do you think it will affect the morale of the other Guardians?!"

Dalton offered a wobbly smile to all the cameras, not sure where to focus his attention.

"I am just impressed at the strength of the Guardians in the branch," Dalton said. "I feel more secure in the Guardians' ability to protect the realms knowing how strong and determined they can be."

"Are you worried one of your subordinates will defeat you in later rounds?!"

Dalton laughed, leaning on Jikia as the blood loss became harder to fight. "I am more concerned about how many other Guardians are so eager to best me in the ring."

"No more questions," Jikia said shortly, leading Dalton away as they called after the Guardians, wanting to conduct full interviews and pick apart every feeling they had about the first round of the tournament.

Unfortunately, they had to cross a large plain in front of 1B Stadium to reach enough privacy for Keito to shift into his animal form and take them back to the Treneke Wolf Tribe. Keito had to move slower than before, worried about Dalton's compromised balance. When they came upon the wolves and the tent they had left up from the previous rainstorms, the pack greeted them excitedly, yipping and howling when Tarrena announced they had won the first round.

Jikia immediately set to making the Guardians food and collecting herbs that would help them heal and recuperate their energy. The five men wandered toward the hot springs, all of them keeping a careful eye on Dalton, more worried about his inability to balance than their own wounds.

After some debate about Dalton being able to sit in the hot water without passing out, they decided it was best to wash quickly and return to the pack, eager to get some rest, despite the early afternoon hour.

They had barely entered the tent when Jikia shoved full bowls of dark green leaves and meat in their hands, demanding they eat everything in the bowl before they were allowed to crawl into their sleeping bags. By the time they had finished eating, Dalton was the only one reclined on his sleeping bag, the others feeling tired, but awake enough to sit around and chat lightly. Xana had also joined them in the tent, leaning against Hanyi's shoulder, mostly-silent.

"I still can't get over how, the moment we leave the stadium, the tournament feels like a distant memory," Mitoki mused.

"I call it post-fight fatigue," Hanyi declared.

"No, Master Linnel was the one who called it that," Keito corrected. "Our masters used to believe that our brains enter such a state of heightened stress that we try to move past it as quick as possible once the adrenaline wears off."

"But you all did very well," Jikia said. "I'm very proud of you."

"My ears are still ringing from the stadium," Eclipse said. "It's so quiet out here now."

"Yeah, it should not be this quiet," Hanyi said. "Why are we not celebrating?!"

"How would you celebrate winning a round before?" Dalton asked quietly, resting on his side with his arm folded under his head.

"We would get drunk," Hanyi stated simply.

"You would get drunk? While injured?" Tarrena asked with an incredulous laugh.

"Correction, *he and Hector* would get drunk," Keito said. "Sometimes Jacob and Sadee would as well, but the masters and I had too high of a tolerance and ended up babysitting drunks most of the night."

"Well, I did have this stashed away for celebration," Jikia said, rifling through her bag and pulling out a small bottle of amber-colored liquor. "*But*," she pointed at Dalton, "you can't have any."

"Fair enough. I already feel a bit drunk."

"And you," she motioned to the wolf, "this stuff is toxic to you."

Hanyi lifted a finger, grinning broadly. "Actually, I learned long ago how to avoid that little hiccup being a wolf among humans. As long as I do not pass out or revert to my wolf form, I can metabolize it."

"But you're a horrible lightweight," Keito teased.

"Which means I don't need much!" Hanyi snatched the bottle away from Jikia, opening it and taking a swig, cringing as he swallowed. "Oh, that burns…"

"Give it here," Keito said, also taking a large gulp. "You baby. This is nothing."

Keito passed the bottle to Eclipse as Hanyi rolled his eyes.

"Yeah, compared to your stash, I suppose."

"How do you know about that?" Keito asked.

"…I don't. You just seem like the type that would have a stash." Hanyi turned away from the demon quickly, pretending to hide his guilty expression.

"That explains a few incidents, actually."

Eclipse offered the bottle to Tarrena and she took it with a shy grin, pressing it to her lips and sipping before passing the bottle to Mitoki.

"I better not," he said, patting the bandages around his thigh. "Feeling a little lightheaded myself."

With a shrug, Tarrena took another drink before passing it back to Eclipse, who offered her a gentle smile.

Dalton saw the way Keito and Hanyi shared a knowing grin, though he was not sure if his blood loss made him imagine the way Eclipse and Tarrena were sharing looks.

"You know, before you get too far gone," Jikia said, leaning over to take the bottle from Eclipse, "are you boys planning to stay around here? Do some investigation?"

"I think that would be best," Dalton mumbled. "We can't exactly leave a giant bone creature wandering about."

"I agree," Eclipse said. "We should stick around until we're certain most of the tourists have returned to their home realms, or until we can be certain this demon and…whatever the hell that thing was are no longer a threat."

"Is that okay with you, Hanyi?" Dalton called. "Can we hang out here for a while until we figure some stuff out?"

"Of course," Hanyi said, turning to Xana. She nodded sleepily against Hanyi's shoulder.

"You are welcome to stay as long as you need," she said. "And I know I would feel safer knowing what happened to that thing, as well. Would hate to come across it randomly."

"I'm pretty sure that just about anything could outrun it," Keito said with a shrug. "That thing may have been unfazed by anything we did to it, but it moved like a snail."

"Still, seeing that thing coming at you would be terrifying," Mitoki said.

"We should probably also search for the others of the Opalon Pack," Xana said. "That attack was a declaration of war. This could lead to some radical shifts in the territories and hunting grounds."

"You're right," Hanyi agreed. "We should probably also call our sons back from training. Let them get some experience."

"Dalton, think you'll be up for a little investigation tomorrow?"

"...no." Dalton said, closing his eyes. "I might need another day or so."

"That's fine," Xana assured. "You all could probably use the rest. Tomorrow, the rest of the pack and I will go on the search for the Opalon Pack. Just a little reconnaissance. See what happened to Raina."

"And if we're feeling up to it, we can check the nearby tourist camps. See how fast they're moving out," Keito added.

Dalton could hear their voices fading around him, his eyes drifting shut as sleep began to claim him. Even though his body knew that it would be almost impossible to move the following day, everything in his body was screaming at him to immediately go into the woods and search for the bone beast, desperate to track down the demon that seemed so invested in everything he did.

He felt his very core demanding that he find the demon. But even that need was not strong enough to keep him from slipping into blissful unconsciousness.

Chapter Twenty-Five

Dalton's frustration was not at the slow pace the tourists were packing up their camps, nor the lack of evidence regarding the surviving members of the Opalon Pack or the bone beast. His frustration was hinged solely on the way his body refused to keep up with his intense need to find answers.

The day after the tournament he had been in and out of sleep most of the day. Jikia was tending to him, waking him when she wanted him to drink a bitter tea or eat something to help him recuperate. The other Guardians spent most of the day in quiet rest as well, Tarrena being sure they ate and drank the same bitter tonic, though they were able to go on short walks to stretch out their tired muscles.

The second day, Dalton was up with the sun, rousing the others, eager to begin searching for their foe. Even as the team suggested places to go, looking for any leads, Dalton became fatigued too quickly. He often had Keito carry him in his animal form, irritated that he could not work at his normal pace.

That day, they were unsuccessful at finding a lead as to the whereabouts of the creatures they were hunting.

Feeling better the third day, they pressed on, trying to follow the path of destroyed trees and littered vertebrae to the location of the bone beast. The day grew very hot and Keito had to walk slowly. Dalton tried not to push the demon, knowing he was also tired and injured, but when they exited the forest and came upon a sprawling plain of thick grass that effectively hid the path the creature had taken, he was persuaded to call the investigation for the day and return to the wolf pack.

The Treneke Wolf Tribe aided the Guardians, though they were far more concerned with the Opalon Pack. They returned every day saying that they had seen no sign of Raina or her pack and that the other neighboring packs had not seen her since before the tournament began.

When the fourth day yielded no results once again, Dalton was beginning to feel like they were being toyed with. An uneasy feeling took hold of his gut as the day progressed. By the time he climbed into his sleeping bag, even the gentle sounds of the forest could not ease his anxiety. Therefore, he was not surprised when he woke up in a horrific state of unease.

Once his mind surfaced to full consciousness, however, it was clear something was terribly wrong. Outside the tent, the forest seemed unbearably loud, the gentle song of the birds he had grown accustomed to now a frenzied wailing. The air felt heavy and thick, and the day seemed somehow too dark for the early hour.

He sat up, noting he was the only one left in the tent. He heard the pacing of the wolves amid low growls and muttered concerns. He quickly left the tent, surprised to see a dusk sky hanging over the trees.

"What's going on?" he asked, running to Mitoki and Keito.

"There was another rupture in the realms," Mitoki answered.

"What? When? How did you find out?"

"Just a few minutes ago there were some messengers that came through the territory to tell everyone to stay put," he said. "Seems a dimensional rift opened in the Human Realm connected to the Realm of Light."

"Any damage?"

"He said that the hole opened into a rural part of the Realm of Light, so the worst damage was that a few farm houses were dropped into the Human Realm with large numbers of livestock. Very minimal human casualties from the initial report," Mitoki relayed.

"And only those two realms affected?"

"As far as we know. But the travel streams are broken, so everyone is trapped in their realm for a few days until the streams can be repaired. A lot of people heading home from the tournament need emergency accommodations. The whole thing is a mess."

Dalton sighed. "Explains the heaviness in the air." He looked at the sky once more. "Is the sun *setting*?"

"Yeah...the day passed in about two hours. All the realms are shifting slightly from the rift. Something about the seal being strained..." Mitoki motioned abstractly to Keito to explain further.

"It's just a residual effect of the rift. As some of the realms move, it pushes against the parts of Vestera's seal that are still intact," the demon elaborated.

"Where are Eclipse and Hanyi?"

"Eclipse is with a few of the wolves," Keito started, dropping his head. "They're...trying to find Hanyi."

"What do you mean?"

"No one has seen him this morning," Mitoki said. "Xana doesn't know when he disappeared. None of the other wolves saw him leave. Keito lost a trail to the north, Jikia and Tarrena are following another trail that leads back toward 1B Stadium."

"Hanyi's *missing*?" Dalton snapped. "As in he wandered off needing some time to himself, or he was taken?"

"We're not sure."

"What was on the trail you followed?"

"I thought I picked up Taniya's scent, Raina's daughter, but it dropped after I traveled about an hour north," Keito answered. "Tarrena thought she sensed the bone beast and they've been following that trail for almost an hour. Xana is using her mate connection to him to try and track him. Eclipse went with her and a few others."

"Do you think he was taken?"

Closing his eyes, Keito nodded.

"How could we have not heard, though?" Mitoki challenged.

"Believe me, it's possible."

"If this demon took him, what would he do to him?" Dalton asked, his voice becoming choked with fear as he continued. "Would he kill him?"

"I truly don't know," the demon said. "I don't *think* so, because he seems awfully invested in us competing in the tournament and if Hanyi is killed we would be disqualified. But I cannot think of a reason why he would take him."

"Other than to use him as a lure to lead us into a trap," Mitoki finished the thought.

The Treneke wolves turned their heads quickly when they heard the sound of footsteps approaching. Dalton's stomach tied itself into a knot when he saw Eclipse jog toward them, wolves in tow. He had a bundle of black cloth tucked under his arm and his worried face told Dalton he had not been able to find Hanyi.

"We found a blood trail," he explained, catching his breath. Xana immediately straightened into her human form.

"It led us right to where the Mount of Marconian used to be. We found this."

Eclipse opened the wrapped black fabric to display a wolf skull, bleached an eerie white.

"It's not his," Xana added. "It's too small and too old."

"But it was sitting on this black cloth like an offering," Eclipse added. "Or a trail marker."

"Did the blood trail continue after the skull?"

Eclipse nodded.

"Then let's go. We'll follow the blood trail from where the bone pile was."

"It could be a trap, Dalton."

"Yeah, maybe," he agreed. "But it's also the closest lead we've got. He's baiting us the same way we're baiting him. I don't see any other option than to follow Hanyi's trail and deal with whatever we find there."

Xana let out a shuddered breath, dropping her gaze to the ground.

"Xana, I'm sure he's alive," Dalton said. "We're going to find him and we're going to bring him home. I promise."

Xana looked as though she was about to speak when Jikia and Tarrena returned to the pack.

"We didn't find any trace of Hanyi," Jikia said dejectedly.

"Any luck?" Tarrena asked Eclipse, her voice growing weak when she saw the wolf skull.

"It's not his," Xana said strongly.

"We found a blood trail," Eclipse answered the younger dragon. "Dalton, I'm on board to follow the trail, but I want you to be absolutely certain you feel ready to face this demon. You've been on a frenzied warpath the last few days, and I don't want you doing something rash."

"One of our teammates has been abducted," Dalton said. "We've been trying to find leads on this demon for days, and now he's baiting us to find him. He hurt Hanyi enough to leave a blood trail. I don't know that there is any other course of action we can take. So we're going after him."

"I'm coming with you," Xana declared.

"Xana…" Keito started, stepping in front of her and holding his hand out to stop her.

"Get the hell out of my way, demon."

"If you go there, I know this demon will not hesitate to kill you. His goal is to inflict pain on us and he'll see a means to do that through *you*."

"You *will not* ask me to stay behind, Keito," she warned, her eyes beginning to shine with rage. "I know you wouldn't be foolish enough to ask that of me."

Keito closed his eyes, pained. "Has he told you about what this demon has done in the past? Did he tell you the way he used to toy with us? Jacob lost his *entire* family just so this demon could teach us a lesson, and it destroyed him. I can't let you do that to Hanyi." He tried to place a hand on her shoulder, though she immediately recoiled, her chest reverberating with a menacing growl. "Xana, the pack needs you. Your pups need you. And Hanyi needs you. Which means you need to be safe." His own glare turned icy. "And if I have to, I will find a way to keep you here."

"Keito…" Jikia said, startled by the threat.

"This is not negotiable, Xana," the demon told her. "If you want to help Hanyi, stay alive for him. Do you understand?"

She continued to growl, her eyes never moving from Keito's as her breathing became labored with anger.

Finally, she dropped her head and her growls abated.

"Thank you."

"I'll go with you," Tarrena said.

"No, you will not," Jikia snapped.

"It's the same thing, Tarrena," Keito said. "He's more likely to kill you than fight you."

"Besides," Eclipse added, "there is no guarantee that the demon hasn't sent the bone beast to attack the pack while we go to rescue Hanyi. The pack needs protectors from that kind of attack."

Tarrena wanted to tell the Guardians that her mother could protect the pack while she defended the Guardians, but she knew Jikia would never let her go against such a dangerous foe alone. She had already been heavily scolded for rushing to defend the Guardians when the bone creature first attacked. She knew it was futile to argue against her mother again.

"All of you come back safe," Jikia ordered. "You bring Hanyi home and you bring yourselves back in one piece. Clear?"

"Clear," Dalton agreed. He nodded to Eclipse, who gently set the wolf skull aside, covering it once more before jogging away from the wolf pack and leading the other Guardians on Hanyi's trail.

Hanyi had struggled against the restraints for the duration of his capture, even as he was dragged through the rough terrain of the Beast Realm and dumped unceremoniously amid the ruins of a dilapidated Council Hall in the middle of the plains.

He had tried shifting into his wolf form, but the magical bindings shifted with him, cutting just deep enough into his skin to allow his blood to trickle free. The two that had hauled him to the site tossed him to the ground, one of the men, clearly a demon, lifting a heavy block of stone and placing it deliberately on the bindings that secured Hanyi, keeping him in one place.

"So, what are you going to do now? Kill me? Torture me? Threaten my loved ones? What's on the game plan, today?"

"You think too highly of your importance, Hanyi," a voice said behind him. The wolf froze, a shiver running through his body. He turned his head over his shoulder, seeing the black cloaked figure approach, his step leisurely. "I've reduced you to bait."

"How did you manage to get a physical form again?" Hanyi asked, his tone dark.

The cloaked head tilted to one side.

"It's not done yet, obviously," Yokouro said, pulling his robe to the side to reveal a mass of jutting bone, sunken, cracked skin, and thick red clay packed together and reeking with a stench of rot so strong that Hanyi had to turn away and hold his breath. "But you seem to forget exactly who I am, Hanyi. Mastering a physical form while an incorporeal entity is not a difficult task for me."

"I know *exactly* who you are," he said angrily, grinding his teeth together. "And this time, I'm really going to kill you."

A sound emanated from the shrouded face, like the disappointed click of a tongue.

"Do you really think you'll man up for it this time?" Yokouro asked. "You were the one who didn't have the stomach forty years ago."

"I realize my mistake now."

"As long as you learned," the demon said. "But I know you, Hanyi. As soon as the time comes to strike the killing blow, you'll shrink back like you did last time, and once again I'm going to tear apart all your little friends while you watch."

"You sick son of a bitch…"

A heavy foot of rotting flesh and clay jutted out from beneath the cloak, landing heavily on Hanyi's left leg.

"This is the leg, right?" Yokouro leered, leaning closer as Hanyi cringed under the weight of the foot and the stench emanating from the cloaked figure. "I've often wondered, Hanyi. Do you remember that day? Do you remember every vivid, fiery detail? Or did you block it out to numb yourself to the pain?"

Hanyi growled, turning his eyes into the dark face he knew was behind the cloak.

"I remember *everything.*"

He did not need to see the smile to understand the sudden chill in the air.

"Good."

He removed his foot, retreating a step from Hanyi as the wolf relaxed, shifting his leg carefully around the forming bruise.

"So what's your plan now?" Hanyi asked. "Cause more destruction? Claim that demons are the gods meant to cast judgment upon humans?"

Yokouro laughed. "Funny little school of thought, isn't it? I'm actually disappointed I didn't come up with it myself. But I figured as long as that philosophy was rattling around in the collective consciousness of humanity, I might as well use it to my advantage."

"But you're telling demons that you're working for their benefit. To get them to be seen as equals to humans."

"I don't want demons to be seen as equal to humans," Yokouro scoffed. "Why would I want to put myself on the same level as a pathetic, miniscule ant? Not even an ant, but a squirming, mindless larva that eats anything in its path and claims it controls the universe?" Yokouro shook his head. "What I want is for demons to be seen as the true masters of this universe. And you know that they certainly can be."

He could not help the broad smile that came to his lips when he saw the way Hanyi shuddered.

"But, whether you want to believe me or not, it turns out that there is a series of events I must go through before I can obtain the true awe I am due. So while some things will be the same as before, a few dead tourists here, a leaked video there, slow progression of panic and mayhem, watching that pathetic mutt Keito try to work against me…I actually do have a plan and purpose this time. Not like I did with you."

"We will stop whatever you're trying to do," Hanyi snarled. "You're now in a body we can hurt, and you did a *really* good job pissing us off. We won't go easy on you."

Yokouro barked a laugh. "Were you going easy on me before?"

"I know you're not going to kill me, Yokouro," Hanyi said. "You need me to be on Team Dalton so you can put us in stadiums and watch us squirm."

"It is damn good entertainment," the demon agreed. "And you're right. I won't kill you. Not yet, anyway. Sadly, I do need to keep you around. But…we've got some time to kill before your teammates show up."

"So, typical torture then?"

"We could, if you want. It certainly makes for a more dramatic scene when they find you."

Hanyi clenched his teeth, trying not to roll his eyes. As he was about to tell Yokouro he did not care what the demon did, a low thrumming came to his ears. He tried to look over his shoulder and locate the source of the humming, but could see nothing over the stone block holding his restraints.

It was when the clacking sounded that Hanyi knew what was drawing closer.

He watched as the bone beast walked along the side of the ruined Council Hall, its creaking body passing by the hollow window frames, steady in its stride. The creature walked around the back of the ruins to the fallen wall. Hanyi's heart stopped in terror when he saw the smooth gait of the creature, its head now upright and its body resembling a wolf as a thick mass of red pulsed and glowed within the twisted ribcage.

"How…"

"Made a few adjustments," Yokouro said. "Should pose a much bigger challenge now. Hopefully it won't kill the human Guardians, but if it does I guess I'll just have to change up my plans a little."

"How did you do this?" Hanyi demanded. "This isn't your thing. It's not your style."

"You're right," Yokouro agreed, the statement sitting heavy in the air between them.

Hanyi turned his gaze back to the beast, trying not to shiver every time he heard it inhale with its maddening clicking sound.

"Now, what should we do to pass the time?" Yokouro mused.

The Guardian could not think of anything to say, trying to turn his attention to the demon though it was almost impossible for him to look away from the lurking bone beast.

"Don't worry, I'm not going to feed you to it. That would kill you," he assured. "And, as we've established, I need you alive for the time being." He looked over the restrained wolf. "But not necessarily in one piece."

He stalked closer. Hanyi pressed his back against the stone block, trying to squirm away from his restraints, ignoring the way they cut deeper into his skin as he struggled. When Yokouro was looming over him, he had only one second to consider how he would attack the demon before the same foul-smelling foot emerged from the cloak and made impact against Hanyi's leg. He felt the bone give way and he let out a cry of pain, forcing himself to stay still, knowing movement would only increase his agony.

As the pain bounced along his nerves, he thought he smelled smoke again. Heat spread over his skin, singeing his hair and causing his eyes to run dry. He coughed, the suffocating smoke filling his lungs as a piercing scream sounded in his ears.

"No, no, no, no…"

"So you *do* remember…"

"Yokouro."

The voice brought Hanyi back to the present, the smoke and heat gone, though the sharp pain in his leg remained. He turned over his shoulder to the man that had joined them in the ruins, donning a similar black cloak, though his long hair and vivid violet eyes were exposed. Hanyi knew his heart stopped beating, cold fear coiling around his chest.

"What?"

"The Guardians have reached the first marker."

"Good. Then you better go," Yokouro said, smiling at Hanyi as he removed his foot from atop the broken leg, causing Hanyi to hiss in pain, though he did not turn away from the newcomer. "We can't have you be seen, now, can we?"

The other demon jerked his head back, the two demons that had brought Hanyi to the ruins obediently following the silent command to leave. The demon's eyes met Hanyi's, holding his gaze for two agonizingly long seconds before he disappeared into the shadows of the ruins.

Hanyi let out a shuddered breath, his body shaking in a mixture of pain, shock, and panic.

~/\~

The humans were pushing their tired legs as fast as they could to keep up with Keito, who had taken up the lead when he caught a strong scent of Hanyi's blood. Even though their bodies protested the speed, their lungs burning and their legs threatening to give out on them, they ignored the pain, desperate to get to Hanyi quickly before the demon could harm him further.

They had been pushing so hard that when Keito abruptly halted, the others nearly collided with him and each other as they tried to slow down, finally coming to a stop several paces ahead of Keito.

"What happened?"

"I..." Keito retreated a step, flinching. "I can't keep going."

"What? What do you mean?" Eclipse demanded.

"Did you lose the scent?"

"No, he's...he's close." Keito winced again and took another step backward. "I can't go any further."

"What?"

"There's...some kind of barrier," Keito hissed, bowing his head. "I can't pass through it."

"What barrier?" Eclipse said, stepping forward and wildly motioning his hands in the space between him and Keito. "No barrier. Come on."

Keito leaned forward, trying to take a step but sparks began to ignite over his skin and small cuts appeared on his hands and face as he tried to move.

"Keito, stop!" Mitoki gasped, his eyes wide. The sun had nearly disappeared, making it difficult to see how deep the cuts went or if the sparks had burned his skin.

"What is this? A demon-specific barrier?" Eclipse asked, glancing around the trees for any sign of the edges of the barrier.

"Seems so," Keito said. "He doesn't want me there."

"How are we supposed to fight him if you're not there?" Mitoki said. "Three humans can't stand up to a demon like this. Or that bone-beast-thing if it's there, too."

"...I think that's the point."

Dalton took in a shaky breath.

"What do we do now?"

"You have to go get Hanyi."

"We're not just going to leave you here."

"He's not going to kill me. He just wants to keep me away," Keito insisted. "He's probably worried I'd fly into a rage and try to kill him before he had a chance to show off for you."

"That's kinda what I was hoping you would do," Eclipse admitted.

"You have to do this without me," Keito said. "It's almost dark and I'm sure Hanyi is nearby. My suggestion is to look for a fire. That's most likely where they are. You should be able to see it if he thinks you don't need me to guide you anymore."

"Are you sure, Keito?" Dalton asked. "There has to be a way to break the barrier."

"I don't know that we have the time to try and figure it out. And if he's really set on keeping me away, he will find other ways to do so." The demon hesitated. "It's the way he plays this game. He'll move us where he wants us. What we have to do is find a way to beat him at his game."

"How are we supposed to do that without someone who knows him as well as you?" Eclipse challenged.

"You're going to have to figure it out." Keito glanced around the darkening trees, trying not to let the humans see his apprehension at sending them on alone. "Go get Hanyi. We've got to bring him home. If I can get this barrier down, I'll come after you. If not, I'll be here when you come back."

Dalton hesitated, fighting with himself about whether to take the time to break the barrier or follow the insistent tugging in his gut bringing him closer to the demon and his captured teammate.

"Stay safe," he said. "And if you get through this barrier, you find us immediately."

"I will."

It took much of his willpower to turn away from his demon teammate, but Dalton managed to face the other direction and begin running to the edge of the woods, scanning his surroundings for the glow of a fire. Eclipse and Mitoki followed reluctantly, Keito watching them be swallowed by the shadows, still pushing against the weight of the barrier restraining him.

Chapter Twenty-Six

Dalton's eyes locked on the distant glow of a fire so fast he almost made himself dizzy with the way his head spun around. They had been running along the tree line, worried about entering the large, open plains in the dark when Dalton saw the glow of a fire near what he believed to be a rocky knoll in the fields.

When he turned and began running even faster than before through the tall grass, Eclipse and Mitoki did not question, searching ahead for what Dalton had spotted. It did not take them long to see the distant points of light glowing a dull orange against the black of the dusk.

Their exhaustion forgotten, they ran through the grass, focusing on the points of light growing larger and brighter.

The structure they came across was in ruins, and Dalton could not help but be stunned to see a manmade structure rise up out of the shrubs and tall grass. In any other circumstance, he would have wondered about the building, but he was focused only on finding Hanyi.

He drew his dagger, kicking himself once again for not bringing his gun to the Beast Realm. He could feel a thick power sitting in the air around them. It caused the hair on the back of his neck to stand on end, invisible fingers seeming to guide him through a vacant door frame into a corridor within the ruins. He kept his back to the cold stone wall, inching carefully forward, listening for any sounds ahead.

Eclipse and Mitoki were also on high alert, armed with their own blades and searching for any movement in the darkness.

Following the orange glow of torch lights, Dalton turned a corner to see Hanyi in a corner of a mostly-collapsed room, leaning against a large stone block, the thick restraints slicing through his wrists, arms, neck, and ankles, causing his blood to run down the stone as he rested, his eyes closed and his breathing labored.

After checking to be absolutely certain he could see no one else, Dalton slinked across the overgrown ruins to crouch in front of his teammate.

"Hanyi, Hanyi, look at me," he whispered, gently shaking the older Guardian, noting with the horror the distortion in his left leg.

"Dalton?"

"Hey, we're here. You okay?"

"Where's the demon?" Eclipse asked, also moving to Hanyi's side, searching for a way to free him from the magic bindings.

"I don't know," Hanyi murmured, his brow creasing as he tried to focus. "We have to get out of here."

"Okay, okay, we're—"

A shiver of dread ran up their spines before they even heard the clatter of bones and the deep, pulsing thrum.

Dalton turned behind him, finally noticing the far wall of the building had completely collapsed, leaving a gaping opening to the plains beyond. In the flickering light of the lit torches along what remained of the walls, a menacing, bone face was staring back at them, the glowing red mass within its torso emanating enough light to illuminate how much the creature had changed from the last time Dalton had seen it.

The bone beast placed one sharp paw on a pile of rubble, stalking closer to the Guardians as the chittering of its breath caused them to shudder.

"What the hell?" Eclipse gasped. "What happened to it?!"

The beast opened its jaw made of many skulls and let out a shrieking cry, sounding like the screaming of the dead and the haunting howls of wolves as they fell over a cascade of bones.

"What do we do, Dalton?" Mitoki asked, standing between Dalton and Eclipse, his hand growing sweaty on the hilt of his dagger.

The creature leapt forward, far faster than it had been before, barely giving the humans enough time to scatter and roll out of the way.

"How did it get so much faster?!" Mitoki yelped, leaping further away when a bone paw reached out to crush him.

"Distract it!" Eclipse ordered, briefly tossing his dagger to the dirt and running at the creature when it charged after Dalton. He focused all the magic he could muster into his hands and grabbed at the mass of bones. Trying to use his magic as a vice, he closed his hands as tight as he could, hoping to break the bones apart or sever some of the magical binding that allowed the beast to move, his hands growing hot as he pressed harder and harder against the leg.

With a sharp swipe, Eclipse was tossed to the side, falling heavily to the grass and rolling away as the beast shrieked again.

Mitoki also forewent using his dagger on the large beast as sharp spears of magic erupted from his fingertips to strike the shoulder and neck. Another loud screech sounded as the beast flinched away, turning its head back as it tried to close its mangled jaws around Mitoki. Dalton yanked him out of the way, both of them tripping over the debris hidden in the overgrown grass, remaining low to the ground as they studied the beast.

"That hurt it somehow," Dalton said.

"I think I hit one of the human bodies," Mitoki noted.

Eclipse also noticed the beast's reaction and took up his dagger once more, his other hand glowing with another magic attack as the bone beast turned to him.

It charged forward, its thundering mass shaking the ruins, pebbles and chips of plaster raining from what remained of the ceiling. Eclipse ran toward the creature, ducking under a heavy paw and sliding under the beast's chest, using the same type of attack as Mitoki to pierce at the torso, hoping to hit some of the pulsing, red mass at its center.

Most of the magic absorbed into the twisted, dense bones. But Eclipse knew something had worked when a shriek was followed by the creature flinching, swinging its body away from where it felt the attack.

All coming to the same understanding, the Guardians each distracted the beast while another tried to hit the bodies encasing its neck like a collar or the mass within the ribs. After a few successful hits, the beast began to swivel away from the human that would run forward, lowering its head to charge the Guardian before they landed a hit.

"How do we take this thing down?" Eclipse snapped.

"It's protecting that thing in its chest, so it must feel pain when we hit it," Mitoki noted, watching Dalton dodge another charge from the clattering mass of bones. "We just have to do more damage."

He saw an opening as Dalton twisted away from the open jaws, turning the beast yet again.

He sheathed his dagger and ran at the beast, but instead of delivering a quick blow to the abdomen and retreating, Mitoki leapt up to grab onto one of the bones, the fingers of his left hand slipping free while his right hand became pinched between undulating bones. Ignoring the pain in his fingers, he lifted his other hand in the direction of the pulsing chest, preparing to attack with his dwindling magic.

The bone beast moved, following Dalton again and knocking Mitoki loose before he could properly aim his attack.

When the beast saw Mitoki, it turned away from Dalton and lowered its head to the youngest Guardian, falling heavily forward in an attempt to crush him. Mitoki rolled out of the way, but used his position on the ground to aim his attack at the human bodies once again.

With a frustrated screech, the beast reared back, shaking its head in pain, the bones clicking and moving, rustling like fur as the beast shrieked.

"Eclipse," Dalton said, "follow my lead."

Without asking what Dalton had planned, Eclipse followed the older Guardian toward the beast as it returned to all four feet, turning vacant eye sockets toward the three Guardians.

"Mitoki! Hit the neck again!"

He obeyed immediately, running the opposite direction of Dalton and Eclipse to get a clear shot of the bodies. When the sharp points of magic made contact, the beast writhed, rocking its head back and forth, the bones shifting, trying to climb up the shoulders to encase the weak spots to protect them from damage.

"There! Eclipse! Now!"

Dalton leapt forward, Eclipse using a force field to propel Dalton upward and into an opening in the chest of the creature as the bones skittered upward to protect the neck. Dalton fell heavily among the pinching bones, the creaking and clacking setting his teeth on edge as he pulled himself along the writhing surface, trying to get to the searing, pulsing flesh before the bones crushed him in their twisting spasms.

His dagger forgotten, Dalton pushed himself forward and placed his hands directly on the thick mass of flesh and blood, pouring all the magic he could muster into it. His arms grew hot, the power he often kept locked deep inside him surging to the surface to spiral down his arms and through his fingers to penetrate the flesh, filling the pulsing cavity within the bone beast with sharp, dark energy.

He was suddenly pulled forward, his arms becoming encased in the heart of the creature before he was violently thrown backward, a deafening cacophony of snapping making his ears bleed. His body felt hot and heavy as it fell to the ground before hard, sharp bones pelted his skin, one catching his cheek hard enough to nearly knock him unconscious.

Dalton's ears were ringing, his eyes stinging from the chalky dust and blood that coated his face. He stumbled, coughing, trying to see where he had landed and what was happening around him.

The bone beast had vanished. The torches had been extinguished. Dalton felt throbbing pains in his body where he had been hit, but he could not wrap his mind around what had happened.

Mitoki gently touched the blood dripping from his ears as he blinked the dust from his eyes. Even when he saw the mass within the beast explode outward, shattering the bones of the beast and sending parts flying all around the ruins, he could hardly process what he had witnessed. He coughed as he tried to stand, a dull ringing in his ears.

Eclipse staggered over to Mitoki, placing a hand on his shoulder as he tried to catch his breath around his own coughing.

"You alright?"

Mostly reading his lips, Mitoki nodded in response, his shaking legs moving him over the bone-littered ground in search of Dalton.

Groaning, Dalton sat upright in the grass, his skin sticky with the viscera of the exploded heart. He tried to get to his feet, but only when Eclipse and Mitoki helped him could he stand upright.

"What…h-happened?" he asked, louder than necessary.

"You made it explode," Eclipse laughed in disbelief. "How did you do that?"

Dalton shook his head, trying to shake off the blood and bone from his body. His head suddenly bolted up as he turned to the corner of the room.

"Hanyi."

Half-running and half-stumbling, they went to their teammate. Hanyi was coughing in the dust, wincing in pain from the bruises he could feel forming from the bones that had struck his body.

"Are you alright?"

He could only nod in response.

"I won't say I'm impressed, because this is exactly what I hoped you would do," a deep voice sounded around the ruins, rattling their already shaken bodies as it cut through the ringing in their ears. Dalton was on his feet again, looking around for the demon, his entire body on alert. *"You met my expectations perfectly."*

"Get out here and face us!" Dalton demanded.

"That desperate to die?" The voice let out a mocking laugh. *"Not yet, dear Guardians. I am not ready to meet you face-to-face just yet, nor are you ready to see me as I am. But you have shown me that you are, indeed, what I have been waiting for."*

The plaster and mortar of the ruins, already weakened from centuries of decay and the force of the explosion, began to crack, sending sections of wall and ceiling crumbling to the ground, the front edifice of the abandoned Council Hall collapsing under the power of the demon's voice.

"Well done, boys. Well done, indeed."

Even around his own pounding heart and the ringing in his ears, Dalton heard the loud crack behind Hanyi. The wolf turned, seeing the corner in which he sat beginning to crumble, threatening to send what remained of the roof down on their heads.

"We gotta move this!" Mitoki barked, trying to push the large stone off the restraints.

"Just shatter it!"

Eclipse pressed his hands against the stone, forcing what little magic remained in his tired muscles into the porous surface of the rock to crack the stone, Mitoki doing the same until it shattered, allowing the humans to yank Hanyi away from the tumbling bricks and tiles.

Hanyi tried to move, hobbling as much as possible with his badly broken leg, finally letting out a shout of pain and collapsing to the ground as they cleared away from the rubble. The others also collapsed, breathing hard, turning to be sure they were not in danger of the falling structure.

As a deep laugh echoed among the building, the final pillars and corners caved inward and the entire area seemed to heave a sigh of relief, finally coming to rest among the grass and shrubs.

Overwhelmed and stunned, the Guardians remained still and silent, staring at the rubble as they tried to catch their breaths.

Hanyi wincing in pain and moving to look at his broken leg finally broke them out of their trance.

"Shit, Hanyi," Eclipse said, leaning close to try and see the injury in the dark. "That's bad."

"You think?"

"Is that—"

"Of course it's the same leg he broke before!" Hanyi snapped around grit teeth, the pain becoming more prevalent with the passing of imminent danger. "That son of a bitch thinks this kind of crap is poetic."

"We have to get you back to the pack so Jikia can heal that," Mitoki agreed, pulling himself onto unsteady feet. "Dalton? Are you alright?" he asked, noticing the way Dalton was staring at his hands.

"I am trying really hard not to think about what is all over me," he choked.

"Yeah, don't think about it," Eclipse agreed strongly.

Mitoki and Eclipse helped Hanyi up, each taking an arm around their shoulder to support the wounded Guardian across the plains in the general direction of the tree line. Hanyi hissed whenever he took a particularly hard step or jarred his raised leg too much, making for slow progress. When they were about half-way across the plains, they heard a voice in the distance.

"Dalton?!"

"Keito!" Dalton called. The wounded Guardians stopped, waiting for the demon to find them in the dark. They saw an orb of magic hovering over Keito's shoulder as he ran to them, the illumination cutting through the oppressive dark of the moonless sky.

The demon first checked over Hanyi, telling them to stay put while he found some branches to make a splint for the broken leg. They eagerly rested in the grass, dreading the long trek back to the Treneke Wolf Tribe.

Once Hanyi's leg had been braced with branches and the sleeves of Keito's shirt, the demon hoisted Hanyi onto his back and carried him through the plains, leading the exhausted humans back to the paths that would eventually take them to the relative comfort of their camp.

Once within the trees, Keito turned to Dalton.

"You know, there's a river right over there."

"Huh?" Dalton murmured, his brain too fried to infer what the demon was suggesting.

"I just think you should probably wash yourself off a bit before you get back to the wolf pack looking like a walking nightmare."

Dalton's brain clicked back into gear as his stomach turned and his skin began to crawl with the disgusting realization of what was clinging to him.

He ran toward the sound of water, half-collapsing into the frigid stream with a gasp.

He began furiously scrubbing at his skin and clothes, ignoring the aggravation to his injuries as he did so, or the way his body shivered at the sudden cold. The chill was a relief. He spent far too long scrubbing down his arms until his skin was raw as he thought about the way his magic spilled into the thrumming heart.

Dalton had never known his magic to take the form of dark fire before, and while the image of the gore that likely coated his skin was disturbing enough, it was the memory of flames licking down his arm to destroy the heart that filled him with unease.

He scrubbed his arms until they were nearly bleeding, trying to rid his mind of the image and terrified at how easily the powerful magic had yielded to his command.

Chapter Twenty-Seven

The sun rose slowly into the sky, lighting the final leg of their journey as they trudged back to the Treneke Wolf Tribe. Dalton was nearly in a trance as he followed Keito along the deer path, and it was not until he heard the excited whimpering of the wolves that he came back to the present. He could not help but wonder if he had been sleepwalking through most of their return.

Xana ran to Keito and Hanyi, trying to determine how to hug him without harming him. Hanyi awkwardly wrapped an arm around her shoulders, pressing his head to hers.

"What happened?" Jikia asked, rushing toward them.

"Broken leg," Keito said. "I've got a splint on it, but do you think you can heal it?"

"Bring him inside."

As Keito took Hanyi to the tent, Xana close behind, Tarrena rushed to the human Guardians.

"Are you alright? What happened to you?"

She reached out to touch the edges of Dalton's black eye, though he shied away from her touch.

"I'm...not entirely sure."

"Did you see the demon?"

"No," Eclipse answered.

"The bone beast?"

They nodded somberly.

"What happened? Did you chase it off? Do we need to go after it?"

"It was destroyed," Mitoki said.

"How did you manage that?"

"Dalton blew it up," Eclipse said, not sure how else to explain what had happened.

Tarrena's eyes were wide, her mouth opened to speak, though she could not think of a response.

"Oh."

Dalton let out a long sigh.

"I just want to wash the rest of this off," he said, lifting his damp, stained shirt.

"Okay," Tarrena said, concerned by the dark tone in Dalton's voice. "Why don't you three go wash up and we can talk when you come back."

The wolves watched worriedly as the humans shambled to the tent, heads down and eyes half-closed. They entered the tent to see

Hanyi leaning against Xana as she held him upright, keeping him still as Keito and Jikia reset his leg to be healed. When Hanyi whined at the pain of his leg being put back into position, Dalton scrambled to get new clothes and get out of the tent, the thought of the broken bone moving causing his entire body to cringe.

Dalton was quick to jump into the warm water and scrub his body down once again, not realizing how cold he had become until he felt the pins and needles that came with bathing in the hot springs. Mitoki and Eclipse were also eager to rinse off, but both were too worried about Dalton's apparent stunned state to pay much attention to how clean they were getting.

Upon returning to the tent, Dalton collapsed onto his sleeping bag, falling asleep almost immediately without saying a word. Mitoki told the others he needed to take a walk by himself and disappeared into the trees to be with his own thoughts. Eclipse sat outside the tent, staring at the ground, pondering why the words of the demon seemed to sit in the back of his brain like a thorn he could not dislodge.

Tarrena sat next to him, nodding back into the tent.

"Dalton sleeping?"

"Out cold."

"Keito?"

"Don't know."

"Hanyi?"

Eclipse jerked his head back into the tent.

"He and Xana are sleeping in there, too."

Tarrena nodded, glancing around them to the wolf pack. Many of them were reclined on the ground, sleeping as the morning progressed, but a few remained upright and alert, uncertain if the danger had truly passed.

"What happened, Eclipse?"

He turned his gaze to her. "What do you mean?"

"You guys got Hanyi back. You managed to blow up some kind of weird bone creature. Why are you acting like you just lost something?"

"...I think we did," he said. "I can't explain it. We got there. We fought. We somehow managed to win. And after all that, it feels more like the demon won than we did."

"How so?"

"I don't know. I almost feel like we just solidified his plans. There was this feeling to his words, this understanding that we had passed his test and now he knew that he could move forward in toying with us." He scoffed. "And we just accepted a challenge with a demon we don't know, who plays by rules we don't understand, with politics that protect him more than they protect those he's threatening." He closed his eyes. "It feels like we just locked ourselves in a cage with a very dangerous predator."

Tarrena placed her hand on his, turning her body to face him.

"That's just because you're tired," she insisted. "You all need to rest. Step away from all this and recover some of your strength. When you've rested, you'll feel differently. I see rescuing Hanyi and blowing up a monster made of bone as a big victory."

"I wish I could agree with you." He looked down at her hand on his, unable to stop the small smile tugging at his lips. "But we're going to have to do a lot more than just rest. We need to get stronger. We need to learn more about this demon and what he has planned. We need to know why he's so invested in the tournament and who he has working for him—"

She squeezed his hand, her other hand taking his face, abruptly stopping his rambling.

"Yes," she agreed. "But first, you rest."

He let out a heavy sigh, his shoulders starting to relax as he closed his eyes and nodded.

With the days still passing in inconsistent increments, it was difficult to tell how long the members of Team Dalton slept. Once they fell into unconsciousness, not even the growing sounds of the forest or the playing of the wolves outside the tent could wake them. Keito remained watchful over the pack and the Guardians, assuring Jikia and Tarrena that he would watch over the Guardians if they wanted to get some sleep as well.

When Hanyi was the first to emerge from the tent, Keito watched him worriedly, wanting to ask the wolf what had happened during his captivity, but worried about the answer. When Hanyi disappeared out of sight into the trees, Keito could not help but follow him, trailing after his former partner until they came to the creek, where Hanyi drank the cold water greedily.

With a tired huff, he straightened and turned, jumping with a yelp when he saw Keito behind him.

"You really have to stop lurking like that," he tried to joke, rising to two legs to talk with the demon.

"I needed to be sure you were alright."

Hanyi lowered his gaze. "Yeah," he said. "It was...extremely unpleasant, but I'm okay."

"Do you want to talk about it?"

Hanyi looked away from the demon, silent, his expression conflicted. "Not really," he finally said. "But we should talk about it."

Keito nodded, waiting for him to continue.

"He's not a full physical form, yet," the wolf started. "Some weird mix of dead stuff and clay, it looks like. He said he was working on mastering it." He tried to think through what else the demon had said to him. "He's still on the destruction and demon domination kick, so that's nothing new. But he seemed...focused. More driven somehow, like he had a specific end goal he was working toward."

"That's troublesome."

Hanyi opened his mouth, hesitating. Keito watched the range of emotions passing over Hanyi's face, feeling a shiver run down his own spine.

"What else?"

"I saw them, Keito," he whispered. He closed his eyes tight. "They were with him."

Keito's eyes went wide.

"No, impossible. I would have sensed—"

"Keito, I *saw* them!" he burst. "One of them was right next to me." He swallowed back his terrified tears, letting out a shaky breath. "What does that mean for us? Why call on them to deal with *us*?"

"...I don't know," Keito admitted.

"...what are we going to do?"

Hanyi knew that Keito would be unable to give him a response. The realization that had gripped both of them seemed to silence even the birds singing in the morning sun, as if sharing in their feeling of helplessness.

~∧~

When Dalton finally woke, he felt better despite his thoughts still filled with concerns about how he had managed to defeat the bone beast.

Once rested, everyone in the team sat in the tent and relayed what had happened at the ruins. When asked about his capture, Hanyi merely said that the demon talked about how he wanted to destroy the humans and that it was nothing he had not heard before. With the amount of information circling the tent that morning, no one saw the brief, secret glance Hanyi and Keito shared.

"Do we think it's safe to go home?" Eclipse pressed. "Should we stay here and make sure that he doesn't try anything else?"

"He said he wasn't ready to meet us yet. And Hanyi said he didn't want to kill him because he wants us competing in the tournament," Mitoki pointed out. "I think it might be better for us to go home. We need to regroup, step away for a bit and start coming up with a plan when we can think a little clearer."

"Not to mention I'm going to have to report what happened with the bone beast to the Elders," Dalton added. "Which means a lot of paperwork."

"We do have a lot of work to do outside the tournament," Eclipse agreed.

"There's no news yet on when the travel streams will be open again, but it would at least be best to check in with families and ground yourselves again," Jikia agreed. "Hanyi, will you be alright here?"

"Of course," he assured, wrapping an arm around Xana. "I've got someone watching out for me."

"Then when we have clearance that we can go home, we head back, take some time to process everything, and then see what we can learn about this demon," Dalton said. "We'll meet up before the second round of the tournament and we'll start forming a plan."

The Guardians did not have to wait long for the clearance to return home.

The following morning their breakfast was interrupted by members of Council tracking down Guardians and telling them that the travel streams would be open to Guardians for one day if they wanted to go home before the streams were closed for more extensive repair.

Quickly packing, the Guardians said their goodbyes to the Treneke wolves and followed Hanyi and Xana to the nearest portal building, the long trek passing easily with the prospect of going home and gaining a little distance from the growing magnitude of their mission.

There was a long line of Guardians queuing up to return home, so Team Dalton stopped further back to bid goodbye to their teammate.

"Are you sure you'll be okay?" Dalton pressed.

"I'll be fine," he said. "That bastard said it himself. My most important function was bait. I'm too boring for him to toy with when you're not around." He laughed, hugging Dalton briefly. "And, uh, thanks for rescuing me, by the way."

Dalton laughed. "You're welcome. Not like I was gonna leave you with that demon."

They each said their goodbyes to Hanyi, hugging him and Xana.

"We'll see you in about two months, okay?" Tarrena said. "We'll meet at our house?"

"I'll be there," Hanyi promised with a wink and a playful salute.

"Take care of yourself, alright?" Mitoki said.

"You, too."

"Xana, make sure he stays out of trouble," Dalton teased. She smiled, shrugging.

"I'll do the best I can."

Waving and calling out final goodbyes, the others joined the line slowly filing into the portal building.

As Dalton was showing his Guardian ID to be granted access to the streams, he could not help but notice the colors of the portals swirling in dizzying motion. Normally, the streams were black voids that were almost painful to look at. The bright colors were even harder on the eyes.

"Are they sure it's safe to travel?" Mitoki asked, perturbed by the twisting channels of bright colors.

"They say so," Jikia said, though she seemed less sure herself as she approached the portals.

Trying not to feel dizzy before he even stepped into the current, Dalton moved forward, feeling his body pull, both too fast and too slow, to another light at the end of the colorful portal.

Disoriented, the Guardians stepped out of the current into the chamber that always kept the portals to the Beast Realm open in the Middle Dimension. Dalton waited for the rest of his team and the two dragons before he made his way out of the building, watching other competitors in the Guardian Tournament hurry to catch shuttles and return home. He walked to the shuttle station, eager to return to his wife and daughter, but not wanting to run from his teammates.

He turned when he reached the first shuttle bench.

"I guess this is where we part ways," he said.

"Take care of yourself," Tarrena said, hugging Dalton tightly. "Get some rest, okay?"

"I will," he assured. "You as well. You two must be exhausted taking care of us like that."

"It's a tough job, but someone's gotta do it," Jikia teased, also hugging Dalton. "We'll see you in about two months. Do you have my number if you need to reach us?"

He nodded. "And I have everyone else on file with the branch, so we should be able to reach each other if something dramatic happens."

"Hopefully nothing will," Keito said, giving Dalton a brief hug. "But if you do need me, call me."

"Thank you."

"I better head home," Eclipse prompted, shaking Dalton's hand and hugging him with the other arm. "See what everyone in the family saw about the tournament on the news."

Mitoki cringed. "Not looking forward to that conversation."

The group said their final goodbyes, each taking different shuttles to return home and rest before meeting again for the next round of the tournament and to investigate the demon threatening the realms.

The sun was shining brightly but the rays did not seem to touch the muddied ground, making the clearing appear heavy and dark. There were ten mounds of dirt surrounding a small pit in the center. The pit was outlined by branches that had been lashed together to form a circle, the bark swollen from being soaked in blood. Another line of twisted branches extended from the circle to each of the ten mounds of dirt, and while they were just as swollen with dark liquid, a pulse scurried down each line, feeding into the circle.

For three days the sun refused to touch the clearing as the hooded figure stood at the edge of the shallow pit, muttering, the words dancing over the damp ground as the trees that heard the spell shuddered, their roots trying to retreat from the dark magic.

On that final day, when the clearing was at its darkest, the earth within the pit pulsed and heaved, crevices opening as the movement became insistent, yet erratic.

The words stopped tumbling from the hooded figure's lips and the earth began to bow upward.

A hand broke through the surface, reaching into the cold air with splayed fingers. Another hand soon stretched out of the earth, the fingers digging into the soft, wet soil to pull the head free.

With a pained gasp, the dirt-caked face of a man broke through the earth, his long hair matted with small roots and clumps of dirt. He collapsed on the incline of the pit, still trapped from the waist down. He panted, his muscles straining and his throat whistling as the air passed the dirt lodged in his mouth.

Reaching another shaking hand upward to crawl further, another clawed hand took his, helping him fight the weight of the earth trapping him as he clamored out of the pit to collapse to the ground.

"Welcome back," the cloaked figure greeted.

The man looked up, his chest heaving with labored breaths as his wide eyes took in his surroundings.

"Whe-where am I?"

"Home, Lord Acurala."

"Ac-Acurala. Yes...I remember..." He turned his eyes on the hooded figure before him, squinting to see the face beyond the cloak. "Yokouro?"

"Yes."

"How are you here? How am *I* here?" He turned his hands to look at them, wiggling his fingers.

"What is the last thing you remember?"

"...I was being chased..." he whispered. "...and that's it."

"You were killed, Acurala. Over a century ago."

"*You* were killed."

"About three hundred years ago, yes. You remember that correctly."

Acurala laughed, shaking his head.

"Always have to be first, don't you?"

Yokouro chuckled, reaching into his cloak to pull out another robe, draping it over the shivering demon.

"You resurrected me," Acurala whispered, his brow creased in confusion. "Why?"

"Because I need your help."

"Is—my brother...is he alright?"

Yokouro laughed again. "Oh, you know your brother. He's alive and well. That's actually why I need you." He crouched in front of Acurala. "You know how high-profile your brother is. I need someone with his same cunning, but not as recognizable."

Acurala let out a wheezing sound that resembled a chuckle. "I see. You're on the hunt again."

"Exactly."

"How did you manage..." Acurala lifted his hands. "I've been dead for so long. My bones should be all that's left."

"They were," Yokouro affirmed. "But I happened to watch Rutu pull a very interesting trick not too long ago with a hex beast. I learned quite a lot about how to animate bones. Then it was just a matter of tracking down your soul, which," he let out a broken laugh, "as you know, wasn't that hard." Yokouro motioned over Acurala's body. "Unfortunately, it's not perfect. You're missing a few ribs and your arms are a different length, but I did the best I could."

Acurala weakly pulled himself to his feet with Yokouro's help.

"I suppose I owe you my life."

Yokouro clicked his tongue. "…in a sense, yes."

"Well played," he said. "I assume my brother does not know you did this."

"Not yet," Yokouro admitted. "He's…not as keen about my challenge to these Guardians."

"Guardians?" Acurala repeated. His face brightened in realization. "Does this have to do with Keito?"

"Keito is old news," Yokouro said, waving the name away. "Dalton Teban is my new focus. A human Guardian with some…*unusual* potential."

"I'm intrigued," the other demon said with a dark smile. "Tell me more."

"I need to grow his potential, push him to his highest capacity," Yokouro said. "And then, I have to crush him."

Acurala hummed in thought. "I guess we have a lot of work to do, then. Tell me what you need me to do."

To Be Continued…

~In~
Dimension Guardian: Realm of Darkness
Blind Ambitions